SURF CITY
CONFIDENTIAL

A Beach Book

SURF CITY
CONFIDENTIAL

A Beach Book

DANIEL J. WATERS

This is a work of fiction. Names, characters, places, organizations, events and incidents are either products of the author's imagination or are used fictitiously.

Actual historical or public figures are used in a fictional context with what the author hopes the reader will recognize as respect and genuine affection.

Text © 2018 Daniel J. Waters

All Rights Reserved

No part of this publication may be reproduced, stored in a retrieval system or transmitted in any form or by any means, electronic, mechanical, recording or otherwise without the prior written permission of the author.

Cover Design by Tony Strong,
AnInspiredImage, Boston
Author Photo © Jean Poland Photography

A WHITER SHADE OF PALE
Words and Music by Keith Reid and Gary Brooker
©1967(Renewed) Onward Music Ltd., London, England
TRO/Essex Music, Inc. New York controls all publication rights for the U.S.A and Canada

International Copyright Secured   Made in U.S.A
All Rights Reserved Including Public Performance for Profit
Used by Permission

ISBN 978-0-9883092-7-2

*For Pam, Jessica, Michael & John-
The best Chapters of my Life*

"And although my eyes were open,
They might just as well've been closed."

Whiter Shade of Pale
Procol Harum (1967)

MAY 1967

HER WRISTS, SUSPENDED SOMEWHERE high above her, were on fire.

Her toes were touching the wooden floor but not her heels, preventing her from pushing up enough to take the weight off. A picture flashed in her mind – a girl's pale, gaunt face, filthy basement, tied up in just the same way. Not more than fifteen, she'd figured, but she'd only been on the job a month back then. According to the coroner, they'd been an hour too late.

She tried to open her eyes. There was someone else in the room. She could smell him. She could hear him breathing. Was she naked? She couldn't tell. Maybe. The girl in the basement had been left in her underwear, she remembered. Pink Maidenform bra and plain white panties from Sears.

All she could see was the floor at her feet, stained with something dark and crusted. There was a faint waft of kerosene and the flickering light suggested a fire or maybe just a lantern. Other scents wafted toward her. Rank human smells, rotting fruit and week-old garbage. She worked hard to piece together the fragments in her head. She'd been riding in car. No. She'd been tied up in car. Someone screaming at her from the front seat. Radio music playing in her ear.

"Time Won't Let Me."

There was more, she knew. So much more but it was all too fuzzy and her wrists were on fire. She didn't think it was clothesline or rope. It felt more like fence wire.

"Time Won't Let Me."

The girl in the filthy basement looked at her. "An hour," she said with her slack jawbone and dead eyes. "Just an hour."

The coroner would amend his report putting the time of death at two to eight hours and eventually settle on twelve, but in the choking stench of the basement the detectives had looked hard, making sure she knew it was on her.

She grunted and tried to straighten her back.

There was movement in front of her. Whoever or whatever was in the room was speaking. It sounded like someone shouting underwater. Feet shuffled, boots scuffed, words came closer.

An hour.

"No," she thought. "Time Won't Let Me."

Wait that long.

MONDAY, THREE DAYS EARLIER

ONE
Surf City, New Jersey

IT WAS A LOW, droning sound – the kind of sound that, no matter which way you turned, always seemed like it was heading directly for you. Mickey Cleary was flat on her back on a wooden Craftsman mechanic's creeper, tugging on the oil pan drain bolt to no avail. She banged the adjustable wrench against the corroded exhaust line sending a shower of road dirt and rust flakes onto her face. Mickey closed her eyes, pursed her lips and blew hard to get them out of her mouth. She dug her heels into the tar-patched driveway and inched her five-foot-seven frame out from underneath the car, wiping at her lips with a grease-stained hand. The sound was almost on top of her now. She squinted up into a cloudless sky. A single-propeller biplane with an open cockpit crossed lazily out past the furthest line of foaming breakers, its wavering shadow drifting over the water at the point where shallow, shimmering green gave way to deeper, darker blue.

"DUNES 'TIL DAWN" read the advertising banner fluttering behind it.

Mickey wiped her hands on her cutoffs and watched as the plane continued its flight north, announcing to all the little towns on Long Beach Island that summer at the shore was just a few days away. Mickey got up from the creeper and walked around to the raised hood of the car, silently assessing how much work she had left to do. Her watch said it was after noon and she'd been at it since the sun had cleared the eastern horizon at just after five-thirty. She drained the last of her lukewarm coffee and decided it was time to switch to the bottles of Tab chilling in the tiny apartment's refrigerator. Five quarts of motor oil and a Fram Racing filter, still in its box, sat by the driver's side door. She hoped she had a can of WD40 in one of the unpacked boxes otherwise she'd have to make another trip to the Pep Boys store in Somers Point which would chew up valuable daylight. The Danube Blue Chevelle SS gleamed in the midday sun. The custom painting additions had been done in Manahawkin, a mile south of the Drive-In Theatre, in a warehouse Mickey suspected functioned as a chop-shop as well. The owner had intimated that he might one day need a favor and had done the municipal graphics for a song. She looked at the five-pointed star on the door and the white lettering underneath.

SURF CITY POLICE it read. And beneath it, *"To Serve and Protect."*

She had stolen the quote from patrol cars she'd seen in California and figured three-thousand miles was enough to insulate her from any copyright complaints. The automotive artist, a pint-sized man named Zeke , had added – at no charge he made sure she knew – the word *CHIEF* in bold capitals on both front body panels just ahead of the door seams. She'd gotten to him add the Department's dispatch phone number horizontally across the trunk. The Borough Council had initially balked at the cruiser's purchase but Mickey assured them she was trying to make a statement about law enforcement being current with the times. She had found the Chevelle at an impound auction on Essington Avenue in southwest Philly and, with her department connections, had nearly stolen it for two-hundred-and-fifty dollars. She had promised to do the upgrading and maintenance herself but only when she mentioned that all the other departments on the island would be insanely jealous did the Council finally relent.

Mickey headed toward the outside stairs that led to her second-floor rooms when she heard the crunch of rubber on asphalt. A shamrock-green Ford Fairlane convertible pulled in and rolled to a stop next to her. The big chrome grill and the four headlights mirrored the sun and Mickey shielded her eyes from the glare.

"Ah, good," the driver said. "I was hoping to catch you." Billy Tunell was the mayor of Surf City and he had taken considerable heat, Mickey knew, over her hiring. He turned off the engine and gave her an impish grin. "But I have to say you don't look very chiefly at the moment, my dear."

Mickey looked down at her cutoff blue jeans and her oil-blotched t-shirt. Faded blue block letters spelled out "PRO ERTY of PHIL DEL HIA   PD" across her chest.

"Do you think the Council would spring for some mechanic's coveralls and maybe some garage space with a lift?" she asked.

"Oh, heavens no," Tunell replied. "In fact, I think they'd like you to buy used motor oil, to be honest. We only have the next three months to generate a year's worth of working capital, remember. If you need something, we'll ask for it after Labor Day. If it's been a good summer – and the Farmer's Almanac says it's going to be hot and dry – then we'll attack the budget when the coffers are full." He nodded toward the Chevelle. "I didn't notice the red stripe tires before. Nice touch. Who, may I ask, owned this beauty before we did?"

"Technically, the City of Philadelphia owned it," she answered. "But before that it belonged to a very successful Greek bookie named Costas Vadilius. Vice collared him in a bust over in Fishtown. Ill-gotten gains, including property can be seized, so…"

"Well it looks spiffy. Very spiffy. How's the dirty work coming?"

"Almost done. Oil and filter and new plugs today," Mickey replied. "I need to do a little more tuning up but the engine sounds pretty good. I'm hoping my timing light and spark gap wrenches are in one of my moving boxes. I'm still in the process of unpacking. The AC is a little iffy, though. I'll have to find some Freon, maybe at Pep Boys. "

"You'll pardon me, I hope," Tunell said, "But I really didn't take you for a grease monkey when we first spoke about this position."

"You can thank my dad," Mickey said. "Let's just say I was brought up to be a tomboy and leave it at that."

"Well, I can believe that. You look in better shape than most of the lifeguards, if you'll pardon a man of my years saying such a thing to a woman my daughter's age."

Mickey smiled. She was, she knew, still toned and overtly muscular compared to most women her age. "Not bad for twenty-four, I guess," she said. "And you can thank my dad for that, too. I played every girls sport there was and every boys sport they'd allow. I had barbells in my bedroom. They wouldn't let me wrestle, though. I think could have been a real hardass out on the mat."

Tunell adjusted his aviator sunglasses. "Well. I'm sure your mother must have had something to say about-" He stopped, a fallen look on his face. "Oh, I'm so sorry," he said. "I remember that you told me. It's simply unforgivable of me to have forgotten."

Mickey shook her head. "It's OK," she said. "I don't believe there's much that's unforgivable in this world. Some things harder than others, maybe, but not that. I, like they say, made my peace with it a long time ago." It sounded hollower every time she uttered it and she decided to change the subject.

"So what's 'Dunes 'til Dawn'?"

"Yes, I saw that," Tunell replied. "Spring has its first robin. Summer at the shore has its first aerial billboard. It's a bit of a tradition down here so you should get used to it. There will be one buzzing the beach every half hour starting on Friday. Memorial Day weekend is the official start of the season for us. As for The Dunes, it's one of the more raucous watering holes in the area. Somehow the owners finagled a variance to remain open and serving alcohol after all the other establishments must close. If I'm correct, last call at The Dunes is five-thirty a.m. Thus the slogan. It's a place best avoided, but it's over in Egg Harbor Township and they don't have a standing police force. State troopers out of Hammonton deal with the problems there and they are welcome to them. You might encounter some of the customers, however, as they try and weave their way back here after a long night and a liquid breakfast."

Mickey considered the information. "Is it a rough place? Like a biker bar?"

Tunell tilted his head in thought. "Not usually, although the only murder in recent history occurred in The Dunes' parking lot. Three years ago this Labor Day, in fact."

"An actual murder – down here? I'm impressed. I wouldn't have guessed."

"Oh, yes. Big local scandal. The victim was a, how can I put this delicately, a *flamboyant* local businessman and outspoken public figure who was found dead in his car with a fractured skull. There was no investigation to speak of and no one was ever charged much as less convicted. Almost as if it never happened; perhaps because suspicion fell on prominent locals, including a member or perhaps members of the law enforcement brotherhood, depending on who you believed."

Mickey's eyes widened. "Capped by a cop? Seriously?"

"Who better to pull it off?" Tunell said. "They say doctors bury their mistakes, well..."

Mickey shook her head. "That just blows my mind," she said. "Did they whack him just because he was...flamboyant?"

"There were several theories. But, as I said ...it's like it never happened."

"I had no idea," Mickey replied. "So anybody around here I should be aware of?"

Tunell's nose crinkled. "Oh, we have our share of well-to-do and privileged visitors but they usually like to blend in with the day-trippers and the locals. And, let's be frank, we may have some tourists and summer residents whose business interests aren't necessarily on the up and up but the last thing they want to do is draw attention to themselves. One murder in all these years and it wasn't even on The Island. I'm trusting you to keep that record intact, Chief Cleary."

"That shouldn't be too difficult. So how's the whole female chief thing going, by the way? Are they still giving you guff about it?"

Tunell crossed himself theatrically. "By the grace of Almighty God and the intercession of Saint Jude I finally convinced them to pay you what Pete Graham was making. Otherwise you'd taking home less than Deputy Fairbrother and probably some of the chambermaids."

"Just because I'm a woman."

"A girl," Tunell replied. "That's what they call you, you should know – the girl. How much are way paying 'the girl?'"

Mickey laughed out loud. "Well, I appreciate you sticking up for me. I won't let you down. No murders on my watch. Cross my heart."

"I know you won't. But you have to realize these councilmen are not particularly progressive thinkers. They also pointed out that there are no female lifeguards."

"What does that have to do with it?"

"Nothing. Which is exactly my point. Branch Rickey had Jackie Robinson and I, my dear, have you." Tunell looked out through the windshield then back at Mickey. "Perhaps it not my place to ask but I will anyway. Have you spoken with your father?"

"Not since I've been back," she answered. "I didn't leave on especially good terms and I'd like to get my feet set here before I take on that whole ball of wax."

Tunell reached for the rearview mirror and grabbed what was hanging there. He studied it and then handed it to Mickey. "St. Christopher," he said. "Patron Saint of Travelers, although you should know he's never been officially canonized by the Holy Roman Church. Some journeys, dear girl, are not measured in miles."

Mickey took the silver necklace and looped it over her head. "Do I have to report this as a gift?" she asked with a smile.

Tunell crossed himself again. "Only to Father Joe Feeney under the impenetrable seal of confession," he replied. "Not that you'll have anything to confess, of course. Now do an old gearhead a favor, would you, Chief Cleary?"

"Anything for Your Honor," she said.

"I have to go to Beach Haven. A dancer from one of the, shall we say, theatres of the performing arts in Atlantic City claims one of *my* machines has mangled her, ah, special undergarments leaving her quite indisposed and possibly unemployed. I'll probably be picking sequins out of the dryer drum for weeks. But before I leave, would you start it up for me?" He winked.

Mickey squeezed in behind the wheel of the Chevelle. She looked over at Tunell and turned the key in the ignition. The big V8 roared into life and the heady scent of aromatic hydrocarbons filled the air. Mickey pushed the accelerator pedal and watched the console-mounted tachometer bounce and then climb as three-hundred-and-ninety six horses came to full gallop. Tunell gave her a carrier pilot's thumbs-up and peeled out in a hail of sand, shells and stones. The new Delco radio she'd installed yesterday was on and she turned the silver volume knob until the speakers vibrated and she could hear above the rattle of the chassis and the rhythmic thrum of carbureted compression. WABC out of New York was coming in crisp and clear on the day's fair weather. DJ Dan Ingram was introducing a song he described as "a little off the beaten path" by The Byrds. Mickey listened as "The Girl With No Name" poured out. She let up on the gas and gauged the pitch of the slightly high idle. She knew all the words to the song

and for a moment she allowed herself to think of what had gone before. She fingered the St. Christopher medal and listened to the engine.
 The past was in the past, she told herself. Everything in her life was in front of her now. And even if the past tried to catch her, she mused, looking down at the tachometer, now she had the horsepower to outrun it. She felt a warm breeze from the dashboard vents. The AC still wasn't working right. Time, she thought, to go visit her three new best friends, Manny, Moe and Jack.

♦ ♦ ♦

 The four boys in the car were a living full-page Ford Motor Company advertisement straight out of LIFE magazine. They crossed Division Avenue laughing and whooping. The top was down on the candy apple red Mustang and it swerved as they poked and jabbed at each other. The radio was turned up full blast and The Beach Boys blared out "California Girls".
 "Come on, slow down," the sandy-haired boy in the passenger seat said. "My old man will kill me if I get another ticket. I already have points on my license as it is."
 "I'm the one drivin' so it'll go on my license, moron" said the boy behind the wheel. His hair was dark and long and blew off his forehead in the breeze. He had already started to tan, a benefit of his naturally olive complexion. "Don't be such a pussy, Paulie. Jesus, you think my dad couldn't get your points erased by the time we got to Ship Bottom?"
 "Yeah, yeah, Danny, we all know who your dad is. But my dad's just a guy so I can't pull the shit you can and get away with it." Paulie reached over with a pale white arm and turned down the radio. "Look, let's just go get the beer and head back to the house. We only have four more days before my family moves down for the summer."
 Danny tapped the brakes, pitching the other three riders forward.
 "Hey, Danny, what the f-?" a voice from the back seat cried.
 "Shut up, Del," Danny said. "You wouldn't even be here if it wasn't for me."
 "Screw you, Danny," Del replied. His new Phillies cap was

knocked askew and he took it off to inspect for damage. "High school's over as of last week. You won't be such a big shit in college."

"Careful, Del," said Frankie, the other boy in the back seat. "Or maybe your old man takes an unplanned vacation. Know what I mean?" He cackled and rubbed more zinc oxide on a prominent nose and cheeks alive with a blooming garden of acne.

"Yeah, Del. Better listen to Frankie," Danny said. "There's a lot a garbage dumps in Pennsylvania. A lot of them."

Del flipped up his middle finger and thrust it in between the bucket seats. Danny grabbed it roughly and started to squeeze.

"Hey," Paulie said. "A cop just pulled behind us. Take it easy, Danny. Christ Almighty."

The Mustang coasted until it hovered at the twenty mile an hour speed limit. Paulie adjusted the side mirror pretending to check his hair so he could keep the cruiser in sight. Ten seconds later he saw the single cherry-red roof light start to turn.

"Fuck," Paulie said. "Happy now, asshole?"

Danny flipped on the right blinker and smiled. "Twenty bucks says we don't even get a written warning."

"Yeah, like I got twenty bucks," Paulie replied. "My dad works for the IRS not the friggin' Mafia."

Danny fixed him with a cold stare. "You ever say that word again and your dad won't have to worry about sendin' you to college this fall. *Capisce*?" He glared at him until Paulie looked away. Danny let the car drift to a stop outside a store advertising Fralinger's salt-water taffy and Copper Kettle fudge. "Get the registration out of the glove compartment," he commanded. "And nobody say anything except 'Yes, sir.' Got it, dickweeds?"

They heard the door of the police car shut. A tall, thin uniformed officer approached casually on the driver's side.

"Afternoon, gentlemen," the officer said.

"Hello, Sergeant," Danny said with the confidence of someone who had never been taught to fear authority. "Have we done something wrong?"

"License and registration, please. And it's Deputy, son, not Sergeant."

Danny intentionally fumbled for his wallet and withdrew his Pennsylvania driver's license. Paulie handed him the registration card and he gave them both to the deputy.

"I see that this car is not registered to you, sir," the deputy said to Danny. "Do you have the owner's permission to be driving it?"

Paulie started to speak until Danny shot him a hard look.

"This very nice car belongs to my friend Paul here's father." He motioned toward Paulie. "We're guests of Paul's family at their house right here in Surf City. I asked Paul if his dad would mind if I drove the car and he said he thought it would be alright. I didn't think I was speeding, Deputy."

"May I see *your* license?" the deputy asked Paulie who quickly produced it and handed it across. Danny smiled and readjusted his sunglasses. "You ticked a curb back there and you were swerving a little," the deputy said.

"I'm sorry," Danny replied. "We were goofing around. I know I should have been paying more attention. We'll be more careful, officer."

"Where are you boys headed?" the deputy asked. He looked right at Paulie who froze.

"We're just out to pick up a case of soda to have with our supper tonight. Then we're going to hit the beach," Danny replied.

"OK, I'm going to let you off with just a verbal warning this time," the deputy said. Danny was trying to read his name tag but it was polished brass and the sun was reflecting brightly off it. "But we'll have a lot of pedestrian traffic here starting this weekend. You need to keep your eyes on the road and your hands on the wheel at all times. Are all of you over eighteen?"

Four heads nodded.

"The drinking age may be lower here than across the river but the laws are tougher and the penalties more severe. I see you joyriding again and you'll get a citation and a hefty fine. Could even lose your licenses if I catch you with any alcohol. Understood?"

"Yes sir," Danny said. "Thank you, sir. Have a good day."

The deputy handed Paulie back his license and his father's registration. He looked at Danny's license for a few seconds longer then passed it to him. "You have a nice day, Mr. Ragone," he said. "And please remember that Surf City is nearly seventy miles from Philadelphia and courtesies that apply there may not necessarily apply here." He tapped the driver's side door and walked away. Danny waited until the cruiser had pulled out and past them and pushed the console shifter into Drive.

"Well, well, ol' Barney Fife just made me twenty bucks," Danny said. "Pay up, Paulie. But I guess if you really don't have it I'll settle for a hummer from your sister when she gets here."

"She's twelve," Paulie shot back.

"Yeah, you're right. She probably wouldn't be very good at it. You'd still owe me ten."

Paulie was about to reply when Danny hit the brakes. "Hey, check it out," he said, pointing to a public bench across the street on the beach side. "Take a look at this asshole."

A young man with long hair sat on the wood-and-stone bench. He wore military camouflage pants, an olive drab uniform coat hung open over a white t-shirt with dog tags dangling on his chest. A wide-brimmed jungle-green hat was pulled low on his face. Danny flipped the blinker, checked the rear-view mirror and made a quick U-turn. "Let's go say hello to G.I. Joe," he said and slowly approached, his foot barely on the gas. "Hey man!" Danny called.

"Leave him alone, Danny," Del said from the back seat. "Probably been in Viet Nam or, what's that other place, freakin' Cambodia. Jesus, he's not botherin' anybody."

"Yeah, well he bothers *me*," Danny said. "I read about what these guys did over there. Pisses me off." Danny nosed the grill of the Mustang right to the curb and put it in Park. He grabbed the top of the windshield with both hands and pulled himself up until he could see over it. "Hey, man!" he called again. The figure on the bench looked up, but the face was still in the shadow of the hat's brim. "You were in 'Nam, right?" The figure squared his shoulders and tilted his head a little further. "Well, you're a freakin' baby killer! Yeah, you heard me. Freakin' baby killer." Danny still could not see his face. "Yeah, that's right. Can't even look me in the eye, can you, you sick bastard. Go back to the jungle. Go kill some more babies!"

"Danny, sit down for Christ's sakes," Paulie said. "He ain't hurting anybody. He's just sittin' there." Danny's hand connected with Paulie's cheek hard enough to make a sound. Danny banged on the windshield with both hands and continued to shout.

"How many little gook babies you kill, huh, tough guy? You use a flame thrower or did you just machine gun 'em? You're a freakin' murderer! Get off the street before I run your sorry ass over!"

The figure on the bench rose slowly but did not advance. As the man lifted his chin, Danny could finally see his face. Danny had worked up a gobbet of spit he planned on launching when it came full into view. He stared right at Danny and very slowly smiled. Danny was shocked at how young he looked and swallowed his mouthful of phlegm. The man in the camo pants and the jungle hat remained seated, but he slowly extended his right arm, lifted his thumb and pointed. He tilted his head and closed one eye, as if sighting down his index finger. Danny understood the gesture immediately having seen it innumerable times at home and in his father's club. The man flexed his thumb and jerked his shoulder back mimicking a recoil action. Then he dropped his arm and lowered his head, his face once again hidden in shadow.

Danny slipped back into his seat. Without saying a word, he shifted out of Park and stepped on the accelerator, checking the rear-view mirror several times as he did.

"Paulie told ya to leave him alone," Frankie chirped from the back seat. "Jeez, *Dante*, I thought you were going to shit your nice white pants back there for a second." He began to laugh.

"Eat me, Frankie," Danny replied. "I see him again I'll kick his ass. I know who he is now. Asshole had his name right on his jacket. 'Dunn.' Well, he will be *done* if he thinks he can screw with me." The rear tires squealed as he punched the gas.

Mickey's trip to Pep Boys had been successful although it had taken longer than expected. She knew the extended time it took to "find" the Freon in the stockroom was only a ruse to let the three middle-aged men behind the counter ogle her for as long as possible. She'd parked on the side of the building and they hadn't seen her pull up in a police cruiser. Her badge was in her pocket but Mickey decided she'd save payback for another day.

On her way home decided to cruise by the station house on Long Beach Boulevard. Halfway there the dispatch radio's tinny speaker clicked on and off several times and then rattled off a description of something she hadn't seen yet and wasn't sure she would – an actual crime being committed in Surf City. She flicked on the roof flashers. The business was named, in complete ignorance of its customer base, Ye Olde Surf Shoppe and it was less than a block away. Mickey pulled up and nudged the cruiser's tires tight against the curb. She got out and looked around but saw no one. Then she went inside.

"Eight bills," the owner said. "Eight bills he took. I 'm tellin' ya, I wasn't gone but two minutes. The little punk." Mickey had met him before. He was short with black hair and a neat mustache and he had insisted she call him Mr. D and only Mr. D. She was impressed at the amount that had been stolen. In the close to a month she'd been in Surf City she'd only seen one person actually riding a surfboard and maybe one other person carrying one. There were no customers in the store.

"OK," Mickey asked. "What'd he look like?"

"I dunno," Mr. D replied. "I didn't get a good look. I was inna back inna storeroom. Two minutes I was gone. Tops. Punk teenager. That's all I know"

"We'll find him," Mickey replied. "You just stay here. Eight bills, you said?"

"That's right, Chief. Everything that was in the drawer from the weekend, he took. All of it. Mother of God, these kids nowadays. Remember I told you? I got plans for this place. I need every dollar." What Mickey remembered was an outlandish strategy to open other stores in what he called "surf towns" up and down the East Coast and maybe even out in California. But he was afraid, he'd told her, that the owner of a rival surf shop called the Ron-Jon in Ship Bottom had a similar idea and considerably more working capital.

Mickey walked back outside and jumped in the Chevelle. She turned off the roof lights and motored in second gear for a few blocks, passing out of the little business district and by a string of whitewashed cottages. A few older couples were conversing on the sidewalk and they waved at her. A woman with a baby carriage darted from behind a parked car. Mickey braked and beeped the horn. The woman extended one arm and a middle finger without looking up. Not now, Mickey decided. She made a right turn and saw a boy walking with his head down, hands jammed in a pair of frayed and faded bell-bottom jeans.

Mickey thought he looked about fifteen but was stockily built. He was white, like everyone else she came across, with curly ringlets of red hair. She could tell he was trying hard to appear nonchalant. Trying too hard, she decided. Mickey pulled to a stop and opened the cruiser's door gingerly. The boy kept walking. She hopped up over the curb and onto the sidewalk, her steps at a slightly faster pace than the boy's. Kaylen Fairbrother's police cruiser pulled in behind her. She stopped and waited for her Deputy, pointing at the boy. She hoped he was on his way to a house with a parent at home. Mickey and Kaylen walked side by side behind him for another block. When he paused at a cross-street they stopped.

"Young man," Mickey called out in the practiced deeper register she'd used for perp stops in North Philly. "Hey, young man. Hold on. We'd like to talk to you."

The breeze had come up strong off the ocean and she wondered if he was pretending he didn't hear her or if her words had gotten blown back in the salty gusts that were sending Sno-Cone cups and paper fudge wrappers skittering along the street. The boy froze. Mickey and Kaylen resumed walking. Suddenly, the youth turned around and reached inside the half-zipped windbreaker he was wearing.

A dozen scenarios went through Mickey's mind. She saw Kaylen's hand go his holster.

"Show me your hands," she shouted. But the boy, she saw, was still reaching into his jacket.

"Son," she said even more loudly this time, "I said show me your hands. *Now*."

Mickey noticed Kaylen's holster was unsnapped. Her eyes darted from her Deputy's gun to the boy's concealed hand and back again. They continued to move slowly toward him.

When she looked again, Kaylen had his revolver drawn. Mickey grabbed his hand, staying it, and shook her head. Half-a-heartbeat later green bills came fluttering out from inside the boy's jacket. Then he turned and began to run.

"Stop," she yelled. The boy zigged but there was no place to go except the street or the sidewalk. He chose the latter. Mickey reached over and pulled Kaylen's nightstick from its belt ring. With a flat flick of her wrist she sent it helicoptering towards the youth's feet. It caught him on the back of one leg and the heel of one sneaker. The boy sprawled on the white cement and skidded forward. Mickey ran up and stood over him.

"Just stay down," she said. "You hear me? Stay down. Why did you run?"

"I don't know," the kid whimpered, his face on the sidewalk. "I was scared. I thought he was gonna shoot me."

Mickey laughed. "So you ran? Because, what, you thought you could run faster than a speeding bullet there, Superman?"

"I said I was scared," he replied. "Jeez, it was just a few bucks."

"That's not what the owner says." She prodded him with the toe of her shoe. "OK. Now turn over and sit up." Mickey reached down and picked up a crumpled dollar bill from underneath him. Kaylen came up behind her holding three more. He bent down and retrieved his nightstick.

"Whoa, Chief," Kaylen said. "Where did you learn *that* trick?"

"My dad taught it to me with his nightstick," Mickey replied.

"Can you teach me?" Kaylen asked.

"Sure," Mickey answered, "But first we have to figure out what we're going to do with John Dillinger here."

The boy had his arms around his knees, hugging them. He looked ready to cry.

"Age?" Mickey asked.

"Fourteen. I'll be fifteen on the Fourth of July. Am , am I going to, to prison?"

"I don't know yet," Mickey replied, trying to maintain a serious expression. Kaylen handed her the three bills.

"Well that's half of it," the deputy said. "The rest is probably a mile away the way it's blowing right now."

Mickey looked at the bills. They were all ones.

"This isn't even the down payment on all of it. The owner said the kid hocked eight bills out of the register."

"Yep," Kaylen said. "You have one and I just gave you three. Half of eight is four."

Mickey looked confused until the answer dawned on her. "No. No. You have got to be shitting me," she said. "Eight dollars – that's what this is about? *Eight* dollars?"

"Yeah, eight bills. What did you think, Chief?" Kaylen asked.

"I told ya it was just a few bucks," the kid whined.

Mickey laughed. "OK, OK. Every place else in the world, except here I guess, when you say eight bills it means eight hundred dollars. Eight Benjamins, eight C-notes - not eight fricking singles."

"Well, I guess I just never heard *that* before, Chief."

The wind was blowing Mickey's hair and she kept pushing it

back to cover her right ear.

"What's your name?" Mickey asked the boy.

"Thomas," he answered with a sniffle. "Thomas Fromm."

Mickey tapped her foot. "OK, Tom Fromm, here's how this goes down. You are going to get into Deputy Fairbrother here's police car. He is going to drive you to your house and wait inside your door while you go to your room and come out with ten dollars. TEN, got it?"

The kid nodded, eyes wide. Mickey continued.

"Then Deputy Fairbrother will drive you back to the surf shop where you will first apologize to Mr. D and then you will tell him you are repaying him with twenty-five percent interest got it?" She waited for him to shake his head. "Good. If your parents are home you'll have to explain to them why a police officer is with you. That's your problem. If they're not then it's your lucky day. Fair enough?"

"I guess," the boy answered.

"He guesses," Mickey said to Kaylen. She reached down and pulled the boy up by the jacket's collar. "And if any of your dopey friends ask, you tell them you almost went to the slammer. But this is my one and only good deed for the whole summer. Pass the word. You got that?"

"Yeah."

"Excuse me?"

"Yes, ma'am," the kid said sullenly, dusting himself off.

"Take him away, Deputy," Mickey said with intentionally dramatic intonation. Kaylen pointed the boy toward the Galaxie.

"Before the weekend," Kaylen called as they moved off. "You have to show me that baton thing before the weekend. That… was really bad."

Mickey gave him a questioning look.

"Really bad – it means it's like really a cool thing," he said.

"Yeah, I know what it means," she replied. "I just wanted to make sure *you* knew."

Mickey went back to the Chevelle. Eight bills, she thought. Obviously she had a lot to learn about life at the shore. She started the engine and headed back to finish her grease monkey tasks. On the way she fretted about Kaylen and how quickly he had drawn his weapon. Things could have gone south in a hurry, she understood, and wondered what would have happened if she hadn't been there. It bothered her the whole rest of the way home.

Four hours and three Tabs later Mickey was bent at the waist under the hood of the Chevelle fiddling with the carburetor. She heard a horn beep twice. The big Ford Galaxie cruiser stopped a few feet away. She waved to Kaylen.

"Enjoying the rest of your day off, Chief?" he called.

"What do you think?" Mickey answered and pointed to the tools, boxes and removed parts. She picked up the bottle of Tab and drained the last of it. The Galaxie idled slowly as she approached the driver's side window. "Any other major crimes today in our fair city today, Deputy?" she asked. "I can't hear the radio when I'm under the hood."

"Pretty quiet, Chief," Kaylen replied. "Some kids joyriding in a boss new Mustang ragtop was the only other thing today. And I really only pulled them over so I could get a closer look at it. Like I said, it was a pretty boss set of wheels."

"Did you make any money for the borough?"

"Nah," Kaylen answered. "I let them off with just a verbal. Didn't think it was worth the paperwork. Something tells me we'll have all summer to write tickets for that car."

Mickey blew engine dirt off her hands and wiped them on her shirt. "Did the kid have the ten bucks?"

"He had nine, so-"

"Kaylen, you didn't. You gave him a dollar out of your pocket?"

"He was sweatin' bullets, Chief. I thought he was going to throw up right on the floor mat."

Mickey laughed at the thought. "What did Mr. D have to say?"

"He acted real mad at first. But then he took the money and told the kid he had to come back and do chores around the shop or he was going to press charges."

"Mr. D is nothing if not a shrewd businessman," Mickey replied. She looked out toward the sparkling ocean. "Only four more days 'til the Mongol hordes descend on us," she said.

"Chief?"

"'Til the summer crowds show up on Friday," she replied. "Radio says high eighties and sunny the whole Memorial Day weekend."

"That'll bring the shoobies out. Ever since they built that A.C. Expressway and then the Garden State Parkway it seems like they all get here at once," Kaylen said. "The old two-lane highways were slow but at least they kept the flow of traffic controlled. Now, it's like a giant tidal wave of cars. There's only one road on and off Long Beach Island and by this time Friday the Causeway Bridge will look like a parking lot."

"What time is it?" Mickey asked. "I left my watch when I went inside."

"Pushing five, Chief," he answered. "How long have you been at it?" He motioned at the Chevelle.

"Pretty much all day," she said. "But I got a lot done after our little adventure. Now all I need is a high-speed chase to test it out."

Kaylen smiled. "I wouldn't hold my breath for that," he replied. "Traffic gets so bad during the season you could go faster on foot than you could in a car most days. Fridays and Sundays are the worst, although this weekend it'll be on Monday when almost everybody heads home. Didn't your family ever go down the shore when you were little?"

Mickey blew errant strands of dark hair from her face. "I saw the Diving Horse at the Steel Pier in Atlantic City once," she said. "My dad always said the shore was just for rich people." She held the Tab bottle up and watched a prism of light appear. "Actually, what he said is that the shore was for rich assholes. No offense."

"It's OK, we say that a lot, too. But only during the off-season. So you really didn't know anything about this place when you took the job?"

"I knew that Surf City was at the shore and that the shore was on the ocean. But I didn't know it was on an island until I looked at a map." She peered out at the rolling waves and drew in a deep breath. "And I didn't know the air smelled this way. I guess it's the salt, but now I understand why rich assholes want to come here every summer."

Kaylen turned the engine off. "It's a unique place, that's for sure. The whole island's only eighteen miles long and there's no place wider than half a mile. Shoot, over in Harvey Cedars you can practically spit from the bay to the beach. Who knows why it ever got divided into six different towns but it's just always been that way. Off the island you got Atlantic City just twenty five miles south and then you hit Cape May and then that's the end of New Jersey. There's a lot of little beach towns up and down the Jersey coast but Long Beach Island is just different somehow. Like when you finally get out of the Pine Barrens and hit the Causeway the road rises up and it's almost like you're flying. You cross the bay on those old wooden bridges and the first thing you see is blue water stretching all the way to the horizon. And *that's* when the salt air hits you. I'll tell you, Chief, there nothin' that smells as good as the beach in summer." He stretched out his hand and drummed on the dashboard. "Most of our visitors just come for the day, really, so you know they aren't rich. But all you need is a tank of gas, an old blanket and maybe a transistor radio. The sand is free, so is the sun and the water. Watch all the little bitty kids on the beach this weekend. You'd think they were in Disneyland."

"Maybe you should be our tourism director instead of a cop."

"No, ma'am. I like Surf City just the way it is. I like that my job is keeping it that way."

Mickey laughed. "Well now, remember, it's just you and me for the first week. The summer help doesn't graduate from the New Jersey Patrolman's Academy until next Wednesday and they won't report until the following week."

"We'll be OK," the deputy replied. "Chief Pete and I held the fort by ourselves one season all the way until the end of June."

Mickey knew that Peter Graham had been her predecessor until the long, desolate winters brought with them an increasing fondness for alcohol and a string of minor but disturbing incidents that led to a quiet dismissal and a quick search for a replacement. Mickey figured she owed her job to the suddenness of Graham's departure just before the looming beach season. "You ever hear how he's doing?" she asked.

"Guess he's in something called rehab. Said it probably saved his life. Wants to be some sort of counselor when he's all done with it. Help other cops with the same problems, I guess."

"Yeah, well, cops aren't very good at talking about their problems, Kaylen. That's their problem."

"Didn't your department give you any help after your-"

Mickey cut him off. "What'd I just say, Deputy? I said cops... don't... talk... about their problems." She turned to look out towards the bay. "I'm about done here. I'll get cleaned up and meet you at the station around seven. Enjoy your night off. There won't be very many for a while."

"OK, Chief," Kaylen replied. "Sorry if I brought up something you-"

"Don't worry about it," Mickey replied. "Just be grateful neither of us will have to deal with any of that down here. And Kaylen, I have to ask – do you think you were maybe a little quick on the draw today? He was just a kid. Chances of him packing are-"

"Not likely but not zero either, Chief," he responded quickly. "I left the safety on. But what if it was the once in a million times? I had to protect you and me both, just in case."

Mickey considered the answer and decided to let it go. It was the mention of protecting her that did it.

Kaylen gave her a two-finger salute and adjusted his sunglasses. Mickey stepped back from the cruiser, put her hands on her hips and watched him pull away. Twice in one day painful memories had been dredged up by well-meaning people. The geographic cure had worked for a while but she knew that now time and work would be the only real remedies. This job had been a godsend, she thought, allowing her to return to a career she loved, a life she'd been brought up in - minus the constant danger and emotional stress of being a big-city cop. She thought of how proud her father had been when she graduated from the Academy. He had pulled every string and lever and pushed every button to get her in and she had made it through despite what she knew was a concerted effort to wash her out. Now she hadn't spoken to him in more than a year; didn't even let him know where she went when she left. Mickey figured he still had enough contacts inside the P.P.D. to know she was back and where she was but every time she went to dial the phone something tightened up inside her. She had failed him by quitting. And if there was one thing Patsy had taught his daughter it was that a Cleary *never* quits.

She looked down at her arms and then her legs. There was a soft pink glow that hadn't been there yesterday. Despite her heritage she wasn't particularly fair-skinned and she thought maybe she would look good with a real summer tan. Northern California had been cool and wet most of the time and unlike many of her cohabitants, she had tried to keep her clothes on as much as possible. She was on, she thought, what seemed like her third lifetime. She hoped the current one would turn out better.

TWO
"The Roundhouse", Philadelphia Police Headquarters
Office of the Commissioner
Philadelphia, PA

THE FBI'S DEPUTY DIRECTOR was late and Basil Jablonski was not in the mood for uncertainty. It was never far from his mind that he served as Police Commissioner "at the pleasure" of the mayor and *that* mayor was up for reelection in the Fall. A low-crime summer was always good for an incumbent, he'd learned. A high-crime one, or one with any sort of spectacular violence was, as Marlon Brando put it in Jablonski's favorite movie, "a one-way ticket to Palookaville" for the sitting P.C. He had just put a down payment on a summer home in Margate, a quiet, upscale seaside town south of Long Beach Island. If His Honor did not win reelection in November his retirement would be forcibly accelerated and his nest egg would suddenly develop a large crack or two. And Margate was a very long commute from Palookaville. Always a step-wise planner, Jablonski had initiated some quiet conversations about a job in the private security sector. It was a fledgling industry and he envisioned himself a consultant of sorts. Most of the would-be employers he talked with, however, were in the market for night watchmen or security guards. Jablonski was convinced that providing private security for wealthy or famous individuals was going to be a money-maker someday, maybe just as a reelected mayor was leaving office in four years. At least it would give him more time to work on it, he reasoned. And so while the safety of the citizens of the City of Brotherly Love was his job, the reelection of the Honorable James H.J. Tate was his mission.

Jablonski's office was simply but elegantly appointed. His predecessor had kept the cop in "Top Cop" and the environs had looked on the day of his appointment like a squad room in any one of a dozen local precincts. Jablonski had raised a few eyebrows when he had the office professionally redecorated and added a small room for press conferences. Some of the rank-and-file saw it as grandstanding but as he watched television news and its mobile cameras begin to chip away at the three daily newspapers, he understood the immense power of an image.

The meeting was supposed to start at noon and it was now ten-after. He personally liked the FBI's D.D. but turf and information had always clouded any attempts at collaboration. The Pennsylvania Attorney General was a long-time friend but even Bill Sennett couldn't say no when the Feds requested a Joint Task Force on what they referred to as "O.C.", the new slang for organized crime. Philadelphia was home to two rival Families and after a bloody run of murders and retaliations in the early sixties a sort-of peace accord had been reached. The dons and *capos* were beginning to understand that publicity hurt their enterprise and forced Jablonski to crack down on things he might have otherwise benignly ignored. He was on good terms with the two most prominent actors, the Rocca brothers and solid-waste entrepreneur Danny Ragone. But the truce between them was a brittle one and, in Jablonski's experience, if one were provoked there would be bloodshed. Both were putatively "legitimate" businessmen with fingers that reached far and wide in the tri-state area of Pennsylvania, New Jersey and Delaware. But, Jablonski knew, things were going to change. The South Jersey suburbs were exploding and the ports grew busier every year. And the influx of narcotics and marijuana posed a challenge of unprecedented proportions for all of law enforcement. It was a simmering pot on a good day, Jablonski realized, and he was determined that it would not boil over before the election. And now the FBI and the A.G. wanted to move on making a big show of breaking up the Mafia's hold on the city and stopping them from sending their slippery tentacles further across the Delaware River. If not handled correctly, he thought, it would start a murderous game of musical chairs with both crime families quickly realizing there would be a seat for only one of them when it was all over. Jablonski's intercom buzzed and he toggled the little black switch.

"Director Durkin is here," his receptionist said.

"Show him in, Catherine. And be a good girl and bring us some coffee, would you?"

The paneled door opened and Catherine stepped in. "Director Durkin from the FBI, Commissioner," she said almost reverently. "I'll bring the coffee directly."

John J. Durkin was a tall, thin man who walked with an athlete's swagger. He had light hair streaked with silver, a pointed chin and a pleasantly straightforward manner. His face had the smooth tan of a frequent golfer and he wore the blue-blazer and khaki-pants uniform of a career Fed. Jablonski rose to greet him. "J.J.," he said, "Always a pleasure. Besides timely and full payment of my income tax, what can I do for the Federal Government today?"

Durkin shook his hand warmly and sat down, a leather portfolio on his lap.

"Good to see you, Basil. How are things with the family?"

"Empty nest as of last June. How about you?"

"The girls, Karen and Deborah, are doing well. Still grade-schoolers. We got started a little late."

The door opened again and Catherine brought the coffee in on an enameled wooden tray. "Thank you," Jablonski said. "Please see that we're not interrupted." Catherine nodded, smiled at Durkin and breezed out of the room.

"Your wife allows you to have such an attractive secretary?"

"Doesn't yours?"

Durkin laughed. "My secretary is a two-hundred-and-forty pound man of Armenian descent with a gun who also happens to type eighty words a minute. So, will Officer Walker be joining us today?"

Jablonski pulled open a desk drawer and extracted the bottle with the black label. Durkin poured the coffee. Jablonski added the scotch. He hoped Durkin wouldn't notice the slight hand tremor that he had developed over the last month.

Durkin took a long sip. "I would think a well-publicized campaign to bring down the scourge of organized crime would do well for the mayor's reelection chances, wouldn't you?"

It was not what Jablonski wanted to hear. He shifted his ample bulk in the leather chair. "I think His Honor would prefer a calm several months with a lower violent crime rate, fewer murders and no high-profile wrongdoing, to be perfectly honest. My fear is that any concentrated pressure at this point will panic the major players into making moves that are in neither our nor their best interests."

Durkin sipped again and set down his cup. "I wasn't aware that we were concerned with *their* best interests, but let me say up front that I and the United States Attorney General, as well as the State A.G and the Director would tend to agree with that overall assessment. But we also feel we're at a crux here and that time is of the essence. Even gangsters like to take the summer months off. Now would be the time to move, when their guard is, perhaps, lowered a bit. When their attentions are, perhaps, directed elsewhere."

Jablonski drained his cup but held it tightly in his meaty hand. "The mayor's opponent, as I'm sure you know, is a bit of a bleeding heart liberal," he said. "He'd like the police to be kind and gentle to the murderers and the child rapists and, let's face it, John, that's just not our style. I'm sure the next P.C. might stop short of disarming the beat cops, but I can't guarantee it. My gut," he tapped his protruding belly for emphasis, "tells me we get Hizzoner safely back in office, me safely back at this desk and then you and I can go in with both barrels and clean house."

Durkin proffered his cup and Jablonski poured from the bottle.

"I understand the logic, Basil. I really do. But, as usual, this is coming from way above my head. The A.G.'s office inherited Bobby Kennedy's crusade and it is not about to be seen as dropping the proverbial ball. Between us, it would not surprise me at all if the junior Senator from New York announced his presidential ambitions early next year. He'll win in a landslide, of course, and every Justice Department appointment will be up for grabs. Careers are made when the guard in Washington changes. You know that the annihilation of the Mafia in America is something near and dear to RFK's heart and so does everyone at the Bureau and over at Justice. It's the smart play, Basil. Your cooperation and assistance on this initiative would not go unnoticed or unrewarded in a Kennedy administration. A new president makes hundreds of appointments right after the election. And a big-city P.C. who took on the Mob would make for some very positive spin."

"Spin?"

"Sorry, it's a new phrase out of D.C. Spin is making whatever we do look good and righteous even if it isn't. Like throwing a curve. You put spin on it to fool the batter."

"I don't really have a vote here, do I, J.J.?" Jablonski asked.

"You have a strongly valued opinion which I will carry back all the way to the Director himself. You have my word."

Jablonski poured more scotch into his own cup and took a healthy swallow. He looked at Durkin's cuff links which were embossed with the FBI's crest. "What do you need from me?" he said.

"I'm assigning two agents to be a special liaison with your P.D. It's a new concept we're trying out and you get to be the guinea pig. Basically, you and they will comprise the Joint Task Force on Organized Crime for right now but we'll be adding men from both our ranks as the operation progresses. We think we've got pretty good intel right now,"

"So it's an operation now?" Jablonski chuckled.

"Oh, yes. Operation Trump Card," Durkin replied.

"Catchy," Jablonski said.

"I'm sure a GS-15 was assigned the task of coming up with the name and that he got a merit bonus for his effort. So…can I tell the Director we have your support?"

Jablonski nodded in assent. "And who are these agents you're so generously assigning me?"

"Two guys from the Philly Field Office," Durkin said. "I'll send you their files this afternoon. I'm not really a fan of Neapolitans, but I thought Italian surnames might help with access to informants in certain situations. Sesso and Speziale."

Jablonski chuckled. "Sounds like the name of a Ginzo water ice parlor."

Durkin held out his cup again. Once Jablonski had poured he raised it. "For our freedom and yours," Durkin said, reciting the national motto of Poland.

Jablonski nodded. "*Eire go Deo*," he said, raising his own cup. "Ireland is Forever."

They tapped the cups together, the bone china sounding a musical note.

"So how does a Polack learn to speak Gaelic?" Durkin asked, rising from his chair.

"My first partner was a bloody Mick like you," Jablonski said.

"He taught me some Gaelic. I taught him how not to get shot." He rose from his chair and saluted.

"I'll let myself out," Durkin said. "Best to Mary Theresa."

Jablonski waited until the door had closed before he sat down. One of the pictures on his desk showed two young police officers in dress blue uniforms holding an infant in a white christening dress. He thought about the things that had happened to the three of them in the years since that day. With a trembling hand he poured himself more scotch.

Fifteen minutes passed before he made the decision. Jablonski still had a little of the Johnnie Walker glow when he toggled the intercom.

"Yes, Commissioner?" Catherine asked.

"Get me The Club."

"Yes, Commissioner. I'll let you know when Mr. Kelly is on the line."

Seconds later Jablonski's speaker buzzed.

He punched the blinking button on his phone and picked up the receiver.

♦ ♦ ♦

Surf City

Ronnie Dunn sat on what passed for his front porch. The sun was behind him now as he faced the beach and watched the glistening expanse of flat sand exposed at low tide. Gulls flew in low, flapping and squawking, and the wind flecked his hair with grains of sand. He was still upset that he'd taken the bait; that he'd even reacted; and now a stupid, spoiled rich kid had gotten the better of him. It was a recurring theme, he mused. It hadn't cost him anything this time but for someone whose greatest skill had once been patience and self-control, it was a glaring deterioration. The car had Jersey plates, he'd noticed, and Ronnie hoped the kids weren't locals or full summer renters. Surf City was his home for now and he wasn't looking for trouble. He glanced at the ramshackle cottage behind him. "Be it ever so humble," he thought to himself.

His gaze turned to the slate-grey Atlantic. Sets of waves were breaking gently, sending spray and foam incrementally shoreward. Further down the beach the rock jetty stretched out its long, black arm, the wet boulders catching a glint of the late-day sun. His end of town, as he thought of it, was sparsely built-upon and several city blocks separated him from Ship Bottom, the next town over. The moon was visible above the eastern horizon but the summer equinox was almost a month away. Ronnie watched the ocean and pondered his current state of mind. He would never, he thought, live anywhere but on the ocean. He didn't want a yard with its bushes, its vines and its whining insects. He'd had enough of rain and lush green vegetation and fetid water to last him a lifetime. And when the waves crashed they didn't really sound like cannon fire, he knew. That's why he enjoyed the sound. No more cannons, no more tracers, no more screams in the night. Just the moon, the sun, the sand and the sea. From now on he would always live by the ocean.

Because he was certain of one thing.

He was never going back to the jungle.

THREE
Surf City

MICKEY TRUDGED UP TO the foot of the wooden outside stairs and was about to mount the first step when she heard her name being called. She peered between the risers and saw Loretta LaMarro, her landlady, waving to her.

"Got time for a cold one?" Loretta asked.

"I'm a mess," Mickey replied gesturing to her stained top and flashing her dirty palms.

"Nonsense," Loretta said. "You look wonderful. Come in and cool off for a minute."

Mickey rubbed her palms together and dusted her cut-offs as best she could then walked around underneath the stairs. Loretta had a cigarette dangling from the corner of her mouth and held the aluminum screen door open with a tanned outstretched arm. The spaces between the sandy risers covered her in striped shadows from head to toe.

"I'm filthy dirty and I smell like sweat and gasoline," Mickey said as she approached. "You sure?"

Loretta rolled her eyes. "I taught third-graders for twenty years. Believe me, honey, I've seen and smelled much worse."

Mickey shook out her hair and walked into the cool of the apartment that was just below hers. Loretta let the screen door slam noisily and pulled the inner wooden door shut. The cool air washed over her like a breaking wave.

"Don't say it," Loretta said. "I know, I know; my air conditioner is much better than yours." She pointed to the window where the large, boxy Norge with the fake-wood panel front was rattling the glass in the lower half of a double-hung. Fuzzy dishtowels were stuffed on either side of the unit to make a passable seal with the window frame. "I've asked Mayor Bill but he says it's not in the budget right now. Says all the money's tied up in that fancy police car of yours. If it gets too hot up there just let me know. I have a little leeway with him but I don't want to use it just yet. Come on, sweetie, sit down."

Mickey looked around at the tidy apartment. The furniture, she noticed, had plastic slipcovers on every cushion. Her host watched her take it all in.

"You couldn't hurl it if you tried," Loretta said. "Sit on the sofa and put your feet up." Even the ottoman cushion was encased in clear vinyl, Mickey noticed. She slipped out of her flip-flops, traipsed across the worn woven throw rug and settled into the sofa. The plastic was cool and sticky against her skin.

Loretta walked to the refrigerator. "I keep it pretty well stocked even though I only nip occasionally. Too early for Scotch?"

Mickey chuckled in surprise.

"Maybe a little," she replied. "The guys on the squad used to make fun of me. Their usual was boilermakers and there I'd be with a Tab or a Fresca. *When* I got invited, which wasn't very often. Once in a while I'd have a beer just to get them off my back."

Loretta pulled on the horizontal silver handle and the door of the big Kelvinator swung open. A cloud of condensation appeared briefly around her and then dissipated.

"Beer it is, then," she said, peering inside. "Piels, Schaeffer, Schmidt's or Ballantine?"

"You *are* well stocked," Mickey said. She wiped sweat from her face and patted her hands dry on her shorts. "Ballantine, I guess." Mickey heard the clink of a glass bottle.

"I'll have the same," Loretta said amidst more clinking. The refrigerator door shut with a loud metallic click. "I used to like Piels mostly because I like Bob and Ray and they did the voices of the cartoon guys on their commercials." There was a softer metal-on-metal sound, instantly recognizable as a bottle opener, followed by two pops. "What were their names?"

"Bert and Harry," Mickey replied.

Loretta walked the short distance from the kitchen to the sofa and handed Mickey the sweating bottle. "Want a glass?" she asked. "And how does a nice young girl like you know that?"

Mickey reached for the bottle and touched the cool brown glass to each cheek.

"I watched a lot of baseball with my dad on the television. I know as much about beer as I do about batting averages. I could sing all the jingles in my sleep."

Loretta sat down and raised her bottle in a mock-toast. "Baseball and Ballantine," she sang softly.

"Baseball and Ballantine," Mickey replied a little off-key. They sang the next lines of the jingle together.

"What a combination, all across the nation, Baseball and –"

The both took a quick swig and continued.

"Ball-aann-tiiine."

Loretta laughed out loud and a tiny burp escaped. She covered her mouth in embarrassment then composed herself and took a small sip. She dabbed at her watering eyes and studied the red and white label with the three intertwined rings. "Jim was always a Ballantine man," she said. "After he died, I started drinking it just to remind me of him." She reached for the ashtray on the table beside her and took a quick draw, exhaling the blue smoke slowly. "I don't suppose you drank Ballantine with your dad?"

Mickey smiled and picked at a corner of her label with a thumbnail. "No, I can't say that we did. He always wanted me to be able to hold my own with the boys and then later with the guys, but I don't think I ever took a drink in front of him."

Loretta reached for a pack of Bel-Air Light Menthols and proffered it.

"No, thanks," Mickey replied. "I might have taken a drink or two when my dad wasn't looking but I never got started on cigarettes."

Loretta turned the pack over. "They have these coupons that you can collect, now. Like S and H Green Stamps, which I also save. Another fifty years or so and I'll have enough to buy a yacht I can tie up at the marina down in Holgate."

Both women became quiet, Loretta studying the Raleigh coupon and Mickey peering down the neck of her bottle. Then each took a generous swallow.

Loretta stubbed out her cigarette and set the pack down.

"So tell me," she said. "Do you have a boyfriend or somebody special? I know it's bold of me to ask."

"No, not at the moment," Mickey replied. "I swore I'd never date a cop and then cops were the only people I was ever around. Well, them and the criminals. And where I was living in California really didn't lend itself to relationships in the usual sense. As for now, I'm not sure how it would look for the Police Chief to be seeing someone even if there *was* someone."

"What do they call it now – the dating *pool*?" Loretta asked. "Well, let me tell you, honey, that the pool on Long Beach Island is pretty shallow most of the time. You need to look for some rich, single doctor or lawyer who's here for the summer, I think. It should be easy. If you see someone you like you could just arrest him for something. Loitering, maybe, or not using a turn signal. Be a cute story to tell your kids someday. Now me, I'm too old for a romance, but the mayor and I do keep company sometimes, since we're both widowed. Mostly we talk about our spouses and reminisce about married life. That probably seems strange, doesn't it?"

Mickey took another drink. "No, I think it's sweet. Where did you teach?"

"At a little Catholic grammar school in a little town on the other side of the state. I was one of only three lay teachers there. The rest were Franciscan nuns. I was probably a first crush for a lot of little boys, I suppose. But I loved it – it was the most wonderful job in the world. I can remember almost all of them and often think of what they might have grown up to become. Doctors, writers, teachers maybe? I was just one little blip in their lives and so the other thing I always wonder about is whether any of them remember me."

"Oh, I'm sure they do. I remember my third-grade teacher and I know I didn't have a crush on her."

Loretta almost snorted up her last swallow. "And who was that, may I inquire?"

"Sister Innocentia," Mickey replied. "Although I don't think there was anything innocent about her. She smoked like a fiend and swore like a stevedore. I thought she was wonderful. I always got the feeling that for her the choice was either the convent or reform school."

Loretta got up and headed to the refrigerator. "I'm having another. You?"

Mickey held her bottle up to the sunlight filtering through the window. "I have to be at the station at seven," she said and peeked at the round wall clock with the black Roman numerals. "I think I can have one more, maybe."

Loretta popped the tops on two more bottles and brought them over.

"You got a little sun, I see. "It looks good on you. I've got a chaise lounge you can borrow. Lay out in your bikini if you want."

"No bikini yet," Mickey replied.

"Well, we'll have to remedy that," Loretta said. "You may be doing a man's job but you are still a young woman."

"They call me 'the girl', the councilmen do. Did you know that? 'The girl.' Mayor Billy told me."

Loretta shook her head. "They're old and foolish and anything new scares them. I spent my life around children and what it taught me was that the future is like a train. You can't slow it down and you can't stop it. And if you stand on the tracks like those old farts, well... And you, whether you like it or not, represent the future. You think their wives don't secretly love that gun on your hip?"

Mickey reflexively reached down. "I guess I never thought about it."

"Not the gun – the power it represents. These women see you with a gun and they start getting ideas."

"You don't mean-"

"No," Loretta laughed, "Although I'm sure most would think about it once or twice a day from what I've seen. " She sipped her beer. "I mean they start thinking about having a little power themselves. A career or a life outside of domestic bliss. That's what has these codgers pissing in their boots. You're not just a woman with a man's job, honey. You're a woman with power in a man's world. That's why they call you 'the girl.' To try and diminish you – to diminish that power. Because it petrifies them."

Mickey studied the sweating bottle and took a small swig. "I've had to be one of the guys for a long time," she finally said. "It was important to my dad and so that's just how it's always been for me. I didn't do it for power or to prove a point."

"How old were you when your mother died?" Loretta asked.

Mickey looked at her.

"Mayor Billy told me. It's OK. It must have been so hard for you, is all I'm saying."

Mickey put the bottle to her lips but did not drink. Then she placed both hands around it in her lap. "I was fifteen," she said quietly. "And it was really hard for me but it was worse for my dad. I had a brother who died of cancer before I was born. So when my mom passed away I felt like I had to make sure Dad was alright. I had to be tough for him. My becoming a police officer was the most important thing in the world to him for a long time. Like I said, power had nothing to do with it."

"Mayor Billy said your dad is a policeman as well."

"*Was*," Mickey replied. "He got shot on the job and had to take disability. Being a cop was almost all he had left and then even that got taken away."

"You raised yourself, didn't you?"

"I don't mean to make it sound like he neglected me. It wasn't like that at all. But he taught me the things *he* knew about. Which were guy things and cop things. Cars and sports and how to make it through the academy. He did the best he could."

"I'm sure he did," Loretta said. "But, you are not a *guy* and, please excuse an old lady's foolishness here, but you need to remind yourself of that. I don't mean wearing mascara or false eyelashes or acting demure. You are the Police Chief after all. But that's not all you are Go out on a date, wear a dress, go buy a damn bikini if you want. And if anyone doesn't like it well then you know where to tell them to go. That's part of your power as well. The world is changing for us, honey. You just got pushed to the front of the line."

Loretta inhaled deeply and continued.

"Oh my," she said. "I guess I'm not really a two-beer broad and I've overstepped my bounds already, but being the chief is *what* you are, sweetie, not *who* you are. You are a grown woman with smarts and guts. They only person who can hold you back is you."

* * *

Mickey looked at the pictures hung neatly on the wall. A young couple in wedding clothes; a younger Loretta with permed blond hair standing on a boardwalk in a flowing summer dress; a handsome dark-haired man in a Navy dress uniform.

"You never had kids of your own?" Mickey asked

Loretta dropped her chin. "I had hundreds of kids, sweetie. And I loved them all like they were my very own. It was all I ever needed."

They drank in silence for a few moments. The air conditioner sighed, shuddered and then shut down.

"In just a few days," Loretta said, "this town will be packed with shoobies basting in Coppertone. You'll be very busy but I want you to remember what I said."

"OK," Mickey replied, "OK, but I have to know. What's with this whole shoobie thing?"

"Shoobies?" Loretta replied. "Oh, tourists, honey. Especially the ones from Philly, no disrespect. Pale as skim milk, usually wearing sandals, black dress socks and undershirts or housecoats and shower caps to the beach. They would bring their lunches with them in a shoebox. So first they were called 'shoeboxers' and then they became just shoobies. It's not a compliment, in case you were wondering."

"That much I got," Mickey said.

"So, as I was saying, you either have to find a nice local guy in the next four days or wait until Labor Day when the season ends and then arrest your doctor or lawyer before he gets to the causeway and escapes."

"I don't see myself with a doctor or a lawyer," Mickey said.

Loretta took a long swallow and wiped her lips with the back of her hand. "OK, so no cops, no doctors, no lawyers. Who does that leave – fishermen?"

Mickey crinkled her nose in distaste.

"Yeah, no fishermen either. I get that. Fireman maybe? There's a few of those around."

"Not big on red suspenders," Mickey said. "And besides, they're the same as cops for the most part."

"You're not leaving much to choose from. If you tell me what you want I can at least keep an eye out for any likely prospects. I'm a retired schoolteacher, not a recluse."

"You make it sound like shopping for a car."

"It's not that much different." Loretta answered. "Just beware of trade-ins and ones that have been in damaged in accidents." She let the thought hang in the air.

Mickey polished off the remainder of her Ballantine and looked again at the clock which was just about register five-thirty-five. "I guess what worries me is that I've been through a lot and I've seen things that most people would never see or want to see. I think it's made me different than I used to be. It would be hard for someone to have to deal with that every day. Someone who hasn't seen it or hasn't experienced it themselves. They couldn't, like they say now, relate. And I guess there's the whole power thing now that I didn't really think about."

"A strong man will be attracted to that power, not intimidated by it. A strong man will *respect* it. That's the person you look for."

Mickey wiped the bottle against her cheek and peered down the neck. "I have to keep a certain distance to do my job, though. You understand that, right?"

"Distance is fine, but I don't want you to be lonely," Loretta said. "I think that's what I'm most afraid of, that I'll be lonely. I think that's what Mayor Billy is afraid of, too. But we're older now. You're a young, very attractive woman. You put the uniform on but you have to remember to take it off now and then." She gave Mickey an impish grin. "And just between us girls, when is the last time you…? You know."

Mickey reached for her flip-flops and stood up. She smiled back at Loretta. "Long enough that I might have to read the manual again."

"Bikini," Loretta said and drank the last of her beer. Mickey slipped her toes into the pink rubber sandals. Loretta took the empty bottle from her hand and brought her face close to Mickey's.

"You know, you might have to let what you're looking for *find* you," Loretta said. "But when it does, you have to be ready to take a little risk. You have to be willing let go a little bit; to give if you want to get. That's how it works, sweetie. You can't always be in control. OK? You can be one of the guys when you're wearing your gun. But save a little time for Michaela, OK?"

Mickey nodded and wondered if the second beer had been a mistake. A sea of emotions was suddenly churning inside her. Loretta's concern was sincere and even for someone who had never had children it was also, she realized, maternal. It had been such a long time since her own mother or, really, any woman had whispered in her ear or dried her tears or given her advice or consolation. So many years now she'd spent building a shell like the ones she saw on the beach every day.

Loretta touched her on the shoulder. "I'll pick up some Tab and some Fresca when I go to the market. If you need someone to talk to you knock on that door. Anytime, right? Unless there's a green Fairlane in the lot." She winked.

Mickey nodded again and without speaking shuffled toward the door, the sandals *thwack-thwacking* against her bare heels with each step. Loretta stayed where she was and Mickey let herself out. Once back in the fading sun she climbed the wooden stairs slowly, looking first at the bay close by and then across to the rolling coamers out on the ocean in the opposite direction. The sea was several different colors all at once. She stood at the deck railing, letting the salt breeze caress her face for several minutes before finally going inside. Mickey shucked her flip-flops and checked the clock. When she sat on the old four-poster bed she realized the second beer might have been ill advised. "Fifteen minutes," she told herself and pulled both pillows beneath her. In less than a minute she was asleep.

* * *

Something didn't seem right but her mind was moving slowly and she couldn't figure out what it was. "Better wake up now," a woman's voice said. "Sleepy time's over. Open your eyes."

It took a moment for her to realize that the voice she was hearing was her own.

None of the three girls moved. She hated to disturb them. They looked so peaceful, all lying so perfectly still. It was very cold, but they had fallen asleep with their little jackets on. Of course, she reasoned, that's why they didn't take notice.

"Look," Mickey said to them. "Look. *Their* eyes are open. All three of them. They want you to wake up and play with them." The girls acted as if they couldn't hear her but she knew they could. "Come on, girls. Here's Linda and here's Betsy and even Chantrell – they're awake and they want to play. It's time to get up now." She reached a hand out to touch the hem of a dirty pink coat. "Oh, you've spilled something. It's OK. Don't worry. We'll get it cleaned up. You'll be good as new soon." Mickey looked down and saw the sticky dark liquid on her fingers. There was a siren blaring somewhere. That will scare the girls, she thought. She bent close to them. "I'm sorry," she said. "Oh, I am so sorry."

"It's alright," her mother said. "Don't be sorry. It wasn't your fault. You can stop crying now." Mickey buried her head further and sobbed louder. Her mother stroked her hair. "Now, now, little black Irish, that's enough tears for one day. That's enough tears for a whole week. Maybe for a whole year, even. Stop your crying now, love. Stop your crying and open your eyes. Lord knows you're knackered but it's time to wake up. Wake up now, darlin'. Time to open your eyes. Open your eyes, Michaela. Open your eyes."

* * *

Mickey woke with a start. She could hear blood pounding in her ears with every heartbeat. She sat up and looked at the clock by the bedside. Only a short time had passed. She relaxed. The dream had been vivid and seemed to last much longer than the time that had actually gone by. She had not dreamt of her mother in months. But she had smelled her perfume – *Wind Song* – and felt the warmth of her body. She heard the lilting, musical way she talked. Mickey tried, but found she could not remember what her mother had been saying to her or why she'd been crying. It had made her happy to feel the slender but strong arms around her again. It had made her feel safe. But now she could not recall even a single word. There were tears in her eyes and on her cheeks, she realized, and she wiped them away with the bedsheet. And there had been something else in the dream, she knew. But it was out of reach now and even the comforting sense of her mother was rapidly fading.

Mickey got up slowly. The pillow was wet and the skin of her arms shone with tiny beads of perspiration. She touched her forehead and found it moist as well, brushing away strands of clinging hair. The bed had a roomy queen-size mattress but only one side showed any sign of compression. She didn't remember getting undressed but dirty clothes lay in a heap on the floor. She walked toward the cramped bathroom and caught sight of herself in a long oval wall mirror. Mickey stopped. She usually avoided looking at herself naked but now Loretta's words came back to her. She turned and squared her shoulders, taking in the image and allowing for a moment the thoughts she usually dismissed. The athletic curves, the flat tummy, the ample breasts, the way her dark hair caught the sunlight and turned it red. Loretta was right – the woman in the mirror was who Michaela Cleary really was underneath everything she tried to cover it with.

"Yeah," Mickey said as she moved to the tiny shower. "Most definitely not one of the guys."

FOUR

MICKEY LEFT HER APARTMENT and slipped back over the bay on the causeway to the mainland so she could wind out the tightly tuned engine on the long straightaways of the Garden State Parkway. She had all the windows down and the empty wooden shotgun rack vibrated behind her. She loved the blue-green glow of the gauges, the long, horizontal speedometer and the feel of the shift knob in her hand. The asphalt was dry and there was hardly any traffic, so she floored the accelerator and marveled at the G-force a big combustion engine could generate as it pushed her back against the seat. She hoped she didn't encounter any bored Staties or Ocean County Sheriff's cars on this milk run but at least she was in uniform and had all her credentials in order. Even her inspection sticker was up-to-date.

The cruiser was performing better than she anticipated and she kept passing turnaround exits until finally deciding it was time to head back to Long Beach Island. The car handled superbly and she was thankful she wouldn't have to tweak the suspension again. Mickey throttled down and exited the Parkway, cruising back onto Highway 9. At lower speeds the Chevelle behaved like a caged animal, seemingly ready to spring at the first chance. She passed a sign for Sunshine Park, the nudist colony in Mays Landing and several ubiquitous advertisements for Zaberer's Restaurant in Atlantic City. She followed the old asphalt to the causeway and the wooden bridges until she was all the way across the bay. She rolled into the town of Ship Bottom which was at the approximate center of Long Beach Island. Mickey downshifted again and motored slowly until she hit Barnegat Avenue. She turned south towards the tip of the Island instead of north toward the station, wanting to enjoy the summer night just a while longer. Each little beach town she passed was almost the same but then not quite. Long Beach Boulevard was the main drag but the road jigged and jogged as the bay took little bites of the island and then spit them back out. Neat little "salt-box" houses, some with the living areas raised on pilings, were tucked side-by-side. There were a few grass lawns but most owners gave up and their tiny yards were squares or rectangles of bleached and broken shells. She crossed into Long Beach Township, then continued to Beach Haven where the owner of the Sea Spray Motel gave her a friendly wave. The paved road ended south of the Holgate Marina which berthed the pricey boats capable of negotiating the Inlet and the big swells of the open ocean. There were a few tourists, she noted, but not many. Most of the human activity was centered on making each little town ready for the onslaught of visitors. Mickey turned back north. Out her window on Little Egg Harbor Bay she could clearly see the three white masts and flag-festooned rigging of the land-moored schooner *Lucy Evelyn*, one of the Island's biggest tourist attractions. Each town had its own little business district with markets and souvenir shops and salt-water taffy stands. Ocean City had its Boardwalk, she knew, but the nestling of the small municipalities right next to each other reminded her of the neighborhoods in Philadelphia – each with its own character and identity. She passed a Long Beach Police cruiser who recognized her and whooped his siren. She flashed her cherry-toppers in reply. The Chevelle's engine purred as she covered the last few miles of the straight, two-lane road and pulled the cruiser into the gravel parking lot behind the red brick shadow of the Surf City Police Department.

Inside, Kaylen was at his desk completing the log book.

"That shouldn't take you very long," Mickey said as she passed him.

Kaylen chuckled. "Spent an hour looking for a lost dog after I left you," he said.

"Find him?"

"Her," Kaylen answered. "And yeah. Keeping company with the neighbor's poodle. There might be some funny looking dogs running around in a few months."

"And they call it puppy love," Mickey said.

"Hey, I actually have that record," Kaylen replied, pointing to a stack of 45's on a battered credenza. "You like Paul Anka?"

"Uh, maybe later," Mickey said. She sat down and rested her hands on her desk. "Mind if I ask you something?" she said.

"Anything, Chief. Shoot."

"How come you didn't apply for this job? You're smart, capable; you would've have done a good job."

Kaylen set down his Bic pen and looked at her. "Honestly, Chief, I didn't want it. Too much responsibility, too much politics. It seems quiet now but once the season starts they'll be pestering you day and night. I have plenty to keep me busy and I really like being a Deputy."

"You'd rather be Tonto than the Lone Ranger?"

"No, ma'am," Kaylen replied. "I mean, yes ma'am. But you know what I'm saying. I just know I'm a better Deputy than I would be a Chief. I'm not unhappy. I got along great with Chief Pete and I think you and me are getting along fine, too."

Mickey regarded him for a moment. She'd read his file, knew a little of his background but he was still a bit of an enigma to her. He was twenty-two but could pass for a high-school kid out of uniform. He didn't seem to like to make decisions and acted perplexed when she would tell him to 'use your discretion'. In some ways, she thought, he was a product of another time. He wouldn't, she realized, last an hour on the street in Philadelphia, but maybe he was perfect for a Jersey beach town. And his first instinct had been to protect her, she reminded herself.

"Why don't you get out of here," Mickey said. "You have big plans tonight?"

"Yankees are on the radio," he replied.

She looked at his desk and its surroundings. His blotter was a model of neatness and organization. Behind him on the wall was an autographed picture of Mickey Mantle, all boyish grin and gleaming teeth. "To my friend, Kaylen Fair Brother," a neat black cursive exclaimed. "Best Always – Mickey #7". Her deputy's general environs, she noticed, were dominated by the baseball icon. In addition to the picture there was a broken piece of a wooden bat, a scuffed baseball with the date "5/15/64 – YS" hand lettered between the red laces, a Topps Mantle card from 1960 and, close by, a Roger Maris card with a thick black "X" drawn over the brooding, crew-cut visage of the young outfielder. Mickey took it all in for a moment and wondered what other treasures he had.

"I take it you're a Mantle fan," she said finally.

"Guess you could say that, Chief. I like the Yankees but I'd like any team Mickey Mantle played for. I think he's the greatest player who ever lived. And he's a great person, too."

"Maybe the Phillies could pick him up in the off-season."

"No, ma'am. The Mick would never, ever leave the Yankees. I'd say he'd retire before playing for anyone else even if they tried to trade him, which they wouldn't. Mantle is loyal like that. A lot of guys aren't but he is."

Mickey smiled. "You get to see him play in person?"

"A few times," Kaylen responded. "New York City's a long drive and the Bronx isn't a great place to park but I've done it. I've seen him more when the Yanks play the Senators down in Washington. I can afford better seats there, too. Yankee Stadium is really expensive."

Mickey folded her hands on her desk. "I kind of like Connie Mack Stadium, myself. My last beat was in North Philadelphia so it's familiar territory. And parking's not a problem when you have a squad car and a badge. Neither are tickets or good seats."

Kaylen raised his eyebrows. "If the Phillies play the Yanks in the Series I'm riding with you," he said.

"Not holding my breath, Deputy. Not after '64. I think it took everything out of Gene Mauch," she replied referring to the Phillies late season collapse and their long-time, cigar-chomping skipper.

"You could be right," Kaylen said. "So who's your favorite player?"

"Jim Bunning's my favorite pitcher," she answered. "And Johnny Callison is my favorite everyday player. Like you said – when they're in the World Series we'll take the Chevelle, park right at the gate and sit behind home plate. You'll be able to count the hairs on Mantle's arms."

"I'll hold you to that Chief. But that means I have to start rooting a little for the Phillies now. On the sly, of course."

"Got it," she said. "Well, at least have a beer and hot dog while you're listening to the game. That's an order, Deputy."

Kaylen rose from his chair. "I can stop at the A & W on my way home for the hot dogs. And I think I have might some Ortleib's in the fridge, so I guess I'm all set."

Baseball and Ballantine popped into her head for a split-second and then departed. "OK," Mickey said. "Tomorrow we'll start planning strategy for the long weekend. Maybe a couple more lost dogs, some jellyfish stings and some D and D's will be the worst of it."

"The lifeguards will start moving in tonight and tomorrow," Kaylen said. "Mostly they're college kids living together on their own in rentals, so when they're not on the chair we usually have to keep an eye on them. Last summer one of them got into trouble with a girl who was a little bit young."

"How young?"

"Thirteen."

"Yeah," Mickey said. "That's young. What happened?"

"Well, to be honest Chief, she did, you know, look – uh – more, um, *developed*?"

"Got it. So how did you handle it?"

"Well, her dad goes to the lifeguard's place and hauls her out before anything happens. Then he beats the tar out of the lifeguard and he's… *old*. Like probably forty. Luckily, Chief Pete shows up before he kills the kid."

"What'd he do?"

"Told the dad to go home and keep quiet. Said he would have done the same thing. Then he drives the kid over the bridge and leaves him at a phone booth in the Pine Barrens with a dime to call his folks. Tells him never to set foot on the Island again."

"That's it?"

"That was it. Never heard another word about it."

"No police brutality rap? No lawsuit?"

"Nope. I asked Chief Pete about it. Said I should forget it. It's summer at the shore."

"I don't know that we'll be handling it that way anymore," Mickey said.

"We didn't arrest a lot of people," Kaylen said. "Chief Pete, he said it was bad for business. Usually we just set them straight, sobered them up or kicked them out – one of the three. He said we had a lot of leeway down here. That's what he called it, leeway. Kind of like what you did with that kid today."

Mickey scratched at the back of her neck and thought again

about the drawn gun and how little leeway a bullet provided. "That was different," she replied. "From now on, just check with me if you have any questions about leeway, OK?"

Kaylen nodded.

"OK, now, hit the road. You don't want to miss the first pitch."

"Yes, sir Chief," he replied. "I mean ma'am."

Mickey nodded as he turned to leave and then said, "Deputy? How about we save the Chief stuff for when we're in public. Otherwise, just call me Mickey."

"I'll try, Chief. Might take me a bit, though." He patted his pocket for his keys and walked out the door.

* * *

Mickey watched him leave. The little station got very quiet. She looked at the two jail cells and wondered how long it had been since either had even been locked. She had been skeptical that a two-man department was feasible for nine months of the year but in the three weeks she'd been on the job she realized not all that much happened in a beach town during the off-season. She understood why Chief Pete might have turned to the bottle, not out of stress but out of boredom. She wondered how long she would last. Her last day as a Philadelphia policewoman would never leave her, she realized. No matter how hard she tried to leave *it*. She wondered if this job was just the first phase of her own rehab, her own recovery. Surf City was a long way from North Philly, she thought. A long way from 20th and Aramingo. But it made her consider if anyplace would ever be far enough?

Mickey looked at the phone then at the wall clock. Her father would be done with dinner and in his chair. He would have the Channel 10 news on waiting for John Facenda to make sense of the world for him, for Tommy Brookshier to tell him how many games the Phillies were out of first place and for Herb Clarke, with his awful toupee, to predict what tomorrow would look like through his apartment window. She put her hand by the phone and tapped her index finger. What would she say when he answered, she wondered. How would either of them start? She moved her hand away from the phone and toggled the desk radio for Long Beach Island Dispatch.

"Go ahead, Surf City," a pleasant woman's voice said.

"Chief Cleary on duty, Dispatch. SCPD 1. "
"Copy that, Chief. Have a quiet night. Dispatch out."
Mickey clicked off the radio and stared at the phone. Tomorrow, she thought. Tomorrow would be a better day to call. She grabbed her keys and headed off for evening patrol.

The proprietor of Beachfront Liquors was gritting his teeth. If it got much worse he was calling the cops, he decided. William Wayne Wanamaker was a shoestring relative of the famous Philadelphia department store family. He had the benefit of the mellifluous name but absolutely none of the money, a fact he bemoaned to any customer who would listen. He kept a gold-painted statue of a perching bald eagle he'd bought at a John's Bargain Store on his counter, mimicking the gilded two-and-a-half ton sculpture that was the centerpiece of the downtown store's magnificent rotunda. A hand lettered sign hung from the ceiling above the cash register that said, "PAY ME AT THE EAGLE".

Beachfront Liquors made Wanamaker a good living. Several beach communities were "dry towns" where no liquor or beer sales were permitted. It was a throwback to the Quaker days and the famous "Blue Laws" which, in some places, would not allow even toy pails or shovels to be sold on Sundays because they were technically implements of work which was forbidden on the Sabbath. He had been called Billy or Bill until the eighth grade when his growth spurt sputtered. From the time he entered high school he was christened – and had since remained – Little Willie Wanamaker. He was thankful he had avoided Wee Willie Wanamaker, thinking that the three consecutive W's of his given name were never going to connote commercial success. To the locals and the long-time summer renters he was just Little Willie.

The four kids had all come in together and they smelled like a brewery. They wanted a case of beer and Willie figured they had polished off at least that much already — six twelve-ounce beers apiece for kids that were clearly not used to handling that kind of quantity. Three of the kids seemed to be more-or-less OK but the fourth was a loud-mouthed prick the others seemed to be afraid of.

"You have to sell to us if we're legal," the tall, dark-haired prick said.

"I'm afraid you're wrong, sir," Willie replied. "I am bound by law to refuse service to anyone who appears inebriated. You boys didn't drive here, did you??"

"No, sir, we walked here," one of the other three said. He was a skinny, pimply kid with a Phillies hat.

"Don't call this dipshit 'sir'," the tall one said. "His job is to sell us beer if were legally allowed to buy it. Jesus, he looks like a freakin' pygmy." He turned to Willie. "You get those clothes at the Boys' Department at Sears?" he asked. He began to laugh and then belched loudly.

"Let's just go," the pimply one said and the other two moved toward the door.

"Just fuckin' wait a minute," the loudmouth said. "If I told you who I was you'd sell me anything I wanted, sure as shit." The s's were sounding a little slurred and Willy was afraid the kid was going to puke right there in his store.

"I'll sell you a six of Schmidt's," Will said finally. "But that's it. And then you have to leave."

The tall loudmouth reached into his pocket, fumbling with a crumpled pile of bills.

"Schmidt's is horse piss and you know it. Better be cold," he said.

Willie grabbed the beer from the small showroom cooler and placed it on the counter. The kid laid out the bills. It looked like there was a hundred bucks at least. Willie pulled out a limp fiver and pushed the stack back.

"Change?" the kid asked. His breath reeked of onions and garlic.

"They're returnables," Willie answered. "You'll get your deposit when you bring the bottles back."

The kid fumbled with the bills and stuffed them in his pocket. "Del, grab the beer," he said. One of the other kids picked it up with both hands and they moved slowly toward the door.

"You gotta be Jewish," the loudmouth said on his way out.

"German," Willie replied. "And you boys have a nice night, now." He rang up the sale on the ancient register and pushed the cash drawer closed. He walked to the window to make sure they weren't getting into a car and watched as they weaved away on foot. There were no other people on the street and Willie decided it was near enough to closing to start locking up. His business mantra had always been "the customer is always right even when the customer is an asshole," but it had been tested tonight.

Willie was flipping the sign in the front door when he saw the Police Chief's car drive by. He gave her a big wave and was surprised when she slowed and pulled over.

Willie liked the new Chief. He was surprised like everyone else when the announcement was made – he'd had no idea there were women police officers who carried guns and arrested people. He figured they just answered phones or took dictation. But this one had actually come around her first week and introduced herself, which impressed William Wanamaker greatly. Plus, she was a looker. He liked her dark eyes and her dark hair which she kept kind of short but without it looking butch. He liked the way she filled out her uniform, especially the top floor. He bet she'd look good in shorts. The way he figured it, a good looking lady cop was good business for Surf City and that meant good business for him. Mayor Tunell had warned him that she'd been a street cop in Philly and had been in a few scrapes; at least one that involved gunfire and fatalities. To Willie, it just made her more interesting.

He wiped his hands on his store apron and stood in the doorway.

"Evening, Chief Cleary," he said.

"Mr. Wanamaker," she said in reply. "Closing early?"

"Just a few minutes," Willie said. "Long day, you know?"

The Chief nodded. "Any problems the department can assist you with tonight?"

Willie had an idea. "I just refused service to four teenagers. I don't think they were very happy about it."

"Underage?"

"No, they were legal," he said realizing he'd never checked a driver's license to make sure. "But looked like maybe they'd had a few already."

"They weren't driving, were they Willie?"

"No ma'am," Willie answered. "I watched 'em leave just to make sure. They were walking a little crooked but they were walking."

"Which way?" the Chief asked him.

"North on Long Beach. But then I think they turned."

He watched the Chief look around the store. "Do you take the cash from the till home with you?"

"No," he said. "I put it in a little safe I have in back. The lady from the bank comes and picks it up for me."

The Chief walked around eyeballing the premises. "What's in back?" she asked.

"The big walk-in cooler where we keep the cases and the kegs. Pretty cold in there. You want to see it?"

"That's OK," she answered. "Another time maybe."

"Alright, then," Willie said. "Appreciate your stopping, Chief."

"Just looking out for you, William," she replied, her eyes still darting around the premises. "You ever been robbed?"

"Nope. Never. Not even close. Not really that kind of town if you catch my drift."

"Yeah," Mickey said with a little laugh. "That's what I hear."

"You gonna check out those boys?" he asked.

"I might drive north a couple blocks first," she said. "Just to make sure they got home OK." She fingered her nightstick. "I'll keep an eye on the place tonight. In case any of your customers get thirsty."

"Thanks, Chief," Willie said. "Anything I can do for you, you just let me know."

"I'll keep that in mind," she replied and strolled out the door.

The glow of a fire on the beach at the far end of town caught Mickey's attention. She flipped off the headlights as she approached the borough limits and slowed, letting the idle speed keep the cruiser in motion. Beach blazes were prohibited by ordinance between the Memorial and Labor Day weekends and somewhat frowned up the rest of the year. But what she spied wasn't exactly a conflagration, there weren't any signs of a beach party and no one had complained. All she saw was a lone figure silhouetted against the ocean by the firelight. Something small and metallic flashed intermittently, mirroring the flames like a lighthouse beacon. The figure - she couldn't really tell whether it was a man or a woman – appeared to be sitting or perhaps kneeling on the sand and remained nearly motionless. The only sound outside of the engine came from the surf and the snap of the wood as it was consumed. Mickey thought the silhouette turned its head to follow her as she cruised slowly by and there was a brief moment when two red circles appeared, like an animal in the woods caught in a flashlight's beam. It reminded her of the night she had arrived in Surf City, emerging from the dense and almost surreal darkness of the New Jersey Pine Barrens. Every curve had revealed nocturnal creatures with shining eyes moving in the dense brush just off the roadway, frozen by the headlights. It was the most foreboding place she had ever seen and she remembered not ever wanting to venture there in darkness again.

Mickey decided she'd stop and make the acquaintance of the fire's sole attendant. Maybe remind him or her about the ordinance that would go into effect in a few days. But just as she was ready to turn off the ignition the dispatch radio crackled. She had to think for a moment which way the address was from her location but then she pressed the gas pedal, turned her headlights back on and sped away. The AM station she had tuned in was playing The Rolling Stones' "Ruby Tuesday". The last line she caught was about life being unkind. She turned right at the bay road and hit the roof lights.

Ronnie Dunn stirred the fire with the tip of the blade, the burning driftwood crackling and sparking with the disturbance. The weapon had accompanied him home from Southeast Asia strapped to his leg, negotiating one military transport and two commercial airline flights without attracting notice. The other things he'd sent stateside or brought back with him in his duffel had been carefully selected and now were tucked safely away but still accessible should the need arise. He still marveled at how easy it had been. He could have probably mailed a Huey helicopter home if he'd had the time and the right wrenches. They were all instruments of war, the hardware of extreme violence, but on the nights when he could sleep, he slept easier knowing they were close by.

The moon was getting small and high. Thin brush strokes of white clouds glowed and a shimmering highway of light rode on the incoming tide. He could hear the waves, not quite thundering yet but pounding with renewed energy as the lunar gravity pushed them back toward the land. Ronnie sat in a familiar crouch, one he'd spent countless moonless nights in, scanning the blackness around him with eyes and ears, one finger always on the trigger. A car with what Ronnie recognized as a powerful engine drove past on the dusty beach road. It seemed to slow for a moment but did not stop. He watched the tail lights glowing arterial-red in the night. Once they had disappeared he retrieved the joint from the sand and inhaled, feeling the familiar burn in his lungs. He held it and then blew the smoke out slowly, letting it rise in tandem with the column of white from the fire.

Ronnie thought more about the kid in the convertible. It occurred to him that he had fought for his country just to insure that stupid people like the kid could shout stupid things at the top of their lungs without fear. The irony of the boy's words now seemed humorous to him. If he would have stopped spewing hate for just one minute Ronnie would have told him. Yes, terrible things were done in war but Ronnie hadn't done them. He'd sacrificed himself and his career in an attempt to stop them. He carried home no shame, no guilt, and no lingering doubts about his actions. He had been what he promised to be when he took the oath. He was honorable, he knew, even if his discharge papers said otherwise.

The two girls could not have been more than fourteen and they were clearly terrified. Both clutched small "wet-look" purses to their chests. The blurred circular arc of a streetlight threw all the standing figures into stark relief and cast conflicting shadows on the asphalt. The location was several blocks off the beach road and the few small cottages nearby were dark. Mickey counted four large motorcycles but only three leather-vested figures. Red pulses from the cherry toppers bounced off the chrome of the bikes giving the scene a strobe-light effect. Mickey left them on and got out of the cruiser.

"You girls alright?" she asked as she approached. They didn't answer. They didn't look at her. They were looking at the three large men who surrounded them. Mickey recognized their expressions. "Frozen watchfulness" they'd called it at the academy. It was a telltale sign in several bad situations but most often it was seen on the faces of abused children and people who were being held or transported against their will. Mickey had seen the same face on an abducted young girl in the front seat of a car once and never forgot it.

"Girls?" she asked again. "You OK?"

"We got a problem here, officer?" one of the three men asked. He was portly and had a bushy, unkempt beard which looked like it could harbor baby birds. The other two men were thinner and hard looking, with bare arms to the shoulders and a crude art gallery of monochrome tattoos up and down.

"It's Chief, not officer," Mickey corrected, "And you tell me if there's a problem. Or better yet, how about you let these girls tell me." She reached for her nightstick with her left hand and unsnapped her holster with the right. She saw the three men tense.

"Well, okay then, *chief*," one of the thinner ones said. When he turned toward her Mickey could see dog tags around his neck. The other thin one crossed his forearms and adopted a defiant stance, arms crossed on his chest.

The one with the dog tags spoke again.

"We made the acquaintance of these two lovely young doves as we were riding home after assisting a stranded motorist we came across down in Holgate," he said. When he smiled Mickey could see that he had perfect teeth. "After exchanging names and some polite conversation they expressed an interest in seeing our organization's HQ and learning more about our code and our customs. For their Social Studies class, I believe. That right, girls?" He fixed them with a stare. They clutched their purses tighter and darted glances at Mickey. Identical small smiles that weren't smiles at all appeared on their faces.

Mickey fingered her baton. "I see. Well, how about you three gallant gentlemen just step aside and let the ladies come stand by me." Neither of the girls moved. "I did mean *now*," Mickey said.

After several silent seconds the trio shuffled their heavy black boots and moved a small distance away from the girls who shot through the opening toward Mickey. The two thinner men leaned in slightly so the girls would have to brush against them as they did.

"Go stand by the car," Mickey told them and took a step toward the motorcycles. "No rice burners, I see," she said. "Very patriotic. Now, I count four bikes and only three of you. Where's your fearless leader?"

"I'm the leader," the portly one shot back.

"No, you're not," Mickey replied. "The fat guy is *never* the leader. The enforcer, maybe, but never the leader." He scowled at her.

One of the girls coughed and Mickey turned to see the missing fourth rider walking around the Chevelle. She immediately didn't like the geometry of the situation and so backed up toward the girls to make sure all four men would be within her zone of fire.

The one by the cruiser walked slowly, almost shambling, and kept his gaze on the vehicle.

"Some pretty heavy wheels for a meter maid," he said. "Surf City must be doing quite well for a town with a purely seasonal economy. If I might ask, will any real police officers be joining us tonight, ma'am?" The other three laughed and shook their heads – just a beat too loud and too long, Mickey thought. Now she was certain this one was the honcho. She ignored the taunt, knowing it was a test. She'd faced down street gang leaders in similar situations. These guys, she decided, weren't anything she couldn't handle. She took a small step towards them.

"So my read on the situation here is that you and your motorhead brothers here may have been planning to entertain these two very clearly underage girls at your little clubhouse in the woods. Perhaps without their complete cooperation or consent. That sound about right?"

"Underage?" the leader said. "Why, they assured us they were both eighteen. And that they were majoring in Psychology at Rutgers. We thought a visit to our organization's base of operations would be more like field work than entertainment. Wouldn't you agree? Chief?" He nodded toward the lettering on the Chevelle's front panel.

Mickey's pulse rate began to drop. Whoever he was, she now knew, at least he wasn't stupid and he wasn't drunk or hopped up. And if he wanted a fight he'd have picked it by now. She took her hand off her nightstick.

"And what is the name of your, um, organization?"

He smiled and turned his back toward her. She understood the double meaning of the gesture. He was answering her question and he was letting her know that there would be no altercation tonight. She looked at the leather vest. Stitched on it were silver letters that said "Sons of Satan" arcing above a menacing red

Devil's head with a protruding long and forked tongue. The letters "MC" were stitched below it

"Nice," Mickey said. "Let me guess. Hell's Angels was trademarked, right?"

"Different branch of the service," he said, facing her again.

"Well, in case anyone else asks about field work, where exactly is your local headquarters?" Mickey asked.

He pointed toward the mainland and the vast pine forest. "In there somewhere," he said. "I'd tell you to follow the signs but unfortunately there aren't any." He walked toward his bike but kept a respectable distance from her. She saw him better in the streetlight's glow now. Clean shaven in contrast to the others with not a handsome face but not an unattractive one either. He mounted his motorcycle. The other three did the same.

"Maybe we'll come visit you in Surf City this weekend," he said. "Now that we're all acquainted."

"You might want to call ahead," Mickey replied. "In case we want to arrange a little welcome reception. I hear Margate's nice. Wide streets, lots of motorcycle parking. Could be a better choice for you."

He shook his head at some inner bemusement, kicked the bike into life and peeled out. His compatriots followed, gunning their engines as loud as they could for as long as they could in what she took as their parting message.

"Both of you, in the car," she said to the two girls and opened the rear door.

The girls looked even younger and more vulnerable in the harsh glare of the cruiser's interior dome light.

"How old are you two?" Mickey asked. "And don't say eighteen."

"Thirteen," one replied with a quivering lip. "We're both thirteen. He fibbed. We never said we were that old."

She looked at their clothes. Skimpy halter tops over barely existent breasts. Short skirts and dressy shoes with thick heels and soles.

"You know what they would have done with you, right?"

They nodded their heads and then both began to cry. Mickey looked around the front seat for a box of tissues, finally locating one in the glove compartment. She handed it back.

"Alright. I'm going to take both of you home now. What you

tell your parents is up to you. But unless it's on the beach and in the daytime, I see you dressed like this again and I'll arrest you for indecent exposure or maybe even for solicitation. If you want to dress like hookers in ten years, I don't care. But all I better see from now on is shorts, t-shirts and sneakers. Got it?"

"Got it," they said in unison, clear snot bubbling from both their noses.

Mickey turned the dome light off. "Oh, and if one of those guys so much as winks at you this summer, you call the station and let me know right away." Two heads bobbed in assent. She fired up the engine and looked out the window. A light in one of the older cottages down the street winked off. It must have been, Mickey assumed, the guardian angel who called it in. It amazed her sometimes, the thin line that divided everyday life from unspeakable tragedy.

On the short ride to the small side-by-side houses she puzzled over the bikers' leader. She ran the things he'd said through her mind. Definitely educated, she figured, maybe even college. Probably not long out of the military, along with at least one of the others, given the dog tags and the terms and abbreviations he casually dropped. He hadn't backed down but he still managed to show her respect when she hadn't backed down either. Mickey hoped he'd taken the hint but, she told herself, she knew what to do if he didn't.

THE BEN FRANKLIN CLUB
Center City, Philadelphia

Jablonski tapped the bell. An oblong wooden panel slid open and a face appeared.

"Sorry, we don't serve Polacks anymore. Just passed a rule this afternoon."

All Jablonski could see were smoothly shaven cheeks and small white teeth.

"And you think I would eat here if I'd known it employed a dirty Irish dog like you as the maitre'd?" Jablonski replied. "I heard the seven-course meal is a six-pack and a potato."

"Yeah, but let me tell you, it is one fucking grand potato," the part of a face said with a laugh. "What can I do for the most powerful man in Philadelphia?"

"You can let me in for starters." A bolt moved and the heavy wooden door opened. Jablonski stepped in and was ushered quickly to a small alcove. "Good to see you, Dave," Jablonski said.

"At our age, old friend, it's better to be seen than to be viewed," Dave Kelly replied. He stood five inches shorter than Jablonski but he embraced the bigger man aggressively. Kelly was trim and tanned. His tuxedo jacket was immaculate and his pants bore scalpel-like creases. His bearing was almost imperial. Kelly had been one of Jablonski's closest childhood friends. They had matriculated through Our Lady of Good Counsel's grammar school and then on to Archbishop Carroll High School together. Kelly had ascended from busboy to head waiter to maître'd at Center City's exclusive Ben Franklin Club in record time. He'd been in that position for over twenty years now and had acted as a go-between for power-brokers both political and criminal, often jesting there was little discernible difference between the two. His visible role as a servant was almost comically reversed for in reality, Jablonski knew, he wielded considerable power, having final say on memberships and controlling who got tables and dining times and who didn't. His discretion was legendary and it was said he had accumulated enough inside knowledge to elect half the politicians in three states and to imprison the rest.

"You still running the place?" Jablonski asked.

Kelly bowed. "I am but a humble knight-of-the-napkin," he answered. "And you're a little early."

"I thought we'd have a minute to talk," Jablonski replied. "Any notables here I should be aware of?"

"You picked a good night," Kelly said. "Most of the muckety-mucks are home packing to go down the shore on Friday. You wearing a vest?"

Jablonski smiled. "I assured both my guests that our meeting would be both informal and off the record."

Kelly's eyebrows arched. "Those two at the same table? You should frisk both of them. Too bad we don't have a metal detector."

"Now what message would that send?" Jablonski said with a thin laugh. "I need a quiet summer out of those two greaseballs. I'm being what they call *pro*-active."

"Either one of them would kill you soon as look at you," Kelly replied. "You want me to suggest the wine?"

"Yes, but make sure it's something I can stomach."

"Chianti is getting quite popular these days," Kelly said. "I'll pick a nice one, for a Dago Red that is. I didn't realize you had developed such a cultured palate, Basil."

"Ha, you were the one that had me drinking the altar wine in sixth grade."

"Ah, those were the days, weren't they? Nothing like a chalice of cold Manischewitz blackberry right before Midnight Mass, eh?"

"As I remember, you fell asleep with the incense thurible still burning and set little Timmy Lannon's cassock on fire."

Kelly shrugged. "He got over it, obviously. Became a priest." He peeked a look outside the alcove and hustled Jablonski to a private dining area.

"They'll have their guys with them you know," Jablonski said.

"I got some cannoli in boxes I'll take out to the cars. I'm not running a soup kitchen here, you know."

Jablonski rearranged the chairs to his liking and took a seat. Kelly moved the antipasto plates and the silverware.

"A little bird told me you just bought a cozy love nest down on the beach in Margate," Kelly said. "Or maybe it was Avalon. You know how birds are."

"Don't forget the cannoli," Jablonski replied. "You been hearing anything?"

Kelly shrugged. Then he leaned in. "A lot of talk about gambling – the legal, Vegas kind – coming to Jersey. Atlantic City, probably. Still years away but the rats are scurrying already." He spied an errant crumb of biscotti and plucked it from the otherwise pristine linen tablecloth. "The local goombahs are worried about the New York goombahs taking it from them. They know there's no way two small organizations can fight them off. One of your guests tonight – flip a coin – probably shouldn't buy any long-playing records." Kelly straightened up. "Just table talk, you understand. Probably doesn't mean a thing."

There was a rustle of activity. A heavy-set man in a suit that looked a decade out of style walked in. He nodded to Jablonski.

"Danny," Jablonski said without getting up. He pointed to one of the empty chairs. The man glanced quickly around the room and sat in the other chair.

"Carmine coming?" the man asked.

"I wanted to talk to you first," Jablonski replied. He heard Kelly close the door.

TUESDAY

FIVE
Surf City

THE BEACH HOUSE WAS quiet when Danny awoke. He dragged himself from the wrecked bed, stumbling from one room to another until he realized he was alone. The air was thick with the smell of stale beer and puke. His boxer shorts were wet and reeked of ammonia. He put one hand on the wall as he maneuvered himself back toward the guest bedroom. There was a narrow trail of dried vomitus winding from the little half-bath to the side of the bed. Danny felt the sheets, pulled them back and then looked in disbelief at the large, irregular stain on the mattress. Jesus, he thought, he had peed himself and the guest bed.

The room looked pretty well trashed, although nothing appeared broken beyond repair. With a pounding headache that was trying to blind him, Danny began picking cigarette butts and beer cans off the tile floor, although each time he bent over his head threatened to explode. A small Day-Glo purple wastebasket held a sickening soup of beer, bile and partially digested pizza from Rose's Tomato Pies. He dropped the trash in on top of it. Danny gagged several times but came up empty. He pulled off his soaked underwear and staggered toward the master bathroom, hoping there was aspirin in the medicine cabinet. As he passed through the kitchen he saw a large piece of tablet paper taped to the new white Frigidaire. A black Magic Marker lay on the counter. Danny shuffled in and squinted until he could read the handwritten block lettering:

YOU ARE SUCH AN ASSHOLE! WE TOOK THE CAR
FIND YOUR OWN WAY HOME
HERE'S PHONE NO. FOR CLEANING SERVICE – YOUR DAD
CAN PAY THEM   555-0515

He pulled off the note and crumpled it up. "Fuck you guys," he said to the empty kitchen. The refrigerator's compressor kicked on noisily as if in reply. There had been a lot of drunken arguing the night before, he remembered. His knuckles were bruised and he had the vague recollection that he might have punched Paulie a couple of times before passing out. Danny leaned on the Formica-topped center island and looked at the clock. It was almost three in the afternoon which meant he'd been unconscious for over twelve hours. A few more dry heaves buckled him. When he recovered he started opening as many windows as he could find. The air that flooded in was hot and salty but at least it was fresh. He couldn't believe they'd left him there in a pool of his own piss. They were lucky he hadn't choked on his own vomit or swallowed his tongue, he thought. They were lucky he wasn't dead. The phone rang and for a minute Danny debated answering it, then moved down the hall towards the salvation of some shampoo, some soap and a hot shower. He'd deal with his former friends later, he decided. Oh yes, he and his family would certainly be dealing with them later.

*　*　*

By six-thirty Danny was feeling like a human being again. There was still a dull throb at his temples but the six-inch split down the middle of his skull was finally gone. After his clean-up he'd gone back to sleep on the Ianuzzi's big waterbed in the master bedroom. His stomach was settling and he started to think about getting something to eat for supper. The phone had rung several more times but he continued to ignore it. Better they think he was gone, he decided. Not that he planned on going anywhere. Some minor detective work had turned up the key to the liquor cabinet and Danny was pleased to see it was already well-provisioned. His teenage drinking had been mostly cheap beer, but he'd been sipping red wine at family dinners and weddings since he was ten. He was sure he could handle the refined experience of hard liquor. Scotch sounded the most expensive and there was a full half-gallon bottle of one called White Horse which Danny figured must be the top-shelf stuff if they were buying it in that large a quantity. He'd even found a red hardbound Bartender's Guide in case he wanted to get creative. He could buy mixers at the market so at least he wouldn't have to deal with the weasely little prick at the liquor store again. The cleaning service was scheduled for Friday morning. Danny had doused the guest-bed mattress with half a bottle of Windex and flipped it over. The sheets and his clothes were washed and now tumbling happily in the little Kenmore dryer. He'd pulled the guest bedroom door shut but left the windows in it open. He sure as hell wasn't going to clean it for the cleaners. The rest of the house looked fine, so if his old buddies were giving him the run of the place 'til Friday he was okay with that. He'd rifled through Mr. Ianuzzi's bureau and found a couple of Playboy magazines in his underwear drawer. In Paulie's mom's bedside table he'd discovered a white plastic vibrator which, he decided, he would take with him when he departed and then mail to Debra Ianuzzi as an anonymous Christmas gift.

Yeah, Danny thought, screw those guys. The guest room was out of sight and therefore out of mind. He wasn't going to be invited back anytime soon, so he planned to make the most of Paulie's hospitality for the next few days. On Friday morning he'd call his dad and either have Shots come pick him up or one of the Atlantic City guys drive him back home to Philly. He toyed with the idea leaving a deuce in Paulie's bed before he left but decided against it. Revenge, his old man had always taught him, was a dish best served cold.

It was now well past seven in the evening. Mickey had spent the rest of the day handling municipal paperwork and petty politics. Mayor Tunell had called a half-dozen times for trivial matters and she'd had to send Kaylen out twice to deliver the triplicate forms. It seemed like they were doing everything except police work. She'd gone out on a couple of minor calls and sent Kaylen out on a few others, mostly nuisance issues. The mayor had sent over food from the Tasty-Freeze but the cartons were still unopened and the ice in the sodas had melted.

"Is it always like this right before Memorial Day?" she asked. Mickey's desk was a mess and she started riffling the papers trying to find some way to organize it. Finally she just stacked all the forms and folders in a pile and set the big brass paperweight on top.

Kaylen was standing by the door. "Yeah, there's always a lot of last-minute stuff but once he season starts they pretty much leave us alone."

Mickey was beginning to understand why Kaylen had not pursued her position.

"Did Mayor Tunell tell you about his idea?" Kaylen asked.

"Which one? He's had about twenty since I got here."

"Beach tags."

"Oh yeah," Mickey replied. "Like people are really going to pay for the privilege of just being on the beach." She shook her head. "That'll never happen. Hey, I was looking for your red Mustang when I was out cruising the loop. I didn't see it anywhere on the streets or parked in anyone's driveway. You didn't scare off any paying tourists now, did you? "

"I was actually pretty nice to them so I don't think so. I'll keep an eye out for it, though." Kaylen stood up, put on his uniform hat and adjusted the brim. "Want me to gas up the Chevelle for you?"

Mickey laughed. "Sorry, Charlie. You don't want the big desk," she pointed to her little wooden workspace, "You don't get to drive the cool car."

Kaylen nodded. "10-4, I understand. Uh, Chief?" Mickey looked up from her papers. "I saw the log book. Anything I should know?"

"About what?"

"About motorcycle gangs," Kaylen said. "Here on the Island."

"Are the Sons of Satan a gang now?"

"Well, I guess they call themselves a club," he replied. "Do you think we'll have any trouble with them?" It was the most worried Mickey had seen him.

"I don't know," she answered."I suggested they ride elsewhere and focus their amorous attentions on women instead of children. I guess we'll see if they got the message."

"You know, there was that town in California," Kaylen said. "They rode in and took it over."

"Hollister," Mickey replied. "But that was, what, thirty years ago? And I think most of the stuff written about it was exaggerated or just made up. I mean, it wasn't exactly like the Mummers or the Shriners hit town but it also wasn't a riot like it got reported. You worried about these guys, Kaylen?"

"Nah," he replied. "Just wondering is all. I'll let you know if I see them in town again." Then he walked out.

Mickey looked at the clock. She hoped to finish up by eight so she could get the rest of her belongings unpacked and tidy up her three-room apartment a little. It looked, she thought, like it had been ransacked. The black desk phone sat at an accusing angle almost daring her to pick it up. She'd get some air first, she decided, and then maybe she'd call Patsy when she got home. The Giants had beaten the Phillies 3-1 then night before with Jim Bunning taking the loss. Mickey thought Bunning was on his way to the Hall of Fame someday but Patsy had always been a doubter. Maybe, she thought, she could talk to her father about Bunning.

* * *

An hour later Mickey gave up. She'd managed to choke down one of the cold cheeseburgers but the fries were a limp, lost cause. She slurped warm, watery Coke from the cup until the straw buckled. It was only Tuesday, she reasoned. She could finish the rest of the paperwork tomorrow. The radio had crackled with a few calls but nothing she needed to go out to assist with. A Good Humor ice cream truck had broken down on Division Street and the driver was unable to turn off the jingly song blaring continuously from the vehicle's speakers. It was straddling the borough line between Surf City and Ship Bottom. Kaylen wanted to know what to do. She asked him which town the truck's engine was in. When he said "not Surf City," she gleefully radioed Ship Bottom's duty officer that it was his problem. He muttered something about payback being hell and clicked off.

Shortly after, Kaylen radioed in and told Mickey she should go and enjoy her night off. She signed out with LBI Dispatch, locked the station doors and fired up the Chevelle. She was, she decided, going to watch the sun set behind the bay from the narrow wooden deck outside her apartment. Maybe she'd invite Loretta up to share the view. She hadn't much appreciated having to lug all her stuff up the brine-stained stairs but once that job was done she was happy being on the second-floor and the little breeze it provided.

    The car shifted smoothly and she liked the constant vibration the engine produced, especially in low gear. As she eased up Long Beach Avenue a figure caught her eye. A youngish-looking man sat on a bench, a bicycle propped against it. He had long hair but appeared clean-shaven and was dressed in what looked like old military issue clothes. A round camouflage-print hat obscured his eyes and she could see what had to be dog-tags around his neck. Surf City, as far as she knew, had no homeless people and she had yet to encounter or even hear about an actual vagrant. She kept her speed steady at fifteen and watched him as she rolled by. Once she was past, she kept him in her mirrors for as long as she could. He didn't seem to move but then there was just a subtle tilt of the hat which told her he was tracking her as well. Mickey thought about stopping but decided she'd had enough for one day. He wasn't doing anything illegal or suspicious. She could ask Kaylen about him in the morning, she thought. A convoy of delivery trucks was ahead of her, bee lining for the causeway road in Ship Bottom and back to the mainland. The Island was like a ship, she mused, getting provisioned for the long summer journey. She heard the ice cream truck's tinny song close by so she detoured a few blocks to avoid any chance of getting involved. If Kaylen couldn't handle such a simple matter using his own discretion, she figured, then she needed to look for a new deputy.

    Mickey cranked up the Delco AM for the last few blocks of the ride home. She had to punch several of the oblong silver buttons until she hit on a song she wanted to hear. California had changed her musical tastes, she knew, but then it had changed a lot of things about her. She couldn't really say if any of it was for the better. The Byrds were crooning a heavily electrified version of the Bob Dylan folk tune "My Back Pages". Mickey pulled into the apartment's lot next to a familiar Fairlane. She shut off the grumbling motor and sat in the cruiser, singing along with the radio until the song was over. She was so much older then, she thought.

♦ ♦ ♦

The scotch was definitely the high-end variety, Danny decided, although he knew he really had nothing to compare it with. He reasoned that only the really good stuff would burn your throat and make your eyes water. He'd taken the first glass straight over ice but then switched to mixed drinks. First, Club Soda, then 7-Up and finally Ginger Ale, which seemed to work best at taming the blast of fire when he swallowed. Danny wondered what all the fuss was about – the alcohol wasn't even touching him and there was a generous dent in the big bottle already. He'd have to remember, he thought, to fill it back up with water before he checked out.

Danny poured himself another tumbler and thumbed through the Playboys, rubbing absent-mindedly at his crotch. He might not be drunk, he realized, but now he was definitely getting horny. He could, he figured, walk to one of the local places. If he met some agreeable chick he'd just bring her back to the Ianuzzi's house to bang. Tell her it was his place, even. He started to laugh – wait 'til the three dipshits found out that instead of shafting him they'd provided him with a night they could only dream about. As he finished his drink he felt pretty certain that's how it was all going to work out. He got up and went to the bar. He wanted to be good and loose when it was time to turn on the charm. He popped the cap off another of the green soda bottles, poured it and added the scotch right from the jug. He was pretty much a pro now, he decided, and he didn't need a shot glass to get it right.

The ship's wheel clock in the foyer said it was just after ten p.m. Danny spritzed on some of Paulie's Hai Karate cologne, checked his hair in the bathroom mirror and decided he was ready to roll. On a white plastic cutting board in the kitchen he spied a long, tapered knife in a black plastic sheath used, he assumed, for slicing lemons and limes or maybe filleting fish. Danny thought about the guy on the bench and slipped it into his hip pocket. He finished the last of the drink in one gulp, pushed the back door open and stepped wobbily out onto the flagstone patio. He'd spent a lot of time salivating over the centerfolds and now he was surprised at how dark it was. He steadied himself on the redwood picnic table, took a few deep breaths and started walking to where he figured the beach road should be.

After what seemed like only just a few blocks, Danny was wondering which turn had been the wrong one. The town was ridiculously small and yet somehow he'd managed to walk too far one way or the other. Now he didn't recognize any of the dark little cottages or the roads and the only streetlight looked to be fair distance away. His head was foggy but Danny thought he had to be closer to the ocean than he was to the bay. He could hear the surf booming somewhere just out of sight. He followed the sound down a deserted alley littered with seagull crap and rotting clams until he finally saw waves, inky black and rolling. He walked the alley until he came to what looked like a slightly larger road hoping maybe he could ask a passing car for directions or even a ride. He wasn't at the beach yet but if worse came to worst he figured he could just sack out on the soft sand and find his way back in the morning. He didn't think he had ever felt so tired. He passed another dark and shuttered summer cottage and kept moving. It was like being in a goddamned ghost town, he thought. Then he heard the sound of tires and a big engine – way bigger than the Mustang anyway - approaching. He hoped it wasn't a cop. If it was they'd have him cold for public intox and then he'd have to call Petroni to bail him out. His old man would definitely kill him.

The approaching headlights hurt his eyes and he used his palm to shield them from the glare. The White Horse Scotch was churning in his belly. He put out his thumb and edged closer. "He's gotta see me," he mumbled to himself. He'd ask for a ride, not directions, when the car stopped. He'd tell him or them or whoever was in it exactly who he was if it came to that. He'd tell them who his father was and that their assistance and their silence would be generously rewarded. And he definitely had to remember not to puke in their car. Danny waited until he thought he heard the engine slow and then stepped out toward the road.

Ronnie Dunn had watched the dark blue police cruiser slow as it passed him and then move on. She had marked him right away, he knew. Six months ago he would have been motionless, invisible. But invisibility was a skill and once not practiced it could not help but deteriorate.

He rose from the bench. There were so many things that could give you away – the random glint off a barrel, the movement of a single palm frond, an errant ray of moonlight striking a dime-sized circle of polished glass. He had used all of them and more to his advantage. But now, he couldn't even keep his head still long enough to avoid a passing patrol.

Ronnie straddled the pink, rust-scarred Huffy and noticed that both tires needed air. Through his fatigue pants he adjusted the handle on the long blade secured to his calf. Then he snugged the chin string on his hat and pedaled slowly off toward the beach road and the dark security of home.

WEDNESDAY

SIX
Surf City

IT WAS WELL PAST the midnight hour when the objects of Jeffrey Silverman's desire were firmly within his adolescent grasp. The topless Heidi Abramowitz was allowing him the opportunity to indulge in an activity he'd fantasized obsessively about through one winter and two bottles of Jergens' Lotion. WIBG was playing through the tinny speaker on the little black Silvertone transistor radio and Englebert Humperdinck was crooning out "Please Release Me", a sentiment urgently shared by Jeffrey's tumescent anatomy. The previous several hours had been a symphony of suggestion, cajoling and, finally, a crescendo of shameless pleading. The last effort seemed to please Heidi and she had simultaneously doffed her shirt and Maidenform with a practiced ease. Then, suddenly, just as he thought he heard her moan with pleasure, she pushed him away.

"OK, there's something down there. Now I'm sure of it."

Heidi Abramowitz covered her freckled breasts with the green 'Kelly for Brickwork' t-shirt, much to the frustration of the fully clothed and now painfully engorged Jeffrey Silverman.

"I don't see anything," he said without looking. Her scent was an inebriating mix of sweat, Chantilly and Sea & Ski. "Let's get back to-"

"No. You go see what it is," she insisted and pulled the shirt back on. "Otherwise we're going home." The boy raised himself to a standing position.

"OK. Where?"

"In the water, down by those broken pilings. Go, Jeffrey, go see what it is."

The boy trudged off down the flat, darkened stretch of beach, his prospects and his stiffy deflating at roughly equal rates.

Mickey hung up the phone. The dream had been another Technicolor one but she couldn't remember any of the details. Something about dolls again, she thought. Touching her head she noticed her hair was moist and matted. Her thin t-shirt was damp and stuck to her breasts and shoulders. Mickey pulled off the clinging bedsheet and dropped her legs over the side. She locked her elbows, pushed up with both arms and headed for the bathroom, willing herself awake. Sunlight streamed in, refracted by four small glass-block windows over the rust-ringed porcelain tub. In the medicine cabinet's cloudy mirror the natural light threw the tiniest of lines on her face into unflattering relief. At first she thought the ringing telephone was just part of the dream. Now, after hearing the news, she could only wish that it was.

* * *

Mickey pulled the Chevelle police cruiser up as far as she could onto the dunes. The air-conditioner was working better but she was aware of a thin line of sweat forming across the top of her forehead, just above her non-municipal-issue Wayfarers. She palmed the crown of her campaign-style hat, which lay on the empty bucket passenger seat, lifted up on the door handle and eased herself out. She intentionally left the red cherry-toppers rotating although the engine was off. The smell of the salt-air was tangy with something foul and familiar.

"Sorry Chief," Kaylen said. "Figured you would want to know right away."

"So do we know who called it in?" she asked as she closed the car door and began to walk.

"Dispatcher said it sounded like a kid, but probably an older kid. Maybe like a teenager. Real nervous on the phone. Wouldn't

ID himself and hung up before she could get anything else from him."

"Did she record the call?" Mickey asked. Kaylen's look told her that calls were probably not routinely recorded on Long Beach Island, an idea she might mention to Mayor Bill. Kaylen's normally pale skin looked a shade whiter and sweat stains ringed the underarms of his uniform blouse. His ever-present patina of Coppertone was augmented with a dab of zinc oxide on his nose and his uniform cap was tilted back on his head.

"Run it down for me again," Mickey said.

"OK, but do you mind if I sit down for a sec, Chief? I'm really not feeling all that well." Kaylen took a seat on one of the wooden pilings that were driven into the beach at the edge of the road. Their main function was to hold the dunes in place and provide a picturesque nautical image at the same time. Each was about the circumference of a telephone pole and they were lashed together in two's or three's with heavy braided rope. Undulating sections of brown wooden snow-fence guarded the path to the beach. Kaylen perched on the piling nearest the road. His Galaxie cruiser, recently washed and still dripping water Mickey noticed, was parked ten yards away, obstructing pedestrian access to the egress point.

"Pull it together, Deputy," she said. "Just tell me what we've got."

Kaylen took a breath and squinted up at her. "It's bad, Chief," he said slowly. "I've never seen anything like this before. I mean, it's really bad."

"OK, then let's just go have a look," Mickey said. She noticed that Kaylen did not move. "You did secure the scene, right?"

He nodded without looking up. "Feel like I might need to heave, Chief," he said. "Can you give me another minute?"

Mickey spread some of the beige sand and broken shells on the edge of asphalt with the toe of her shoe. "OK, well, just come down when you're ready, I guess," she said.

Mickey Cleary never heaved, no matter how bad it was. She was a third generation cop, she reminded herself. Whatever it was, she knew, she had surely seen worse. Her soles slipped awkwardly in the sugary sand and she pumped her arms for balance. There were whitecaps offshore and a small knot of people milling behind a makeshift rope cordon a good twenty yards further down the beach. She was surprised to see an older man in Bermuda shorts and a floppy canvas hat standing knee-deep in the surf by the ruins of an old pier. Then she recognized Doc Guidice, the retired G.P. who also acted as the Island's coroner. He was poking in the water at something with a piece of driftwood. The pungent aroma mingling with the ocean breeze, she knew immediately, was decomposition.

Guidice, when she'd first met him, had taught her how to pronounce his name correctly. "Like Judah-Jay," she remembered him saying. "Think Judas without the 's' and Jay like jaybird." At her approach he straightened his back and looked at her.

"Hell of an eye-opener, huh, Chief?" he said with a crooked smile. "Grab a leg and we'll pull him up on the sand."

Mickey stepped into the gently foaming surf and watched as the wetness quickly wicked its way up her khaki pant legs to just below her knees. It really was bad, she realized. She now understood Kaylen's queasiness. Mickey took three quick breaths and swallowed hard, willing the little that was in her stomach to stay there.

"Ever think about wearin' shorts ?" Guidice asked. "This *is* a resort town, you know. Nothing wrong with a summer uniform." He bent back down and grasped a soggy, sock-clad ankle.

Mickey leaned over to do the same. "I have ugly legs," she shot back. Guidice tilted his head up and narrowed his eyes.

"Now I'm bettin' that's a lie," he said. "I am still a doctor, you know. Technically retired, but fully licensed in two states and pretty good at human anatomy if I do say so myself."

Mickey grunted as they dragged the heavy, lifeless form up the inclined shore, a trail of indented sand and leaking bodily fluids snaking behind them. The low tide had passed and the waterline seemed to inch slightly shoreward with each lapping wave. Once out of the water, Mickey surveyed the carnage and started making mental notes. Young white male – late teens or early twenties, maybe. There were socks but no shoes. She saw multiple contusions and abrasions, especially around the belly and chest. Probably multiple rib fractures and a couple of broken long bones at least. Fairly standard stuff until you got to the shoulders. Guidice was poking again with the driftwood. The young man's head, it appeared, had been nearly severed. A crescent-shaped cut revealed pale white neck bones; they and a few strands of sinewy muscle were all that held it to the body. The shiny cross-cut windpipe drained a pink, foamy fluid mixed with sand and seawater. A shock of long, jet black hair lay matted to the intact but dented skull, the face puffy and bruised. In the heat, the seawater was quickly evaporating, leaving a film of brine on the olive skin.

Guidice dropped the driftwood stick and put his hands on his low back. "I'm guessin' he fell out of a boat and the prop must 'a got him," he said. "Big prop, I'd say. Charter boat maybe. Probably report it that way for the State. Shame. Good-looking young man before this happened to him."

"You know him?" Mickey asked, clearly surprised. "A local?"

"No," Guidice replied."More of a non-resident summer visitor." He rubbed his palms together to clean the sand off them. "Terrible, terrible accident. It's the reason why I sold my boat, Chief. *That* – he pointed toward the surf - *that* out there is the damned Atlantic Ocean. No telling what can happen to you once you clear Barnegat Inlet and get out past the jetty. You're enjoying the view, maybe one beer or one Grasshopper too many, and a beam wave or a big wake slaps the hull. *Bam*, next thing you know you're in the drink. If there's so much as a light chop or a moderate swell, nobody's gonna see your head bobbin' out there 'til it's too late."

Mickey looked at the old doctor. He had a strange expression on his face. His gaze met hers and held it.

"Really?" she said. "So you think all... *this* is from a boating accident?" She tipped up the brim of her hat and felt the cool of the freshening offshore sea breeze on her cheeks. She looked back down at the mangled body. "I mean, look at the neck. It's a pretty clean cut for a propeller blade."

"Y'ever seen the size of a prop on one of the charter boats or the big Chris Crafts? Plus, lots of fishies with teeth out there. Something could've gnawed on him while he was in the water. Crabs usually go right for the eyes in my experience. There are predators galore just out past the breakers, you know."

"You mean like a shark?"

"Oh, Chief," Guidice replied, "Now I didn't say anything about any shark. And if I were you that's one word I wouldn't use around here. But hell, even blowfish have chompers that'll take your finger off. And a flounder's jaws are like rows of little serrated knives."

Mickey took off her hat and fanned herself several times before putting it back on. The old doc was working her hard on this one, she knew. "You're telling me you think this was all from an accident. A boat accident."

"Really be best all around if it was, Chief," Guidice replied. Mickey noticed his eyebrows rise almost imperceptibly. "Especially given the identity of the unfortunate victim."

At the academy Mickey had been taught to assume foul play in every unexplained death. It was standard procedure as far as she was concerned whether your jurisdiction was one square mile like Surf City's or a hundred and forty-two like Philadelphia's. She shook the sand from her own hands then smacked them together several times and looked out at the cloudless horizon.

"And so who exactly *is* the unfortunate victim?" she asked."Did you find some ID?"

Guidice rubbed his forehead then brushed away some clinging grains and bits of shell.

"No wallet or license," Guidice replied, "But, trust me, Chief, this is one Mister Dante Ragone."

"Danny Rags?" Mickey said, her voice rising with recognition of the name. "Can't be. This kid is-"

Guidice cut her off. "Dante D. Ragone, *Junior*." His eyes narrowed and he looked intently at Mickey. She suddenly felt cool and sweaty but fought the urge to sit down. Her head was spinning with a dozen unpleasant thoughts. Doc Guidice's gaze never left her. He leaned in and almost whispered, "We say this is anything *but* an accident and things will get real complicated real fast, Chief. In case you haven't noticed, we're just a little drinking town with a big fishing problem. We're not very good at complicated." He pulled the sun-bleached and salt-splattered hat off his head and smiled. "Be glad to help you with the report if you'd like. I'm a pretty good typist, too. I'd need to go home and get my bifocals, though."

Mickey drew in a deep breath. Small sand crabs were emerging and starting to crawl over the body. From the corner of her eye she could see Guidice watching her. The next thirty seconds, she knew, would set the tone for her term as the law in town, whether that term was ten more days or ten more years.

"So as Coroner, that's your stated opinion?"

Guidice's eyes narrowed. "Death by misadventure," he said. "Accidental, so no post-mortem required."

Kaylen was walking toward her, his loping gait graceful and smooth despite the uneven surface. She waved at him to come over.

"Chief?" Kaylen said as he approached her. "You want me to get the kit?"

"No, not now," Mickey replied, "we need to get this body off the beach pronto, before any more rubberneckers show up. " She drummed her fingers on her gun belt. "Call the Fire Station. Tell them to find a body bag and bring it down here right away. Load it in the back seat of the Galaxie."

"Wouldn't the ambulance be-"

"It would," she replied. "But it'll just draw more attention. Which is not what we want right now." She looked at Guidice. "I don't suppose you have a morgue close by, do you, doc?"

His face crinkled. "Chief, I don't even have an office anymore. And the nearest funeral parlor with cold storage for stiffs is in Harvey Cedars. I got one of those new Sears icemakers, though, if that'll help. Crushed or cubed, your choice."

Mickey shook her head. "Harvey Cedars won't work. I need to keep it in town, where I have control over it." She turned to Kaylen. "Load it up and take it to the liquor store. Go in through the back. Put it in the big walk-in cooler, up off the ground. And tell Willie to make it as cold as possible in there without freezing anything."

"Well you and I both know he won't let us do that, Chief. Willie is a-"

"Yes, he will," Mickey interrupted. "Tell him I know about the high-schoolers and the tall-boy cans of *Colt .45*. And *nobody* - not you, not the firehouse guys and certainly not Willie - says another word about this no matter who asks. Any and all inquiries come directly to me. You got that?"

"What about the people over there?" He pointed toward a group elderly shellers who were just outside the thin rope cordon.

"OK, if they ask, just say we can't release any information until we find the next of kin, but we think it was a clammer from Forked River who fell overboard two days ago."

"I didn't know there was a-"

"There wasn't. But *they* don't know that. And that's what

they'll repeat which is all we care about right now. It will buy us some time."

Kaylen appeared to process the information for retelling. "Clammer from Forked River. Got it."

Mickey adjusted her hat. "Now, I need to go make some phone calls. Stop back at the station when you're done." Mickey looked at Guidice, whose face bore an enigmatic smile. "I have to bring in the State Medical Examiner on this one, Doc," she said. "No offense."

Guidice nodded wistfully. "I understand, Chief. It's your call. And, just so we're clear, no offense taken." He picked up the piece of driftwood and studied it. "Been quite a while since we had any real excitement around here anyway." Then he walked slowly toward the water.

SEVEN

NEW PALERMO SOCIAL CLUB
South Philadelphia

THE HIRSUTE BELLY HUNG out over the waistband of the beltless slacks and peeked from underneath a yellow Ban-Lon shirt. Two parallel mint green stripes ran vertically down the front, framing the sweat rings below both arms.

"Get the fuckin' car!" the huge man shouted. "And get my fuckin' gun. The automatic." He was prowling around the small back room. A poker table lay upset in the middle of the floor, blue-backed Bicycle playing cards and plastic betting chips scattered about. Dante Donatello Ragone – "Danny Rags" to his friends, enemies and members of local, state and federal law enforcement – paced back and forth in a lather. His eyes were red but the crying had been brief. Rage had soon consumed him, pushing out any other normal human emotion.

"Who ever done this – they're *dead*!" Ragone wiped spit from his mouth and continued pacing. "It's the Rocca's. Gotta be. Mother of God, didn't he just sit down last night with me and Jablonski and promise a quiet summer? Carmine's been waitin' to make a move like this. Shares *gnocchi* and *risotto* while he's plotting something. Agrees to a holiday cease-fire and then attacks. " He pounded his fist.   "I want him dead. And his schoolteacher brother, I want him dead, too. And I want their balls cut off while they're still breathin' and brought to me on a plate."

A thin man in an impeccably cut sharkskin suit waited for a lull in the storm. He lit a cigarette, released the blue smoke through pursed lips and saw an opening.

"Juice says he's sure it was a boating accident. We're checking on who he was hanging out with down there."

"Some kids from school", he said. "Boating accident, my fat, hairy Sicilian ass," Ragone said. "He ain't ever been on a boat that I know of. Can't even swim." He pulled a fresh pack of Lucky Strikes from his breast pocket and tore at the cellophane and foil. He tapped the pack three times, withdrew one cigarette and patted his pants for his lighter.

Arthur Louis Petroni, the man in the sharkskin suit, pointed to an end table which had somehow remained upright during the fracas. A Zippo lighter with an enameled Italian tri-color lay on its side. Ragone grabbed the lighter in one hairy paw and flipped the top. It opened with a familiar click. He spun the thumbwheel several times until a blue flame flickered. Petroni waited until he saw the tip of the butt glow red before he began speaking.

"Danny," he said slowly, "Nobody would hit Little Rags. You gotta know that."

At the sound of his son's nickname, Ragone gave a heaving sigh and collapsed into an overstuffed leather chair. He looked up at Petroni with bloodshot eyes. "He wasn't part of any of this," Ragone said, voice breaking. "I sent him to that fancy prep school just so he'd be out of it. He wore a jacket and a tie every day there. He was gonna go to St. Joe's this fall." Petroni watched as the rage ebbed, slowly but surely, letting the sadness and hurt start to trickle back in.

"We'll check it out just to make sure," Petroni said evenly, "but Juice did good work for us for a long time. He's one of our guys even if he is a civilian now."

Ragone wiped at his eyes with thumb and forefinger and looked at Petroni. "A lot of the work Juice did for us was saying things weren't something when they was. Let's not forget that."

Petroni nodded. "Like I said, we'll check it out. As it happens. the new Police Chief in Surf City has a connection to an old friend of ours."

"Yeah, who's that?" Ragone's composure was returning. Petroni could see the wheels starting to turn again.

"Patsy Cleary," Petroni said, withdrawing a pack of his own preferred brand, Pall Mall's. "His daughter Michaela – she goes by Mickey – she took the job there couple weeks ago." Ragone considered the new information.

"I thought she was walkin' a beat down at K and A. It was inna paper."

Petroni blew out a wispy smoke ring and watched it disappear. "Kensington and Allegheny isn't what it used to be, Danny," he said, referring to the eponymous intersection. "And that was a while ago." Petroni took another slow drag. "She was involved in a shootout down there. Some little girls got killed. Right after that she turned in her badge and just disappeared. She was on our radar because of Patsy but we lost her until she turned up in Surf City. Like I said, I'll make some calls and check it out."

Ragone crushed his cigarette on the tile floor and placed his hands in his lap. "This girl, this Mickey, she don't know nothin' about what happened with us and her old man, right? I mean, she ain't got no axe to grind, no ideas about, you know, *fare una vendetta*, right?" He mulled the thought. "A cop. You know a cop could do it and get away with it if they wanted. You remember a few years ago… down there?"

"I remember. But I doubt Patsy never told her about his work for us." Petroni was secretly disappointed that he hadn't made the connection himself. It was an intriguing idea, maybe even a good possibility, but he thought it best to let it lay for the time being. Danny was able to survive, Petroni realized, exactly because he saw all of the connections and the potential advantage had or, more importantly, the danger it posed.

"Yeah, well, we gotta think about all the possibilities. She could'a found out on her own. See if she has any ties to Carmine. She was in North Philly, right? Carmine's got eggplants that still work for him up there. Check them out, too." He paused and adjusted his pants. "How's Patsy these days, anyway?"

"Not so good I think since that slug shifted near his spine. Sits in a chair mostly is what I hear."

"He shouldn'ta done what he did. He didn't give us no choice."

"That is true," Petroni said. "He took the deal and he knew the consequences."

Ragone looked at the floor. "He lost his boy, didn't he?"

Petroni nodded solemnly. "Little Mikey," he said. "Seven years old. Lymphoma. It just about broke Patsy. And the medical bills…" Petroni paused for effect and turned his palms upward.

"Thank God we could help Patsy out with them. Until he became ungrateful, of course."

"And you said the girl's name is – what? Michaela? What kind'a name is that for a girl?"

"Yes, Michaela, poor kid. Born a year after Mikey passed. I think they call it a replacement child. Right down to the name." Petroni tapped his ashes onto the floor.

Ragone shook his head. 'That don't matter to me. I wanna know is she a straight-shooter? I mean, who paid her bills when she was on the job? Who lined her pocket?"

"She was clean as far as anyone knows," Petroni said. "But I guess that shooting and those little girls really messed her up."

Ragone remained silent, his thick brow furrowed in thought. Then he spoke. "If she's the one that done this -" He put index finger and thumb to his lips and raised his eyes. Petroni knew well what the gesture meant. It was the kiss goodbye.

A little chill ran through the lawyer. "I'll tell you what," Petroni said. "Forget the phone calls. I'll drive down the shore myself. Today. Acting as your attorney, of course.

"Shots, too," Ragone said.

Petroni nodded. "I'll talk to Juice and then I'll get her to release the bod-" He stopped. "I'll tell her to let me bring Little Rags home."

Ragone took a stuttering breath and began to sob uncontrollably. Petroni watched him with a mixture of pity and fascination. He had never once hugged another man.

He wasn't about to start now.

EIGHT
Surf City

KAYLEN FAIRBROTHER WALKED IN through the back door of the brick station house. Both holding cells were empty as usual, their doors swung open wide. Mickey had turned on all three of the ancient table fans. Faded slips of red ribbon were tied to their grates and they oscillated slowly and asynchronously. They faced away from the paired desks so as not to disturb the mountain of paperwork on top.

"Well, I think we can safely assume that Little Willie isn't very happy with either of us right now," Kaylen said and sat down.

"I don't care," Mickey replied. "That body needs to stay in *my* town and therefore in *my* jurisdiction until I can get the M.E. from the State here. I don't expect Willie to be happy. I do expect him to be quiet." She watched as Kaylen removed his hat and hung it on a peg to the right of the autographed Mickey Mantle picture.

"That's what I told him," the deputy said. "I said if he blabs you'd make sure he wouldn't be selling anything but Yoo-Hoo for the next five years."

Mickey smiled. "Well, I didn't say it exactly like that but I like it. Mickey Mantle, he drinks Yoo-Hoo, doesn't he?" she asked, deciding she needed to talk about anything else for a minute.

"No," Kaylen replied with a serious expression. "Just regular milk or regular chocolate milk. Yoo-Hoo is Yogi's drink. The Mick respects that."

Mickey nodded. "Have we heard anything from the Ragone family?" she asked.

"Oh, yeah," Kaylen said, reaching for a slip of notepaper in his breast pocket. "A guy named A. Louis Petroni called City Hall and asked them to release the body to him. City Clerk told him she didn't know anything about any body to release." He arranged some paper clips in a line on his desk blotter. "Do you know where the State Medical Examiner is and when can he get here, Chief? If I could tell Willie something he's likely to be less excitable."

"Guidice says he thinks Dr. Galasso is on vacation somewhere in one of our neighboring beach communities right here on the Island," Mickey replied. "Maybe up in Loveladies or Harvey Cedars. I'm waiting to for a call back from his office in Trenton to confirm."

Kaylen inched his chair closer to the desk. "Anyway, Chief, this guy, this A. Louis Petroni, he says he's the attorney of record for the Ragone family and he's coming here to claim the remains. Told the clerk he'll have some kind of a writ." He handed the little paper to Mickey, who committed the name to memory and then immediately crumpled it and tossed it into the wastebasket.

"If and when he shows up, you send him straight to me. Or better yet, radio me with your 10-20 and I'll come to you. Understood?"

Kaylen nodded. "Got it, Chief," he said. "You mind if I put on some music?"

"Go ahead," Mickey said almost absent-mindedly. "I'll need to figure out a way to stall this Petroni guy until we can find Dr. Galasso and get a proper autopsy done. Man, I just promised the mayor a quiet summer and now we may have a murder on our hands."

"Murder?" Kaylen said, clearly surprised. "I thought Doc Juice said it was a boating accident. No doubts whatsoever, according to him."

"Juice?" Mickey asked, raising her head.

"Doc Guidice. I guess Juice was what they called him back when he was growing up over in South Philly." Something tickled at the back of Mickey's brain. She let it tease her for a moment then moved on.

"Kaylen," she said. "Do you really think this was a boating accident? I mean, you saw the same body I did, right?"

Kaylen did not look at her when he answered. "Big speedboat

propeller could do that, I think, Chief. A Merc 350 has a huge prop or maybe even something' smaller if, say, there was twin engines and twin screws. Seen them cut sea robins in half like with a knife. The prop on a fishing boat's even bigger. It'll take the tail off a dolphin."

"I checked with the State and with the County," Mickey countered. "There are no boats registered to the Ragone family."

"Probably out with locals or maybe summer renters," Kaylen said, his voice a shade weaker. "I'd sure be laying low if a kid fell out of my boat and drowned, I'll tell you that. Considering who his dad is."

"What do you know about his father?" Mickey asked, leaning forward a little.

"I've seen his name in the papers, Chief, same as you. Sounds like he might be a gangster from what I read."

"Yeah, but he hasn't been nicked for anything yet," Mickey replied. "Hauls away the city's garbage on contract if I'm not mistaken. As far as anyone can prove, he's just another successful business man."

Kaylen busied himself with some papers. "Yeah – and if he's just another successful business man then Mickey Mantle is just another right-fielder." He stood up and went over to an RCA Victor record player which had seen better days. Shuffling through a stack of 45's he selected one, centered it on the squat spindle then started the turntable. The plastic arm lifted, rotated and set the needle on the edge of the record. Ricky Nelson's "Poor Little Fool" poured scratchily out of the single speaker on the front.

"Ricky Nelson?" Mickey asked. "Kaylen, it's 1967. Don't you have any Zombies, Strawberry Alarm Clock; any Doors? Ricky Nelson is just so, so ….I don't know, so Fifties."

Kaylen looked hurt and Mickey immediately felt bad. "I don't really care for any of that pothead acid music, ma'am," he said. "Ricky Nelson, Mickey Mantle – they're the kind of people kids should be looking up to, not these long-haired dope fiends. They're even starting to show up in Major League Baseball now."

Mickey noticed that her deputy looked genuinely distressed.

"People need heroes, Chief. Real heroes. Every boy should want to be The Mick. Every girl should want to marry Ricky Nelson. Would you want a sister of yours to show up one night with, with Jim Morrison as her prom date?"

There was more color in his face than she'd seen in three weeks.

Mickey laughed. "Kaylen," she said, "I think the fact that you even know Jim Morrison's name means there might hope for you yet. Times change, people change – and besides, nobody's ever exactly what they seem or who they say they are. I've heard Mantle has an eye for the ladies and a maybe taste for the hard stuff."

Kaylen's's pink cheeks flushed even redder. "The Mick is a married man with kids. Hell, he rooms with Maris and Hank Bauer during the season so if you think there's any funny business going on there, well you're just dead wrong, ma'am. Mickey Mantle is a genuine American hero."

Mickey sat back in her wooden desk chair, springs squeaking as she did. "I'm sorry I said that. I really am. I believe in heroes, too," she said. "But heroes are still just people like you and me. They make mistakes, they make bad choices, they do things they shouldn't do. It doesn't make them less heroic, Kaylen. It just makes them more human."

Kaylen looked at her in disbelief. "You ever seen The Mick hit a home run?" he asked.

"Only on TV," she answered.

"Well if you saw it in person," he said slowly, "you'd know there isn't anything human about Mickey Mantle."

The background singers crooned Ricky out and silence hung in the air for a moment. Mickey thumbed her badge and smiled. "OK," she said, "OK, maybe Mickey Mantle isn't human, but the rest of us certainly are. You got anything newer in that stack?"

Kaylen's tense expression relaxed, "You like The Tremeloes?" he asked.

"Well, I guess I like 'Silence is Golden'," Mickey lied. Kaylen all but leapt from his chair to put it on. "Say," she continued while he sifted through the records, "Speaking of long hair, who's the guy in the fatigues and the jungle hat? I saw him hanging around downtown last night."

"Oh, him? That's Ronnie Dunn," Kaylen answered without hesitation. "Got back from Vietnam few months ago. Rumor has it something maybe got shot off, but nobody's sayin' exactly what or where."

"So is he a local?"

"Yeah, kind'a. He went to Holy Spirit High School over in Absecon. He was a big jock there – football, baseball, track. Pretty much Mister All-Star in everything he did. Joined the Army right after graduation and then got shipped to Viet Nam after that. Somethin' real bad must've happened, that's all I know. Somebody said he took a bullet but he still came home with a Dishonorable Discharge. Not even a Purple Heart or medal or anything. He lives in an old bungalow way down at the far end of town. Must be getting a nice disability check 'cause he doesn't seem to have any job. And he wears those camouflage pants and that green hat all the time, even when it's hot out."

"He ever have a beef with anyone. Like maybe Little Danny Rags?"

Kaylen still hadn't turned around. A melodic electric guitar riff heavy with reverb filled the empty air between them.

"Not that I know of," Kaylen replied quickly. "Ronnie mostly just rides that old girls' bike around town and hangs out or sits on the beach looking at the ocean. And I think, Chief, he might smoke that mary jane sometimes, too. But he really doesn't bother anyone and so nobody bothers him. 'Course, who would want to bother a guy who carries an eight inch knife?" He turned toward the stack of records.

The Tremeloes finished their four-part harmonic crescendo. Mickey rose without a word, exited the station house's rear door and hopped in the Chevelle. The glare was blinding so she adjusted her sunglasses first and then the windshield visor. The Chevelle had a broad, dark-blue tinted stripe across the top of the glass but its effect at the moment was negligible. Mickey squinted as she pulled out of the pitted asphalt and gravel trapezoid that functioned as the station's parking lot. She looked at the high gloss wax finish on the Galaxie, its single red dome light sparkling in the climbing sun. Kaylen had been happy when Mickey had cut her deal to get the Chevelle and she knew he was meticulous about his cruiser. She thought he said he had been cleaning the interior when the call about the body came in.

When Mickey got beyond the main beach paths the road was as much sand as asphalt. Irregular black patches of sticky pitch bubbled in the sun, tiny versions of the LaBrea Tar Pits she had seen during her self-imposed exile in California. An old man in knee-high black dress socks and Roman-style leather sandals crossed in the rearview mirror. "A shoobie," Mickey thought to herself. Sand and shells crunched under the tires. Every few yards the wheels would slip a little bit and Mickey slowed down. After what looked like the end of any organized residential zoning she spied the dwelling her deputy had described. This was, she now realized, directly across from where she'd seen the fire on the beach two nights earlier. She parked the cruiser twenty yards away and rolled down the window. The ramshackle dwelling she saw wouldn't qualify as a bungalow even on a good day. Its strake board construction and peeling whitewash paint made it look like one of the lifeguards' dory boats turned upside down and then squared off at bow and stern. Double pane wooden sash windows were open top and bottom to the day's prevailing breeze. What had probably once been curtains flapped intermittently through the apertures. Mickey regarded the front of the structure. It had, she noticed, a makeshift porch constructed of slatted wooden shipping pallets laid end to end. Driven in or perhaps bolted to the flimsy lumber at one corner was a rather new-looking white flagpole. Perched atop it was shiny brass eagle, its wings spread majestically, head turned in profile. An American flag snapped smartly with each gust of the sea breeze. It looked as new as the flagpole. But there was something wrong about it and it took her a minute to determine what it was. The flag, she noticed, was flying upside down.

Mickey pushed open the shack's half-unhinged door with her nightstick. The sun was not yet high enough to illuminate the interior and it took her eyes a moment to adjust.

"Ronnie? Ronnie Dunn?" she called. "Hello. Anybody home?"

There was no answer. As her pupils dilated she took stock of what appeared to be the place's main room. A threadbare carpet remnant covered much but by no means all of the tilted board floor. There was no TV or radio that she could see. The room had a slight but not unpleasant smell – one very familiar to her. As she moved farther in she called again.

"Ronnie Dunn? Chief Cleary, here, Surf City Police – just checking on things. You here, Ronnie?"

Again, silence. There was a large green shape at the far end of the room. As Mickey approached she saw what it was: a camouflage- patterned bivouac tent was set up, taut strings tethered to the floor with eyelets screwed directly into the boards.

The flap was closed. Mickey took several steps forward until she was directly in front of the tent. She leaned over and gingerly pushed open the flap with her nightstick. She craned her neck to peer inside when she heard a creak and felt the floorboards move.

"Looking for me?" said a voice from behind her.

Mickey wheeled and exhaled sharply. She grasped the nightstick with both hands. Ronnie Dunn was standing in the shack's doorway. The ocean glittered jewel-like behind him. The jungle hat was on his head. He was wearing olive drab fatigue pants but no shirt. Several pairs of dog tags hung from his neck down onto his tanned and hairless chest. No scars or tattoos that she could see. She pegged him at six-one and a lean but smoothly muscular buck-eighty. At first she was startled by the youthfulness of his face and voice. Then he gazed straight at her. His eyes, she thought, looked a hundred years old. Straight, light brown hair touched the tops of his shoulders. He had black rubber thong sandals on his feet, but they didn't look like the kind that came from Woolworth's on the boardwalk in Ocean City. She backed up a step and lowered the nightstick.

"Startled me there, Ronnie," she said.

He stared at her without answering. His right hand was buried in the pocket of his pants. His opposite arm hung down concealing his left hand behind him. Mickey let the nightstick slip from one hand but did not let it go. She tried to strike what she hoped was a non-threatening pose.

"Nice place you got here," she said, forcing a smile.

Ronnie continued to stare at her. When he shifted from one foot to the other she saw what was in his left hand. Kaylen Fairbrother had been wrong – it was more than just a knife. It was a bayonet

Mickey slowly became aware that music was playing somewhere behind her. She thought she recognized The Doors' signature organ riffs and Jim Morrison's whiskey-scarred vocals.

"I do something wrong?" Ronnie asked.

"Not that I know of," Mickey answered.

"Then exactly why are you here, ma'am?"

Once a soldier always a soldier, Mickey thought. Or maybe it was just the typical kid from a Catholic school –a type she knew all too well.

"Deputy Fairbrother said there were a few local residents that were worth getting to know."

"In case a dead body washes up on the beach, you mean?"

Mickey slipped the nightstick back in its belt ring. "Look," she said, hoping to strike a conciliatory tone, "Let's not get off on the wrong foot. I really just got here and-"

"You really just got here three weeks ago," Ronnie replied. "Three weeks and two days, ma'am, to be exact. So it seems I must not be high up on your list of people worth getting to know."

Mickey shrugged. "OK, fair enough – but two things: first, can you please put down the blade and, second, stop calling me ma'am. We're probably about the same age. How about Chief Cleary or just Chief for now?"

He laid the bayonet on the floor but did not step away from it. "Let's try one thing at a time, ma'am," he said without smiling. Mickey exhaled loudly.

"Is there a place we can sit?" she asked.

"Not really," he replied. Ronnie eased down into a squat so effortlessly that Mickey figured he'd done it a million times, probably in much worse environs. She tried to do the same, her nightstick tapping the floor as she did.

"I'm just here looking for answers," she said. "I've got a dead kid who looks like somebody tried to cut his head off." She glanced at the bayonet. "You've got a weapon that could do it. Problem is, the rest of him looks like he tackled a Mack truck." Ronnie appeared as if he could stay in his crouch all day, she thought. She was already becoming uncomfortable. He met her eyes without replying so she continued. "That didn't happen down there on the beach."

"Fell out of a boat is what I heard," Ronnie replied. "Could be, I suppose. Takes a flyer off the side or over the stern transom; maybe that long hair gets caught in the prop or he gets hit by another boat who can't see him bobbing in the water. Only takes a second. I saw a guy get sliced in half when a Huey helicopter tipped over on landing one time." He shrugged. "Good an explanation as anything else."

"Are you telling me you think that's what happened?"

"I didn't say that, ma'am," he replied.

"How long were you in Viet Nam?" Mickey asked.

"Now I never said I was in Viet Nam," Ronnie answered. "Could it be you know more about me than I think?" Mickey started to get up. Ronnie didn't move. "You slowed down to eyeball me downtown last night, Chief. You were watching me."

"Yeah and you were watching me back."

"Well, some of my skills are a little rusty,"" Ronnie replied.

"You know who the kid is?"

"I don't know his name," Ronnie said. He began to trace with his index finger on the dusty floor between his knees. Then he looked up. "But I did interact with him briefly earlier in the day yesterday."

"I hadn't heard that," Mickey said. "But I appreciate the fact that you're telling me before I found out on my own." She looked around. "You really don't have a place to sit somewhere?" she asked.

Ronnie smiled. "I'm not much on accommodations, ma'am," he said nodding to the tent.

"You really… sleep in there?"

"Only when it rains and the roof leaks. Then I cover the mattress and the furniture in the bedroom with a tarp and I bivvy out here. I've slept in a lot worse places than this, ma'am."

"Would you mind standing up?" Mickey asked.

"You want to arrest me?"

Mickey let out a sigh. "No, I don't want to arrest you unless you tell me that you got crossways with this kid and then used the skills the United States government taught you and *that* bayonet to do what I saw this morning. Then, I suppose, I would need to arrest you. Otherwise, I just want us to talk eye to eye."

Ronnie nodded and eased out of the squat without visible effort. He kicked the weapon toward her feet. "Check it out if you want," he said. "But I'd like it back when you're finished. I use it to cut driftwood and stir the fire."

Mickey looked down. "When I was a beat cop," she said slowly, "I had to make a lot of rapid personal assessments about who the good guys were and who the bad guys were. Who I could turn my back on and who I couldn't. So, I'm going to leave it right there for now while you tell me about your encounter with the deceased."

"Don't you mean the victim?" Ronnie asked.

"The term victim presumes homicide or manslaughter, accidental or otherwise."

Ronnie rolled his eyes. "OK, Chief Cleary, I'll tell you about my brief encounter and then you can decide what to do with me and my driftwood knife."

"Listening," Mickey said.

"I was, as the guilty always say, just minding my own business on a bench a couple blocks up from the surf shop. This car pulls up – brand new Mustang convertible – and this kid, the dead one, he's driving. So he pulls over and stops right next to me. Starts yelling things. And not at all nice things, ma'am. In fact, quite nasty things I'd have to say."

"Like what,"

"The usual 'Nam shit people who didn't or wouldn't go like to say. Called me a baby killer and a disturbed individual. Asked me if I stabbed them or just machine-gunned them. He then strongly suggested I vacate the public space I was occupying immediately or he would 'run my sorry ass over' is I think how he phrased it." Ronnie shook his head. "Very poor manners for a young man. Especially in public and to someone who's served his country in battle."

Mickey drew in a breath. "And how did you respond. What did you say back?"

"Nothing," Ronnie answered. "I just smiled and I did this-" He extended his arm and pointed at her with his finger, then repeated the act of sighting down his arm and pulling back his shoulder.

"And how did he respond?"

"He shut his mouth and he drove away."

"See him after that?"

"No, Chief Cleary, I did not. Stupidity is still not illegal although it is very often lethal."

"The car didn't happen to be red, did it?" Mickey asked.

"Yeah, it was red," Ronnie replied "Candy apple red."

"Passengers?"

"Three other guys, probably around the same age I'd say. High school kids, most likely. They didn't look too happy about the whole thing. Like they were embarrassed by this kid or pissed off or maybe both."

"They say anything?"

"Not a word. The kid behind the wheel was clearly the alpha dog."

Mickey tugged at her hair. "I think my deputy might have actually pulled them over a little earlier. Nothing bad; they got off with a just a verbal so unfortunately we don't have any paperwork that would help ID any of the companions. Have you seen that car or any of the other kids since?"

Ronnie shook his head.

"Neither have I." Mickey stepped over the bayonet and took a step toward him.

"You forgot something," he said, looking at the weapon on the floor behind her.

"No I didn't," Mickey replied. "And you say you don't know who the dead kid is?" Ronnie cocked his head.

"Negative ma'am. Expensive clothes, expensive car, bad attitude toward the locals – describes ninety-nine percent of the summer crowd right there."

Mickey laughed. "Yeah, well his name is Danny Ragone." She looked at Ronnie for any hint of recognition.

"Is that supposed to mean something to me?"

"His father is a businessman across the river."

"Kind of rings a bell," Ronnie said. "Might have seen something about him in *The Inquirer* or maybe it was the *Evening Bulletin*. I read the ones people leave at the luncheonette sometimes. If I remember right, the phrase 'reputed mob boss' usually accompanies his name. That might be a problem. Especially if the angry young man didn't fall out of a boat."

"That's exactly what I'm afraid of," Mickey replied. "Did anybody see you have this little altercation?"

"The street was deserted and so was the beach. And it was over pretty quick. Couple of minutes. It's not like it happened in front of a crowd of onlookers or anything. Be different if it was this time next week."

Mickey rubbed at the back of her neck and walked past him. "I think you and I will need to talk some more about this but I don't want to do it down at the station right now. I'm going to try and find the car or one of the kids who was in it. I think that's the best place to start."

"Then I am not a suspect, I take it?"

"Our coroner's official opinion is that it was an accidental death. Which means I can't prove there's been a crime committed until I get an official post-mortem," Mickey replied. "So for the moment, nobody's a suspect."

"Are you going to tell me not to leave town like they do on 'Dragnet'?"

"I've seen your wheels," Mickey answered. "I'm not too worried you becoming a fugitive. Be better if you stuck around, though. And no more fires after Thursday night. Summer ordinances will be enforced starting Friday."

Ronnie angled his head slightly. "I'm willing to go one klick further, Chief Cleary, if you're willing to take a chance, that is. Emil's Tavern is just over the Causeway in Somers Point. You pick up two pizzas. One cheese, one sausage. And a six-pack of Ballantine – beer, not ale. Make sure you get it from the back of the cooler not the front. You can wait 'til after dark. Park down the street. I know some people that you don't. I'll hear some things that you won't. Maybe I can turn up a useful rumor or two. Maybe not. But it's pretty cheap intel if I do." He fingered the dog tags. "Sun's not down 'til almost eight-thirty now. Give it about an hour after that."

Mickey looked around the empty room. "Need some time to shop for furniture?" she asked.

. "Couple of beach chairs and a folding table OK?" Ronnie answered. "And one more fire before the shoobies arrive."

"That'd be a regular dining room suite for this place," Mickey said and began to walk out. "It's my shift tonight, so maybe I'll just bring the pizza. Can't be contributing to the delinquency of a citizen, you know." She walked to the door.

"You don't want to take the bayonet?"

"You'll need it to cut the driftwood."

"A K-BAR knife would work better but I didn't bring one of those back with me."

"Why would it be better?" Mickey asked.

"Bayonet has a three-sided blade. So the hole it makes won't close itself. It's designed for stabbing not cutting."

"Thanks for the lesson in deadly weapons. But you know what's interesting? You're probably the only professionally trained killer on Long Beach Island and I'm crossing you off my list first."

"Chief," Ronnie said. "It's got nothing to do with me. I've seen enough violence And I've seen it up close and personal. I'm finished with it."

Mickey turned toward him. "Then how did you know?"

"About the body?"

"Yeah, about the body. How did you know it was the kid from

the car?"

Ronnie shuffled his feet. He dropped his chin but raised his eyes to meet hers. "I don't really sleep very much. I like the fact that now I can enjoy the night. I can keep my eyes open because I want to, not because I have to to stay alive. And I like walking next to the ocean when it's as black and smooth as the sky. You don't have sand in your shoes yet, but you will."

"You saw the body on the beach, didn't you?" Mickey said. "Why didn't you call it in?"

"Now wouldn't that have seemed just a little too convenient, considering the day's events?"

Mickey pondered the thought. "Yes," she said after a moment. "It would have. And you would be at the top of my list instead of crossed off it. Did you see anything else, any*one* else?"

Ronnie shook his head. "I thought it best to return to base. The sit-rep was clearly FUBAR at that point."

"FUBAR?"

"Grunt slang. Fucked up beyond all recognition."

"But you knew I'd be here, didn't you?"

He nodded toward the bayonet. "Sooner or later," Ronnie replied. "I saw you on the beach this morning."

"I didn't see you," Mickey said.

"I said my skills were rusty. I didn't say they had disappeared."

Mickey adjusted her hat. "And you think you can find something that would help me?"

"Maybe I just want free pizza and beer."

Mickey paused. Now she did turn around to look at him. "OK," she said. "Let's assume I'm willing to take that chance for really no sensible reason that I can think of at the moment. Answer one more question for me. You mentioned your skills. What was your job, you know, your specialty when you were in uniform?"

Ronnie cocked his head to the side and squeezed one eye shut. He drew a breath then let it all the way out and made a double-clicking sound with his cheek.

"I was a sniper, ma'am," he replied.

NINE

Cottman Avenue Garden Apartments
Northeast Philadelphia

IT TOOK SEVERAL MINUTES to cover the eleven feet between his easy chair and the front door. There were days when he thought he could actually feel the slug which, the doctors told him, was perilously close to his spinal cord. He was convinced that extreme movements would result in the paralysis his neurosurgeon at Jefferson Hospital had warned him about. Patrick Aloysius Cleary, "Patsy" to most people he knew, settled his atrophying gluteal muscles on a red plastic stool and reached for the doorknob.

The buzzer was being pressed repeatedly now. He pulled open the flimsy wooden inside door and peered through the torn screen on the metal storm.

A man in a tailored suit and a narrow tie stood on the stoop.

"Sergeant Cleary," he said. "Top o' the mornin' to you. How is our old friend of the family today?"

Patsy recognized him immediately. "What do you *want*, Artie?" he replied.

The man at the door hesitated. Patsy knew how much A. Louis Petroni hated being called Artie. The meager effort at a pleasant tone disappeared immediately

"I assume you've heard," Petroni said.

"Heard what, Artie? You know I don't get out much."

"Oh, that slug still bothering you?" Petroni asked. "After all these years? I guess payback really is hell. And, yes, I'd love to come in and reminisce about old times but unfortunately I only have a moment."

"What do you want, Artie?" Patsy asked again, shifting on his stool.

"I see your Mickey has been promoted from beat cop to beach cop," Petroni said. "So it surprises me that you haven't heard the bad news."

A little chill ran up Patsy's endangered spine with the mention of his daughter's name. He held his breath and waited.

"Little Rags was found dead on the beach this morning in Surf City."

Patsy suddenly felt as if the room temperature had dropped ten degrees.

"Yeah, well give Danny my condolences," he said flatly. "Accident, I presume."

"At this point I'd say that presumes a lot, Sergeant Cleary," Petroni replied.

"Kids are civilians, Artie. Everybody knows that. Nobody would come after Danny's kid. They'd have to be crazy."

"Let's hope that turns out to be the case," Petroni replied. "Things could get ugly, otherwise. And since we're on this sad subject, it's possible I might need a little favor."

Patsy wiped a bead of sweat from above his eyebrow. "I'm in no position to do favors, Artie. You guys made sure of that."

Petroni ignored the remark. "I'm on my way down the shore to bring Little Rags home. That is, if the local constabulary will let me. The woman I talked to in the City Clerk's office was, shall we say, a trifle less than helpful. I'm sure it's just a misunderstanding that I can easily straighten out in person. But just in case…"

"What're you askin', Artie?"

"All I'm saying is that if the need arises you might hold some sway with members of local law enforcement. Nothing more than a phone call and maybe a little fatherly advice."

"Michaela and me don't really talk that much," Patsy replied. "Not since Eileen passed away. I didn't even know she was back from California 'til last week."

"You're all she has left," Petroni said. "Maybe this is God's way of letting you two patch things up. Could be some good comes of it all around."

Patsy let out a laugh. "God's way, Artie? God's way? Let's just wait a second and see if you spontaneously combust into flames for sayin' that, why don't we? If things were supposed to go God's way you'd be takin' it up the ass in Frankford Prison right now 'stead of drivin' around in that Coup de Ville Danny Rags gave you." He pointed at the car double parked on the narrow street.

Petroni chuckled. "It's actually a Jaguar S Type Sedan, Patsy, and I'd wager its book value is a lot more than yours right now. But let's get something straight. I am a legal professional, admitted to the Bar in three states. I earn every penny I make. And I don't suck the public tit like you do with that fat disability check you cash every month."

Patsy's face flushed. "Yeah and how'd I get disabled, Artie? You were a slimy Ginzo fuck when you were a kid and you ain't never changed. You just dress better now is all." He waited for Petroni to answer. It took several seconds.

"I've caught you at a bad time with some very distressing news, Patsy. I'm sorry. I'm on my way to assess the situation in Surf City personally on Danny's behalf. I'll make sure I let you know if you can be of any assistance to the Ragone family during this most difficult time." Petroni said this without a glimmer of unpleasantness. "And I'll say hi to Mikey – oh, sorry, I meant Mickey, for you. I'm sure she misses being closer with her dad."

Patsy pushed himself up to as close to a standing position as he could manage. "You stay away from my little girl, Artie" The pain in his lower back felt like the business end of a tenpenny nail. Petroni turned and without another word strolled to the idling car. Patsy grabbed the door frame. With one hand he steadied himself and with the other he pushed open the storm. "I said stay away from my little girl. You listening to me, Artie?" he shouted into the street as the big sedan pulled away. The thin, dented door rattled and slammed when he let it go. Two boys from the neighboring apartment were playing pimple ball on the cement stoop. They looked up at him.

"It's OK, boys," Patsy said through the screen. "But I got a buck for whichever one of you eggs that car if it ever comes back here."

It took several minutes for Patsy's hands to top shaking. How long had it been, he wondered, since he'd said the words *my little girl*? How long since that little girl had called him Daddy or even Dad? It wasn't her fault, he knew. It was his. He was the one who made her fill the hole Mikey's death had torn in his heart. He was the one who gave her the impossible load to carry. Eileen had seen it and tried to protect her. But in the end all he'd done was to drive both of them away. They were kind enough to call Eileen's death "natural causes" so the life insurance would pay out but Patsy knew that watching *her* little girl be slowly pulled away from her was not a natural cause. Neither was the bottle of Four Roses or the packet of Seconals he found and then hid before the doctor arrived. For a long time he was able to blame it all on losing Mikey and no one ever questioned his right to grieve or the manner in which he did it. He'd been able to convince himself, Patsy realized, that he had a good excuse for everything.

Among the pictures hanging on the wall across from him was one of Michaela on the day of her First Communion. In all the others, he noticed, she was wearing a uniform – baseball, basketball, field hockey and finally, a police officer's. Only in the one, he thought, did she really look like his little girl.

Patsy maneuvered slowly to the tiny kitchenette where the beige Bell telephone hung on the wall. He picked up the receiver and dialed "O." When she came on the line he asked the operator to connect him with New Jersey Information for the 609 area code.

TEN

THE PINE BARRENS
Southeastern New Jersey

TRAFFIC WAS LIGHT AND two hours had gone by quickly. Cruising south and east on State Route 72, A. Louis Petroni, Esq. had a stop to make. It would have been faster, he knew, to take the recently completed Atlantic City Expressway but he preferred the solitude and nostalgia of the old and pitted asphalt two-lanes. The Black and White Horse Pikes were not continuous roads but rather amalgams of local and state highways originally conceived to lead beach-seeking tourists from Philadelphia's Ben Franklin Bridge all the way to Cape May, the southernmost tip of the Jersey shore. His business was further north, however, and so he'd taken the Walt Whitman Bridge and the old Marlton Pike until he hit his present thoroughfare

His visit with Patsy Cleary had soured his mood. He felt he had certainly gotten the better of the encounter but it had also dragged up the indelible memories of schoolyard tormentors chanting "Farty Artie" until he bawled. It pleased him to know that, if he chose to, he could have those who'd made his young life miserable killed and dismembered by any one of Danny's button men, with little more fanfare than ordering cannelloni for take-out. This thought, the sunshine through the tinted windows and the smell of the Jaguar's rich leather brought a thin smile to his lips. He tuned the radio to an FM station – there were only two he could get reliably – and watched the landscape change as he motored along.

Except for the occasional farm truck hauling produce and the scattered roadside stands selling ripe Jersey tomatoes, the road was deserted. Petroni checked his watch and scanned the right side of the highway. A telephone pole with a thick black wire descending diagonally told him what he needed and he downshifted smoothly as the tires made a popcorn sound on the gravel of the unpaved shoulder. Petroni got out and, by habit, surveyed the road for observers or threats. Seeing none he walked from the idling car to the phone booth which was listing several degrees off plumb. Even with the natural solitude he closed the door and turned his back towards the old highway. Fishing a dime from his pocket he dropped it in the circular slot at the top, lifted the receiver and dialed a number he seldom used but always remembered.

"Thass' shoor a nice coor you're drivin'," the voice on the other end said after eleven rings. Instinctively Petroni ducked his head crouched. The voice laughed. "Just fuckin' with ya is all. Can't see no coor. Heard the tars, though."

Petroni straightened up. Billy Bowker, he knew, was a fourth generation Piney, as tough as rebar and twice as useful.

"I may have a package for you to process in the next few days," Petroni said. "It might need special handling."

"We can do that," Bowker replied. "Fars happen all the time round here. Don't usually leave much behind. You want to stop by? New batch of brandy ready. Put hair on that skinny eye-talian chest a' yours."

"I'll be there in five minutes. Put the dog somewhere this time, OK?"

Bowker cackled. "You ever get that spunk outta yoor pants leg?"

"I had to burn them," Petroni answered. "Fifty dollar custom-cuffed and pleated from Lit Brothers. Maybe you should deduct it from the bill."

"Maybe you should wear shoorts," Bowker said without humor and hung up.

Petroni scanned through the smeared, dust-caked glass and opened the folding door. The Pine Barrens were intimidating even in daylight. Sunlight filtered between the tall trees but the sense of remoteness was palpable and terrifying. No wonder legend said the Jersey Devil lived here.

Two more turns and a quarter mile of oiled dirt road brought the shack into view. Bowker stood on a cinderblock front porch, a half-empty canning jar in one hand, a shotgun in the other. Petroni looked at the two rutted tracks that led up to it and decided to park the Jag and walk the hundred paces. Shoes were cheaper to replace than shocks and a transmission.

Bowker sipped, almost delicately, from the jar as he approached. Ninety paces in he brought the shotgun up. Petroni stopped and pulled open the suit jacket to show he was unarmed. Bowker nodded and Petroni covered the last of the ground.

"Don't trust me?" he asked.

"Don't trust nobody," Bowker answered. "S'why I'm still draw'n air'."

"This package may be a problem for you – I just want to make sure you know that ahead of time." Billy Bowker had been disposing of bodies for most of his adult life. The Pines weren't really as barren as their name implied. The acidic soil was perfect for rapid decomposition and the general air of foreboding kept most searchers and even law enforcement at bay. The pitch pines and the scrub oaks hid tiny hamlets and shotgun shacks like the one Bowker lived in. The locals had long-resented the term "Piney" as derogatory and Petroni knew better than to utter it in Bowker's presence, but lately he was sensing in them a growing pride in their isolation and their other-ness. Bowker, he knew, reveled in his status as an outsider and a true backwoodsman. The apocryphal legends of in-breeding and bizarre social and sexual practices only added to the Barrens' reputation as a place where "civilized" people dare not tread. The Barrens also were riven with swamps and areas of pygmy pines and cedar forests where the water ran a blood-tinged red, ideal for concealing crimes both great and small. This suited people like Bowker, and those who dealt with him, just fine. He'd handled some notables for Petroni and the other East coast families, mostly rivals and inconvenient witnesses. But Petroni knew he also was dealing with some new clients, namely the small but increasingly violent motorcycle gangs that were looking to carve out fresh criminal territory. Both groups of outsiders would have to be dealt with, Petroni was sure, in the years to come. He hoped his ties to Bowker would make him a valuable resource when that time arrived.

"So, will it be wigglin' when I git it?" Bowker asked. The sun lit up the jar in his hand sending a prismatic spectrum onto the shack's door.

"Hard to say," Petroni responded. "We may not need you at all if everyone plays their cards right." He tapped one shoe against the heel of the other to shake loose the sandy dirt. "We would need you to be ready to take delivery on short notice though. Think you can hold off coon hunting or whatever it is you boys do for a few days? We'll provide a *per diem* for the trouble if you want."

"What the fuck is a purr deem?"

"It's money every day for doing nothing. Figure a hundred."

"Hunnertwunny," Bowker said. Petroni had assumed he'd come back with a hundred and fifty and so he quickly nodded his head in assent. Bowker took a long swig from the jar and wiped his mouth with a wrist as thick as Petroni's ankle. "And the clock starts now."

Petroni turned and walked briskly back to the Jag. Bowker was reliable but he was also as close to feral as any human being Petroni had ever met. Years of living on the outskirts of society had bred in him a predatory cunning that suited his line of work but rendered him all but unfit for human companionship. If the stories Petroni heard were true, there was also a deep current of sexual sadism that made even the old *capos* shake their heads. It would be simpler and so much cleaner if business could be conducted without him.

* * *

Saint Mary of the Angels Preparatory School
Haddonfield, New Jersey

The tap on the door made him look up. A boy with stiff, straw-colored hair and a pock-marked complexion stood at the entrance to the classroom.

"Sorry, Mr. C.," the boy said. "But there's a guy down at the front entrance says he needs to talk to you." He nodded to the boy and put down the Calculus finals he was correcting. The school was quiet. The seniors had graduated the week before and the only students on campus were those taking exams.

The slap of his leather soles echoed in the stairwell as he descended and approached the glassed-in main entrance. Just inside the front door stood a burly man in his forties. He was dressed nicely and wore a tan London Fog raincoat despite the sunshine and warm temperatures. The teacher knew immediately what this meant.

"Do I have time to straighten my desk up, maybe grab my briefcase?

"We should probably get going," the man in the raincoat said. The teacher nodded. He had played the role of hostage several times before during negotiations and knew the requirements. The extra money it brought in every few months was nice, especially with the paltry salary and retirement benefits the diocese provided. He hoped either Donahue or Marquart would be able to proctor the Algebra final scheduled for the following day. He walked out into the glare and saw a baby-blue laundry truck parked in the circular drive next to the alabaster statue of Mary Magdalene surrounded by long-winged archangels. The driver's seat appeared empty. He walked around to the rear and two cargo doors with painted-over windows opened simultaneously. The faces inside were familiar.

The burly man helped him in. "I know the drill," the teacher said and proffered his wrists. Once they were bound he looked for a place to sit down as the doors clanged shut. The burly man stopped him.

"Slight change in plans today," the burly man said this as he buttoned up his raincoat and pulled a white plastic sheet from one of the laundry bags. Then he unbuckled the teacher's belt and roughly pulled his recently purchased Slax N' Jax polyester trousers down to his ankles

"Is this really necessary, boys?" the teacher asked.

It was then that he glimpsed the pearl handle of a barber's straight razor. His bladder let go and he began to retch.

ELEVEN
Surf City

KAYLEN FAIRBROTHER PULLED THE Galaxie cruiser into the marked diagonal space in front of the Ebb Tide Motor Hotel. It was the place he referred to as his house although the two connecting rooms he rented on the second floor were never intended nor zoned for permanent residence. Eddie Giacometti, the owner, only charged him rent on one of them. By Eddie's calculation, there was value in having a steady "police presence" at the establishment. The mere sight of a "cop car", as Eddie called it, tended to discourage even teenage loiterers much as less actual criminals. The Ebb Tide was rarely at full occupancy, even in-season, and Eddie's yearly loss on the property seemed to keep the IRS less interested in his other more lucrative ventures. Eddie's eye, he had told Kaylen, was on the future; when the small rhomboid of land the motel occupied would be worth fifty times what he had paid for it. Kaylen didn't see the same future for any place on Long Beach Island but he was getting a free room and so he let Eddie dream anything he wanted without argument.

Kaylen took the outside stairs two at a time. There were only two floors so from the little balcony that encircled the top one he could look out towards the Atlantic, only three blocks away. From the back side he could see the bay, a full block closer. He kept one of the exterior doors dead-bolted and he let himself in through the other. The window-mounted air conditioners rattled incessantly but managed to keep the interior cool even during the heat of the day. Kaylen reflexively went to the connecting door and surveyed the adjoining room. He took stock of all his prized possessions. He did this every time he came home and figured he could do it from memory if he ever had to. A fence from Atlantic City he had once arrested told him that old baseball junk – *memorabilia* was the word he used – would someday be worth a fortune. Kaylen thought he was crazier than Eddie.

Seeing nothing amiss, Kaylen went to the small refrigerator and pulled out a Royal Crown Cola. He used the opener mounted on the door frame to pop the cap then took the bottle and sat down in the easy chair he had rescued from his sister's basement. Cold sweat on his brow mirrored the condensation on the glass bottle. The seasick feeling returned. Kaylen rubbed at his eyes with his free hand. He wasn't a good planner, he knew. He wasn't good at knowing what to do next in an unfamiliar situation. This wasn't turning out the way he expected. Three sips into the soda he stood up and walked to the little couch his mother called a davenport. Reaching underneath he extracted the crumpled uniform blouse, trousers and socks. He carefully removed the web-knit belt and brushed some dark flecks from the brass buckle. The belt he left on the floor, the clothes he carried to the laundry hamper and stuffed them in. He grabbed two towels from the bathroom and stuffed those in on top. Then he pulled the bag out of the hamper and cinched it with the drawstring. For a moment he was torn on which way to exit. He locked the exterior door, walked to the inside one, opened it and stepped into the musty hallway. Twenty steps later he was descending the ragged carpet-runner with the faded palm trees on it. Doreen, the front desk clerk, was thumbing a lobby copy of Photoplay magazine.

"How's Deputy Fairbrother today?" the rotund woman asked brightly. Of her layered chins, only the upper one was sunburned.

"Just fine," Kaylen answered. He had forgotten to wipe the rime of perspiration from his face, he realized. "Gotta do laundry before the shoobies and the renters get here."

"You should really have it dry-cleaned and pressed," Carol chirped. "They'll even pick it up and drop it off right here at the desk if you ask."

Kaylen gritted a tight smile. "Not on a deputy's salary," he said.

"Suppose that's so," Carol replied. "Have to wait 'til you're Chief, then, I guess."

Kaylen pushed open the glass door. The tinkle of the tiny bell affixed to it sounded much louder inside his head. "Sure," he said as he walked out into the sunlight. "Someday when I'm the Chief."

♦ ♦ ♦

Third Street and Indiana Avenue
Fairhill Neighborhood, North Philadelphia

The shadow of the gothic spire of St. Bonaventure's Catholic Church cast an accusing finger over the decaying landscape of North Philadelphia. The once busy industrial area was graffiti-covered and strewn with trash and empty liquor bottles. Abandoned warehouses and pockmarked row homes dotted the empty streets where trolleys once rolled beneath sparking overhead cables. The homeless, the hopeless and the helpless crouched in rusted doorways or peered through broken windows.

Frank McCusker had been a patrolman for only three months but he knew two things: that the man lying on the sidewalk was not from North Philadelphia and that the man on the sidewalk was dead. The jacket, tie, socks and shoes were untouched. McCusker patted down the body and found the man's watch and wallet equally undisturbed. He radioed in the call and then went back to the body. There was a single bullet wound in the center of the pale forehead but no blood in the back. The front of the new-appearing trousers was stiff with a crimson inkblot of dried blood. It was his first real murder scene but it did strike him as oddly composed. Then he noticed something even more unusual: sprinkled around and underneath the stiffening corpse were what looked to rookie Patrolman Frank McCusker suspiciously like piles of beach sand.

♦ ♦ ♦

Shamong Township, NJ
The Pine Barrens

Petroni made one more stop at the last working phone booth on the old highway It was more disheveled than the previous one with only the paper spine of the Bible-thick phone book remaining and crude graffiti gouged deeply into the steel counter. There were, however, two dimes in the lever-action coin return. Petroni took this as a good omen although the day was slipping away from him, he realized. At this rate he would barely make it to Long Beach Island by five. He was certain no beach town municipal offices would be open a minute before or after that. Petroni took his found money and dialed another number he knew by heart.

"Fairview Cleaners," a raspy voice answered.

"Yes," Petroni intoned without introduction. A rattle-trap truck came into view heading West and Petroni turned his face away. "I'm going to need an item dry cleaned this evening. And I'll need it picked up and delivered."

On the other end of the line, Petroni knew, was one Tomasino "Tommy Shots" Caputo. He was Danny Rags' senior button man. The moniker came from a tendency to use more bullets than necessary when carrying out a hit. To cops and *capos* alike he was known simply as Shots. "Got an address?" Caputo asked.

"Let's discuss the details at The Anchorage. This item may need special handling. It's a dress uniform."

"They all process the same. Take me a little while to get the truck cleaned up. Whaddya say about nine?"

"Nine will work nicely. You know The Anchorage?" Petroni asked.

"Sure. I know the place," Caputo replied. "Seven for a dollar."

"How was business today?"

"Not too bad," Caputo said. "Just a local customer needed a clean and press. Had to drop the merchandise off in a bad neighborhood, though."

"Hazards of the business," Petroni replied.

"Yeah, right. Hazards," Caputo said before letting loose with a cough Petroni thought must have produced at least some lung tissue. "See you at nine."

Petroni hung the receiver back on the scarred and dented hook. As he opened the groaning bi-fold door he heard coins drop and stopped to fish them out. Two nickels. He was still ahead on the day, he figured.

◆ ◆ ◆

Surf City

The Surf City Police Station was stifling when Mickey arrived so she propped the back door open with two empty yellow Pepsi-Cola bottle crates. She sat down just as Kaylen's cruiser wheeled into the lot, spraying gravel against the open door. Mickey waited until he had entered and settled himself at his desk before speaking.

"In a big hurry, Deputy?" She thought he looked a little distracted.

"Sorry, Chief," he said. "Still getting used to the V-8 power in that Galaxie. Can't figure why you didn't want it – it's a honey. You hear from the M.E. yet?"

"No, not yet."

"How about this Petroni guy?"

"Thankfully, no. He's going to be a pain in our asses, I guarantee it. The longer it takes him to get here the better." There was silence for a minute. "You got family nearby?" Mickey asked, shifting the subject. Kaylen smiled at the question.

"Well, Chief, Mom and Dad live in Tuckahoe. Dad sells appliances at the Sears Store in Ocean City. Got an older sister in Atco. She works for a State Senator's office."

"What's her name?" Mickey said. After nearly a month she realized she knew what was in his employment file but almost nothing of her deputy's personal life.

"JoLynne," he said. "Dad wanted Jolene and Mom wanted Linda, so they just split the diff."

"Pretty name," Mickey replied. "Married?"

"Not a lot of eligible bachelors in Atco, Chief," Kaylen answered. "She's hoping the Senator will run for Congress and she can go with him to Washington, D.C. where the prospects are better."

"Good plan," Mickey said. "I remember my dad took me to the Atco Dragway one Sunday. I got to shake Big Daddy Don Garlits' greasy hand down in the pits. I think top fuel funny cars were running that night, too. Nitro injected. I couldn't hear right for a week but it was worth it. I still remember the noise and the smell. You want to sign out now?"

Kaylen looked momentarily flustered. "Um, I was wonderin' if maybe, if it's not a big deal or anything, if I could take tonight's shift and then maybe be off tomorrow night instead. It was real quiet last night and I really don't feel tired at all. I mean, you're the Chief so it's up to you, but I'm happy to work again."

"Got a hot date tomorrow night?" Mickey asked.

"No, Ma'am," Kaylen replied. "Just some personal stuff to take care of."

Mickey thought of Ronnie Dunn's peculiar invitation. "OK," she agreed. "We might as well get our own stuff done before the shoobies arrive in force." She stood up. I have to get my shotgun out of the rack and secure it. Want me to get yours while I'm at it?"

Kaylen almost leapt up. "No, ma'am, Chief," he said and stepped toward the open door. A trickle of sand had blown in and settled on the faded linoleum. "I'll get 'em both and lock 'em up. You go have a night off. Like you said, there won't be very many for a while."

Mickey sat back down and waited for him to return. The two twelve-gauge Remington's went into the station's wall rack and she heard Kaylen slip the bar and snap the big Master padlock closed. "Jam up and jelly tight," he said.

"Kaylen, do you know a place over the bridge called Emil's?" Mickey asked

"Yeah, it's a good place," he replied. "Probably best pizza on or off the Island. They sell beer in bottles but it's cheaper on tap by the pitcher. They also have a great shuffleboard table but you usually have to wait a while to get a game."

Mickey nodded. "I'm not much of a bar athlete," she said, "Do they deliver?"

"No, but you can take out as long as you go there in person to order."

"Maybe I'll treat myself," Mickey said. "Close as I'll get to a home-cooked meal." She walked to the door and stopped. "Make sure to keep a close eye on Little Willie's place tonight, OK."

"I'll stop by special," Kaylen answered and gave her a two-finger salute, Boy Scout style. She thought he looked relieved at the request.

"Kaylen?"

"Yeah, Chief?"

Mickey took a step back into the station. "Funny thing. The kid on the beach. Was he the one driving the red Mustang you pulled over yesterday?"

The thin line of pink in his cheeks disappeared. "I think he must have been, Chief, now that you say it. I wasn't even thinking about that. I guess the shock of seeing the body like that and all."

Mickey thought of an old trick her father had taught her. "Yeah, that can crowd out a lot of other thoughts. But you must have seen his license, right?"

"Yes, ma'am, I did."

"How many other kids were in the car?"

"Three, I believe, ma'am."

"Did you get any of their names or check their licenses?"

"I checked the license of the kid in the passenger seat. The car was legally registered to his father."

"Do you remember what his name was."

"The kid or the father?"

"Either one," Mickey said. She kept her tone soft and deliberately spoke slowly.

"Are you thinking the other kids are somehow involved, Chief?"

Mickey looked closely at her Deputy. It was hard to believe he was being anything but straightforward with her. She didn't think he had it in him to be otherwise.

"Well," Mickey continued, "they haven't come looking for their friend or reported him missing, which is strange. And I haven't seen a candy apple red Mustang around."

Kaylen replied quickly. "But if it *was* a boat accident like Juice says it was then they might have gotten spooked and gone back home, maybe. Chief, am I in trouble for not issuing them a citation? I mean, I really didn't even have a good reason to pull-"

"No," Mickey interrupted. "I'm just trying to piece this together before it gets," she thought of Guidice's cryptic statement on the beach, "complicated." She tried to watch Kaylen's body language but he looked genuinely perplexed and leaned back in his chair. "Do you remember the passenger's name or the name on the registration?" she asked.

Kaylen put his hands on his thighs. "It was a Jersey registration and license," he said. He looked up at the ceiling. "Real Italian-sounding last name. Capuzzi, Abruzzi, Galluzzi, something like that. There were a couple of z's and an i at the end, I remember that. Sorry, Chief, I was honestly paying more attention to the car.

I know that's not very good police work."

Mickey nodded. She had wanted to ask something more but now she could not remember what it was. The dispatch radio crackled.

"SCPD2, please see the woman at the corner of Sunset and Barnegat. She says she has lost her dog. Says Deputy helped her previously. Copy?"

Kaylen leaned over and pushed down the black toggle switch. "Dispatch this is SCPD2, copy. Tell her I'll be there shortly." He looked at Mickey and rolled his eyes.

"Kaylen, how old is the woman who lives at Sunset and Barnegat?" Mickey asked, arching her eyebrows slightly.

"I don't know, Chief," he replied reaching for the keys to the Galaxie. "Thirty, maybe thirty-five."

"Married?"

"Not sure. Looked like she might live there alone, though. Why?"

"I don't want any funny looking puppies running around in January, that's all."

"Ma'am?"

"Just tell her she needs to purchase a sturdy leash," Mickey said and turned. "And be sure to say 'no' if she asks if you want to see her cat. How long to get to Emil's?"

""There won't be hardly any traffic until Friday, so, fifteen minutes I'd say, tops."

"OK. Now, do you know who would have a record of all the property owners' names and addresses in town?" she asked. "City clerk maybe?"

"No, ma'am. That would be at the County Assessor's Office up in Tom's River. Probably about twenty-five miles or so north. You'd have to take the Parkway." Kaylen replied. "Do you need me to-"

"No," Mickey said, "I'll give them a call. I mean, how many z-z-i's can there be on Long Beach Island?" She stopped. "Never mind. Dumb question. I might have to visit them tomorrow." She headed toward the door. "Get hold of me right away if you hear from either Dr. Galasso or this Petroni character, got it?"

"I will, Chief," Kaylen replied. "You go enjoy your pizza. If you get the large one, it's pretty good cold, too." He followed her out the back door, locking it behind them. Mickey watched him get in the Galaxie and drive off. She started up the Chevelle and felt a cooling blast from the finicky air-conditioner hit her full in the face. Then she remembered what troubled her in their previous conversation about Mickey Mantle: Kaylen knew that Danny Ragone was a gangster.

Mickey let the cruiser idle while the information percolated. For a moment she considered calling her deputy back to the station. Nothing made immediate sense. He hadn't denied making the traffic stop and he hadn't seemed evasive when they discussed it. She couldn't imagine Kaylen Fairbrother as a practiced liar or even someone particularly capable of violence even in a situation where that violence might be necessary. She cupped the radio microphone in her hand, her thumb on the "TALK" button. What exactly, she wondered, would she ask him? Had the traffic stop turned ugly? Was there a second run-in with them? And where was the red Mustang and the other boys who were riding in it? She really needed to find out because she figured it had to be one of them who called the body sighting in to the dispatcher. That would explain the nervous-sounding teenage voice. Then she remembered what Ronnie Dunn said: "Alpha dog. The others were embarrassed or maybe even pissed off." So, Mickey wondered, did the pack finally turn on the alpha dog? Maybe some harsh words mixed with some liquid courage and things got out of hand. Did they beat the shit out Danny Junior and leave him somewhere or maybe pushed him off a jetty or someone's boat? If they did, she reasoned, then they would have good reason to be nervous. And an even better reason to disappear.

Mickey took her thumb off the microphone button and set it down on the seat next to her. Something still didn't add up but now she felt guilty about thinking Kaylen might have intentionally deceived her. She pushed in the clutch, slipped the cruiser into gear and decided to make one more stop.

It wasn't yet six o'clock yet but the sign in the window of Beachfront Liquors said "CLOSED". Mickey rapped on the thin metal screen door until a face appeared. "Closed" mouthed Willie through one of the narrow glass panes on the inside wooden one.

Mickey held her badge close to the screen and said "Open".

She heard the rustle of a chain and the turn of a bolt and the door opened inward. "Just checking on my merchandise," she said pleasantly. "Now you can show me the cooler."

Willie shuffled and wiped his hands on his dirty store apron. Mickey followed him to the back. He pulled a large circular handle and the cooler door swung open. Small cumulus clouds of condensation billowed out. The body bag was set on a large rack of shelves. Cases of beer in cans and bottles sat on the cement floor, having been moved to accommodate it. Mickey went to the business end and tugged on the zipper.

"Jesus!" Willie cried holding his nose. "That's worse than the Stink House in August."

"Put a slice of orange under your nose," Mickey said pointing to a sack labeled Indian River Citrus leaning in a corner. "Cop trick for floaters." Willie moved for the sack and Mickey surveyed the remains. She looked at the violent near-decapitation and tried to picture the bayonet she had seen. A tiny sand crab scuttled across the torso. Mickey zipped the body bag shut. Willie returned with a slice jammed in each nostril. "What time do you open tomorrow?" she asked him.

"Eleven," he answered in an understandably nasal whine.

"Make it noon," Mickey instructed. "I'll be here at eleven to claim this."

"You can't do that," Willie protested. "That costs me money."

Mickey pointed to the two adolescent boys hiding behind the big cardboard Miller High Life sign, each clutching a six-pack. "*That* will cost you more," she said. "I'll be at that back entrance at eleven sharp tomorrow – and so will you. Got it?"

"Yeah, I got it," Willie said. His small frame and thinning hair made him look older than he was, Mickey thought. She noticed the spidery nest of broken veins on his nose and wondered if he might be drinking up some of the profits.

◆ ◆ ◆

Woodland Township, NJ
The Pine Barrens

Petroni sat behind the wheel and looked at the two nickels. He had turned off the Jag's engine and put the windows down. His decision to take the old highways had been a sound one until the overloaded flatbed Ford had tipped and spilled its cargo of early Florida-grown melons across both lanes. Now he found himself hemmed in by a noisy busload of migrant workers behind him and a Hammonton Township police cruiser on the barely existent shoulder. A front-end loader was on its way, he'd been assured, but Petroni knew he would conduct no official business in Surf City today. He looked at his watch. Shots would get nervous if he was overly late which meant either he might vamoose or he might get drunk. The latter was at least workable. There was still a little while until sunset but the vast forest of dense pines had sucked the remaining light out of the sky. The officer had turned on the cruiser's headlights and side spotlight, illuminating a lurid tableau of shiny, fragmented rinds and smeared wet pulp.

Surf City

The second-floor apartment had come rent-free with the job but Mickey's attempts at homemaking had been, she decided, not quite up to *Better Homes and Gardens* standards. The basic furnishings, which had also come with the deal, were clean but threadbare. The bed was comfortable and she had decided to forego the supplied sheets and pillowcases and purchased her own. She had left California with almost nothing of real value but the money in her bank account in Philadelphia. Communal existence frowned on personal possessions and so, besides t-shirts, sneakers, cut-off jeans, socks and panties, and her mechanic's tools, she'd had to restock her life almost from scratch. The Free Peoples City of Love had run on a market economy that was summed up neatly by a sign posted on a hollowed-out redwood that marked the commune's entrance – "Admission - Gas, Grass or Ass."

Grass had been plentiful both as a staple and as a cash crop. Band roadies from San Francisco and L.A. made regular "shopping trips" to their grove. There had even been a thank-you note from one of The Mamas and the Papas' managers extolling the quality of the product. The commune had two working vehicles, the requisite finger-painted Volkswagen bus and, for some incongruous reason, a Lincoln Continental convertible. She was able to avoid the brothel existence only because she could ably repair both of them and was called upon regularly to do so. As for the price of admission, only grass and gas were truly valuable commodities. The last, Mickey thought sadly, was cheap only because it was so plentiful. By the time she left, she had come to believe that the "square" world, in all its ugliness and brutality, was actually more honest and that the idyllic existence she'd tried to escape to was, in the end, nothing but complete and total bullshit.

Mickey gathered up some clothes and her one pair of leather beach sandals. Between Sears and F.W. Woolworths, resupplying her wardrobe had been laughably cheap. Loretta had stocked her refrigerator and pantry with homemade pastas and sauces when she was at work.

Mickey had some acquaintances, she realized, but she no longer had any real friends. Patsy was her only family and they had become nearly strangers since the shooting and her desperate flight to escape the memory of it. She looked at the picture of Eileen Cleary propped on the nicked and water-ringed coffee table. Mickey had her same copper-colored hair and her same dark eyes. Even the same pattern of freckles on the dark-toned skin. "Little Black Irish" her mother had called her when she was small. Now, for one clear and several very unclear reasons, she was going to pick up pizza and beer and share it with an armed man she'd known for less than thirty minutes, and at his place to boot. She could call it police business, she supposed, even though now she was off duty. He said he might uncover some information that would help her. She'd bring clothes but would arrive in her uniform, just in case she changed her mind. And, she decided, she was definitely bringing her gun.

The red plastic RCA radio Loretta had given her was turned on low and Mickey recognized the smooth delivery of WFIL evening disc jockey George Michael. She thought it was uncanny the way this particular "boss jock" was able to lead in a song and never talk over it, his last spoken syllable almost kissing that of the first lyric. Her apartment building, on Shore Avenue, put her close by the bay. Through the open window she heard the lapping of water against the wood pilings and the metallic clang of halyards against sailboat masts. Loretta was shuffling busily around below. She thought about Ronnie Dunn. A little boy in a warrior's body was the description that occurred to her. She wondered if he knew anything more than he was saying; or if he really could find out something that would help her. Maybe, she decided, he just wanted the company of someone who wasn't a tourist or a retiree. Not to mention free pizza and beer on the borough budget. This last thought made her smile. She listened to the song George had cued up. The Young Rascals were on again, this time singing "Lonely Too Long." Mickey thought maybe the DJ was sending her a message.

   She left the radio on, smoothed her uniform and grabbed her change of clothes. She dismissed her thoughts about Kaylen as the result of the crooked cops she had known in her former life. She just couldn't imagine him wandering very far from the straight and narrow. He was too much of a Boy Scout. One look at his desk had told her that.

   Michaela Eileen Cleary stood by the apartment door, listening until the song finished. Then she switched off the light, pulled the door shut and headed for the stairs.

TWELVE
Surf City

MICKY SPIED THE FIRE on the beach before anything else. She put the Chevelle in Neutral, turned off the engine and rolled to a stop. Ronnie Dunn's beach shack was dark, its façade faintly lit by the blaze across the road. She laid her nightstick on the seat, opened the driver's door, stepped out and then closed it as gingerly as possible. She glanced at the house and then walked toward the dancing flames. She left the pizza and the beer on the back seat. There was that same sweet smell on the breeze that had been inside the house. Two years in California had made her, if not an expert, at the very least a connoisseur. As her eyes adjusted she saw Ronnie, back in that deep crouch, staring into the fire. He seemed transfixed and did not react to her approach until she stepped on a shell. It cracked underfoot with a sound like a twig snapping.

Ronnie reached for a stick in the sand. Except it wasn't a stick, she realized. It was his bayonet, glinting in the firelight. His face now illuminated, she saw a feral, black look in his eyes. He was tensed in a fighting stance, one foot slightly in front of the other to maximize balance. Mickey reached for her holster and then stopped. She raised her arms slowly until they were even with her shoulders.

"Ronnie Dunn," she said carefully. "It's Mickey, Mickey Cleary. We met earlier today. Chief Cleary? Surf City Police? Just here to say hello. Beer and pizza, remember?" She raised her hands higher. Whether it was the gesture or the light reflecting off her badge, Ronnie's visage changed in a heartbeat and he looked stricken. He stuck the bayonet in the sand and stood up.

"Kind'a startled me," he said. "Probably not a good idea as a routine."

"Yeah," Mickey replied. "I know what you mean. Hard to turn it off when they work so hard to teaching it to be a reflex. Sorry. Maybe I should have hit the cherry tops and run the siren, huh?" She brought her hands to her sides.

"You didn't draw your sidearm, Chief," Ronnie said. "In a different situation that might've been a mistake."

"But this is not a different situation, right."

"Right," he agreed. "Not this time. Not with me."

"Okay, I get it." Mickey exhaled a sigh. "I come bearing gifts. Pizza and beer from Emil's. Had to stand at the bar and drink Pepsi while they baked them. In uniform, you know? Not like I stood out or anything. And what kind of local moron hits on a cop? Anyway, it's in the cruiser. Want me to go get it?"

Ronnie walked out of the fire's circle of illumination and returned with two rusting beach chairs - the kind, Mickey noticed, that barely kept your bottom out of the sand. They opened with a painful sounding creak and he set them next to each other. He motioned for her to sit and then did the same.

"You ever been out on a night patrol?" Ronnie asked.

"I was one of the first four women ever allowed to walk a beat. You know that was only going to happen in the light of day and with backup both seen and unseen, as they say in church. I did some ride-along nights in a blue-and-white, though. Couple of drug and numbers raids that scared the crap out of me. First time I heard a round go by my head I nearly peed myself. I'm not ashamed of that. I probably don't have to ask about you."

Ronnie stirred the sand with his foot. "First month in-country I led one, walking point at some riverbank village. I didn't worry so much about being shot. I worried more about the traps and the mines. Panji traps, tiger traps. There was one called the Venus Fly trap – the spikes were angled both ways and so if it got your legs you couldn't get them out. Some guys just shot themselves right there." He reached down and brought a burning joint to his lips, inhaling deeply. "Anything that had spikes they'd smear with their own shit – so even if you could extricate, the gangrene set in almost before you were evac'ed." He took another toke, the end glowing brightly with the draw.

"That's not a Camel, now is it?" Mickey deadpanned.

"It is imported tobacco, yes, but perhaps not Turkish." Ronnie replied after exhaling. "Correct me if I'm wrong, Chief, but I get the distinct impression that you may not be a novice."

Mickey stared into the flames. A driftwood log shifted and kicked out a little shower of sparks. "I spent over a year in a commune just outside Arcata, way up where the redwoods are. Planted it, harvested it, dried it, rolled it, smoked it; did everything but deal it."

"Well, this may be a little more, um, intoxicating than anything currently available domestically," Ronnie said. "It could also be a bit overpowering if you're not used to it or if you've been away from it for a while." Ronnie toked again. "Or if you're on watch."

"Change of schedule," Mickey said. "Actually, I'm off duty until oh-eight-hundred tomorrow."

The Galaxie made a few cruises down Long Beach Boulevard and then back up Barnegat Road on the bay side. Few of the summer places were occupied yet and most of the year-rounders were older or retired and tended to pack it in early. The same scintillating blue glow lit up scattered downstairs windows as Zenith's, Motorola's and RCA's pulled in the three broadcast stations out of Philadelphia with rabbit-ear antennas wrapped with tinfoil. Kaylen cruised the cross streets until it got dark. He pulled in behind Beachfront Liquors. Little Willie's place shared a back lot with Ye Olde Surf Shoppe. Kaylen had only been inside the surf store once and had been shocked to see cans of Sex Wax for sale right next to swim trunks and boogie boards. It wasn't until the end of that summer that he found out what it actually was.

There were no lights on the back side of either store but there were two salt-pitted garbage dumpsters. Kaylen clicked off his headlights and rolled up behind them leaving about thirty feet of darkened asphalt. He surveyed the surrounding blocks and then pulled the cruiser back. With three spins of the wheel he executed a perfect K-turn and backed up toward the dumpsters, angling toward the surf shop side. The reflections of the brake lights and back-up lights glowed brighter as he inched closer. He shut the engine off and stepped out, again checking for pedestrians or other vehicles.

Kaylen had left just enough room to slide his slender frame between the Galaxie's stout rear bumper and the dirty receptacle. He put the key in the trunk lock, turned it and popped it open. He carefully opened the lid of the dumpster and found what he hoped would be there – a half-empty sack of discarded papers, assorted business refuse and some old clothes. He lifted the sack out and placed it in the trunk. Then he transferred the contents of the laundry bag to the sack, pushing them as far to the bottom as possible. This accomplished, he slung the sack back into the dumpster and carefully closed the lid. The filet knife he dropped deep in the corner of the other dumpster. Then he eased the trunk down until the latch clicked. Kaylen slid out from behind the bumper and got back in the cruiser. He sat for a few minutes, checking in all directions for possible observers. He did not turn his headlights back on until he was three blocks away.

"So, do you usually socialize in your uniform and weapon?" Ronnie asked without looking away from the small but crackling fire.

"I did bring a change of clothes but I wanted to make sure I wasn't just delivering a take-out order first." Ronnie half-smiled at this.

"Do I really look like the kind of person who would order pizza and beer and have it delivered by the local Chief of Police?"

"You look like the kind of person who wouldn't be afraid to," Mickey said. "You look like the kind of person who might enjoy the irony."

"Yes and yes," Ronnie replied. "I'm not afraid and I do enjoy a little irony."

"Like a cop watching you smoke a joint?"

"For starters. Or, you know, it might just be some home-rolled pipe tobacco. From, let's say, Delaware," Ronnie replied after exhaling.

"And maybe I'm Barney Fife."

"I bet you carry more than one bullet."

"Let's hope we don't need to find out."

Ronnie took another smooth draw. "So is it just you and Deputy Dawg all summer?"

"No," Mickey replied. "There'll be some probationary candidates from the Patrolman's Academy here starting next week to help us out and get some experience on the job. But I doubt I'll have many nights off once the season starts." She kicked at the sand and looked toward the darkened shack. "Is there a light in there I can use to change?"

"There's a Coleman on the table I got just for you. You know how to-?"

"I know how," Mickey said. "After a year of living off the land, you'd be surprised at the things I'm capable of doing."

Ronnie flicked a glowing ash. "So was it a communal Garden of Eden kind of deal or more like the free-love camps they wrote about in the magazines the Army gave us?"

"Well, there was definitely a lot of, yeah, love, but trust me, none of it was free," Mickey replied. "Payment always came due. I'll be right back." She pushed herself out of the chair and walked toward the shack, unbuckling her gun belt as she went.

Kaylen was feeling better. He patrolled the little town in concentric rectangles. With slightly less than a square mile of jurisdiction, it didn't take very long. He made sure each pass gave him a sightline to the back of the surf shop and the liquor store. Once he thought he saw a light flickering inside Little Willie's but the next drive-by showed it to be dark. If he saw something again, he thought, he'd have to get out and investigate. The dumpsters in back looked undisturbed. He had hit them with the high beams from a block away and was satisfied that he'd been the last visitor. He was, he mused, the only law in town, although technically Surf City was a borough. Town cop sounded a little tougher than borough cop. The idea to have the Chief take the night off had come out of nowhere but Kaylen was pleased at its success. He thought he'd handled her questions pretty well. Kaylen checked his watch There was a little portable television at the station; he could still catch the eleven o'clock news.

The Anchorage Tavern

Somers Point, NJ

"Danny's called three times already," the man at the table said as Petroni squeezed into the opposite bench. "Bartender's startin' to take notice." The lighting in the old bar was lousy and threw sinister shading on the man's already coarse features.

Petroni had his back to the dark wooden bar. Arrayed in front of Shots Caputo were seven small, tapered glasses, only one of which still contained any beer.

"Unavoidable delay," Petroni said. "It was a mistake to take the two-lane."

"Black or White Hose Pike?" Caputo asked, referring to the equine nicknames of two old South Jersey highways.

"Neither," Petroni replied as Caputo drained the last glass and pushed another bill from the stack of dollars toward the end of the table. I took old Route 72. I don't know why anyone takes the Pikes anymore."

"So how are the Bowker boys?" asked Shots.

"Only saw Billy," Petroni replied. "That was enough."

"Dumber than a bag of hammers, that one," Shots said as an aging waitress scooped up the dollar bill. "And mean as a motherfucker."

The seven full replacement glasses arrived quickly and Petroni waited until the waitress shuffled away before speaking. "So Danny didn't bother to wait for me to check this out I gather?"

'You know what he says. Somebody punches you, you punch 'em back right away so maybe they think twice about punching you again."

"Frankie Numbers was almost a civilian. He only did the books."

"Danny said it was a message to Carmine."

"We don't even know if Carmine had anything to do with this." Petroni rubbed at his forehead as one by one the seven ounce glasses were drained.

"That's why he picked Frankie. If it wasn't Carmine then they didn't lose anybody really important. If it was," Shots shrugged, "Well, then, it's gonna be a long summer. And now he's got it stuck in his head now that Patsy's girl had a hand in it. On her own or maybe with Carmine. Payback's a bitch and all. So you know what that means." He tilted the glass up and slurped the last of the foam into his mouth. "Maybe you can slow this thing down a little bit and I can go home. But Danny's the boss – not like either of us are gonna argue with him when he gets like this."

"I'm hoping this goes a different way. Juice swears it looks like an accident but I'm not sure that's not just because it's what he wants it to be."

"He's still carrying that around with him, idn't he."

"We have to assume he's got a soft spot for Patsy and the girl," Petroni said.

"Hope that doesn't cloud his judgment." Caputo downed another glass.

Petroni reached for his cigarettes. "If the girl lets me have the body I think that'll be enough for Danny to hit the brakes. But if she doesn't….." He tapped out a Pall Mall and rolled it between his long fingers. "If it's the hard way, then I want you to deliver the package cold. I don't want Bowker having any fun with this one."

"Who says it being cold will make any difference?" Shots asked, the rim of a new glass already at his lips. The contents were gone in a heartbeat. "He'd screw a snake. Shit, Artie, he'd screw a woodpile if he thought there was a snake in it." The next glass was in his hand. "When will you know?"

"Tomorrow," Petroni said, wondering why the waitress hadn't asked if he'd wanted to order anything. "If it's a delivery then we'll do the deal tomorrow night and be on the road before anyone's wise."

"But you'll make sure Danny's good with this, right? Waiting a little?"

"He will be. I'll call him from the motel pay phone as soon as I check in."

"Make sure he knows I was here and ready to do it, OK?"

Petroni looked at the glasses. "Don't worry, Shots. I'll tell him I had to hold you back."

"Another thing. I was thinkin' if we have to do it maybe we should plant some drugs in the car. You know, set up a bad cop story if we need it. Fuckin' newspapers eat that shit up whether it's true or not. I brought a little bag of horse just in case."

"That's why we pay you, Shots." Petroni pushed out of the cramped booth. "I'll meet you across from the Ebb Tide Motel around noon tomorrow with the plan. I'm sure you'll need to, uh, sleep in." Caputo pushed another dollar past the empty glasses as Petroni walked out.

THIRTEEN
Surf City

MICKEY TRIED TO ASSES her appearance but noticed there were no mirrors anywhere. She thought of a book she'd had to read in English class at Maria Goretti, "Pride and Prejudice." The people in it kept referring to their houses as "my humble abode." Looking around she figured if any place met the definition of humble abode it was this one. The card table with the Coleman lantern on it looked like the one her Dad kept in the basement. The two lawn chairs set by it were rusting at the arms and the joints and were laced with frayed plastic webbing that had perhaps once held color. That there was a working toilet and sink and not just a hole in the ground amazed her. She had almost tripped in the dark hallway over a long black case covered with a blanket that looked like it came right off a barracks bunk. She wondered if her cut-offs were too short; if her t-shirt was too tight. She hadn't really thought out her wardrobe choices, limited as they were. The she fluffed her hair, slipped on the leather sandals and walked out toward the beach. She'd at least try, she thought, not being one of the guys.

* * *

Kaylen was seated in his chair, leaning back, when the phone rang.

"Surf City PD," he said smartly. "Deputy Fairbrother speaking." The voice on the other end was unfamiliar but friendly and the caller identified himself as Chief Cleary's father, Sergeant Patrick Cleary of the Philadelphia Police.

"No sir, she's not here at the moment. She has tonight off." A pause while he listened. "Yes sir, I'll be sure to tell her you called when I see her in the morning." Another pause. "Yes sir. I'll tell her it's very important. What's that, sir?" Kaylen leaned forward and took his feet off the desk. "No, sir. I haven't seen the gentleman yet. Yes, sir. I'll make sure the Chief knows it's police business." He set the receiver back on its perch atop the black rotary phone. The little television was warmed up and Kaylen reached to increase the volume. News anchor John Facenda looked even more concerned than usual, his owlish visage pinched in a mask of worry, his sonorous baritone delivery a minor chord lower. Kaylen leaned in to listen.

"Even though Cherubini had no overt criminal ties, his execution-style murder in North Philadelphia could be a return volley, perhaps from reputed South Philadelphia mobster Dante Ragone who, WCAU confidential sources tell us, recently suffered the loss of a family member. Details are sketchy but we'll try to have more on this story on tomorrow evening's broadcast.

If the revered newscaster said any more, Kaylen did not hear it. He got up from his chair and paced the office. His feeling of finally having thought something out right was evaporating. He looked at Mickey's desk and knew he should call her right now. Then he looked at the items on his own. It was just leeway, he thought. Leeway and using his discretion, just like she told him to do. And maybe it could all still go away, he told himself. It could all still just go away.

After a few minutes he looked up the number for her apartment phone and dialed.

"*Now* you're off duty," Ronnie said, extending the burned down joint. It was still long enough for him to hold with the tips of his thumb and forefinger. Four or five more tokes, Mickey calculated, and then they'd need a paper clip or a pair of tweezers.

"Is this a test?" Mickey asked. "As far as I know you could be working undercover for the State Attorney General's office."

"I don't work for generals anymore," Ronnie replied after exhaling a held breath. "I have the papers to prove it." Mickey reached for the quickly diminishing joint and put it to her lips. She inhaled slowly and deeply, stoppered her windpipe, then just as slowly breathed out.

"Definitely imported," she said with a rasp.

"Thailand, if you must know," Ronnie said taking it back. "Pretty close to Delaware." He reached into his pocket and withdrew a silver surgical clamp no bigger than a child's safety scissors. Mickey heard a faint click as he pincered the unlit end of the rolling paper with it.

"Are we at war with Thailand?" Mickey asked.

"We are at war with everyone," he replied, "including ourselves."

Ronnie's voice had taken on a subtle weariness, Mickey thought, or maybe it was just the dope. She settled into the beach chair and felt the cool, smooth sand against her bottom. The fire was mesmerizing and she was already starting to feel the buzz. He was right, she thought – it was strong stuff.

"So what does it say on the papers that prove it?"

Ronnie offered her another toke. "Couple more hits and maybe I'll tell you," he said. "That way I can say you were in an impaired mental state and misunderstood what I said. It's called plausible deniability."

"Who would I tell?"

"I don't know. Somebody looking for Kurtz."

"Wait a minute, who's Kurtz?"

"Kurtz was the hero of a book I read while I was being informally detained. The person with the answer to the question no one wanted to ask."

"I think you just lost me," Mickey said. He didn't acknowledge the statement.

"It says on the papers I was given that I am Other Than Honorably Discharged from the United States Army for a violation of the Uniform Code of Military Justice Article 128 which forbids, and I quote, 'assault with a dangerous weapon or any other means or force which is likely to cause death or severe bodily harm.'"

Mickey let it float in the air with the sparks and the pounding of the surf.

"So, what, you struck a superior officer, I assume?"

"You assume wrong, Chief. That's the joke," he replied. His voice was calm and flat. "I struck a subordinate, a recruit, a grunt, an FNG. That's Army slang for-."

"Fucking New Guy," Mickey interrupted. "It's cop slang, too. So you what - slapped him, like Patton did at that field hospital?"

"How do you know about Patton?"

"My dad loved military history. Studied it. Talked about it all the time. From Constantine to Pershing, from Patton all the way up to Westmoreland. Even old Schwartzkopf. All the names, all the battles, he was like an encyclopedia. His favorite was Constantine, because he became a Christian and fought the Turks."

"Was your dad a soldier?"

"No," Mickey replied. "He was a cop. Like his father before him was a cop. And his father before him was a constable over in Ireland. So I was never going to be anything else, obviously."

"I'm sorry," Ronnie said. "How long has he been gone?"

Mickey looked at him. "Gone? He's not gone, soldier boy. He got shot on the job and cashed out on full disability. He lives in a two room apartment up in the Great Northeast."

"You kept saying 'was' so I just figured-"

"You figured wrong." Mickey reached her hand out for the joint. "And I really didn't come here to talk about my dad. I'll say we're currently estranged and leave it at that. But my mother is dead, so you don't have to ask about her." She took a long drag and handed it back.

"I didn't mean to-"

Mickey stared straight into the fire. "I don't want to talk any more right now. It's been a difficult day. Tell me about something. Tell me about the Pine Barrens."

Ronnie snuffed the burning joint in the sand then blew the clinging grains off it. He sat quietly while Mickey watched the flames, her hands rhythmically gripping and releasing the flat metal arms of her chair.

A. Louis Petroni signed his own name to the desk register and surveyed what passed for the Surf City Hotel's lobby. There were two rummage sale chairs and a cigarette-burned and water-ringed coffee table with magazines that looked like they'd been there since Eisenhower was president. The night clerk was of about the same vintage with sun-weathered skin and two perfectly circular bald patches in his gray crew-cut hair. Petroni passed him a five.

"Anybody calls on the pay phone, no matter who they ask for; you come get me, OK?" Outside the open jalousie window a neon signed buzzed and crackled. "I NEVER SLEEP" glowed a garish purple in curved glass tubes against the soft black night. The old man nodded. Petroni had thought about staying further south down in Wildwood where there were better hotels like the Sans Souci or the Chateau Bleu. But that risked running into fellow businessmen – friendly or otherwise. The Shore was always neutral territory but after the events of the last twenty-four hours, Petroni figured all bets were off. He padded down the narrow hallway holding the cartoonishly large key fob in one hand and a small leather valise in the other. He glanced at the gold Bulova on his wrist. Danny never went to sleep before midnight. He'd call precisely at ten 'til. Any negotiations would be easier, he thought, with his boss on the brink of exhaustion.

Ronnie paused in his meandering description of the Pine Barrens and its populace and looked at Mickey. "Too much detail?" he asked.

Mickey shook her head. "So why does anyone go there?" she asked.

"It's a place you go to disappear. Whether you want to or not," he replied. "It's as close to a no-man's land as you'll ever see. Full of unusual creatures, wild and domestic, two-legged as well as four. So is it OK if I ask you something now?"

"It's possible I might be a little stoned," she replied. "So nothing I say can be used against me in a court of law. Agreed?"

"Agreed," Ronnie answered. "How long were you a cop?"

"I'm still a cop," Mickey answered, "I'm just not in uniform or on duty at the moment. Oh, and I put the pizza on your lovely dining room table and the beer in that thing that looks like it might have once been a fridge."

"Great. So now we can talk, right?" He looked at her profile, the way her dark, reddish hair reflected the firelight and the shimmer of her eyes. She was still tense, he recognized, her jaw clenched and her neck muscles tight. Finally she turned slightly toward him. "You just keep talking for a while," she said. "I may not say anything but I'm listening. Start by telling me why the Army thinks that you're less than honorable."

"*Other* than honorable," Ronnie corrected. "It's an important difference."

Mickey nodded but did not reply.

Ronnie took out a Zippo lighter. A blue and red Octofoil insignia was on the brass case in bas-relief. He flipped the top open and thumbed the flint wheel until a small blue and yellow flame appeared. He cupped the lighter and put the joint in his mouth, sucking audibly until the glow held. Then he snapped the case shut. The sound that it made, he mused, was one that millions of men would recognize instantly, even in the dark. Ronnie took a sharp draw and slid back in his chair. The exhaled smoke hung in the air for just a moment and then disappeared on the soft breeze.

"So I'd been in-country for about eighteen months. There really wasn't any formal sniper program at that point. Just guys shooting coconuts out of the trees for fun or beer or cigarettes. We were called marksmen or sharpshooters but we started referring to ourselves as snipers; kind of because it was an old military term but mostly because it just sounded so much badder. I was with one of the riverine units on the Mekong Delta – what they called the brown water navy. The PBR's had heavy machine guns and small arms but we found we could pick off Charlie hiding on the shore or in the palm trees using an M-16 and a scope. Some guys were naturally better shots than others and after a while it just got to be our main job. That was fine with me. I wasn't very good at the hand-to-hand stuff the way some guys were. It didn't take the Army long to figure out that this was something they could develop for tactical purposes. They started talking about sniper units and sniper schools and better scopes and using the new M-14's they'd ordered. So they shipped me back to Fort Bliss to field test a new long-range scope and rifle combination. We were drinking at a bar off-base one night and I hear this guy talking at a table nearby. Pretty drunk and getting really loud. He was talking about all the gooks he was going to kill and what he'd do to the women and the girls. I should have let it go but I didn't. Maybe because I'd seen so much shit already and I was getting ready to go back and I just lost it. I cracked him in the skull with the butt of my sidearm, which I wasn't even supposed to be carrying. Big brawl after that, MP's, local cops. A real redneck shit-storm. Anyway, they gave him, the guy I cracked, a free pass into Officer Candidate School in exchange for keeping it hushed up. I tried to tell them that he was a flat-out psycho - that all the bad shit that was going on had to stop. That we couldn't send over any more people like this. I told them that this is what was going to do it. "

"Do what?"

A wry smile crossed his lips. He eased out of his chair and onto the sand, his head titled back slightly, his eyes still on the fire.

"I told them that was what was going to lose the fucking war. See, it's really not the hills or the firebases or the NVA body counts like they show on TV that matters. It's the shit that happens when you're out on patrol. First you're scared but then after a while you forget about being scared. You're just numb and then after that something really changes. The part of you that was once human goes away when the smiling mama-san pulls the pin on a grenade and blows herself and two of your buddies to kingdom come." He fingered the dog tags. "Our friend - the victim of an unprovoked assault is what they called him - will be a second lieutenant here in a few months. That means he'll be in-country leading men on patrol by the end of the year. Good men he'll either get killed or worse. Without me and my sixty seconds of stupidity, he never advances beyond corporal or washes out with either a self-inflicted wound or a Section Eight. That's my real crime. And maybe it really does make me something other than honorable."

Ronnie turned. His face was almost childlike in its sadness.

"They kicked me out for attacking the real threat. Talk about irony."

The crashing surf came louder as the tide rolled in. Mickey waited for Ronnie to tell her more. Two tokes and several long minutes later the moon was a quartz circle in an anthracite sky. Ronnie was leaning back on one elbow, the most relaxed posture she had yet observed. He used the bayonet to stir the wilting fire. A fresh shower of sparks issued forth and then flamed out like a sparkler twirled in a child's hand on the Fourth of July. Finally, he spoke again.

"The JAG attorney told me it was either the OTHD or hard time in an Army prison. Bad press was already starting to leak out about burning the hootches with flamethrowers, poisoning the wells and other things you don't even want to know human beings are capable of. The last thing they needed was me testifying in my defense about what I'd seen happen on patrol. They kept me out of the stockade only because they thought they could isolate me better that way. Filing papers and sweeping floors. Restricted to barracks. An MP accompanied me when I went to the can and one bunked next to me at night. My exit interview with command was basically a message that if I told anyone what I knew or about the deal I'd agreed to, I would be mustered back in, put in a dark hole somewhere and forgotten about. They reminded me that being considered other than honorable rather than dishonorable in the eyes of the government still qualified me for disability pay. Then a staff sergeant broke my little finger."

"These were our guys?" Mickey asked.

"Chief, what you have to realize is that there are no *our* guys anymore. There are just the guys who know the lie and the guys who protect and defend it. What's Pogo say? We have met the enemy-"

Mickey finished it for him. "And he is us."

Ronnie was quiet again and then stood up and shook sand from his palms. "I have to say, I have a lot more respect for you now that I know you were a dope dealer."

"Ah, I told you I never dealt. And the other stuff? That wasn't really me," Mickey said. She held the little clamp and squeezed one more draw from the barely extant joint. "As far as anyone knew it was a chick named Moondancer who did all that. No last name, no ID or driver's license, just a funny Philly accent and a great rack – at least according to some observers." Ronnie reached into his fatigues pocket and produced another rolled joint. "Uh-uh, I'm done," Mickey said. "I hate to use the crappy line but I do have to work in the morning."

"I told you my story," Ronnie said proffering it. "Now you tell me why you quit."

Mickey shook her head. Ronnie went off and scavenged a few more pieces of driftwood and some dried reeds that had washed up along the high-tide line. When he had tossed them into the fire he sat on the sand Indian-style.

"Just so you know, I haven't told anyone that story before," Ronnie said. "Not even my parents. My dad was a Marine, fought at Guadalcanal, so I know what it means to have a legacy to live up to. He hasn't spoken to me in months. Told me to go to the VFW and throw away my ribbons and medals in front of everybody. Told me I was on my own. Broke my mother's heart but you'd have to know him – he's a no-shades-of-gray jarhead and that will never change. Things between us would have to get a lot better before I could even say that we're estranged." Ronnie fell silent. Mickey kicked at the sand with her toes, sending little sprays of it into the crackling flames. Several times she leaned forward and moved her mouth to speak but, each time, she stopped and fell back into the chair without uttering a word.

After several long, silent minutes she began. Slowly and quietly at first. So quietly that Ronnie had to lean closer to hear her above the hiss and pop of the fire.

"It was a really cold, really ugly day," Mickey said. "The damp kind of cold that feels like it goes right through you. I had forgotten my gloves so I had my hands in my pockets a lot. We got a tip that a load of smack was getting ready to be picked up in North Philly somewhere in my territory. Drugs were kind of the hot new thing then, but the local hoods hadn't caught on yet so it was mostly what we called invaders. I was assigned to the Twenty-Fourth and I'm on foot patrol with two blue-and-whites for back up. I was about a block off Aramingo Avenue when I saw a car that I knew right away didn't belong. I radio it in and one of the blue-and-whites picks me up. We stay one block parallel and follow it. You need to realize, the K and A Gang, which is basically the Irish version of the Italian Mafia, had run that part of North Philly since the Second World War ended. But now there's this new element starting to carve out turf and they were decidedly non-Irish. So it wasn't like they were tough to spot. Which reminds me, are there any – and I mean any – people in Surf City who aren't the same color as the sand? No blacks, no Chicanos, no Chinese? Anything here but pale and pink?"

Ronnie shrugged. "Couple of the municipal workers and maybe a hotel maid or two, but they all live on the mainland, not here. Don't try to change the subject."

Mickey held out her hand for the joint. Ronnie passed it to her.

She toked slowly and without taking her gaze from the fire.

"After a couple of passes they pull in behind this little cracker-box apartment building. I mean just a shit-hole. We pull around the front and there's these three little girls – seven, maybe eight years old – playing in what counts as the front yard. Basically it's bare dirt and trash and dog turds with a helping or two of broken glass but they don't care. They have this cardboard box that they're pretending is a dollhouse and they're holding some beat up Barbies. I think at least one of the dolls was missing an arm or a leg. They must have either pulled them out of the trash or somebody found them at a second-hand store. The sergeant sends me to go talk to them. He says 'You're a girl. They won't be afraid of you. Go ask them who's inside.' So I pull my patrol jacket down over my gun and do like he says. It was so cold, and they had on these skimpy little jackets with holes in them and the stuffing coming out but they were chattering and laughing like they were in the toy department at Gimbel's. And, God, they were beautiful little kids. One was dark as molasses, the other two a little lighter but with these big toothy smiles. I almost forgot for a second what was going on inside. I asked what the doll's names are. I can still remember. They said this one's Linda, this one's Betsy and *this* one, this is Chantrell – she's the queen of the other dolls, they tell me."

Mickey passed the joint back and put her hands together, rubbing one thumb slowly and repeatedly over the other.

"I ask if their mommies are inside. They all say yes. I'm about to ask who else is inside when this strung out white girl opens the door and stands on the stoop. She starts yelling at me to get away from the girls. She's got one hand behind her, so I don't know if she has a piece or what. I go to take my hands out of my pockets and she starts screaming louder. The boys in the cruisers are pulling into position when these two really bad-looking dudes come from around each side of the building and head right for me. They guys are still in the car. One of them hits the siren and I can still see the roof lights reflecting off the broken apartment windows. I go to reach for these girls – I was just going to lay down on top of them - but before I can these two guys snatch them up and run up the steps with them. I kneel down to pull out my piece when I hear a bullet whizz over my head. They guys from the cruisers are running and yelling now, heading around the back. They order me to cover the entrance so I get down in a shooter's stance. I can hear yelling and shooting inside. It's crazy. I can hear these little girls crying and the white bitch is coming out the door saying 'they shot my babies' and then she's running right at me with something in her hand so I squeeze off two shots and she just drops. Then the bad guys come out and they've got the little girls held with one arm and pointing big-ass guns with the other. My guys are behind them with every piece drawn telling them to get down. One of the scumbags shoots at our sergeant and our guys just start squeezing off rounds like it's a free-fire exercise. I hit the deck way so I don't take one in the head. A slug goes by so close it ruffles my hair and my hat comes off. The bad guys are stumbling off the porch and I'm yelling at them to put the kids down. One looks right at me and raises his piece so I cap him with another two. And then I see the blood – except it's on the little girl's pink coat. He drops her on the ground – I mean like she was a bag of trash – and starts to run but the guys in the squad drop him within two steps. The other guy is on the ground, too. Everybody wearing a uniform is yelling and hollering and they just keep pumping rounds into these two dirtballs. I mean like emptying the clips and maybe even reloading. Then after what seems like forever it gets real quiet. The air smells like Cordite. The white girl is kind of moaning but all the little ones are still. They look like they're just sleeping but I know, I know, I know they're not. I know they're not sleeping.

Mickey's voice is thick and nasal. Thin trails of clear mucus run from her nose and glisten in the light of the fire and she rocks slightly as she speaks. She snuffles and clears her throat, then wipes her cheeks with one hand.

"They still had the Barbie dolls in their hands," she said softly. "That's what I remember. And the dolls' little dresses, they had blood on them. And the little girls looked peaceful. Like they were just taking a nap with their dollies and they would wake up any time. But, Jesus, the little doll dresses had blood all over them. And the dolls, the dolls had their eyes wide open. Wide open like they were staring at us. Like they wanted to know what happened. Why their little girls were asleep and they were awake..."

Ronnie reached out to touch her hand but Mickey pulled her arms in tight around her and sat nearly motionless except for the rise and fall of her chest with each breath. Finally, she spoke again.

"I don't think I moved until we heard more sirens coming toward us. I touched each of the girls on the cheek and I said 'I'm so sorry, I'm so sorry'. But then there's blood dripping on them. And it's mine. My ear hurts when I touch it and my hair is wet and I realize I'm bleeding like a stuck pig from something. I hardly remember anything else, the ambulance guys, the Hahnemann ER, the debrief, signing a statement, anything. I guess for a few minutes everybody thought I'd bought it." She pulled back the hair over her right ear. Even in the firelight Ronnie could see the missing piece of the upper curve. "Attractive, I know. The ear and the scalp took some stitches to close but they patched me up and sent me back. Looked a lot worse than it was, they said. Hurt a lot worse than it looked, then, I told them."

She let the dark hair fall back. "The guys wanted me to go to a bar over on Delancey with them. It was one of the few times I was ever asked to be included in anything. There still wasn't a women's locker room, so I waited until they were all done changing into street clothes and then I sat there and cried until I thought my eyes would bleed. I didn't care about my ear. I was bawling like a baby over those little girls. I wanted to call my dad but I couldn't let him know how bad I was. Cleary's never cry and Cleary's never quit. He said that shit all the time. So after a little while goes by, I finally get hold of myself. And, even though I was a Cleary, I did both."

The fire was on its last legs. Ronnie hadn't moved other than to take off his shirt and give it to Mickey to blot her face with. The lip of a breaking wave crawled toward them, the ocean murmuring now as high-tide approached. Ronnie stretched out his arm. Mickey grabbed his hand and pulled herself up, turning to face him. The light from the glowing ash and the burning embers danced in his pupils. "Beer's probably cold," she said with a laugh that also contained a small sob. "But I'm sure the pizza's stiffer than a board by now."

Ronnie kept her hand locked in his. "It's better that way. MRE. Jungle-style." Then he let her hand slip free and walked around her toward the shack. The amber light from the Coleman shone feebly through the excuse for a front window. Another wave broke and foamed at Mickey's heels.

"You swear you're not working for the New Jersey A.G.?"

she asked.

"You swear you're not working for Army C.I.D.?" he replied

She took one step and then another one, following him toward the house. Two steps later she heard him singing the opening lines from The Rascals "How Can I Be Sure?"

His voice, Mickey thought, was shockingly sweet and clear.

FOURTEEN

Philadelphia Police Headquarters
Office of the Commissioner

A HOODED DESK LAMP was the only light burning above the ground floor at The Roundhouse. Traffic was light as midnight approached at the intersection of 8th and Race Streets, quiet except for the occasional belch and grind of a city bus or the blare of a cabbie's horn The three men sitting in the otherwise darkened office cast conflicting shadows as their conversation grew more animated.

"I don't care if he was a nobody, he still got whacked in my city."

Basil Jablonski leaned toward the two men who were seated across the wide lacquered maple expanse from him. "Hizzoner is up for reelection this Fall and he ain't going to lose over some Dago blood feud. No offense." FBI Special Agents Charlie Sesso and Steven Speziale both indicated that none was taken. "Frankie Numbers was a friggin' accountant for Chrissakes. He taught friggin' Math at a friggin' Dago high school in friggin' Pennsauken."

"Prep school," Sesso interjected. "It's a prep school. There's a big difference."

"I don't care if it's a Hebrew school for friggin' deaf, dumb and blind kids," Jablonski thundered. "A no-name nobody gets capped and left in plain sight with sand sprinkled around him. And you guys and your friggin' Joint Task Force know nothing – I repeat, *nothing* – about it."

"Could be a ritual killing," Speziale said. "That would explain the getting snipped part. You know, a religious cult or something like that. There's a lot more of that around these days. Druids maybe. Or could even be Rosicrucians."

Jablonski ran a sweaty hand over his face and brought it down hard on the desk. "It ain't no friggin' ritual murder, OK? Frankie Cherubini got whacked 'cause Danny Rags' kid washed up dead on a beach down the shore. End of story. Now what we have to do is make sure that's where it stops."

"Our informant on LBI says the boy's death was probably a boating accident, " said Sesso, "but apparently the local authorities want it to go to the State M.E. and they're holding on to the body until an autopsy confirms C.O.D." Speziale nodded.

"What local authorities?" Jablonski asked.

"Local P.D. in Surf City is what we're getting. New C.O.P. wanting to set the tone, maybe."

Jablonski looked incredulous. "First, you two knock it off with all the initials crap. You want to tell me Long Beach Island, you say Long Beach Island. Second, you're telling me that a piss-ant cop in a piss-ant beach town is calling the shots here?"

"Apparently so," Speziale said. "And Surf City is a borough, not a town. Just for the record."

"OK, it's a borough. Now who is this guy and what in God's name does he think he's doing messing around with this?"

Sesso raised an index finger. "Actually, it's a girl not a guy. A woman, I guess I'm supposed to say. She's been the Chief there for less than a month. You might know the name. Michaela Cleary? D.O.J. says she graduated from your academy and was P.P.D. for a few years. Left the force for unknown reasons maybe a year, year and a half ago? "

Jablonski rocked back in his chair. "Yeah, I know the name. I just can't friggin' believe it. I walked a beat with her father, Patsy. He's got a little history with Danny Rags himself. Jesus Christ on a crutch."

"Looks like she's within her jurisdiction to hold the body, anyway," Sesso said. "As long as it stays in Surf City, that is. You know anything about this Michaela?"

"Yeah," Jablonski laughed, "I used to bounce her on my knee and she could kick both your sorry jacket-and-tie asses even on a bad night." He rolled his chair as close to the desk as his ample midsection would allow. "They tried every trick in the book to fail her out of the academy. She just gave it back in spades. Lost a brother to cancer before she was even born. She was like son *and* daughter to Patsy and Eileen, God rest her. Mickey - that's what they call her - Mickey was in that shootout near K and A when those three little girls got killed. After that she just disappeared. And when I say she disappeared, I mean she friggin' e-*vaporated*. Turned in her gun, turned in her badge and was gone. Even Patsy didn't know where she was. I never figured we'd see or hear from her again in this lifetime."

"What's her father's connection?" Speziale asked.

Jablonski paused before answering. "Patsy was in the wrong place at the wrong time," he said. "Took a slug in the back from one of Ragone's shooters. It's still there, I think. Docs all said it was too dangerous to get it out. Got a commendation and a full disability rating, but I'm sure Mickey holds Danny Rags responsible. This better to Christ not be payback for some ancient friggin' history."

Speziale leaned in. "Come on. There's no way that she-"

Jablonski cut him off. "Don't say anything you can't be certain about. Now, you two goombahs get your federal asses on the road down the shore and find out what the Christ is going on. I'll make a call to Danny Rags first and then to Carmine Rocca and try to broker something like a truce 'til we can sort this mess out. Jesus, I just got this settled, I thought. You boys ever heard of the Gulf of Tonkin?" They shook their heads. "Go look it up. A great Polish philosopher once said if you don't know history you end up repeating it."

"We'll leave in the morning," said Sesso, rising from his chair.

"You'll leave tonight," Jablonski replied and remained seated. "And I'll say a novena to St. Casmir."

"Who's St. Casmir?" Speziale asked.

Jablonski chuckled. "Patron Saint of Polacks. Protects us from you dumbass Wops."

Neither agent laughed.

"If we're leaving tonight, I gotta call my wife and let her know," Sesso said.

"Use the phone in the next office," Jablonski replied. "Like I said, I got some calls to make myself. And there can't be a record of any of them."

Surf City

The knock on the door of Room 100 at the Surf City Hotel came at four minutes after midnight. Petroni followed the old man to the pay phone and waited until he saw him return to the front desk before closing the folding door.

"Well that certainly makes it more complicated," Petroni said, his hand cupped over the receiver. "Just keep clear of me and Shots and try not to look like a Fed this time. You can pick up some cabaña wear in Ocean City and pretend you're tourists from Bristol. Black socks and plaid shorts is always a good look. Just try and stay out of the mix." Petroni scanned the lobby for patrons or loiterers and saw neither. "I talked Danny into twenty-four hours. Let's be happy with that. I think there's a good chance this can be resolved through diplomatic channels." He fingered the coin return slot and came up empty. "OK. No, I don't think that's necessary. I'm pretty sure old Sergeant Cleary isn't going anywhere soon." Petroni checked the lobby again and opened the door. The old man lifted his head from his copy of *The Sporting News*. Petroni reached into the pocket of his bathrobe, the same style he'd read Sinatra wore, and plucked out another five spot.

"'Spectin' any more calls tonight?"

Petroni shook his head. "Will you be here in the morning?" he asked.

"Connie gets here 'bout eight," the old man replied.

"Good. Come knock on my door at seven. And there's another five in it for you if you bring hot coffee. *Capisce?*"

"Yessir. Seven on the button. With coffee."

Petroni walked the thirty paces to his door thinking about Billy Bowker. He sincerely hoped Michaela Cleary was a reasonable woman.

The sweat on his neck glistened and danced, reflecting the lamplight. Mickey watched as the individual drops tracked diverging paths down his chest. The metallic taps of three sets of dog tags chimed with their shared rhythm. She pushed them against his breastbone and the room quieted. The muffled creak of the floorboards under the mattress waxed and waned. His eyes were closed.

"It's OK," she whispered. "It's OK now."

Mickey had always been able to detach herself from the act and had never felt shame in that. But something was very different in this moment, she realized. She was anything but detached. The darkness was a cocoon that kept everything beyond it at bay. If there was a world outside the rim of light that bathed them, it didn't matter. All that existed was illuminated. All that mattered was within her reach. Nothing could touch them as long as they were touching each other. All her energy, emotional and physical, was being channeled, concentrated. It wasn't just pleasure, although it was certainly pleasurable beyond anything she could remember. All the heated exploring that led to this moment had been unhurried, as if time had been paused just for the two of them. Mickey had lost track of the minutes – or maybe it was the hours – that had passed. They were two bodies moving synchronously, not just connected but hard-wired to the same circuit with the same jolt of current flowing through them.

Mickey tried to wait but the sensations opened a fault line deep within her and as she panted through the earthquake and then the aftershocks, their dark little world went out of focus and there was nothing but being and feeling. Opening her eyes she understood the little death she had just experienced and wondered how anyone survived such ecstasy. She became aware that Ronnie was moving faster now, his breath warm and wet in her ear. He had not said a word.

"It's OK, baby," she whispered. "Baby, it's all OK now." She didn't know what it meant, only that it was true.

Ronnie's body shuddered and he let out a gasp.

Music was playing. Had it been playing all along? Jefferson Airplane. Or was she imagining it?

She put her hand on Ronnie's back and pulled him tight against her, locking her legs around his.

His weight was on her now and his breathing slowed. She felt a warm rain of perspiration falling on her face from his, just an inch above her. When she moved her hand to wipe it away she realized they weren't beads of sweat that were falling.

They were tears.

THURSDAY

FIFTEEN
Surf City

PETRONI WAS ALREADY IN his Sinatra bathrobe when the knock came. The old man was good to his word and he held a small Bunn brand glass pot in one hand and a slightly chipped ceramic mug in the other.

"Phone never rang all night," he said and proffered the mug. Petroni held it while the old man poured. The aroma was rich and heady. Too rich to be instant, which was what Petroni had been expecting. He took a sip and reached for another five.

"From Horn and Hardart's, downtown Philly," he continued. "Best in the city if you ask me."

Petroni did not ask him. He just slipped him the bill.

"Shower and the can are at the end of the hall. Hang the plastic seashell on the door so we know if you're in there."

"Are there any other guests?" Petroni asked.

"No, but Connie has a bladder situation goin' on. No sense flashin' her. Her heart ain't much better. I'll keep the pot warm at the desk if you need a refill."

Petroni closed the door and sat at the room's little desk. From his valise he brought out a sheaf of legal documents which had no bearing on his present business but looked impressive enough, he hoped, to scare someone into acquiescing to his demands. It was an old ruse but it would be better for everyone involved if it worked.

Mickey awoke the second time on the mattress alone, covered by a crisp percale sheet and the barracks blanket. The first time had been much earlier and only briefly. She had found herself enfolded in the warmth of his body. He was awake and looking at her intently. When she smiled he had kissed her softly, almost chastely and she had drifted immediately back to sleep.

Mickey propped up on her elbows and surveyed the room. Her clothes from the previous evening were folded tightly and neatly by the doorway. Her uniform hung on a steel hanger hooked on a large spike driven into one of the wall boards. Her sidearm was next to the bed and smelled of fresh gun oil. It was strapped into its holster with the leather belt coiled like a sleeping snake around it.

The shower had some stains of uncertain origin but the water was hot and little hotel soaps and shampoo bottles were jammed in the wire caddy. Towels with a green stripe and *Holiday Inn* stitched in white cursive lay nearby.

Once washed and dried, Mickey put on her uniform and buckled up her gun belt. The shack was silent. Morning sunlight peeked in the windows but she heard no movement. She walked out towards the front room. The card table was still set up but only one lawn chair nestled by it. On the table was a large cup of coffee in a white Styrofoam cup. Mickey inhaled the aroma and put the cup to her lips. She wondered if Ronnie had vacated the premises to spare her any awkwardness on her exit. She wasn't at all hazy about the previous night. She felt anything but awkward. And, she thought with a smile, she hadn't needed the manual after all.

Kaylen was a wrinkled mess.
"Sleep in the squad car?" Doreen asked.
"Tried a little stake-out action," he replied. "Thought there might be something fishy going on back behind the Surf Shoppe."
"Was there?" Doreen looked truly alarmed.
"Nah, but I did keep an eye on it until the trash guys came."

"Nice to know you're on our side," Doreen said. "Make you some coffee? Or I got a cold Yoo-Hoo if it's not too early. Couple 'a TastyKakes, too. One of 'em's a Chocolate Junior." Kaylen waved her off.

"I'm going to try to grab some shuteye. If the Chief calls tell her I patrolled a little later than usual last night and just need a couple hours." He wiped at the blond stubble on his face and turned for the inside stairs. "I'll hang the Do Not Disturb sign so Florence doesn't go waking me up. Tell her to go easy on the vacuum – maybe do the upstairs hallway last."

"Hey, Kaylen," Doreen called. He stopped at the bottom step, cocked his head but did not turn around.

"Yeah?"

"When you see Chief Cleary tell her some reporter from one of the city papers called. Wanted to talk to her about the body that washed up yesterday. Says he might just drive down here to check it out. Wondered if we had a room. Says it might be a big story – maybe even get him the Howitzer Prize, whatever that is."

Doreen could not see the little stain of color in Kaylen's cheeks drain away. He threw her a wave and mounted the steps, walked glumly down the hallway and unlocked his door.

Once inside, he alternated pacing and sitting, pacing and sitting, pacing and sitting. He took stock of his adjoining room. It was more treasure trove than museum. All the artifacts were arrayed for only him to appreciate. But the signed baseballs, the game glove with the broken laces in the webbing, the boxes and boxes of trading cards and the autographed pictures that hung on each wall were cold comfort at the moment. It *had* been the right thing, he reassured himself. There was too much at stake to have done anything else. Kaylen retreated to the kitchen and got a glass of ice water, hands trembling as he poured. The knife had been the mistake, he realized. Trying too hard to make it look like something it wasn't. The doc had taken the hint it right away. He'd just overdone it. A little less and they'd all be out looking for a boat; or more likely it would be ruled a death by misadventure and the book on it closed by now.

After a few minutes he doffed his uniform and hung it up neatly. He put on the pinstripe summer pajamas JoLynne had bought him as kind of an inside joke. He waited a few minutes until he had to use the bathroom and once finished, tore a slip of paper from the small tablet he'd taken from the office. Kaylen looked at the plain lettering at the top:

SURF CITY POLICE DEPARTMENT
Peter R. Graham, CHIEF
Hobart 5 – 3434

Maybe the Chief would understand if he called and told her. Maybe she could still help him. But either way, it was Mickey who would take the blame and he couldn't bear that thought. Kaylen picked up the blue Papermate Flair pen and began to write.

She was two steps past him when Ronnie called her name.
"If you're trying to sneak out under cover of darkness, I'm afraid it's a little late." He was sitting in one of the lawn chairs off to the side of the rickety porch. He stood up holding an identical Styrofoam cup. There was a white bakery box at his feet. "Grab the doughnuts, would you?"
Mickey picked up the box by the crisscrossed twine. Ronnie grabbed his chair and then stopped. "Unless you want breakfast out here on the lanai," he said. The boyish grin was the closest she had yet come to seeing him really smile.
"Yeah, let's sit out here," Mickey replied. "Better view. Fresh air."
The sun was now just over the eastern horizon. The Atlantic was calm with only baby waves gurgling on the beach. White-winged seagulls stood one-legged on pilings or scurried on the beach picking at unlucky sand crabs and jellyfish marooned by the outgoing tide. Ronnie brought the other chair out and set it by his.
"Did you really clean my gun?" Mickey asked as she sat down. Ronnie was slipping loose the string to open the box.
"Yeah. Oiled it, too. Hope you don't mind. Old habit. It needed it, though. Sand and salt will foul it pretty quick down here."
"And my clothes?"
"Tunell's All-Night Coin Laundry over in Beach Haven. I had to take a couple of dimes from your uniform pocket for the dryer. Hope you don't mind." He held up the box. "The best cream doughnuts come from a little bakery called L & M way over in

Riverside, but that was too far to go. These are from DeLuca's. I got half powdered sugar and half crystal – wasn't sure of your preference."

Mickey reached for one and then leaned forward to take a bite. "Granulated," she said with her mouth full. "I wouldn't be able to get powdered sugar out of my uniform blouse." Ronnie wolfed two down doughnuts almost simultaneously and followed with a generous gulp of the coffee. Mickey tapped her feet on a broken pallet slat. "What did you mean about sand in my shoes?"

Ronnie wiped powdered sugar from his face with the back of his hand and reached for two more doughnuts. "It's a local expression. Means once you really love the shore you never want to leave it. People who have to move away always want to come back. Some say they keep beach sand in their shoes just to remind them."

"I didn't think that was how you meant it."

Ronnie swallowed the fourth doughnut. "I didn't, exactly. I meant that there are all these unwritten rules and interconnections here that you have no idea even exist. Some of our residents and visitors are like the sand crabs. They sneak in and out of their little holes so fast you don't even know they're there. But while you're looking at the ocean they're picking the place clean right under your feet. The Nazis went to Brazil. The Mob goes to Long Beach." He paused to slurp more coffee. "Your dead body is going to be a real problem."

Mickey brushed sugar off her pants and listened.

"Look, there hasn't been an actual murder *on* the Island in over forty years so that's really an unlikely possibility. But, misinterpretation of intentions by people who regard killing as a business necessity - well, now that's a way different problem."

"All I'm doing is holding the body for the State M.E. Once it's in his hands I'm out of it and Surf City is out of it." Mickey said.

"Yeah, well, that's the best case scenario. But also the least probable. This won't just be about one dead kid. This will be about power in New Jersey and Philadelphia and who controls what here and there for the next thirty years."

"OK, in Philly I understand the turf issues but look around," Mickey said, "What's there to control? The salt-water taffy market? Seashell necklaces and funnel cakes?"

Ronnie patted his hands to shake off more sugar. "Try beachfront property, zoning rights, building permits and a dozen other things people will pay for. My friend Tony says they're going to legalize gambling down in A.C. within ten years, maybe less. The big boardwalk hotels are dying. If they could legalize prostitution they'd do that, too, but a gambling casino is something else."

"Yeah, casinos in Atlantic City – right," Mickey replied. "Craps tables and the Miss America Pageant. Bert Parks emceeing at a strip club on his night off. What would they do, take bets on the Diving Horse?"

"Strip clubs they already have. And it's not just the gambling, it's the linen, the trash hauling, the restaurants and the other service industries. Plus all the illegal stuff that naturally goes with it – bookmaking, hookers, drugs. The sand and the ocean are no match for greed. It's really no different than the war. You think we're interested in Southeast Asia 'cause we need jungle property and rice paddies? Defense contractors, politicians and anybody with a screwdriver to sell the military are making one mint after another on the backs of grunts like me and these guys." He grabbed the dog tags.

"And who's this Tony?" Mickey asked.

"Tony Mart. Runs a club over the bridge. Knows nothing and nobody according to him. But trust me, he knows a guy who knows everything and everybody. You want some more intel about what trouble you're in for if you can't put this to bed right away? Go ask Tony. Tell him I sent you. Just take the causeway bridge and start looking for signs that say 'Showplace of the World'. It's about seventy klicks That's my best advice. That and get the body out of Surf City as soon as you can. It's like blood in the water right now. It'll only draw sharks."

"OK, how far is seventy klicks?"

"About forty-five miles. You can take Nine but the Parkway's quicker. You're a cop. Drive fast."

Mickey reached into a pocket for her keys. "And to think I had you pegged as the silent type," she said. She stepped away, trying to save both of them from the awkward moment.

"I just want you to know," Ronnie said. "I mean, I don't usually - I wasn't planning on – it's not why I asked you - "

"Neither do I and neither was I," Mickey replied. "Just for the record." She looked out at the green, glittering ocean. Ronnie stared down at his feet.

"I don't think it was a mistake," he said.

Mickey put on her sunglasses. "No, it wasn't a mistake," she answered. "A mistake is something you regret. We'll just have to wait and see if it was a good idea or not." The keys to the cruiser jangled in her hand.

"There's a nice little restaurant over in Tuckahoe," Ronnie said. "I'd be happy to show you. When's your next night off?"

Mickey looked at her watch. "Tuesday after Labor Day," she said and stepped off the porch. "I'll let you know."

Ronnie laughed. "That's fair," he said. "But go talk to Tony if you can. And get that body out of here ASAP. Sharks, remember?"

"Sharks," she said. "I got it. Hey, one more thing. You know the Sons of Satan or anything about them?"

Ronnie gave her quizzical look.

"I met a few of them on a call the other night. Interesting group."

Ronnie sipped his coffee. "They are that," he said. "I think they're probably harmless. It's not a real big club. Most if not all of them are guys back from tours in Nam. They like the outlaw image but mostly they just can't or don't want to fit back into everyday society after what they went through. A biker club is a lot like a military unit. Brothers-in-arms kind of thing. Maybe with a little petty crime and drugs mixed in. They're definitely guys who are never going to punch a clock or stock shelves at the A&P."

"You know them?"

"I know *of* them," Ronnie replied. "And vice-versa. We don't usually cross paths, if that's what you're asking."

"How come you're not in it? Based on your description, you'd think-"

"I ride the wrong kind of bike," he answered. She pictured his two-wheeled bicycle and laughed.

"That I believe," she said.

"But let me know if they give you any trouble."

"I thought you didn't cross paths."

"We're on each other's radar. Leave it at that. I can pass a word if you need me too."

Mickey raised her coffee cup in mock salute and walked off towards the cruiser. Part of her had really wanted to kiss him, she realized. Loretta would be proud.

SIXTEEN
Surf City

A. LOUIS PETRONI, ESQ. thought he was in especially fine voice today. Equal parts Clarence Darrow and Perry Mason, although the latter had been unceremoniously and lamentably canceled the year before. The Borough Clerk, whose white-on-black plastic nameplate identified her as one Helen Martin, was cowering behind her grate of vertical wrought-iron spindles as Petroni let fly with one Latin phrase after another.

"If this were just a matter of *res ipsa loquitor* I wouldn't be wasting my time. But madam, we are talking about multiple binding legal principles here which include but are certainly not limited to *habeas corpus, in vin veritas, habemus papum* and most importantly *quod Deus vult*! *Quod Deus vult,* my dear woman, the *Agricola agricolorum* of all civil jurisprudence!"

As it was only 8:05 a.m. the poor clerk was the sole employee in City Hall. And at sixty-three years old and only seven months away from retirement, she appeared ready to deed Petroni the building, the grounds and perhaps the entire borough if not the Island. Petroni walked around the tiny tiled lobby trying to suppress a smile at his cleverness. *Quod Deus vult* was the motto of his Catholic high school and meant only 'Because God wills it.' He snapped the papers on the marble counter in front of the grate. "Madam," he said in his most stentorian tone, "Release the decedent's mortal remains forthwith or I will have to find you in *Nolo Contendere* as well as *Nihil Obstat*." This was followed by a wicked and extemporaneous *coup de grace*: "And with either of those, you can kiss your sweet pension goodbye!" At this the poor woman began to sob and Petroni heard a door open. He watched as a middle aged man in khaki pants and a crisply pressed white shirt entered brandishing a bottle of Dr. Pepper in his left hand. He had a graying hair and a malevolent twinkle in his eyes. He thrust out his empty right hand.

"I'm Bill Tunell, the mayor of Surf City. How can we help you today?"

Petroni brandished his business card which the mayor looked at but did not touch.

"Spiffy card," Tunell said. "Spiffy. Great speech, too. You know, I'm an old Notre Dame man, Class of '49. Four years of Latin and two of Greek were required back in those days so, believe me, I am doubly impressed at your *mirabile dictu* command of a dead language. But before you take your papers and leave," he said, simultaneously taking Petroni's arm and low back like a foxtrot dancer, "let me make the following observations. First, *quod culus tibi*. Second, *planus stercoris totalis es*. Now please exit the premises and once you have, please *protinus ad inferos*. Forthwith and with all deliberate speed."

Petroni found himself outside the small stucco building almost before he knew it. He squinted in the morning sun and began to straighten his papers when the mayor poked his head out.

"To save you the trouble of looking it up, let me translate for you: you, sir, are an asshole; you are completely full of shit and you should go straight to hell as soon as you can. I suggest if you have any further business here you take it up with local law enforcement whom I'm sure will find you even more repugnant than I do and will hopefully arrest and incarcerate you if only on general principles. Good day to you, sir." With that he slammed the door. Petroni walked to the Jag and got in. He stuffed the papers in the valise on the passenger seat and started the engine. Now someone was going to pay, he mused. Someone was definitely going to pay.

◆ ◆ ◆

The station door was locked which caught Mickey by surprise. She fumbled momentarily with the keys on her ring then slotted one in the deadbolt. "Kaylen," she called as she entered. The portable TV was on but the volume was turned down. A Clutch Cargo cartoon was playing. The real moving lips on the cartoon heads had always freaked her out and they were still a little unsettling. She went to Kaylen's desk and leafed through his call log. The last entry was at 0715 she noted. And the Galaxie was not in its space. A copy of the Philadelphia morning paper lay on his desk. Mickey scanned the front page for any mention of Surf City and was relieved to find none. She took the Sports section, walked to her desk and sat down. She got on the radio and tried to hail him.

"SCPD 2 this is SCPD Base. Copy?"

Static.

"SCPD 2 this is SCPD Base. Do you copy? Kaylen? What's your twenty, Deputy?"

She toggled the receiver switch a few times then put the hand unit back in its clip. She thumbed her Rolodex for Kaylen's number at the Ebb Tide.

"Ebb Tide Motor Hotel, Doreen speaking," a pleasant voice answered.

"Doreen, this is Chief Cleary. Did Kaylen come in last night?"

"Yes ma'am. He's asleep right now. Said to tell you he was patrolling later than usual last night and needed a few hours of sleep this morning. Had me route room calls here for a while. Is he in trouble, Chief?"

"No, Doreen, he's not in trouble. But if he's not up and at 'em by eleven you go wake him up, OK?"

"Yessiree, Chief. Writing myself a note right here on the guest register. Kaylen -eleven o'clock. He's a good deputy, isn't he Chief."

"He is, Doreen," Mickey answered. "But you are now his official wake-up call. Got it?"

"Got it, Chief. Have a beachy day and thank you for calling the Ebb Tide Motor Hotel!"

A beachy day. She could definitely see Eddie Giacometti making her say that.

Mickey hung up the phone and looked at the paper. *The Inquirer* Sports section was thin but she did notice a story tucked in a corner below the fold.

Mantle Fined for Curfew Violation
A.C. Excursion Costly for Slugger

Regular milk or chocolate milk, she remembered. She'd have to show it to Kaylen.

The bongo-heavy theme song was playing and Mickey tried to remember the names of Clutch Cargo's animated companions. "Spinner," she finally said out loud. "Spinner and Paddlefoot." She turned the set off. The vacuum tubes glowed orange through the hundreds of machine- punched ventilation holes in the beige metal case. A childhood memory arrived unbidden but not unpleasant: Mickey and her father testing the tubes from their little Zenith at the gas station when she was around nine. She had been surprisingly good at figuring out which pins went into which holes. If she didn't want to be a policeman, her father had told her, she could be a TV repairman. They would always need TV repairmen. That was her job now, she thought: fitting the pins in the right holes and figuring out which tubes were good and which ones were bad.

She checked the box score for the Phillies game, stared at the phone and then finally dialed.

Sesso and Speziale sat in a high-backed booth that gave them a view of the entirety of Bill's Luncheonette. They wore the same clothes they had on in Basil Jablonski's office with the addition of some cheap Foster Grants they'd picked up at a Sunoco station next to Olga's Diner in Marlton. Sesso said they were the same ones the guys in Steppenwolf wore.

There was a brisk breakfast business, mostly local teenage girls and a few early arriving lifeguards. Sesso kept his sunglasses on so he could ogle the fresh flesh in the skimpy one and two-piece suits. The lifeguards pretended to ignore them, wolfing Tandy Kakes and Butterscotch Krimpets straight from their cellophane packages or bags of white powdered Donettes, washing them down with quart cartons of whole milk.

"Put your tongue back in," said Speziale. "It's all tiny hiney and jailbait. Probably kill an old fart like you." Sesso sipped his coffee and cut his jelly doughnut in half with a water-spotted knife.

"Where to first?" Speziale asked.

Sesso stuffed one of the halves into his mouth, the jelly sticking to his mustache. "Let's lay low for a while and then drop in on the Chief unannounced. Flash the creds and talk tough. Subpoenas, warrants, wiretaps – all that shit. See if we can get her to slip."

"She's a cop, Charlie. She'll know what we're pulling in a heartbeat."

"OK, then, let's go the other way. Full support, Bureau resources, whatever she needs. We're here to help. Good cop, good cop, get it?" Sesso squeezed the remaining half into his mouth. "We just need to be out of there before eleven." He said when he finished chewing.

"What happens at eleven?"

Sesso hesitated. "Lunch," he said. Then, "OK let's go cruise around and see what's what. But I gotta sit for a minute." He looked down at his lap.

"Jesus, Charlie," Speziale said as new bevy of adolescent girls pushed through the doors, all budding breasts and early tan lines. "You have no respect for yourself."

"I just appreciate the wonder of God's creations," Sesso replied. He dropped another sugar cube in his coffee. "On second thought, I think we should stake this place out. Looks like it might be a hub for suspicious activity." Three linebacker-size lifeguards came in all wearing identical red OCBP sweatshirts and dabs of zinc oxide on their noses. "See?" Sesso said. "Clearly some type of gang activity going on here. Let's observe closely for a while, huh partner?"

They didn't see the young man in the jungle fatigues peer through the window at them and then walk past without entering.

Mickey counted twelve rings and decided she'd give it a baker's dozen when the line picked up.

"Cleary." The voice was at once familiar but different. An older voice. A weaker one.

"Hello? Who is this?"

Mickey paused and for the briefest of moments considered hanging up. Then she drew in a breath.

"Hi, Daddy. It's me. It's Michaela."

She couldn't tell if the silence at the end of the line was surprise or anger.

"Michaela. Is it you?"

"Yeah, it's me, Daddy. It's me." Tears filled her eyes. She felt so stupid, calling him Daddy.

"Are you OK?" Patsy asked. "Michaela, are you alright?" Mickey wiped her suddenly bubbling nose on her sleeve.

"Yes, Daddy, I'm fine. I'm back from California. I got a job at the shore. I'm a cop again. I'm the Chief, believe it or not."

"Yeah," Patsy replied, his voice thickened. "I think I might'a heard that somewhere. They must know talent when they see it."

Mickey laughed, tears and mucus running down her cheeks. She cleared her throat and fought for composure. "I'm sorry I didn't call right away. I wanted to get settled in first."

"It's OK," Patsy replied. Mickey could tell he was on the verge of blubbering. "I understand. Lots to do when you're the new Chief."

"You wouldn't believe it," Mickey said.

"I heard you've had a bit of excitement down there."

"Who told you that?"

"A slimy guinea rat it's been my sincere and lifelong misfortune to be acquainted with," Patsy replied.

Mickey visualized the name on the slip of paper she'd taken from Kaylen.

"A. Louis Petroni?" she asked.

"Did he call you?"

"No, but he left a message that he's on his way here. Thinks he's taking the body out of here before I can get the autopsy done."

"I've known Artie since we were kids. Farty Artie we used to call him. He stopped by here yesterday."

Mickey wiped at her cheeks and took a breath.

"Yeah? Why'd he want to see you?"

"He thought I could get you to help him. Thinks I owe him something."

"Do you?"

There was a pause. "The only thing I owe Artie Petroni is a quick trip to the next life. I told him to stay away from you."

"I can take care of myself, Dad."

"I know you can," Patsy said. "But Artie's always playin' both sides in any deal. Just do what you need to do and ignore him if you can. You think Danny Rags' kid got capped?"

"I'm not sure what happened. It was pretty gruesome. I'm trying to get the New Jersey State Medical Examiner to take this off my hands. I've got several thousand tourists coming my way this weekend and I need this over and done with before they get here."

"I seen that Ragone took out one of the Rocca's guys already. A bottom-rung one, but that's a bad sign. Those assholes are just itchin' for a fight; they have been for months. Just can't wait to show off their firepower, I guess. Danny thinks he's the next Al Capone and Carmine ain't much better. What do you have for back-up down there?"

"I have a good young deputy and some probies coming in another week. If I need them, I have the cops from the other towns and the Staties over in Hammonton. I hadn't heard about another killing. That's got me worried even more now."

"You keep the State Police number handy. 'Member I told you their first Commander was an Army General. West Point man, too. He made those bastards sharper than any military unit."

"Norman Schwarzkopf," Mickey replied. "Right? I remembered."

"Right. I read in the *Daily News* he's got son commanding in Viet Nam right now. Bet he'd rather be in New Jersey, though."

Mickey thought of Ronnie. "I bet," she replied.

"You be careful, Michaela. I had my run-ins with Danny Ragone and his crew over the years. Those goombahs never forget anything. And I mean anything."

Mickey was quiet for a moment. "How are you getting along? How's your back?"

"Good days and bad ones," Patsy answered. "Not too bad today. Might sit out on the stoop for a while. Watch the kids play wiffle ball. Maybe even walk a block to the newsstand for a paper."

"Phillies lost last night," Mickey said.

"Bunning's a bum," Patsy replied.

"He's not a bum. He's going to the Hall of Fame, Dad."

"He's a bum who just happened to pitch a perfect game - one time."

"It was on Father's Day, remember? We listened on the radio." She paused. "I should have called you before I left," Mickey said. "That wasn't right."

"But you're back now and you're OK. So that's what's important." There was a short silence. Mickey heard Patsy take a deep breath. "You watch out for yourself, girl. These guys are just sewer rats in suits. They're always looking to settle some score or another. And if you want to get Petroni's goat be sure to call him Artie; makes him nuts. If you don't mind, I'll call some guys I still know in the Third District, see what they got. If I hear anything I'll let you know. I called and left a message with your deputy yesterday – didn't he tell you?"

"I haven't seen him yet this morning. I'm sure he will."

"I'm glad you called, Michaela. I know I haven't been very-"

"It's good, Dad. You don't have to say anything. I'll let you know if I need something."

"Remember what I said," Patsy replied. "And don't turn your back for a minute on any of them."

"Message received, Sergeant Cleary," Mickey said. "Now I have to go brief the mayor on the status of my investigation. Dead bodies are generally bad for tourism or so he tells me."

Mickey hung up the phone and grabbed her hat and keys feeling like she'd been able to put down a boulder she'd been carrying around for too long. She was about to leave when the phone rang.

"We have a visitor," the mayor said.

Mickey sat down and listened. Tunell told the story of his encounter as only a true Irishman could. Mickey had to laugh at the image of him screaming profane Latin translations at Petroni as he booted him out of City Hall.

"I guess I didn't know there was a Latin word for asshole," Mickey said. "Nuns must have missed that one."

"There's a Latin word for everything," Tunell replied before he hung up.

Mickey was at the door when she heard the sound of rubber on asphalt in the front parking lot. If it was A. Louis Petroni, Esq., she figured he could stew for a few hours longer. At least until she got the body in the hands of the M.E. She keyed the deadbolt and slid into the Chevelle, hoping the brick mass of the station house would muffle its whining idle long enough for her to make a getaway. She pulled out slowly in first gear, staying behind the station's shadow until she was a block away, upshifted and headed for the beach road.

Cottman Avenue Garden Apartments
Northeast Philadelphia

Patrick Cleary put on his most comfortable pants, his roomiest short-sleeve shirt and an old bucket hat from his days fishing for shad or sunfish on the Delaware River. When Mickey was little, he recalled, she was never squeamish about grabbing their wiggling bodies and taking them off the hook, but she always insisted that he throw them back "to be with their fish family." In the bedroom dresser he carefully unwrapped something large and heavy, swaddled in several layers of white handkerchiefs. The keys had a thin coating of dust on them when he lifted them from the ashtray Mickey had made him for Christmas when she was in the third grade. She didn't sound worried, he thought. And that, he knew, could be a problem. He shuffled to his left. Every step was ponderous and painful but Patrick Cleary had always understood the demands of the job.

SEVENTEEN
Surf City

"YOU DO UNDERSTAND THE urgency," the mayor said. "The summer season begins in two days. Blood and sand don't mix, Tyrone Power notwithstanding."

"I expect to have this unfortunate matter wrapped up before the end of the day," Mickey replied. The large black floor fan in the mayor's office had an oscillating function that blew Mickey hair sideways every seven seconds.

"The Philadelphia papers and news stations could turn this into front page news if you don't."

"The body will be in the possession of the State Medical Examiner before suppertime, maybe before lunch. Once it's out of Surf City the story goes away."

The mayor rubbed at his temples. "I have a lady friend who works at the Ocean County offices. She's going to mimeograph a list of the names of the property owners. Perhaps your erstwhile deputy will be able to recognize one of them."

Mickey nodded and rose from the wooden chair that faced the front of his desk.

"That will help," she replied. "I can pick it up-"

"I will go and retrieve it for you," Tunell replied. "I want you to focus all of your attention on putting this matter behind us as quickly as possible. I'll release a statement hinting that it was a death by misadventure."

"But we don't know that," Mickey said.

"We don't know that it was anything else, either," the mayor shot back. "Occam's razor, my dear. The simplest answer is usually the right one."

"You mean the most convenient."

"I mean the least complicated for all parties involved."

Mickey laughed at the word. "Does the Ragone family own any-"

"None," Tunell said. "My lovely friend did manage to get a look at the R's and there are no properties in Surf City or on Long Beach Island deeded to anyone named Ragone."

"OK, Mickey said. "I'll let you know as soon as I hear from the M.E."

"One more thing, if I may," Tunell said. His manner was hesitant.

"Anything, your honor."

"Another good friend of mine tells me – and only me – that your patrol duties may have kept you from getting enough rest last night." He arched an eyebrow. "I've already had calls from all four of the Borough councilmen asking if we needed a more – how shall I put this? – *experienced* law enforcement presence to handle this."

"You mean 'experienced' as in possessing a couple of testicles?"

Tunell's face flushed. "Well, perhaps an indelicate rendering of the conversation but not an inaccurate one. I told them I stand by you and your experience and I meant it. Just remember what a very small town this is and, as the song says, the night-"

"Has a thousand eyes," Mickey finished.

"Good," Tunell continued. "You understand. And do give my regards to Anthony."

"Now how did you know-"

"He's what one might call a silent partner in my burgeoning Laundromat empire. And as such, not a bad source if you want to inquire about dirty linen and how to clean it. Make sure you let me know the second the deceased is outside the city limits."

"You'll be the first person I call," Mickey replied. The she paused. "I can handle this. However it shakes out, I can handle it. Let me know when you have the list of homeowners and I'll have Kaylen look it over. Finding the kids who were in the car is the key to solving this. I'm sure of that. I just need a place to start."

"Our local sawbones says boat accident. Why can't it be that simple?"

"When everybody wants it to be one thing it just gets under my skin that maybe it's something else. Regardless of who they are or what they do, the poor kid and his family deserve the truth about whatever happened."

Tunell smiled. "I think you'll find, my dear, that the truth is rarely pure and never simple. Or so said Oscar Wilde."

"I'll have to take your word for it," Mickey said and headed out the door.

* * *

Mickey sat in the cruiser for several minutes and then radioed central dispatch. The little office in Beach Haven fielded calls for the six boroughs and townships that stretched the length of Long Beach Island. In another week there would be two more dispatchers assigned to handle the huge uptick in calls that arrived with the tide of tourists. On duty today was Arlene, a former Registered Nurse from Stratford who lived with her husband on the Island and, Mickey thought, always sounded happy.

"Copy that," her staticy voice replied. "Ship Bottom will provide back-up for Surf City. Give us your twenty, please."

"Headed for Tony Mart's in Somers Point. ETA thirty minutes. Don't plan on being there very long."

"Copy, Tony Mart's. Send Tony regards from Beach Haven's finest, Surf City One. And see if he has any extra tickets for Mitch Ryder. Love that guy."

Mickey clicked off and turned on the cruiser's radio. She rolled down the driver's side window and let the wind blow back her hair. She kept waiting for what a girlfriend in California referred to as "fornicator's remorse" to set in but for the moment, she thought, she was OK. If it had been a bad idea, then it had been the best bad idea she'd had in a long time. The Zombies were singing "She's Not There" on WIBG. Mickey thought of A. Louis Petroni, Esq. sitting in the station parking lot and smiled.

♦ ♦ ♦

Ronnie pedaled the old Huffy two-wheeler back home, dragged it through the sand around to the back and leaned it against the generator. He loosened the corded tie-downs on an olive drab tarp and pulled it back. The chrome on the Enfield Interceptor caught the sun. Ronnie read the company's motto – "Made Like a Gun" arcing above the business end of a wheeled cannon barrel on the stamped-metal logo. The motto, he knew, also had a rejoinder, "Goes Like a Bullet." He took the tarp and used it to cover the bicycle and then rolled the four-hundred pound motorcycle to the asphalt. It would seat two, uncomfortably, but not if he needed to pack support. Except for the chrome, it was matte black thanks to a newer powder-coating process. Built in 1964, he'd bought it from a Piney at a shack in the woods some miles outside Hammonton. Ronnie immediately met the man's asking price because he hadn't looked like the kind of person one wanted to dicker with for very long. The man had offered to take a gun or guns in trade, but, he insisted, only if they were military-grade, had been used in combat and had actually killed someone. Having seen up close the effects of high-velocity projectiles on human flesh, Ronnie had sworn he didn't own any.

With both wheels now firmly on the tarred road he kicked the bike into life. The smell of gasoline from the single carburetor gave him an unpleasant flashback: a soldier with a flamethrower on his back and a man running down a path. He let it pass and climbed on.

Mickey could not remember the last time she had sung along with a car radio. The Grass Roots had just instructed her to live for today, which seemed like reasonable advice at the moment. She loved the "Sha-la-la la lala" part. Now Buffalo Springfield's "For What It's Worth" was on.

She turned it off. The picture was back in her head and it wouldn't go away.

Jesus Christ, she thought. Not again.

The cardboard box they'd turned into a dollhouse. The smudged and nicked-up Barbies. Chantrell, the queen, with blood congealing on her plaid jumper.

Mickey pulled onto the soft shoulder as soon as she crossed Manahawkin Bay, sat in the running car and wept.

Tacony-Palmyra Bridge
Delaware River

Patsy couldn't understand how everyone could drive so fast. The '57 Chevrolet Bel-Air still had plenty of power but every car, truck and motorcycle on the road passed him like he was standing still. Many made known their displeasure at having to weave around him with blaring horns and upraised middle fingers. Patsy pushed the accelerator a little harder and told himself to relax. He could have sold the car years ago for what was then a pretty penny. He doubted he could even give it away now. The old Esso "Highway Map of New Jersey" was spread out on the big front seat next to him. Parts of it were torn along the folds making it difficult to manage with one hand. If he could just find Highway 9, he figured, he would be OK. The pimply kid at the Sinclair station in Tacony had tried to steer him to the Atlantic City Expressway and then something called the Garden State Parkway. The names alone told Patsy he didn't want to be driving on them. He shifted in his seat again hoping to ease the ache in his spine. He wished he'd brought a bottle to piss in so he wouldn't have to pull over. The tires whumped on the tarred seams of the narrow two-lane steel arch span that would dump him in Palmyra on New Jersey Route 73. His prayer of avoiding a bridge-opening had apparently been heard. He sighed with relief when he the Bel-Air passed the buzzing metal roadbed grates of the two drawbridge leaves and approached the line of yellow tollbooths. The nickel he handed the collector left only pennies remaining in the car's flip-out ashtray. Patsy cracked the fly-window and felt better with the little breeze it generated. He hoped the tires were OK. He had no idea if there was air in the spare.

Surf City

Petroni knocked on the front door of the station. A little white clock face with movable black hands pointing straight up at noon hung in the square window under lettering that said "BE BACK AT." The sun-faded pattern told him the hands had not been moved in years. The film "High Noon" popped into his head along with its song. Truer words, he thought to himself. He was not about to be forsaken by Mickey Cleary. He walked around the building, trying to peer into the dusty windows with the bars on the outside. He jiggled the handle on the back door. He was being disrespected and he knew it. His phone call to Danny Rags had only inflamed instead of calming the grieving moron, Petroni thought, and he had immediately wanted another one of Carmine Rocca's foot soldiers taken out. Petroni had preached patience, saying he would have it all settled by nightfall. Had Danny Rags blustered on any longer he would have run out of dimes. But he knew what Danny was really demanding was a sacrifice. A blood sacrifice to atone for the loss of his son. Maybe all that remained was to determine who would fulfill that bargain.

Petroni returned to the big Jaguar sedan. The interior was already heating up in the bright sunshine. If that's what it came down to, he thought, the idea of giving Billy Bowker a little bonus was beginning to look better already.

EIGHTEEN

Somers Point, NJ
"SHOWPLACE OF THE WORLD"

THAT'S WHAT IT SAID right there on the sign. Mickey pulled the cruiser up and turned off the engine. The place looked like one big building to which a much smaller one had been joined clumsily at the hip. Atop the larger structure was a huge sign that read TONY MART'S. The letters, she figured, were easily ten feet tall. On the top border a narrow sign said, "Follow The Arrow To" and ended with a curve and an arrowhead triangle. Large, clear light bulbs dotted the whole thing. Mickey thought it must be an impressive sight at night.

She looked at her eyes in the rear-view mirror and slipped on the Ray-Ban's. The balled up Kleenex's went under the seat.

"Levon and The Hawks Starting Memorial Day Weekend!"

This sign was nailed to the smaller building which looked like the entrance. As she approached she saw a colorful poster advertising Mitch Ryder and the Detroit Wheels in a few weeks. Mickey walked through the large saloon-style doors and into the musty and dimly lit Showplace of the World.

"Help you ma'am?" a young man asked her. Mickey thought he looked at about fifteen.

"I'm Chief Cleary from the Surf City Police," she said. "I'm looking for your boss."

"Levon's in Atlantic City meeting with some producer," the boy answered.

"I don't mean Levon," Mickey replied. "I need to talk to Tony."

"You just met the boss," a voice from behind her said. "At least that's what the guys all call him." It came from a thin man in a tie-dye t-shirt and faded bell bottoms. His shoulder length hair was scraggly but kempt and he was barefoot.

"Yeah, and if that's Tony Mart then you're Bob Dylan and I'm-"

"Linda Ronstadt," he said.

"Hmm. Never heard of her," Mickey lied.

"She fronts the Stone Poneys right now but you'll be hearing her name soon enough all by itself. California band. Big in L.A. but someone from Jersey probably wouldn't know them. I'm Doug Doucette, Double D around here. I'm Tony's floor manager. Tony's not on premises at the moment so-"

"How old are you, kid?" Mickey asked the young-looking boy.

"Seventeen," he answered. "Just graduated high school."

"Got a work permit?"

"Oh, he's not an employee," Double D quickly interjected. "He just hangs out. Tunes guitars, sits in with the band if one of the guys has the brown bottle flu and can't rehearse. That kind of stuff. I think he'd sweep the floor if we asked him."

The boy inched away.

"Sounds gainfully employed to me," Mickey said to Double D. "Be a shame if the New Jersey Department of Labor needed you to shut down right before Memorial Day so they could check on your child-labor compliance issues." She looked at the boy. "What high school?" she asked.

"Freehold," he answered. "But I start classes at Ocean County College in the Fall." Mickey looked back at Double D.

"You know, I think Tony might have come in while we've been visiting. Let me go check," he said and walked away.

"You any good?" Mickey asked the boy.

"Levon and the guys say so," he replied.

"What's your name," Mickey asked. "So I can come see you when you're-"

"What brings an important Police Chief all the way from Surf City to my humble abode?" a voice boomed. Mickey turned to see a heavy-set man with wavy black hair and an impressive mustache striding toward her. When she glanced back, the boy was gone. "Tony Marotta," he said extending a recently manicured hand, "a.k.a. the world famous Tony Mart. To what do I owe this honor and pleasure?"

He's a charmer, Mickey thought. "Any chance for a quick sit-down in some place a little more private?" she asked. Tony made a sweeping gesture with his arm then led Mickey to a cramped office behind the smaller of the club's two main stages.

"Homemade anisette?" he asked, producing a bottle of brown liquid from a squeaking desk drawer. Mickey shook her head as he poured a small glass for himself. "Let me save you some time and trouble, my dear." He sipped slowly and dabbed at his lips with certain daintiness. "I know why you're here. And please send my best to your honored mayor. But let me be forthright. I'm just a businessman, an entrepreneur, if you will. A purveyor of musical entertainment and legal libations to those of age. As to the matter that concerns you, I don't know. I don't want to know. I don't need to know. And if you ask me if I can help you the answer will be 'No'. But so your trip here is not wasted, may I offer you some complimentary passes? The Female Beatles are here next week."

Mickey smiled. "I was told that although you don't know anything, it's possible you might know someone who knows something. The name of *that* someone would be extremely useful and would keep you out of any further discussions." She took off her sunglasses and hoped her eyes looked better than they felt.

"That someone, as you call him, unfortunately does not exist in this case." He sipped at the liquid which looked paler in the shaft of sunlight that now cut across the room. "Something terrible has happened. How this has happened we don't know. Conclusions have been reached, perhaps in error, and many theories abound. There are people, and I know I don't have to tell *you* this, but there are people who will use this, this – *incident*, if I may, to embark on courses of action that will be of benefit to them and their cronies, both in terms of monetary enrichment and, of course, power of a kind." He looked into the half-empty glass as if an answer floated there. "You are in a difficult position. You have, perhaps, been counseled to minimize things as a way of keeping the peace but you see that course of action, again perhaps, as in conflict with your sworn duty to enforce the law and maintain order. This I can understand."

Tony drained the last of the anisette in one gulp, inhaled deeply and leaned back in his ancient desk chair. "Let me tell you this:

the genie is not yet out of the bottle. But he has both hands on the rim and will soon be free if the stopper is not quickly replaced. The chances of a deliberate act, in my humble opinion and experience, are quite small. Perhaps even non-existent. But very often, people seeking power and money acquire it most quickly through conflict." He set the empty glass gently on the desk. "They may choose to create the conflict but they would prefer for the conflict to create itself. An accident, perhaps, a momentary lapse in judgment or even an unfortunate misadventure. If you value *my* advice, then it is to follow the example of another great Roman, Pontius Pilate, and wash your hands of this completely and quickly. The longer you don't, the more the situation can be taken advantage of by unscrupulous individuals and the more you will be dragged into a battle that is not of your making. I am a showman and so I understand drama. Better to ring down the curtain as soon as you can and send all the actors home. Should any interested parties inquire, I will vouch for your diligence and, more importantly, your impartiality."

He dabbed again at his mouth with the linen napkin. "Now, you are a very lovely girl for not being of Italian descent. Such loveliness should never be threatened or endangered. My friends in the music business are calling this the Summer of Love. My advice to you, as they say in L.A., is to see that only love is made here this summer, not war. I assume it was Ronald Dunn that sent you to see me?" Mickey nodded. "I thought so. Good kid. They broke him though, the Army did. Whether it was the jungle or the *facacta* discharge they gave him, who knows? He was like, ya know, Jack Armstrong, the All-American Boy before he joined up. God, ya should'a seen him throw a baseball, catch a pass or run a race. 'Ronnie the Rocket' they used to call him. I thought for sure I'd be watching him play for the Phillies by now or maybe even the Iggles. He used to sing Sunday Mass at St. Elizabeth's. But now…" Tony folded his hands in front of him and fell silent.

Mickey stood. Tony remained seated.

"Thanks for the information" she said.

"But I provided no information," he replied. "Only opinions which, you may have heard, are like assholes – everybody has one."

"And they all stink. My dad used that line a lot. OK, if anybody asks, that's what I'll tell them," Mickey said.

Tony suppressed a laugh. "No one will ask," he said. "And give my regards to his royal highness, the Laundromat King of Long Beach Island." He lifted his hand in a friendly wave.

Mickey walked out of the office to find the boy waiting for her. He's just so damn skinny, she thought.

"You're radio's been going crazy out there, ma'am" he said. "I think maybe they might be looking for you."

Mickey mumbled something and hustled for the door.

Fifteen minutes later the Chevelle was a blue blur, flying over the causeway bridges, siren wailing and cherry toppers flashing. Arlene was calling on the radio saying someone named Doreen need to talk to her right away; that it was a real emergency and that it somehow involved Deputy Fairbrother. She braked hard and made the left toward Surf City then accelerated again past the neat squares of crushed seashell "lawns" and into downtown. There was just enough foot traffic that she had to slow down to avoid the oblivious pedestrians with their shopping bags and beach umbrellas. When a clear space opened ahead of her she gunned the Chevelle and laid on the horn for good measure. Outside the Ebb Tide Motor Hotel a queasy feeling settled in her gut. She whooped the siren a few times and drove up on the sidewalk until she was as close as she could get.

* * *

Doreen was standing in the tattered lobby, her face a mess of red blotches and tear-matted strands of recently dyed hair.

"I can't go in there," she half-sobbed.

"Doreen, what's going on?" Mickey asked.

"I did what you said," Doreen replied. "I called to wake him up at eleven but he didn't answer. I thought maybe was in the bathroom or taking a shower so I waited and called again at eleven-fifteen but he still didn't answer so, so I went up and knocked on the door."

"Doreen," Mickey said a little louder, "Just tell me what happened. Where's Deputy Fairbrother?"

Doreen was small and portly. A yellow housedress hung on her A-frame body like a tent. Her sloped shoulders carried a heavily pilled pink sweater whose sleeves reached only to her chubby forearms. She seemed incapable of answering directly and continued in a stuttering monotone narrative interrupted only by snot-wiping swipes of her right hand.

"I knocked for five minutes but he didn't answer the door. All I could hear was the TV on real loud. So I waited and then I, I – please don't tell Mr. Giacometti a'cause I'm not supposed to have one – I used a pass key to open the door. Then I ran down and tried to call you." Doreen was staring straight ahead either afraid or unable to make direct eye contact.

Mickey led her to one of the worn vinyl chairs and eased her into it. Then she got down on one knee and put her face directly in front of Doreen's.

"Where's Deputy Fairbrother, Doreen?" Mickey asked. "Is he here?"

Doreen Kuzma squeezed her eyes shut and pointed an index finger upward.

"OK," Mickey said. "Stay right here. Is anyone else upstairs right now?"

Doreen shook her head without unclamping her tightly contorted visage.

Mickey patted her on the hand, rose from her kneeling position and walked to the inside stair risers. She could hear the sound of the television from above. She unsnapped her holster and drew her pistol as she hugged the inside wall of the staircase. The TV noise got louder when she gained the first landing. She listened for movement. Hearing none, she took the second set of steps and paused at the interior hallway.

Only the sound of the television.

"Kaylen," she called. "Kaylen, it's Mickey. Chief Cleary. Kaylen, you OK in there?"

There was no reply so she grasped the pistol with both hands and extended her arms in front of her. She covered the twenty paces to the open door and peered in. An Aunt Jemima Syrup commercial was playing on the color picture tube of a new-looking Motorola Quasar. The turned up volume echoed against the walls and the patterned linoleum floor.

"Kaylen?" Mickey said again. She pushed the door hard on its hinges to make sure no one was lurking behind it.

Two more steps and she could see him. He looked like he had fallen asleep watching something. Mickey relaxed for a moment.

She looked for a light switch and found it to her right on the wall. An incandescent lamp glowed overhead and an ancient ceiling fan with dust-covered wooden blades began to turn. She spoke his name again, softly so as not to startle him. Then she saw the pillow and the blood.

"No, no, shit, shit, *shit*," she mumbled and brought the gun to her side. Each step closer told the story in greater detail. She put her hand on Kaylen's neck hoping for a pulse. She'd seen suicide attempts where the bullet traveled under the scalp or through a hollow sinus, stunning the victim without causing major damage. The skin was cold and there was no pulse. Mickey holstered her gun and knelt down next to the couch.

"Oh, Kaylen, buddy," she said with a heave. "Jesus, Kaylen. What the *fuck*?"

♦ ♦ ♦

Ronnie parked the Enfield behind the double storefront that housed Mary T's Notions & Sundries and Faunce's Soda Fountain which was hawking a sugary drink called Take-A-Boost with free samples outside. He slipped on the fatigue hat and mounted the outside stairs of the empty apartment that occupied the space above the Surf City News Agency, catty-corner from the motel. Pressed against the beige stucco and beneath the overhang of the flat, guttered roof he became nearly invisible.

Two men in shirts and sport coats were clambering up the wrought iron steps of the Ebb Tide's furthest corner. Ronnie saw the flash of holstered side arms as they reached ahead for the railing. A woman inside the entrance to the motel was crying hysterically. When Ronnie looked up again a room door at the far end of the second floor was open and one of the sport coats was stepping inside.

♦ ♦ ♦

Sesso pulled his piece and shouted "FBI!" into the darkened room. All the shades were drawn and at first he wasn't sure what he was seeing.

"Holy Mother of Christ," Speziale said a step behind him. "Look at all this shit."

The trove of souvenirs was like nothing Sesso had ever seen.

He put his back to one wall and let Speziale enter with cover. Then he pointed to the connecting door. They maneuvered around the plastic display cases and tables and bookended the portal. "FBI" Sesso said again. "We are armed and we will fire." They both listened for movement or reply but there was none, only the loud music of a TV jingle coming from the other room.

* * *

At the sound of a voice Mickey spun around and grabbed her weapon. Speziale entered first.

"Freeze, motherfucker," she said, leveling the barrel at his chin

"Ah, good Christ," he said.

Sesso followed just behind, his gun now braced with both hands in front of him. He stopped when he saw Mickey locked in a shooter's stance. Her eyes darted back and forth between the two of them. After a moment both men's arms came down together.

"Police." Mickey said first.

"FBI." Sesso and Speziale replied almost but not quite simultaneously

"Both of you, drop your weapons," Mickey said. "And I mean right fucking now."

For an instant the words hung in the air until Sesso spoke. "FBI, Chief. We're lowering our weapons and I suggest you do the same before something extremely embarrassing happens here." Mickey held her stance

"Tell me what the fuck are FBI agents doing in Surf City?" Mickey asked, her gaze hard on the shorter Sesso who was obviously doing the talking for both of them.

"Easy, Chief". Sesso answered. "It is Chief Cleary I assume. Ease that barrel down and we'll tell you."

Sesso and Speziale holstered their pieces. Only then did Mickey lower her gun so it pointed just below Sesso's knees.

"Now, who are you guys?" she barked. "And, again, what are you doing in my town and in this apartment?"

"Special agents Charlie Sesso and Steven Speziale, Federal Bureau of Investigation, Philadelphia Field Office," Sesso responded. "We're both going to reach in slowly and show you our creds." They produced their matching badges and ID wallets and handed them to Mickey, who looked at them and then at the two men several times before handing them back. "This is your deputy we're also going to assume?"

"How about you let me ask the questions first, OK?"

There were approaching sirens outside and Mickey glanced toward the window.

"She already called for back-up," Sesso said to Speziale. "Jablonski said she was a smart cop."

Mickey was momentarily confused. "How do you guys know Jablonski?" she asked.

Before they could answer there were footsteps on the stairs and then pounding down the hallway. Behind her two Ship Bottom officers entered with guns drawn.

"Nobody move," the younger officer said. Mickey recognized his voice.

"It's, OK, I've got this, Al," she replied.

"Oh, jeez, Mick," she heard him say. "Is that Kaylen?"

The young officer grabbed a small metal trash can and vomited into it. Sesso pointed to a hook on the wall. A neatly ironed deputy's uniform was on a wooden hanger, badge affixed and recently polished. A gun belt with its empty holster lay coiled on the small wooden table beneath it. The shiny brass name tag was set next to the holster, resting on its clasp like a museum display card. "K. T. Fairbrother" stood out in etched black relief.

Mickey was trying to hold it together but the sudden presence of the emetic aroma was clinging to her like a wet sheet. A second Ship Bottom officer appeared at the door. Mickey turned to him.

"Dale," she said, "Get your partner and his bucket out of here. I've got the scene. Thanks for helping me out."

"Sure, Mick," he replied and helped his colleague to his feet. "We'll be downstairs. You OK with these two?" Mickey nodded and they and the bucket disappeared through the door. Mickey turned on a small table fan and her head began to clear.

"Ah, not to make a big deal of it, Chief, but actually *we've* got the scene," Sesso said. Mickey thought his partner looked confused but he didn't speak.

"And how exactly do you figure that, Agent-"

"Charlie Sesso," he responded. "Like I said, both Steve and I are assigned to the Philadelphia F.O. and we're part of a Joint Task force on organized crime with Philly P.D. We report directly to

Commissioner Jablonski whom we met with last night. I believe you also know him or, at least, he indicated he knows both you and your father."

The air was clearer but Mickey's mind was racing. She knew what he was doing. Using their first names. Personal connections. Family ties. Just two good cops that are on your side. Nothing to worry about. Something, she knew, was definitely wrong.

"The only organized crime in Surf City is the price of suntan lotion and summer rentals," she snapped. "What are you guys really doing here?"

The one named Steve shot her new friend Charlie a look. "This is certainly not how we'd prefer you to learn of it," he said, "but your deputy was a C.I. for us. We came down here specifically to meet with him on a matter of some importance."

"Kaylen Fairbrother was a confidential informant for the FBI? You can't really expect me to believe that-"

"Feel free to call Commissioner Jablonski yourself to verify if you'd like. He expressed to us a certain personal fondness for you and a deep respect for what you've been through."

Now Mickey was reeling. This guy was good, she thought, although his partner was acting as if this was all news to him. She looked at Kaylen's body.

"I've got evidence envelopes and bags for his hands in my cruiser. I'll be right back. Don't touch anything. I'm waiting for the State M.E. on another case – looks like he'll need to handle this one as well."

Sesso nodded. "Certainly appears to be a suicide."

"Appears?" Mickey replied. "As opposed to what?"

Sesso shrugged. "As opposed to something else. Forensics are a cop's best friend. Have you secured the weapon? I assume we'll find the deputy's service revolver somewhere close by."

Mickey hesitated. "I haven't touched anything but his neck checking for a pulse. I'll get my evidence kit. As I said, don't disturb my scene."

"Wouldn't think of it, Chief," Sesso replied. "We'll just take a peek in the other room until you get back. Hands off, like you said."

Mickey looked at Speziale. "Do you always let him do the talking?" she asked.

"I'll let you know if I have something to say," he replied. "I

usually find listening more productive in these situations."
Mickey turned and walked to the door wondering what exactly he meant by "these situations."

Ronnie pressed his back to stay in the shadow of the roofline. After they talked to Mickey he watched as the two Ship Bottom cops get back in their car and, after several back-ups and pull-forwards, head south toward Division Avenue. He pulled the slender spotter's scope from his breast pocket and glassed the surroundings. A man standing just off the knot of bystanders caught his attention. He was dressed like a tourist Ronnie thought but then he realized that was wrong; he was dressed like someone who wanted to *look* like a tourist but really didn't know how. He'd gotten the black, over-the-calf socks right but the shiny brown wing-tips gave him away. Ronnie was sure he wasn't a cop or a Fed but he knew he didn't belong. And he seemed quite interested in the activity at The Ebb Tide.

♦ ♦ ♦

After filling out several sheets of paper and sketching a crude diagram Mickey produced a bulky Polaroid Land camera and took pictures from several different angles. The flashbulbs sizzled and then crumpled with each one. Sesso watched as she took a sheet from a narrow closet and placed it over the lifeless and stiffening form. He didn't like the Chief's tone or her demeanor but he kept a concerned, sympathetic look on his face. "Is there a funeral parlor in Surf City?" he asked.

"No," Mickey answered. "He'll have to be taken to McTear's in Loveladies. I'll call the owner and tell him to get a hearse here right away."

"I'll go with the body," Sesso said, "And Steve will stay here to help you finish securing the scene." He saw Mickey look at her watch and a dismayed expression appear on her face. Sesso checked his own: it was well past eleven.

"I'll be there shortly after you," Mickey said to him. "Nothing happens until I get there. Is that understood?"

Sesso ground his teeth a little but spoke softly. "I understand,

Chief. I can fill you in more about the deputy's role in our investigation at that time. McTear's you said?"

"Yes," Mickey replied. The owner's name is Frank. I'll call him from the lobby so he understands as well. I have to check on something important but I'll be right back. I want to be here when they take him out."

"OK, we'll say it's your scene, Chief Cleary, but it is a federal investigation. We're here to give you our full support and whatever resources the Bureau can provide. Given the circumstances, the M.E. may want to cede jurisdiction to the Bureau and its superior forensics capabilities. Just to be on the safe side." Mickey muttered something he couldn't make out. He watched as she laid her hand on the deputy's covered shoulder.

She knelt for a moment then stood and walked out.

When she had gone Speziale turned with his palms upraised. "Charlie, exactly what the fuck was that?"

"Grab the uniform," Sesso said. "I'll explain later."

Mickey hung up the phone at the front desk and put her arms around Doreen.

"I'm so sorry, Chief," she hiccupped. "I should have checked on him. Maybe I-"

"There's nothing you could have done, Doreen, Nothing. I'm sorry you had to find him that way." Doreen let out a muffled sob and leaned against the outer door. Mickey walked outside to the Chevelle. A tanned older man in a light blue-striped seersucker suit approached her.

"My office tells me you've been looking for me," he said. "I'm Dr. Gene Galasso, the State's M.E. I understand you have a body you want me to look at?"

Mickey was momentarily flustered but quickly recovered. She reached out to shake his hand. "Sorry about wrecking your vacation, doc. I'm on my way to pick up the body I contacted you about but now there's another one upstairs here I need you to handle as long as you're in town." Galasso looked confused. "Do you know McTear's Funeral Home in Loveladies?" she asked.

"Yes. It's only a few blocks in from our place on the beach, actually," he said.

"They're sending a hearse."

"For which body?"

Mickey realized she hadn't thought it all the way through. The hearse would have to take Kaylen. It would either have to come back for the kid or she'd need to figure out something else.

"The one upstairs," she said. "I know it's confusing, but now I have two bodies. The one I originally called you about and this one which I just discovered. You can examine the scene if you want. There's a federal agent upstairs who can help you. I'll be right back. Please don't let them take the body out before I get back here." Galasso still appeared confused.

"I usually don't need to be involved in deaths from natural causes."

Mickey couldn't help herself and laughed. "I'm sorry," she said. "I'll explain everything when I come back. But I can assure you, natural causes have nothing to do with either one."

♦ ♦ ♦

Petroni figured he had waited long enough and was on his way back to City Hall to confront the mayor again when he saw the commotion at The Ebb Tide and the Police Chief's distinctive squad car. He watched her get in and roll away slowly down the street. Without lights or siren, he noted. Petroni downshifted the Jag into second and followed several car lengths behind. She made a couple of lefts and then pulled into a parking lot behind two adjoining buildings. He idled as she walked up to the back door of the one on the left. Then he put the Jag in Park and opened the door.

♦ ♦ ♦

Ronnie watched until the hearse pulled up. One of the sport coats had stepped outside and appeared to be scanning the small crowd of onlookers. Along the Mekong River, Ronnie's platoon had avoided annihilation several times by realizing quickly enough when friendly appearing villages were waiting VC traps. "Feeling the vibe," one of the machine gunners had christened the preternatural feeling that things weren't right. He thought of the small group of people clustered in or around the Ebb Tide at the moment. Several seemed to be decidedly out of place. He figured he'd watch and wait until he saw Mickey's cruiser again but now he was most interested in the two gun-toting sport coats he'd first spied sitting at Bill's Luncheonette. To the casual eye the hubbub was just tragic small-town excitement and nothing else. But Ronnie knew there was something else going on. Something churning like a storm offshore. He couldn't say exactly what it was or when it would manifest itself, but he was, he realized, definitely feeling the vibe.

NINETEEN
Surf City

THERE WAS A SMALL line of impatient patrons waiting in front of Willie's Beachfront Liquors when Mickey drove by. Some looked at their watches, one or two cupped their hands against the store windows trying to peer inside. An older woman at the end of the line wore a large, floppy hat and it rotated slowly like a sunflower as she followed the cruiser's path past the storefront and around the corner.

Mickey had to bang several times on the door before Little Willie's face appeared in the square glass pane. She heard him jiggling the lock.

"Come on, Willie," she said. "Quit stalling." The door was still not open when she felt a shadow cross her back. Her hand went to her holster as she turned around. A man in a shirt and tie was less than two feet from her. He had slicked back thinning hair which was gray only at the temples. It looked like a dye job, she thought. The little dents on his nose told her he usually wore glasses. In his left hand he held a legal size paper which flapped in the freshening breeze.

"Chief Cleary," he said. "I assume you know who I am."

"I don't have any idea who you are," Mickey replied sharply. "But you better show some ID pretty quick or someone may have to ID *you*." The man looked shocked and stepped back.

"I left a message with your deputy yesterday of my arrival and my urgent need to speak with you about Dante D. Ragone, Jr., the decedent whose remains you illegally commandeered yesterday and are illegally holding at present."

Mickey kept one hand on her holster and put the other on her hip. "I'd be a little careful there counselor about leveling accusations based on hearsay and tenuous assumptions."

"Ah, so you do know who I am."

"I'm a law enforcement professional making a rapid and accurate assessment of identity and motive based on prior information. A. Louis Petroni, Esquire, legal eagle for Danny Rags. Didn't the kids used to call you Artie? My dad said they-"

"Where is the body, Chief Cleary?"

"You have a writ?"

"I have a *right*. A grieving father has a right. What you've done is-"

"Completely within my purview and in my jurisdiction. And you know it. So if you think I'm going to start quivering over a piece of paper and some high school Latin you can go back to South Philly right now and tell Danny Rags he sent the wrong guy."

Petroni was about to answer when Little Willie came around the corner, a ring of keys in his hand. He looked like a badly made bed.

"He here to help you move it?" Willie asked. "'Cause I ain't touchin' it. That's bad juju. "

Petroni stepped forward but Mickey blocked him. "Mr. Petroni was just leaving." she said.

"Not until Mr. Petroni sees the body," Petroni replied.

"Who's Mr. Petroni?" Willie asked. "*This* yutz?"

"I am the Ragone family attorney and I demand to see the decedent's remains."

Mickey held her arm out. "Stay right there, Artie" she said. "The State M.E. is waiting for this body at a mortuary in Loveladies. If he says there's nothing for him to investigate after seeing it, you can have it. I'll even help you load it in your trunk. Your car probably fits at least one body, maybe two, huh, Artie?"

"Meet you inside, Chief," Willie said. He unlocked the door and disappeared.

"Alright, let's go," said Petroni. "Ladies first."

Mickey sensed something was wrong as soon as they passed the Schlitz display by the counter. There was trickle of water was on the cement floor. She followed it towards the walk-in cooler in the back. The trickle became a puddle and the puddle became a lake as they approached the heavy insulated door. The exhaust fan was running at high rpm's and a frosty mist billowed from the open door. Inside, Willie was cursing.

"The City's gonna pay for this," Willie shrieked. "All of it. I ain't coverin' none of this. No way. Not when I did you a freakin' favor, Chief."

Mickey stepped inside. Her shoes made a slurping sound with each step. Scattered on the cooler floor were dented and empty beer cans and toppled cases. Foam mixed with condensation and the interior smelled like a frat house carpet after a party.

"You can't possibly mean to tell me," Petroni was saying.

Mickey said nothing because there was nothing to say. The body bag was gone.

"Don't look at *me*," Willie said. "I just got here and ain't been in here since closing yest'day afternoon. And I locked it up myself."

Petroni was blathering about filing a motion with the Circuit Court judge and throwing out terms like malfeasance, criminal negligence and dereliction of duty. Mickey instantly developed a screaming headache and could not seem to hear herself think. Finally it all became too much.

"Shut up, Artie," she yelled. "You too, Willie. I don't know how this happened but whoever is responsible is in for some bad shit, that much I promise." She walked to the cooler and then back to the counter. "You're shut down the rest of the day," she barked at Willie. She looked at Petroni. "You give me a number where I can reach you and you sit by the phone until I call you. You give me six hours to get the body back and it's yours. Promise. But if you start making any phone calls that start with 215, the deal is off. Same thing if I start seeing black cars with Pennsylvania plates come across that causeway."

"I really don't think you're in any position to-"

"Take it or leave it, counselor."

Petroni shrugged. "Six hours. Mickey. Seeing as we're on a first name basis now." He patted his pants for his keys. "I'm at the Surf City Hotel. They'll put the call through to my room."

Mickey waited until he exited. "Who else has access?" she asked Willie.

"The old lady has spare keys but she's at her sister's in Waretown," he answered. "That's it, I swear."

"Button it up and go home," she said. "And make sure you can show me both sets of keys next time I ask."

"But I got customers outside," Willie whined.

"Tell them the cooler broke down. Nobody likes warm beer."

Mickey walked out into the noonday sun and fired up the cruiser for the short trip back to the Ebb Tide. She just hoped she didn't run in to the mayor.

* * *

The last thing Mickey had wanted to do was send the two FBI agents with Kaylen's body. But now, she knew, she had bigger fish to fry. She'd made a cursory check of the rooms at The Ebb Tide and sealed the doors with yellow tape. Eddie Giacometti asked if the city was going to reimburse him for lost business. Doreen was almost catatonic and Eddie wouldn't let her leave early.

Loveladies Neighborhood
Long Beach Township

The interior of McTear's Mortuary & Crematorium had not been updated since the 1950s, Sesso surmised. He watched as the owner and the M.E. lifted the body bag on to the steel embalming table and unzipped it. Decomposition was already starting and old man McTear opened a window and pulled the chain on a ceiling fan. The M.E. brought out a little tape recorder and a bulky Polaroid from a black satchel he'd carried in. He took some shots with the Polaroid and then set it down. Then he pulled on some cheap looking rubber gloves and his hands disappeared inside the bag.

Sesso had brought in the uniform and gun belt. While McTear and the doc were fussing with the corpse he rummaged through the pockets. He removed the deputy's wallet, a few crumpled dollar bills and a set of keys and put them on a tray. He checked the blouse pockets and found a folded piece of paper. He peeked over at the embalming table. Both men were still hunched over the bag. Sesso angled his back to them and unfolded the note. He thought briefly, but only briefly, about what he should do. A door opened and he heard Speziale's voice. He slipped the note into his coat pocket without a word.

◆ ◆ ◆

Mickey stopped at the station. She had called McTear's to let them know there would not be a second set of remains coming today. She spoke briefly with Galasso who seemed concerned about the involvement and subtle pressure from the FBI in what he considered at present a State and local matter. She placated him with a promise to take it up with their superiors as soon as possible. She asked about the evidence kit and was shocked when he said that Agent Sesso had taken the sealed case for safekeeping until Galasso was ready to take it back to his laboratory in West Trenton.

It was starting to slip away from her, Mickey thought. And now she was by herself. She decided to go find the mayor and let him know the body was gone, just not in the way she intended. Then she'd go look for Ronnie.

◆ ◆ ◆

"I'm starving," Speziale said as they drove back from the funeral home. "I mean, come on, three hours for a guy that obviously shot himself. Should'na taken more than five minutes to make that call. What was he doing?"

Sesso checked the rear-view mirror and made a series of right turns. "He thought our Chief Cleary was going to deliver another body for him to examine. Rags's kid you have to figure. Then old McTear gets a phone call and says the M.E. can head back to his beach house. That there wouldn't be a second body today."

"There's a burger place," Speziale said and pointed over the dash.

"Let's get a room for tonight and call Jablonski," Sesso replied. "I'm working on an idea. Then we'll get some grub."

"There's another place in Surf City," Speziale said. "Or the Sea Spray in Beach Haven. That's real close. It's not fancy but it's clean."

"Let's go to Ocean City and stay someplace nice. PPD's paying, so maybe the Port-O-Call. They got a good restaurant there. Steaks."

Apparently placated, Speziale sat back and yawned. Sesso fingered the note in his pocket and decided it would keep for now.

Old Marlton Pike
Lakehurst, NJ

Yansick's Garage had one ancient pump, no actual garage bay and sold Atlantic gasoline for 24 cents a gallon. Patsy Cleary handed the restroom key back to the snaggle-toothed woman who sat behind the counter. It had a Studebaker hubcap attached to it and clanged when she dropped it next to her. "Four dollars and fitty," she said. Patsy handed her a five.

"How far to Long Beach Island?" he asked.

"A ways," she said. "Probaly be there just before dark figurin' one more stop for gas and drainin' your dragon."

"Can I have my change?' Patsy asked

"Surcharge," the crone answered, which made Patsy laugh.

"Surcharge? For what?"

"Directions."

Patsy grabbed a new road atlas from a wire display stand and started to leave. "Directions," he said to the old woman and shook it at her.

Surf City

Mickey looked at her watch. Her planned quick stop at the station was going on two hours now. And other than the morning's doughnut, she hadn't eaten anything all day.

She boxed the last of Kaylen's desktop baseball souvenirs and any other personal effects she could find. She felt bad about going through his drawers, but other than his Yankees collection his effects were as much a cipher to her as he had been. She wasn't buying the informant crap the two Guinea feds were feeding her. She'd tried Patsy's apartment but got no answer. She was hoping he could call in a few favors and get her some dope on either one of them. Sesso was the one that worried her. If she didn't reach Patsy by six, she thought, she'd have one of the local cops do a welfare check on his place. A call to Jablonski's office was answered politely but she was given the "he's in a meeting" kiss-off. She got a little further when she called back said she was his niece – she *had* called him Uncle Jabo when she was little – and got to leave a message to call her as soon as he was out. And she had Mayor Tunell working on findings Kaylen's parents or his sister to break the tragic news. She hadn't seen or heard from Ronnie since she'd left his place that morning. A drive past his shack showed no signs of him. Mickey moved to the wall and took down the signed picture and placed it in the box. She looked at Kaylen's stack of 45's and felt a mix of sadness and anger welling up. She just couldn't figure what angle the Feds were playing with the C.I. bullshit but she knew that somehow she was the one being played. She was certain that Sesso had made up the story on the spot just based on his partner's reaction. But why go to all that trouble for something she knew they couldn't possibly back up. She sifted through the stack of records, put one on the player and tapped the ON button. That's when the phone rang.

"I have the solution to your problem, I believe," a man's voice said.

"Doc?"

"I doubt your phone is wiretapped but I hope you'll forgive me if I don't identify myself formally."

There was a static crackle as the tone arm dropped and the needle met the vinyl. The Young Rascals poured forth, still unsure.

Mickey turned down the volume and sat at Kaylen's desk.

"Tell me you have the body," she said.

"I said I have the solution to your problem. I never said I have the body or any body, for that matter."

"What is the solution to my problem, then?"

"You have a very short time to cast oil on the troubled waters, as it says in the Bible. If you act intelligently things will return to something like the status quo and a lot of unnecessary bloodshed will be avoided."

"What do you want?"

"Meet me tonight, after dark obviously. I will have arrangements in place and I will bring what you need."

"Where?"

"At our old friend Barney's parking lot. You can use the cruiser but no lights or flashers and do come by yourself. If I see other cars or officers our deal is off."

"It's a State Park," Mickey said. "It closes at dusk."

"The gate will be open. Go to the far end and wait. You wouldn't listen once. Try to do better this time." The line went silent.

Mickey replaced the receiver. She clicked on the police band and raised Central Dispatch.

"This is Surf City One. Tell Ship Bottom One I need them to

watch the ranch from eight until about nine. My twenty will be at Barnegat Light."

"Copy that, Surf City One. Wait. Ship Bottom is down a man. Beach Haven will have to do it. Eight to nine by Beach Haven. Copy that." Arlene was having a long day. "And Surf City One?"

"Yes, Arlene?"

"So sorry about Deputy Fairbrother. Nice kid. Dispatch out."

The record had reset itself and Mickey turned the volume back up.

Complicated, she remembered. That was the word he used. And we're not very good at complicated.

Ocean City, NJ

The lights on the Port-O-Call Motor Hotel sign shined an iridescent aquamarine in the fading light even though it was still half a mile away. The gray sedan with the two men in the front seat slowed. The single motorcycle rider gunned the throttle and pulled alongside them. Sesso looked over but the sun was now just above the horizon and all he could make out was a silhouette. The bike stayed with them for a few seconds then braked suddenly, made a hard right turn and sped off.

"What was that asshole doing?" Speziale asked.

Sesso puffed on a Raleigh. "Who the fuck knows? Let's get checked in, make some calls and then spend a little of Mayor Tate's money on dinner."

Speziale rolled the window down all the way to clear the curling blue smoke."You want to call Jablonski or should I?"

"You can," Sesso answered. "But let's you and me go over what we have first." The hotel's vertical sign had a smaller illuminated PARKING one just below it. Sesso braked and looked for an empty space. "We'll stop at the bar on the way in. Get a drink and watch the sunset."

"The sun sets on the bay side," Speziale replied.

"Then we'll watch the tide go out."

"But the tide will be coming in."

Sesso blew out more smoke, rolled down the window and tossed out the butt. "Stevie," he said, "I love you like a brother but you are without a doubt the most annoying Dago I have ever known. For that, the first round's on you."

TWENTY
Surf City

THE OLD MAN WAS on duty when Petroni got back to the Surf City Hotel.

"Here a little early, aren't you?" Petroni asked.

"Shirley's got a bladder infection. Has to go every ten minutes else she pees her britches. Then she smells like the trough in the men's room at Connie Mack."

Petroni pushed a folded five across the desk. "I have to make some calls. Be nice if they weren't all toll calls."

"I'll make sure I wipe 'em off your bill, if that's what you mean."

"That's what I mean," Petroni replied. "I'll let you know when I'm done."

"Big business deals I 'spose? You look like the type."

"Yeah," Petroni said as he turned for the hallway. "You could say that."

* * *

Shots Caputo was stretched out on the bed in Petroni's room when the lawyer opened the door. "Make yourself at home, why don't you?" Petroni said. He closed the door behind him and set the chain. Caputo doubled the pillow under his head.

"Just be glad I work for Danny and not Carmine," Caputo said. "Or this little conversation would be over already." Petroni scanned the room. The only window was plugged with a bulky air-conditioner.

"The old man let you in?" Petroni asked.

"Does it matter?" Caputo replied. "I'm in, aren't I?"

Petroni did not see a weapon but knew that it was rare for Shots to be unarmed. Even in the company of supposedly trusted associates. He sat down in the wooden chair by the writing desk.

"So help me out here," Caputo said and put both hands behind his head. Petroni relaxed a little. "Now, you and Danny both think that Patsy's kid is the one did Little Rags. But you think she didn't count on him washing up on her beach?"

"It makes the most sense at the moment," Petroni said and loosened his tie.

"What doesn't make sense to me is that she called the M.E. 'Course now that the body's disappeared…"

"Yes. I'd say that was rather too convenient, wouldn't you? Gotta giver her credit, though. Shifts suspicion from her pretty quickly. Makes it look she tried to do the right thing."

Caputo sat up and reached into his pocket for his pack of Winston's. Petroni tensed visibly.

"Relax, Artie," Caputo said with a chuckle. "Jesus, you gotta trust somebody." He withdrew a cigarette and took a pack of matches from the table by the bed. Petroni took a deep breath while he lit it. "But that assumes that she knows we were the ones shot Patsy."

Petroni arched an eyebrow. "We?"

"Yeah, OK, Artie, that she knows *I* was the one that shot Patsy. On Danny's orders. Happy now?" Caputo took a couple quick puffs. "So this is *un fare vendetta*, like back in the old country - you hurt my dad, I hurt your kid. It's a pretty gutsy move. She'd have to be sure Danny would go after that rat bastard Rocca. But Jesus, Artie, Patsy took that slug how many years ago?"

"Danny always says revenge is a dish best served cold," Petroni replied. He rose and crossed to the tiny closet making sure Caputo could see his hands. He peeled off his shoes, slipped on the Sinatra robe and sat back down. "I told Danny I think he was right. You know him and his instincts. Now that I've been here and met her, I think she did it herself or she at least helped get it done."

Caputo took a slow drag and blew two perfect smoke rings. "This ain't about something else, is it Artie?"

"What is that supposed to mean?"

Caputo picked up the amber glass ashtray and tapped the cigarette on it. "You've hated Patsy Cleary since we were kids. When he welshed on the deal the first thing you wanted to do was grab the girl – what was she then, eleven, maybe twelve?"

"That has nothing to do with this," Petroni replied. He took his own pack of Pall Malls from the desk and lit one.

Caputo stubbed his out. "Even smart lawyers have feelings," Caputo said. He picked at something on his nose several times. "Hot or cold, payback is a powerful thing."

Petroni blew smoke out through his nostrils. "My feelings aren't the issue here. Little Rags is dead and that can't go unanswered. I got it straight from Danny. He said if she did it take her out. Didn't even blink. Can you handle it or are *your* feelings about capping a girl an issue here?" Several airline miniature bottles of gin were lined up on the desk. Petroni opened one and sipped.

Caputo laid back down and rubbed his eyes. "When?" he asked.

"As soon as we can," Petroni answered. He drained the bottle in one swallow and reached for another. "I don't want her dead, though. Definitely not dead. Not even dying if you can help it. I think our friend in the Pines deserves a little live entertainment before he finalizes the arrangements." A thin smile crossed his face. "Bowker will be there to accept delivery tonight. Let's hope he hasn't started on the 'shine yet."

Caputo raised himself from the bed and smoothed his wrinkled shirt and slacks. Petroni downed the second bottle of gin. "I figured this is the way it would go," Caputo said. "I got something in the works already. I'll call you when it's done,"

Petroni shook his head. "No. Stop here on your way back. Leave a message at the desk that the shirts have been delivered. And give the old man a five. I'll pay you back tomorrow." Caputo nodded and went to the door. He unhooked the chain and looked back at Petroni.

"If you happen to talk to Juice in the meantime, don't mention this conversation," Caputo said. "And go easy on the gin. A drunk *consigliere* won't be of much help." He opened the door and quietly departed.

A. Louis Petroni usually thought of himself as the smartest guy in any room but he was surprised at how this plan was advancing almost on its own. His contacts in the State Senate and Atlantic County assured him that casino gambling would be up and running sooner than later. They had it all figured out. Forget the ponies at Garden State and Freehold, they said, this was going to be Las Vegas with a white sand beach and a sparkling blue ocean instead of a crappy desert and a few cactuses. The high rollers would be standing in line to get in. They were already lining up big money guys in New York who wanted part of the action. They were even discussing the need for a bigger airport and direct rail lines. The graft alone would be worth millions. And Petroni saw himself in the middle of it or maybe – just maybe - at the top of it. Danny would never cut him in, he knew that. But if Danny got tied to the unsolved murder of a police chief at some opportune time, well, there just might be a managerial vacancy to be filled. Petroni smiled the smile of someone who was sure he was going places. He picked up the phone and dialed the old man at the front desk. "Send me down some tonic water," he said and glanced at the plastic cups. "And a real glass. A clean one, preferably." He was tired and the gin was starting to percolate. Petroni puffed on his Pall Mall and relaxed a little. His work, he decided, was all but done.

PORT O'CALL MOTOR HOTEL
Ocean City

"You're shitting me," said Speziale. "No. Jablonski's never going to buy this. No way in hell will he think the girl is good for this. She's a cop, Charlie, for Chrissakes."

"Might not be the first time something like this happened down there. The name Harry Anglemyer ring a bell?"

"No."

"Look it up on the 'fiche when we get back to Philly. I'll buy you some fudge on the boardwalk for the trip."

"I don't understand," Speziale said. "What does fudge have to do-"

"Forget it," Sesso replied. He reached into the pocket of his sport coat and pulled out the folded note. "I liberated this from Deputy Fairbrother's uniform blouse while we were at the funeral home." He handed it to Speziale who carefully unfolded it and then held it under the table lamp to read.

"No fuckin' way."

"Read it out loud," Sesso prompted.

"I had to protect Mickey. I'm sorry. K.T.F."

"Better than a smoking gun," Sesso said. "A deathbed confession or, at the very least, a deathbed implication."

"You're sure he wrote this and not you, Charlie?"

"Easy there, partner," Sesso replied testily. "We can have the graphics lab compare it to samples from his entries the police logbook. I'd bet the pen and the tablet he used are still there at his place. There will be no doubt, I guarantee it. We break this one and we're not Field Agents for very much longer, *capisce*?"

Speziale rubbed a hand over his face and handed back the note "Jesus, this is just too much, Charlie."

"What's too much?" Sesso countered. "Ragone has her dad shot and damn near paralyzes him when he won't do collections anymore. She waits a long time, gets herself another job in law enforcement, sees an opportunity, whacks the kid and everybody including Danny immediately blames it on the Rocca's. She's a full-blooded Mick. What does she care if the noble descendants of Caesar kill each other over it?"

Speziale seemed unable to comprehend it all. The three martinis he'd downed at the hotel bar weren't helping. "I don't know, Charlie. Lot of what-if's and long-shot coincidences here if you ask me."

Sesso held up the note and raised an eyebrow.

"OK, so what do we do?"

"What *you* do, pal o'mine, is call the Commissioner and calmly explain what we have uncovered and what we believe to be the correct course of action."

"Which is what? That note'll never hold up."

"Which *is*, we find and interview Chief Cleary later this evening and then hold her for questioning in the demise of Dante D. Ragone, Jr. We can take her back to Philly tomorrow or we can let the State Police pick her up. Lock her in her own jail cell – that, Stevie, would be what's called poetic justice."

"But now there's no body, remember. Isn't there a little thing called *habeas corpus*?"

"Just proves my point," Sesso replied. "She, or maybe it was the deputy, took the body and disposed of it. Who knows, could be shark food by now. The ocean's a lot bigger than some landfill. Anyway, she's off scot-free without this note. I admit it's circumstantial, but it's still pretty damn incriminating."

"So why don't we just go back there right now?" he asked. "Talk to her, see what she has to say. I think there's way too many loose ends to lock her up, Charlie."

"Because Hizzoner's steaks will get cold if we do that. It may be a long night. We'll think much clearer on a full stomach." Sesso reached into a breast pocket. "I got this from the Ebb Tide." He produced a signed Mickey Mantle rookie card. Then he fished for something in the opposite pocket and held it out to Speziale. "This one's Mantle's 1964 Topps card," he said. "Take it, it's yours."

Speziale grimaced. "Nah, you keep it Charlie. I wouldn't feel right."

"*What*?" Sesso asked with a measure of incredulity. "Wouldn't feel right about what? Soon as the kid's buried all that baseball crap is going straight to the dump, some Goodwill box or his parents' attic. It's not like it's worth anything."

"Nah," Speziale said again. "You keep it. I'm more of an Eagles guy myself. You know, Chuck Bednarik or Pete Retzlaff. Now, what about ruling out other suspects? What about Patsy Cleary or even the Rocca's? Maybe it was just an accident?"

"From what I hear, Patsy's lucky if he can get to his own bathroom. He ain't smart enough to mastermind this and definitely not mobile enough to carry it out. Trust me partner, one of these days they'll find him dead in that apartment, five feet from where he pisses. Let's start with the girl. If it doesn't pan out we'll move up the chain from there. Few ruffled feathers, maybe, but no real harm done, right?"

Speziale massaged his brow. "OK," he said. "Let's go downstairs and eat. But no more liquor. I have to think this through."

Sesso refolded the note. He put it and the Topps card into his pocket.

Surf City

Mickey was startled to see Ronnie, leaning on a motorcycle behind her Chevelle.

"Really, I have to ask. How'd you ever talk them into *this*?" he said, nodding at the car. "In high school we called these suicide machines."

"Put a kid behind the wheel and it would be," she replied. "Anyway, I told them the crowds were getting younger and that they would respect a cop in a muscle car a lot more than one in a Ford like their old man drove." She pointed a thumb at the motorcycle. "Did you get that bike just to impress me?"

"Well, I got it *out* just to impress you."

"Well, it's working so far," she said. "Indian?"

"Nope. Enfield, 1964, made in England. 750 cc, twin engine, single carburetor. Climb a brick wall with it if you wanted to. Any luck locating your package?"

"Good news travels fast."

"There are a lot of tourists in town for this time of year in case you haven't noticed."

"A couple with badges," she said.

"All of them armed and dangerous by my recon," he replied. "You look tired. You eat supper?"

"Just on my way to grab something. I have a lead on my package I have to check out in a little while."

"Need a military escort?" he asked. "Well, ex-military, anyway."

Mickey laughed. "I'm still a cop in case you've forgotten. Fast car, powerful gun, trained and licensed in the use deadly force. I'm not exactly a damsel in distress."

"I never said that. I'm just saying we learned quick in Viet Nam that Charlie could go out alone because it was his jungle. This *isn't* your jungle – not yet anyway."

"Concern noted and appreciated. You might scoop the loop a few times around here while I'm gone. Still no sign of the red Mustang or the other kids in it. You can deduct the bike as an undercover expense."

"Nice that you assume I pay taxes."

"Nice that you assumed I was a dope dealer."

Ronnie smiled. "OK, but at least file a flight plan. Where's your LZ?"

"My what?"

"Your landing zone. Where are you going?"

"Barnegat Light."

"Kind of isolated out there at night. You sure you-"

"I'm sure," she said. "But I gotta get something to eat. Cream doughnuts and coffee will take girl only so far."

"Sorry about your deputy. I lost a few friends that way. Usually after they got home. You never know what somebody's really carrying around inside them."

"Doesn't make sense," Mickey said. "Not like he was someone who had a deep, dark secret or anything."

"We *all* have deep, dark secrets. But sorry nonetheless. Let me go grab you something and bring it back. Five minutes."

Mickey looked at her watch and then at the sky. "OK. Just not cold pizza and warm beer, OK? I'm only falling for that once."

Ronnie brushed his hair from his forehead and pawed at the sandy asphalt. Then he turned away and mounted the Enfield. It grumbled to life and left the scent of gasoline heavy in the air. It reminded Mickey of her father.

TWENTY ONE
Surf City

RONNIE KNELT IN FRONT of the open black case. He wrapped the more delicate parts in sections of oilcloth and put them in a dusty camouflage duffel bag. He'd gassed up the Enfield after leaving Mickey the burgers and Coke. He had lied to her about what time the sun set, exaggerating by a good thirty minutes at least. He opened the little compact and smeared the greasy mixture on his face, then on the backs of his hands. He traded his shorts for fatigues and pulled a long-sleeved green tactical over his head. He left the Coleman lit on the table and the stereo playing. Then he slipped the black thongs on his feet and walked out the door. He hoped he would have enough time.

The bay road took longer but it kept him out of sight for a while. The water was already dark and there were enough clouds to at least muffle the moonlight. Once he was out of Surf City he flaunted the speed limit only when he could see there was no traffic or parked cars in all directions ahead. He would have, he thought with some humor, a difficult time explaining to a patrolling beach cop what he was doing with the bag that was parachute-corded to the seat behind him. As he headed north, the only route left to him was Long Beach Boulevard which split the island like a spine. He cruised through North Beach without seeing anyone but had to slow down when a police car in Harvey Cedars decided to follow him. He half-expected the flashers when he approached the Loveladies neighborhood but it turned onto Ladybug Lane and disappeared. He saw only one other vehicle as he cleared Loveladies and the Boulevard became Central Avenue. Once he hit the numbered streets he accelerated and veered left onto Broadway which took him into Barnegat and dead-ended at the state park in the fading shadow of the one-hundred-and-sixty-nine foot lighthouse. Ronnie killed the engine and walked the bike to a dilapidated section of brown snow-fence and then laid it behind a dune. The bottom half of the lighthouse was painted white and still caught some of the last rays of the dwindling daylight. He unhooked the heavy bag and slung it on his shoulders, back-pack style.

Ronnie scanned the lot for any vehicles or activity. He circled the lighthouse twice at a distance then approached the entrance alcove in a low squat, taking the last twenty yards in a jungle crawl. Despite its rich history, the lighthouse was generally ignored by the locals and tended to only on occasion by the State. Vandalism was rare and so a *laissez-faire* attitude had settled around the edifice. The wooden door inside the entry alcove was already ajar when Ronnie reached it. He slid it open only enough to pass through the camo bag and then squeezed his thin frame inside. He pushed the door closed from the inside and set a large metal trash can against it, less as a doorstop than as an alarm.

He mounted the metal spiral staircase with its grated pie-shaped steps. There were two-hundred and seventeen of them between him and the lamp room. The center support pole creaked and swayed slightly as he ascended.

The lighthouse had been deactivated in 1944 and the Fresnel lens long-ago removed. Ronnie felt a cool breeze as he approached the lamp room and kept his head down when he finally mounted the last step. He found the place where he would have the most space, sat in a cross-legged Indian position and placed the bag between his knees. There was a little remaining ambient light but he didn't need it. It interfered with his concentration. He closed his eyes and unzipped the bag. Placing his hands inside he unwrapped and withdrew each piece in the exact reverse order from which they had been placed. He kept his eyes shut and worked without pause or effort. Each part fit together with incredibly small tolerances. Only an occasional click or the sound of sliding, oiled metal marked his progress. When all that remained was the Redfield 3-9x telescopic sight Ronnie opened his eyes. Then he rose to one knee and inched around the circular concrete floor until he found the view he was looking for. The M-14 weighed almost nine pounds but to Ronnie it was as weightless as one of his own arms.

◆ ◆ ◆

Mickey felt an odd sense of calm as she cruised the Boulevard. An occasional shopkeeper gave a friendly wave as the neon lights or megawatt bulbs of hamburger joints, salt-water taffy stores and souvenir shops wavered and then winked on. She passed The Ebb Tide and had to look away. All four windows in the Chevelle were rolled down and the wind whooshed through unimpeded causing the shotgun to rattle in its rack. She was beginning to understand the subtle magic of a beach town at night, she thought. What it was that put sand into people's shoes. As she followed the Boulevard north she breathed in the salt air and the unmistakable and uncapturable fragrance of the beach. Her scanner was on with the volume at a whisper. The Delco glowed. The AM tuner was set at the 770 mark, WABC out of New York, which the big antenna pulled in clearly. Summer songs played as she crossed each imaginary municipal division. Bruce Morrow was DJ'ing with his plugged-nose delivery. He liked the older stuff and Mickey thought of Kaylen. The Syndicate of Sound was pumping out "Hey Little Girl", a hit from the previous summer "Cousin" Brucie informed his listeners.

The academy had taught her about the "golden hours", the first forty-eight after a crime that usually decided whether it would ever be solved. She knew she had about twelve hours left and the clock was running. Her call to Petroni promised a resolution by midnight.

Long Beach Island was a barrier island, a fact she'd read in a black leather-bound volume Collier's Encyclopedia at the borough's tiny public library. Barrier islands came and went all the time, it said. Giant hurricanes, beach erosion, sea level changes – it was really only a matter of a few feet which determined whether it existed at all. In fifty years, someone at the U.S. Geological Survey had predicted, it would a giant sandbar; in a hundred, it would be the seafloor. Fifty years, a hundred years, forty-eight hours, she thought. Maybe none of it mattered that much in the long run.

She imagined Billy Tunell and his hundreds of washing

machines and driers underwater, covered in barnacles and being explored by perplexed skin divers someday.

This reverie carried her all the way to Old Barney, as the light was affectionately known, at the northern tip of the island. It guarded The Inlet, where the tide swept in and out twice each day and took only the intrepid and the foolhardy out into what Doc Juice had called "the damned Atlantic Ocean," when they had first stood by the ravaged corpse. It seemed like a lifetime ago right now.

The long triangular gate marking the entrance to Barnegat Light State Park was open half-way. She thought no one was there until her headlights caught the reflection of an older model station wagon with large wooden side-panels. Big enough to haul a body bag, she thought, and relaxed just a little. She killed the radio. A man stepped from the wagon as she approached, his hands raised in front of him in the classic "don't shoot" position. He had on a short-sleeved shirt and a faded fishing hat. Dark shorts and tennis shoes completed the ensemble.

"See, no flashers, no siren," Mickey said as she got out. She remained behind the car door just long enough to quietly unsnap her holster strap.

"You're a good kid, Mickey. You always were." Juice took one step and then stopped.

"You have my solution back there, Doc?" Mickey asked.

"I'm sorry about all this, kid. I really am. I tried to tell you. I tried really hard but you're just like your dad. You both worry too much about doing what's right and, when you look at it, sometimes what's right turns out to be all wrong." It concerned Mickey that he wasn't walking toward her. It was like he wanted her to come to him.

"Anybody with you, Doc?" she asked. "Anybody around back of the car maybe, or hiding inside it?"

Guidice put his arms down. "I never forgave myself for Mikey. All these years and I never did. I want you to know that. I think about it every day. Things were different back then. We didn't have all the fancy tests we have today. We had old tests and old docs and we flew mostly by the seat of our pants."

An image was forming in Mickey's head. A man standing by a hospital bed.

"Ninety-nine times out of a hundred, a kid with swollen glands has a virus or strep throat. I treated Mikey the way I treated a thousand other kids who all got better. But he was that one. That one where the swollen glands don't get better. Because it's not a virus or the strep, it's childhood lymphoma and by the time you figure it out it's too late."

"You were at my dad's bedside after he got shot. Why were you there, Doc?"

The little remaining light was fading fast and Guidice had moved to his left which took him further from the glow of Mickey's headlights and deeper into darkness.

"I tried to tell your dad what would happen, same way I tried to tell you. But you're just like Patsy. You see what you see and you decide you're right and after that nobody can tell you anything, even if it's to keep you safe."

"They shot my dad, didn't they?" Mickey said, louder now. "Danny Rags and that scumbag Caputo. They're the ones that shot my dad, aren't they, Doc? Why? Because he didn't do what they wanted? "

Guidice backed up until he was pressed against the grill of the wagon.

"They paid for your brother's treatments, kid. Thousands of dollars in doctors' and hospital bills and they paid them all. They used it to set the hook and then they reeled Patsy in like a fish. And when he wouldn't do a favor they asked they collected on the debt."

Mickey's head was swimming. She put her hand on the butt of her pistol and screamed into the blackness. "What did they want him to do? Tell me, you motherfucker or I'll shoot you right now. I swear to God."

"He was supposed to shoot another cop who had evidence on Danny. Just to send him a message. He didn't even have to kill him. Just get his attention. And he wouldn't do it, the dumb shit. He wouldn't do it. So they sent Patsy a message instead. I'm sorry, kid. I liked both of you."

"You worked for them. All these years. You worked for THEM. You *still* work for them, don't you?"

"All I ever did was fill out some death certificates. That's all. I never hurt anybody. I told you I'd sign one for you but you and your shanty-Irish stubbornness wouldn't have it. None of this would be happening if you'd a' listened. Like I said, I'm really sorry kid but now there's nothing I can-"

"Turn around you shamrock-shitting bitch." Mickey heard the raspy voice somewhere behind her. "And take your hand off your piece."

She pivoted on one foot to see a small man with a craggy face, wire-rimmed glasses and a large gun muzzled by a silencer. "You think you can call *me* a scumbag, you clap-ridden Harpie whore? I let your old man live with just a permanent reminder but you're gonna wish I'd killed you right here when you find out what you're in for next." She saw him lower his angle so the muzzle pointed toward her legs. She reached for her gun.

♦ ♦ ♦

The first thing they'd taught him in tactical weapons training was to never put your face close to the scope. The recoil would take out your eye in a hundredth of a second. Ronnie watched the scene below unfold with a detached calmness. His breathing slowed and his heart rate dropped. He had mistakenly focused on the man by the station wagon. Only the glint of car headlights off of a pair of metallic-framed glasses alerted him to the figure moving stealthily from behind the dunes. His index finger was on the guard, steady as the becalmed sea. He saw Mickey turn and in the same instant he caressed the trigger. The man with the glasses was saying something. It was never wise to put off the business at hand, Ronnie knew. Too much could go wrong in such a short period of time. He exhaled slowly and, when his lungs were empty, he squeezed.

* * *

Mickey hit the asphalt hard, her cheek finding broken shells and sand. The crack had been deafening. She instinctively felt for her legs fully expecting to feel shattered bone or pumping blood. She wasn't surprised that there was no pain yet – the shock, she knew, was too great for few seconds. A second crack and the ground exploded not ten feet from her. She curled up in a ball and started to inchworm her way toward the cruiser. At ground level she watched the scuffed whitewalls of the station wagon squeal past her and into the night. Gingerly she got to her knees. A quick survey told her all her parts were intact. There was a clanging metallic sound in the distance like someone banging a wooden spoon on a cheap metal pot. She pushed into a crouch and held her gun out in front of her, pointing it blindly into the darkness. "Police officer!" she yelled as loud as she could. "Stay where you are!" Her ears were still ringing as she stood up but she thought she heard someone calling her name.

TWENTY TWO

Port O' Call Motor Hotel
Ocean City

STEVEN ANTHONY SPEZIALE HAD been Charlie Sesso's partner, if such a thing existed inside the Bureau at all, for two years. Now he sat at the hotel room's fake-wood desk and watched the white surf break fifty yards from the darkened boardwalk. Charlie's swiping the dead kid's baseball cards had shaken him and now his conversation with the P.C. had rattled him even more. He didn't even want to think about the on-the-spot informant fantasy.

"Keep your eye on Sesso," Jablonski had said. "It's possible he has friends we don't know about." The call hadn't gone all that well. He should have made Charlie do it since it was his big, complicated theory. Jablonski said that if the note looked genuine they should bring in Mickey Cleary for questioning just to clear things up. When Speziale asked if that meant *hold* for questioning, the P.C. gave a non-committal "use your judgment if you think she's a flight risk."

The whole thing was making him a little sick to his stomach. Charlie had laid out his theory that Mickey Cleary was exacting revenge for her father's shooting which had been ordered by Ragone. But, Speziale wondered, where did Charlie get that information? The plot, if that's what it was, seemed a bit elaborate for what may have well been just an accident. It also occurred to him that either the Ragone's or the Rocca brothers could be looking for an excuse to start a shooting war. In Speziale's experience, the winners always ended up with more turf, more power, more money and fewer competitors. He looked down and realized he was wringing his hands, "Friends we don't know about," the P.C. had said. In Bureau parlance, "keep an eye" was equivalent to "don't turn your back." And now they were going to question Mickey Cleary in her own police station. It was almost surreal, he was thinking, when Charlie knocked on the door.

Barnegat Lighthouse State Park
Barnegat, NJ

"Hold your fire," Ronnie was saying. "Mickey, Chief Cleary, hold – your –fire."

Mickey felt like a balloon filled with hot water had burst in her head. She brought the gun to her side and dropped to a sitting position. She was certain she was deaf in one ear.

Ronnie loomed above her, a fearsome-looking military rifle slung on his shoulder, black and green camo paint smeared on his face. Her hearing started to come back.

"You're OK," she heard him say. "You're not hit. You're not wounded. You're OK."

"Did you-"

"The real morons always want to make a speech," he said. "I could have had dinner up there and still had time to make the shot. He had a weapon trained on you. What if we say I made a citizen's arrest with extreme prejudice?" She saw him smile. "Can you stand?" Mickey nodded.

"I have to call this in," she said. Her lip was swollen from hitting the deck and the words came out a little thick.

"I think that's probably a bad idea right now," Ronnie said. "We'll just leave this piece of shit here for the shellers to find in the morning. We need to get you back before whoever set you up tries it again."

"It was Guidi," she struggled with the sound. "It was Guidi-, it was Juice."

"Yeah, but the old man was just the bait. We need to account for the bad actors right away and then we can call for reinforcements. The station is probably the safest place right now." He took her arm and helped her up. The world was back in focus now and she could hear the ocean smacking against the long rock jetty far out in the dark.

"I think I'm OK to drive," Mickey said.

"I have to ditch this somewhere," Ronnie said, twisting his chin to indicate the rifle. "I'll follow you back and then I'll pull off at my place. Lock yourself in the station and stay away from sightlines through the windows or doors. Then call the cavalry. There's no telling who's corrupted so I'd start with the State Police." She nodded again. "I'll meet you there. Don't let anyone in unless it's me. Got it?"

"Copy that." She replied.

"And stay off the radio. Somebody thinks you're already dead and if you have a scanner then maybe they have one too." He helped her to the still running Chevelle and closed the door once she was in. "I've got more ordnance under my floorboards," Ronnie said. "I'll come prepared."

Mickey put the cruiser in gear and drove slowly toward the rusting gate. Without thinking she turned the Delco back on. The Doors leaked out of the speakers, sultry as the summer night

Surf City

They parked a block away and walked through the warm night air, Sesso in the lead by two steps. "Don't see her cruiser," Sesso said.

"Not like you could miss it," Speziale replied. "Did you catch the red stripe tires and the chrome mag wheels? This little town must be rolling in dough to afford that. Anyway, who's going to inventory the Deputy's rooms now?"

"I'll ask the Troopers to do it. Let the State handle all the personal possessions crap. We don't have time to go looking for family members or deal with them squabbling over it. Not that there's much to squabble over." Speziale thought of the baseball cards but said nothing. "Besides, we don't have any official connection so less paperwork for us, right?"

"Wait, I thought he was a confidential informant," Speziale said as they approached the back door of the station. The pause lasted long enough for him to understand all he needed.

"That's was off the books," Sesso said. "I thought I was pretty clear about that."

Speziale did not reply. Sesso tried the door. "Locked," he said, as if it wasn't obvious. He reached into his sport jacket. "Block my sightline and keep an eye out for any rubberneckers. This won't take a minute." Speziale turned his back and scanned the darkened and deserted streets. He heard the plaintive scraping of metal on metal and then the twist of a lock. Light poured out from the open door. "Inside, quick," Sesso said. He closed the door behind them.

"B and E, Charlie? Seriously. Like we couldn't get a warrant? We are the fucking FBI, remember?"

"We're operating under the auspices of the Joint Task Force on Organized Crime at the moment with direct reporting to the P.C. We'll update the D.D. after we've got the whole story. A warrant could tip our hand."

"And what hand is that, Charlie?"

"Look, Stevie, I laid it out for you once. We're not going to have a bloodbath over this kid's premature demise. Mickey Cleary had motive and opportunity. Let's see how it plays out, OK partner?" Sesso looked around the room. He pointed to a desk chair and an old wooden visitor's chair. "You cover the front door," he said. Speziale settled in. He kept his back to the wall and made sure he could always have Charlie in sight.

The headlight on the motorcycle flashed twice in her rear view mirror. Mickey turned off onto a side street as Ronnie pulled alongside.

"On second thought," he said over the grumbling idle, "I'll go with you and then double back."

Mickey shook her head. "You need to lose that weapon and the camo paint," she said. "I am the Chief of Police. I am going to my own police station. I am armed and, right now, really pissed off and therefore dangerous. I think I can handle this."

"In the jungle, the worst things happened when you relaxed, when you thought you were safe for the moment. When you thought you were on your way home."

"Yeah, well Surf City isn't exactly the jungle but I'll keep that in mind."

"Good song," Ronnie said.

"What?"

"On the radio." She hadn't been paying attention. "My favorite actually."

Mickey leaned forward and recognized the funereal rhythm of Procol Harum. "That I never would have guessed," she said. He tapped his forehead with his index finger and sped off.

Mickey turned off the radio and hit the gas.

Surf City

"Surrender your weapon, Chief Cleary," Sesso boomed. "FBI."

"What the-"

"Surrender your weapon and sit down, Chief. Slowly, with your left hand. You know the drill." Mickey did know the drill, but from the other side.

"You assholes can't be serious," she said as she unsnapped her holster and extracted her gun. She held it by the barrel and handed it forward.

"Lay it on the desk," Sesso said, declining to handle it. Speziale watched from his chair, right hand at his waist." Mickey knew what that meant.

"I want to see some paperwork right now," Mickey snapped. "You guys are so far over the line here."

"*We* decide where the line is, I'm afraid, Chief. So just have a seat. Paperwork's in process but we're working under the mandate of the Deputy Director and the Philadelphia Police Commissioner."

"You're full of shit," Mickey replied. "Get Jablonski on the phone."

"Chief Michaela Cleary," Sesso said, "You are under arrest for the premeditated murder of Dante Ragone, Junior, on or about the twenty-third of May of this year. Under the new federal Miranda guidelines you have the right to remain silent. Any statement you make can and will be used against you in a court of law. Do you understand your rights as I have described them?"

"I have the right not to be detained by a complete dickhead like you," Mickey replied.

"I'll take that as a 'Yes,'" Sesso said. He pulled a chair up and sat opposite her. She could hear Speziale shifting in his chair, drumming his fingers on the wooden armrest. Something was amiss between the two agents, she sensed, and she wondered if she could exploit it.

"It's over, Mickey," Sesso said. "We know you killed the kid. We know you did it to punish Danny Rags for plugging Patsy. We know you rigged it to look like an accident, or maybe not. You've seen enough homicides. I'm sure you could lead even the State M.E. wherever you wanted him to go. I have to admit, in its own way it's pretty fucking brilliant. You hit Danny Rags where it hurts. You maybe start a mob war so more of the Ragone's and the Rocca's get whacked – less Wop bastards to deal with, am I right? An onus with a bonus, you might say. Maybe it even blows back on Danny enough to put him away or get him taken out. Like I said, pretty fucking brilliant. But your deputy, now we figure he helped you or maybe he just caught on to what you were doing. So either you staged his suicide or maybe he just couldn't live with having to cover it up and really did eat his gun."

"You are completely out of your mind," Mickey said. She turned toward Speziale who tensed and leaned forward. "You'll take the fall real hard along with your partner when this goes south," she said. "And it's going to go south in a big goddamn hurry. I know you're not right with this. Both of you get up, walk out, drive back to The Roundhouse and tell Jablonski, or whoever it is you're really working for, that it just didn't pan out. I'll do my part to save your careers only out of loyalty to the shield." She thought for a second that Speziale was going to go for it but he looked at Sesso and then leaned back, avoiding her stare.

"Now I know why they loved you at the academy," Sesso said. "Just one big bottle of piss and vinegar. Word is the Bureau is looking to recruit its first female field agents. Without this little complication we could'a maybe helped you with that."

"You never had any intention of helping me with anything," Mickey replied. She measured the distance to her gun. Sesso, she figured would have to reach around his portly belly to draw. She felt certain his partner would not shoot her in the back. She was betting he would not shoot her at all. Sesso was speaking again but she was calibrating the time and the distance and the sequence of movements in her head.

"...but you didn't count on poor Deputy Fairbrother dropping a dime on you post-mortem." Mickey looked at him. "Ah, *now* I've got your attention, I see. You won't be such a Chatty Cathy after I show you this." He reached into the outside pocket of his jacket. Mickey flinched and moved forward.

"Ah-ah-ah," Sesso said. "Just relax and let me read this. Deathbed confessions are highly admissible as I'm sure you know." She watched as he unfolded a heavily creased slip of paper. He held it up so she could read it then turned it toward himself and read it to her. "I had to protect Mickey," Sesso said. "So simple, so straightforward. Tucked in his uniform blouse right behind his spit-shined badge. Ironic, in a way, don't you think?"

"It's a plant and you know it." She turned again to Speziale. "Let me guess. *He* found it and showed it to you after you left the scene." Speziale had the frozen look of someone watching his parents argue, she thought. "Time to be the *good* cop here, Stevie," Mickey said. The distress in his expression was plain.

"I'm the agent-in-charge here," Sesso said. She turned back to him. "But Agent Speziale will not hesitate to use deadly force if you resist. I can assure you of that." She heard the chair scrape as Speziale stood up. "Now," Sesso continued, "Nice and easy. Stand up, put your hands behind your back and turn around slowly." She saw him pull the cuffs from his belt.

"The set-up didn't work," she said. "Caputo's dead and Juice is probably in the middle of the Walt Whitman Bridge right now. You and whoever your real boss is are done." Sesso looked startled but only for an instant.

"Turn around, Chief," he said. "Now."

She did and saw that Speziale had drawn his weapon. He was sweating profusely and was shifting from foot to foot. "It's OK, Chief," he said. "It's just 'til we get this thing figured out. I'll look after you."

She felt the cuffs hard and cold on her wrists and heard the familiar snap of the lock. Sesso's hand was on her shoulder. "Let's go, Chief," he said prodding her toward the open cell door. "I'm sure you run a comfy place with clean sheets and pillow mints. Just step in and sit on the bunk. Probably best if you don't say anything right now." She shuffled into the cell and stood at the bars as Sesso clanged the door shut. She did not sit down.

"OK, have it your way," Sesso said.

Speziale holstered his gun and took a step forward. "Charlie, what the fuck is going on here? What's she talking about with Caputo? That's Ragone's trigger man."

Sesso produced a handkerchief from his pocket and dabbed his brow. "Stevie," he said with a tiny laugh, "I love you like a brother." He picked up Mickey's weapon with the cloth. "But you are, without a doubt, the dumbest Dago I ever met."

In the small confines of the station the first shot was loud and echoed thunderously off the brick walls. Mickey counted three altogether and saw Speziale slump to the floor, a mixed look of pain and surprise still on his face. She watched Sesso pick up the telephone and dial.

♦ ♦ ♦

A. Louis Petroni was on his third J & B Scotch miniature, with two empty cans of Schweppes' Club Soda in the trash, when the knock came. He still hadn't heard from Shots. The liquor had damped his anxiety but not removed it. He felt relieved that there would be good news shortly.

Petroni walked to the door and loosened the chain. He opened it a crack and saw the craggy visage of the old man.

"Call came for you – didn't want to be put through. Left a message, though."

Petroni reached two fingers out.

"Fella who called said don't write nothin' down. So I'm s'posed to tell you this exactly." He issued a phlegmatic cough and continued. "Package secure but delivery plans have changed. Driver unavailable due to serious illness. Need help loading package at local station. Said make sure I remembered to say 'station' when I give you the message."

The three scotch and sodas were not helping Petroni process but in a minute he thought he understood. He reached in his pockets but both were empty. "Fresh out of fins," he said.

"No sweat," the old man replied. "This one's on the house." Petroni closed the door and moved to the bed. He doffed the Sinatra robe and started dressing. He'd pack his bag when the work was done.

He walked down the hallway and past the front desk where the old man sat, again with a copy, maybe the same copy of *The Sporting News*. "I'll be back later to check out," Petroni said.

"I'll be here to help you," the old man replied with a crinkled smile.

♦ ♦ ♦

Ronnie sat on the floor breaking down the rifle into as many components as possible. It would, he knew, take a while to dispose of them in different spots but between the ocean and the bay there was no shortage of places. He'd had it shipped home in separate parcels, each a week apart. It was only fitting, he thought, that he retire it the same way. Scott Mackenzie was on the crappy plastic AM radio.

The case would be the biggest problem. But he'd worry about that later. Scott was singing about a new explanation. Ronnie laughed at the word and realized he might have plenty of explaining to do in the next few days. But right now he needed to be a person in motion.

Patsy flipped on the high beams and squinted at the road signs. He had made it to Highway 9. The traffic was light and he was passed only now and then by cars not going that much faster. Oncoming traffic was almost non-existent. He had studied the map closely at the last pit stop and the grilled cheese and coffee had given him all he needed to go the remaining distance. The attendant at the gas station had delivered Red Ball service and topped off the tank. Patsy felt the old juices flowing. The pain in his back was like lying down on a shooter marble but it was more than tolerable. Even his vision seemed more acute. The darkness of the Pine Barrens enveloped him but keeping the brights on along the lonely road allowed him to see the signs in plenty of time. He matched each exit with the memorized map in his head - Toms River, Barnegat Township, Tuckerton. He had his window down and in the air he could smell a whiff of salt air and stagnant water.

A colorful roadside placard announced "L.B.I. 7 Miles." Patsy's palms were wet on the wheel. He reached over and patted the .38 nestled in the crook of the bench seat. The half-hour it had taken to clean, oil and load it now seemed like time well spent. "L.B.I.," he thought. An image of Eileen seemed to appear in the windshield reflection as he passed beneath one of the sparsely spaced lights mounted on the telephone poles. For an instant he could see her smile, dazzling white against her dark skin and hair. And with it the image of his daughter – same bright smile, same dark hair. Little Black Irish, Eileen had always called Mickey. L.B.I. Seven more miles to Little Black Irish. A green sign with white lettering appeared.

> Rte. 72 Ship Bottom
> Long Beach Island
> Next Right

Patsy eased off the accelerator and looked for the poorly lit intersection. The big steering wheel took both hands to turn. The road was pitted and bumpy but he pressed down on the gas pedal. He leaned forward, trying to peer past the headlights into the darkness. A few miles further and the ocean announced itself – vast, black and almost invisible. Pulling him like the tide. Patsy felt the planks of the wooden bridge tapping on the tires. He was almost there.

TWENTY THREE
Surf City

"YOU HAVE NO IDEA what you've done," Sesso said after replacing the phone in its cradle. "I sure as shit hope it was worth it. You might have evened the score but now Patsy is going to have to grieve for both of his kids. That'll kill him long before that bullet in his back ever does."

Mickey inhaled deeply and spit through the cell bars, catching Sesso on the cheek and neck. After a moment's hesitation he laughed and wiped at it with the handkerchief. "You should have been a guy," he said. "'Cause you really got balls, honey." Sesso carefully folded the cloth hanky and left it by Mickey's service pistol. He walked up to the bars and faced her. "You'll enjoy our friend," he said. "Way out there in the Pine Barrens, where no one can hear you scream." Mickey wanted to spit again but her mouth had gone to cotton. Sesso backed up a step. "A word of advice, if I may. Billy Bowker likes it pretty rough so the less you struggle the quicker he'll get bored and put you out of what will surely be your misery. Members of the Bowker clan have really warped ideas about what's, uh, normal." A smile creased his face that sent a shiver through her. "Just pray to God his brother isn't there. I think they call it tag-teaming." Mickey sensed he was getting off by taunting her. The cuffs were cutting into her wrists and she struggled to keep control.

"You'll have to try a lot harder if you want to scare me," she said. "Right now all I see is a fat pussy who shot his partner. Know what they'll do to a Fed in a federal lock-up, Charlie? Hope you don't have hemorrhoids. And I heard they knock all your teeth out when you first get there so you can suck it better."

Sesso started toward the cell, his faced puffed with anger. "You stupid c- "

He turned around when the front door opened.

"Jesus H. Christ," Petroni said. "Charlie, what the fuck have you done?"

A faint but ripe smell was emanating from the corner where Speziale lay.

"Stevie had the grand misfortune of figuring it out, Artie" Sesso replied. "He was just a little slow on the draw, you might say. He became a major liability."

"How are we going to expl-"

"Artie, relax. I capped him with the Chief here's gun. The only prints on it are hers." He pointed to the hanky. "Here's how it went down. There was a struggle, she shot Stevie and fled. Who knows where she is. Hiding out in the Barrens, on the run, maybe never to be seen again."

The scotch was wearing off and Petroni tried to assess the damage. "OK. Help me load her in the car and let's get this taken care of."

"Or we could can put the gun in Stevie's hand and shoot her," Sesso said. "Make it look like he returned fire and died in the line of duty. Family would collect nicely on the Bureau's D.B. policy. Least we can do for him kind'a thing, you know? Simpler that way."

Petroni was too angry to be appalled. He knew that Sesso was a loose cannon but this was almost beyond his comprehension. It began to occur to him that maybe Charlie wasn't freelancing. This kind of carnage would only be tolerated with the approval of someone very powerful. A boss. The question was – which boss? He watched momentarily transfixed as Sesso picked up the hanky and moved to Speziale's cooling body. "I hate it when they evacuate their bowels like that," Sesso said. "Happens damn near every time. They don't show *that* on TV, uh?" He calmly located Speziale's weapon and wrapped the dead man's cool but still-pliable hand around it.

"Juice has the body," Mickey said.

"Yes," Petroni replied, "and it's safely on its way to Dadino's Funeral Home in South Philadelphia for a proper Christian burial.

Which is all the fuck anyone ever wanted in the first place." He looked at Sesso. "Now, tell me again why you think we need to shoot her? Nobody's ever going to find her body. Bowker will make sure of that."

"Artie," Sesso said, "I love you like a brother but-"

The back door burst open catching Petroni and Sesso by surprise.

"Hey Farty Artie, you Ginzo fuck." Patsy Cleary stood in the doorway, bracing himself against it. There was a grimace of pain on his face and a .38 Police Special in his hand. "I told you to stay away from her." He raised the .38 and pointed it at Petroni.

"Dad!" Mickey yelled. Patsy glanced over at her. In the split second he did, Sesso cranked Speziale's lifeless arm around and fired.

"Shut up, bitch." Sesso commanded. He leveled the gun at Mickey. "Or it'll be one tap to the head for you and another one for dear old dad." He left the gun in Speziale's hand, dropped his arm and walked toward Artie. Patsy was moaning and gurgling on the floor, a port wine stain spreading on the right side of his chest. Sesso pushed the big man's feet inside and closed the door. "Alright, help me get her ready to go," he said.

"Shit, Charlie, how are we going to explain all this?"

Sesso laughed at something but Petroni had no idea what.

"Oh, don't worry, I'll think of something," Sesso replied. For an instant Petroni felt the whole scene stop, as if suspended in time. As someone whose profession was defined by words and where guilt or innocence was often a matter of inflection and tone it struck him that Sesso had used the singular simple future contraction "I'll" instead of the plural "we'll." When time resumed, Sesso had the cell door open and Mickey pushed down on the bunk. "Don't bite, don't bite," he warned and stuffed a washcloth into her mouth. "Grab something to tie her feet," he ordered.

Petroni pulled a brown electrical extension cord from the desk fan and tossed it in. Sesso began wrapping Mickey's ankles with it. Petroni looked at the desk and decided to wait.

"Alright, Chiefy," Sesso said. "Time for a ride. Artie, go check outside. We'll put her in the car."

"Whose car" Petroni asked.

"Well, not a Bureau car and if you don't want to get pulled

over driving a police car, I guess that leaves yours."

Petroni considered this as he opened the back door of the station and peered around. He was amazed at how silent a beach town was before the summer season. They only things missing, he thought, were tumbleweeds rolling down the deserted street. Seeing no one he walked to the Jag, which he had parked in a shadowed area, and opened the trunk. He looked in and frowned then went to the rear door and motioned to Sesso who had Mickey's limp form slung over one shoulder. A stream of muffled grunts accompanied them.

"Bitch is a lot stronger than I thought," Sesso said. "Had to cut her air for a minute to get her to calm down. She'll be alright by the time we get there. Let's go back inside and make sure the scene's controlled. I want to check that Stevie's gun is in the right place."

Now Petroni was certain. "Yes, Charlie, I think that's a very good idea," he replied. They walked back into the station. Sesso pulled the door shut and immediately went to Speziale, obscuring his movements by turning his back towards Petroni.

"Starting to stiffen a little. Be just a second here, Artie."

The scotch had dissipated and Petroni was now thinking with a clarity and a calmness he didn't think he possessed. He saw it all as if in a diorama. It had to be Danny, he realized. Patiently waiting years for any match to light the fuse. Building up crews and firepower to take out Carmine Rocca and have Philly and its present and future turf all to himself. Even using the loss of his own son to do it. That's why Sesso was here, Petroni knew; to make sure the plan went through and anyone who got in the way would be eliminated. He also knew what Sesso's job would be once Mickey was disposed of. The various scenarios ran quickly through his legally-trained mind. He could turn her loose and offer to be a government witness or even become an informant. He dismissed both ideas knowing he wouldn't live a week either way. Mickey's fate was already sealed, he decided. Going against Danny's orders at this point would be just as suicidal. Only one option remained. He picked up the handkerchief first.

"Charlie," he said. "You know I love you like a brother but-"

Sesso snapped his head around and Petroni fired three times with Mickey's gun. Blood and brains hit the wall with a wet sound like *pasta al dente* dropped in a colander. Petroni looked down at Patsy Cleary. His eyes were half-closed but he was still breathing. "Now we're even," Petroni said to him. "You'll be with little Mikey soon." He put the gun and the handkerchief on the desk, turned off the lights and walked out. The surrounding blocks were deserted; the only sounds a distant engine and the boom of the surf on the beach. It was almost done, he thought..

Ronnie stood at the end of the rock jetty. Without a bright moon, the water looked black and angry. Surf spray hit the giant stones and dampened his clothes. He had scattered the remaining smaller parts randomly in crevices and the last piece deep into a fissure near the jetty's end. The rocks were flat on top but slick and he almost lost his balance twice. He would, he decided, fill the case with rocks and drop it off the bridge into the bay off Little Bonnet. But that would have to wait. He watched his footing as he negotiated the black stones, hopping down at the last bit and trudging up on the sand. He had swapped his black VC thongs for sneakers to negotiate the rocks. The sand snuck in with each step and ground under his soles as he walked.

As he approached the road he heard the scream of sirens and the whine of high-performance engines. He ducked behind a splintered piling and watched as two New Jersey State Police cars zoomed by, their single red dome lights flashing, heading in the direction of the little downtown. When they had passed, he sprinted for the shack and revved up the Enfield.

TWENTY FOUR

MUD CITY
The New Jersey Mainland

THERE WERE BIG BOXES of legal files in the Jaguar's trunk so Sesso had dumped Mickey in the big back seat. She was starting to come around, Petroni could tell, and so once they were over the Manahawkin Bridge and the lights became sparse Petroni started talking to her.

"Let me tell you something. The worst day of your life hasn't even begun. You are going to just love Billy Bowker. And I hear the Pine Barrens are especially beautiful at night. So peaceful, so quiet, so completely isolated. I'm the last real human company you're ever going to have so try and enjoy it. "

Mickey was starting to move her legs and kicking with both feet at the leather upholstery.

"Go ahead," Petroni said. "Knock yourself out. But save some for Billy. No just lying there like a dishrag, OK?" He had no idea if Mickey was listening to him but he kept on talking, voice rising slightly in pitch with each passing mile. "None of this had to happen. Do you hear me? NONE of this. This was nothing. This was an accident – no it wasn't even that. But you wanted it to be more. Spoiling for a fight they call it. Why? To avenge your father? Yeah, well how well did that turn out for either of you? He's about to breathe his last and you're about to wish you had."

In the absence of any towns or even hamlets, with their polluting light, the sky overhead was onyx black and the stars shone like Christmas tree lights in a dark living room. Petroni was only half-watching the road, turning his head more and more frequently to shout at Mickey.

"You turned a fucking accident into a fucking war. Now people are dead who didn't need to be. And more will be. Just look at the fucking mess you've made. I tried, Mickey. I tried to give you an out. All you had to do was turn over the body. I tried to give Patsy an out, but he didn't take it either. Lace-curtain Irish – both of you dumb as a sack of spuds." Spittle was clinging to the sides of his mouth and his voice was turning hoarse, but Petroni kept shouting at her.

Mickey became vaguely aware that music was playing. Somewhere close. Almost right next to her. She tried to move and felt the constricting cuffs and the cord lashed around her ankles and almost remembered. Someone was speaking but it was hard to hear it over the music. Was he shouting? Why was there music so close? Her jaw ached horribly and she tried to bite down on the rag to lessen the discomfort. It was becoming a little softer with her saliva soaking it but, as hard as she tried, she couldn't push it out with her tongue. She kicked her bound legs a few times and felt her shoes up against something soft and forgiving. Why was there music? She knew the song. She knew the group. The Easybeats. No, that was wrong. She shifted her hips and tried to push with her back but it only made her neck and her jaw hurt worse. Not the Easybeats. The Zombies. No, that was wrong, too. The talking – it really sounded like shouting - was getting louder. Air was flowing over her. She opened her eyes. Nothing looked familiar. It was the wrong half of a dream. The Young Rascals. No. Only one name, not two. It was right in her ear.

A car. She was in a car and it was moving. Fast. Resolution came quicker now and she kicked and strained against the bonds, screaming a scream that wasn't. Breathing through her nose. Shouting. Her dad, oh God, her dad. Speziale dead in the corner. Sesso and Artie Petroni talking about her. The worst day of her life, he said. Hasn't even begun.

She felt the thrum of the tires and knew they were still on a paved road. She still had - The Outsiders. That's who it was. The

Outsiders.

The Pine Barrens. Someone named Billy. The worst day of her life. She felt sickness rising and forced it back down so she wouldn't choke to death on it.

"Shit," Petroni said and hit the brakes, hard. He had been yelling at the back seat and missed the turn off the asphalt. In the pitch black he couldn't tell where he was. Maybe he hadn't missed it. Maybe he'd missed it by a mile. He would have to drive slowly and look for the phone booth, the only landmark he knew. He jammed the shifter into Reverse and hit the accelerator. The rear end fishtailed and dropped off onto the soft shoulder. Petroni cursed and shifted into first. The rear tire whined at high rpm's without any purchase and there was a burning smell like the brakes were on fire. Petroni shifted into Neutral, set the brake and got out to look, knowing he was wasting precious time. He'd heard distant sirens and figured that could mean only one thing. He looked at the rut the tire had made in the thin soil. Then he grabbed a gnarled tree limb and jammed it underneath. He wouldn't be calling the Auto Club tonight, he thought, and laughed to himself. "Happy fucking Motoring," he said as he climbed back in. The emergency brake released with an audible clunk.

Downtown Surf City

Both State Police cars were parked at the rear of the police station. So were both Surf City cruisers. Ronnie felt a wave of relief. He parked the bike at the far end of the lot and approached the open door on foot.

A large man in a bloody shirt was lying just inside. Ronnie could see one of the troopers bending down close to him. His chest was moving regularly, but slowly. The kneeling trooper was holding what looked like a towel to the man's chest –applying direct pressure, he thought. As he walked closer, arms and hands in front of him, he could hear the trooper's voice.

"Easy there buddy, easy. We're calling the ambulance. It'll be here in a minute. You're going to make it. You're going to be OK. Can you tell me what happened here?"

Ronnie was close enough to hear the man's ragged breathing.

"Hold it right there," a voice behind Ronnie commanded.

"Hands where we can see them."

Ronnie did as instructed and turned around. The other trooper must have been in his car. He wore what Ronnie always called the Park Ranger hat like the D.I.'s in Basic Training wore with the strap hooked under his chin. He looked about his own age, Ronnie thought. "Got business here, soldier?" Ronnie's dog tags flashed in the car's spotlight. "You earn those or buy them at the Army-Navy store?"

"9th Infantry Division," Ronnie answered. "Mobile Riverine Force. May fifteen 1964, March sixteen, 1967. Serial number-"

"OK, that's enough. What are you doing here?"

"Chief Cleary is a friend of mine. I thought she'd be here so I-"

"You know where she might be?"

"No, sir. I don't. I-"

"Well it's a shit show here now, soldier. Back up is on the way. Why don't you just stick around in case we have questions."

Before Ronnie could answer the young trooper dashed toward the door. The older trooper, his hat removed, gray brush cut shining in the light, looked up at him.

"Write this down," he said. The younger trooper, Ronnie thought he caught a name badge that read G. JOO, pulled out a leather-backed notebook and a pen.

"Kidnapped. Daughter. Chief. Going." He leaned in closer to catch the weakening voice. "Where, where were they going?" He put his ear almost to the man's mouth and then looked up. "Pine Barrens," he said. "Someone named Billy."

The trooper wrote it down. "I've got a guy here says he knows-" He turned around but Ronnie Dunn was already gone.

Ronnie heard the ambulance and at least one fire truck rolling. A Ship Bottom police car passed him going in the opposite direction followed by another from Beach Haven. The drivers didn't even look at him. He pulled up at the shack and left the bike on its side on just off the road. Inside he grabbed a zippered "go-bag" with faded U.S. Army stenciling on it. Four items went inside and he was back on the bike just as a third police car, this one from Long Branch, sped past. At Division Street he braked hard and turned right until he hit Barnegat Avenue. The rear tire skidded on a patch of sand when he made the hard left but the Enfield stayed upright. He gunned the motor and slowed only to make a drifting right onto the main road off the island. The he opened it up.

The small bridge crossed Bonnet Island first and then the much wider Cedar Bonnet. At its end the big causeway bridge began and he followed the road over the dark and brooding expanse of Manahawkin Bay. He passed Mud City and felt like he was leaving civilization behind. A few lights mounted on telephone poles provided the only illumination in the gathering gloom. Ronnie throttled the engine up and hoped months of imported tobacco had not dulled his memory, his sense of direction or the way-finding training the Army had spent a fortune on. At a certain speed the wind caused his eyes to tear so much he had to slow down. There were fewer lights now to mark the way and the darkness felt very close. The bike's single headlight reflected off the retinas of animals as he wound deeper into the woods. Approaching the outer limit of the Barrens a line from a poem he read once in high school came to him:

This is the forest primeval

He couldn't remember the rest. But there was something about murmuring pines, he thought.

The Pine Barrens

Petroni felt like he was puttering along, shifting constantly between second and third, looking for the phone booth in the pitch black. He had the passenger side window rolled all the way down and was craning his neck to look for the silver and red rectangle on the shoulder of the road. The high beams were on and wildlife of various sizes and shapes skittered off into the blackness when the light hit them.

He had stopped yelling at Mickey, having almost lost his voice along with his way. Fortunately, she appeared to have worn herself out struggling and was now fairly still with her knees drawn up and her neck bent. He slowed so he could make sure she was still breathing then accelerated gently and drove on.

The phone booth appeared so quickly and so indistinctly that he almost missed it again. He angled the jag to illuminate it and felt sure it was the right one. If it wasn't, he knew, he was miles off course. He inched forward and looked for the gravel turnoff. The Jag rolled over something large and the undercarriage banged against the road. A hubcap bounced off and rolled like a coin to the faded yellow median stripe. Petroni stopped and was about to retrieve it when he saw a lantern waving through the Pines. Bowker. He shifted into gear and made the turn, the coarse gravel crunching and popping loudly. He'd grab the hubcap on his way out. The shack came into view, lit from the inside like a Halloween jack-o'-lantern. Bowker raised his free hand to shield his eyes. Petroni killed the headlights and then the engine.

* * *

Mickey heard voices and the sound of the car door opening.

"Yep, still wigglin', ain't she?" a thick voice with a hillbilly accent said. She heard Petroni answer.

"You'll have your money tomorrow," he said. "But you'll need to pick it up at the usual spot."

"Awww," the thick voice said, "I hate fishin' it outta the shitter at that damned rest stop. Smell 'll gag a maggot. Last time a guy was in thar right before I had to go get it. Hey, looks like you lost a cap off'a one 'a yore tars."

"Yeah," she heard Petroni reply. "It's out on the asphalt somewhere. I'll get it on my way back."

Then Mickey heard the rustle of footsteps. She looked up to see a thickly muscled man with missing teeth and tight curls of sandy hair. She made herself think of how she would describe him to the sketch artist.

"Hi, darlin'," he said. "Let's get you inside and see if we can't switch that rag in yore mouth for somethin' you'll like a whole lot better." Mickey felt herself picked up as if she weighed nothing. She was being carried, she realized, with one arm.

It never left you, Ronnie thought. Never. Not the drilling, not the killing and not the skill or the will to survive. He was trained in dead reckoning and had a good natural sense of direction and so now, even in the thickening blackness, he felt like he knew his way. The bike was going back to where he bought it. If the man who sold it to him was alone it would be difficult but not impossible. If there were others he'd need a whole different plan. That's what the bag was for. Ronnie recalled him in detail. Thought Billy was not a name that suited him. He remembered thinking he was built like a bear, thick through the neck, trunk and hips. The forearms were massive, like Popeye's without the anchor tattoos. But there was something else, Ronnie thought at the time. It wasn't even a physical attribute, it was something deeper. Like he was one or two klicks off being human. He thought about Mickey and pushed the throttle all the way open.

Petroni backed the Jaguar out slowly. He tried not to think about Mickey Cleary and her next few hours. Her *last* few hours. He had given her every opportunity to avoid this and she had refused. His conscience, he thought, was clear. He was not guilty. He was acquitted of all charges. He was free to go.

Petroni shifted out of reverse and went slowly back onto the gravel. He flipped on the high beams again as he approached the asphalt. He thought the hubcap should be right in the middle of the road. He angled the Jag several different ways, sweeping the headlights across both lanes but still couldn't see it. Petroni looked at his watch. He still had his belongings back in Surf City. He'd pick those up and make the drive back to Philadelphia tonight, wanting to be far away when someone stumbled upon Shots Caputo. He would call Danny Rags and describe in detail how he'd not only avenged Little Rags, but cleaned up a messy situation with guts and guile. When it came time to put down roots in Atlantic City, he mused, he'd remind Danny of this and his part in it. Maybe he wouldn't need to send Danny to the slammer to reap his reward. He even thought of a name for it – he'd call it the "shore thing," as in sure thing. His cleverness never failed him, it seemed. He eased the big sedan out onto the road, took one more look around for the hubcap and then shifted into park. He got out and checked the back seat for evidence.

Ten minutes later A. Louis Petroni was winding his way east through the clinging darkness, never able to see further than his headlights.

* * *

Ronnie wondered if picking up the hubcap had been a mistake. But as he watched the car speed off into the night he decided it didn't matter. He placed it against a post at the corner where the asphalt met the gravel as a cairn. The Enfield was behind a large pine tree and the go-bag was on his shoulder. He saw the lights of the little wooden house and started walking. Silently - just the way that Charlie did. The foliage was different, but the sense – the vibe - was the same: he was back in the jungle again.

TWENTY FIVE
The Pine Barrens

MICKEY WAS NOW WIDE awake and frantically trying to come up with a plan. Her wrists felt like they were on fire. The half-animal, half-man she saw sitting in the torn and stained easy chair was drinking turbid liquid from a Mason jar. His eyes had a shimmering glaze that terrified her.

"Good," he cried and clapped his hands. "Now you're all done nappin'. Time to have some fun." What looked like a twelve gauge shotgun was across his lap and a large hunting knife rested on a crude homemade table next to the chair. Kerosene lanterns lit the room casting lurid shadows on every wall. "Comfortable?" he asked.

Mickey's hands and arms were above her head, tethered to a rough-hewn crossbeam that spanned the tilted, off-kilter ceiling. Her ankles were now unbound and she began thinking of how much leverage she could manage if she kicked with one or both legs. She'd been taught things at the academy but those were meant to work on normal people. Billy Bowker – he had thoughtfully introduced himself at some point – was clearly not a normal person.

She saw him take a long swig on the jar, wipe at his mouth and then stand up. "Might as well git to it," he said. He leaned the shotgun against the chair. It was probably a ten gauge she saw now, big and double barreled. He picked up the hunting knife and approached her slowly. "I'll cut you loose if you do what I want," he said. "Or I can leave you strung up and just do what

I want anyway." He had taken the gag out of her mouth but her voice was whispery and her tongue felt like sandpaper.

"Cut me down," she said. "And I'll do what you want." She had to, she realized, play for time.

Billy Bowker laughed. "Yeah, they all say that. Hell, one said she do what I wanted then she tried to bite me in two. I got her head cut nearly off 'fore she unclamped. Still got the scar."

Mickey thought if he held the knife at just the right angle she might be able to use a knee to drive it backwards into him. But he stayed just out of range. The dark stains on the wooden floorboards beneath her feet told her this wasn't his first rodeo.

"I see you thinkin'," he said. "I like that. No fun if it's too easy." He took another drink from the jar. She had been stripped to her bra and panties. The St. Christopher medal was still around her neck. The functioning policewoman part of her brain recalled a victim restrained the same way in a filthy basement in Manayunk. The girl had lived because she'd strung her torturer along long enough for them to find her. Mickey wondered if anyone was searching for her yet. Billy looked a little woozy already and if she could keep him talking and drinking she thought she might still have a chance. He reached his arm out touched her bra with the tip of his knife.

"Just sharpened it today," he said and traced a circle on the fabric over her nipple. "Dull knife just wouldn't do, now would it?" He made a little twist with the tip and the fabric parted. Mickey gasped but quickly realized he hadn't drawn blood. "You do this enough you get real good at it," he said.

"Tell me something that you want," Mickey said. "Tell me exactly."

Billy Bowker licked his upper lip and wiped off brownish drool from the corner of his mouth.

"I really like it when they scream," Billy said. "I like that the best. But not the fake screams. I like the ones that come from way down deep. When it really hurts and when you know it ain't going to stop."

"What do you do to make them scream?" she asked.

"Oh, darlin'," he said just a little more slowly. "Just the most awful, terrible things that can be done with the tip of a knife." He held the blade an inch from her face, so close her breath fogged on it. "With the tip you can just go on and on, for hours and hours 'til even screamin' don't help anymore." She noticed his pupils were dilated and he swayed just a little. He turned the knife slightly and in the polished blade she saw the reflection of something moving behind him. His breath smelled like rotten eggs and stale tobacco mixed with the strong scent of alcohol. He touched the tip of the knife to her breastbone and pressed. The he tapped the medal. "I'll leave this on you 'til we're all done." He had moved even closer and was almost whispering. "Now, the only question I ever ask them is - where you want me to start?"

The spray of hot blood caught her by surprise and she thought, just for a moment, it was her own. Then she saw Billy's face contort and the tip of the bayonet poke through the front of his neck. Mickey brought both knees up and knocked him backwards. Billy Bowker grabbed at his throat, robbed of speech by a punctured windpipe. Red and blue streams ran from his neck, the bright one pumping, the darker one oozing. She saw Ronnie grab the hunting knife and in seconds her arms were free. She peeled the heavy electrical tape from her hands watched as he circled Bowker, who was on his knees and trying to stand. Ronnie went behind him and reached for the handle of the bayonet. Bowker clamped Ronnie's wrist with a massive hand and pulled him over one shoulder. Ronnie was kicking his legs for leverage but like an enraged, wounded animal, Bowker was overpowering. Ronnie hit the floor with a thud, propelled by his own weight and his forward momentum. A pink froth was forming at Bowker's neck, bubbling out and sucking back with each heaving breath. But he did not go down. From his knees he grabbed the loosened bayonet and slashed at Ronnie. Despite the blood and the bubbles Bowker actually got to his feet. Ronnie rolled away from another slash. "Go!" he said to Mickey. "What are you waiting for?"

Billy Bowker was no longer a man. He was a gored bull in the arena. With one hand still clutching his throat he staggered toward Ronnie. A guttural, raging sound came from a place deep in his chest. But he somehow was able to sense Ronnie's presence and moved toward it. Mickey took a step in the direction of the door expecting Ronnie to follow. Then she saw him slip in a blood puddle on the wooden floor and tumble on to his back. Bowker had the bayonet and was still moving, his eyes wild but actions willful.

Mickey moved to the chair and tried to pick up the shotgun.

After having her arms above her for so long it felt impossibly heavy. She realized she couldn't shoulder it so she slid the barrels down onto the padded armrest. Then she knelt down and levered the stock up with both hands. Sighting on the bead between the barrels, she held her breath and pulled the twin triggers.

Surf City

The old man wasn't at the desk when Petroni returned. He fingered his room key and walked down the hallway. He was surprised to find that the door was open. The desk clerk was sitting calmly in the overstuffed chair, the same magazine on his lap. The room, Petroni noticed, was immaculate.

"Figured you might be in a hurry to get back, so I took the liberty of packing your stuff. It's out behind the desk. I'll make sure it finds its way home." Then he smiled and turned a page. "Oh, and by the way, Danny said to tell you that even a pat on the shoulder or a kind word would have been enough."

There were two flashes and *The Sporting News* exploded in a confetti of action photos and box scores. A. Louis Petroni fell where he stood with very little fuss and even less mess. The old man laid down the gun and set to tidying up. He'd keep the robe, he decided. He thought it looked exactly like the one Sinatra wore in Palm Springs.

TWENTY SIX
The Pine Barrens

HE WAS STILL MOVING.

Ronnie was trapped under the bleeding, gurgling, flailing form of Billy Bowker who seemed, impossibly, still sentient.

The shotgun blast had rocked the wooden shack. Part of the load must have caught Bowker but Ronnie knew the shot was high and it had done more damage to the kerosene lamps on the wall than to his adversary. He also knew if it had been much lower he wouldn't be worrying about his current predicament. With his head at floorboard level he could see Mickey's bare feet but with the struggling weight on his chest he couldn't force enough air out to call to her. Ronnie realized that the sheer bulk now pressing might asphyxiate him before Bowker expired.

One bloody hand was clawing at the floor near his head. Ronnie reached for the wrist and pulled. The sound that followed was something straight from a Saturday matinee horror movie – a cross between a howl and a moan. Blood and phlegm spattered his face. Ronnie kept pulling when suddenly the weight tumbled and slid off him and he could breathe. The floor was slick and the air had the awful metallic stench of fresh blood. His feet slipped in it again as he scrambled from underneath the writhing form which was somehow still reaching for him.

Once he could stand Ronnie looked toward Mickey. She was reloading the ten-gauge from a box of shells on the floor next to the chair. He croaked her name and she paused. It seemed to take her a moment to realize he had extricated himself.

"Let's go," Ronnie rasped. "He's done." She pointed.

Bowker's legs were moving and he was slithering toward Ronnie's ankles, driven by some primal force that defied his gruesome injuries. Mickey dropped the shells. They clattered and then rolled away on the canted boards.

"No. We have to put him down," she said in a voice that sounded hollow and far away.

She advanced two steps and picked up the bayonet.

"Let me do it," she said and sidestepped to avoid the still-lunging arms.

Ronnie grabbed the bayonet by the blood and hair-matted handle and took it from her. One of the shattered lamps was on its side against the wall, the orange flame licking at the unvarnished planking.

"You need to get out of here now," Ronnie said and grabbed her arm. She pulled back.

"I have to make sure he's dead," Mickey replied. Ronnie motioned to a camouflage bag behind her.

"I'll make sure," he said and stepped toward it. The prone form continued to writhe in an almost serpentine way, marking bloody inches on the floor with each tortured movement. "Get outside. I'll be right on your six." He handed her the bayonet back. "In case you run in to any tourists," he said.

Mickey hesitated until Ronnie pushed her roughly from behind. Her steps were slow and deliberate despite the proximity of Bowker's clenching and unclenching hand.

"Still wigglin', are you, motherfucker?" she said as she passed him.

Once outside she stood on the dilapidated porch until Ronnie appeared. He pointed to the rutted path. "Follow that until you come to a car hubcap leaning on a broken post and then wait there. He pulled off his green tactical and handed it to her. "Stay low to the ground and be ready to cover your face with that," he said. "It's going to get hot and loud in a minute. Don't stop and don't look back. Just stay low and keep moving. Remember – car hubcap about a quarter-klick on your right. You have to go now."

"What are you going to do?" she asked.

"I'm just gonna pop some smoke," he replied.

Mickey took the shirt and started walking.

"Down!" Ronnie yelled after her. "Stay down."

Ronnie watched until her figure was hard to make out and then reached into the bag.

The *m34* was different from other grenades. Nicknamed "Willie Pete", it weighed over two-and-a-half pounds and could be fired from a launcher or deployed by hand if necessary. Ronnie reached in and withdrew the canister. It looked like giant, tiled dreidel with a black handle. He judged how far he could lob it. In the light from the open doorway he saw the red lettering and the painted yellow band around the midsection.

There was still movement inside the shack and an animal sound that he recognized as suffering and rage. He could no longer pick out Mickey's crawling form. Ronnie stepped toward the door and was shocked to see Bowker upright and shuffling forward. His ragged breathing produced a small plume of pink froth with each exhalation. Ronnie stepped back off the rickety porch, pulled the grenade's pin and with the underhand motion of a pitcher tossing to first, rolled it through the doorway and into the path of the oncoming specter.

* * *

Mickey dropped to her knees in the coarse foliage. Blunt manna and panic-grass brushed her exposed skin and clumps of peaty moss clung to her palms and knees as she pressed forward, the bayonet in her right hand. Mickey was grunting with each move forward now. The spongy peat suddenly gave way to a large stand of Pennsylvania sedge which whipped at her face as she crawled through it. She had no idea how far a "quarter-click" was but she hoped it wasn't much more than she had already covered. The air was heavy and now alive with insects. The fighter-plane whine of mosquitoes was everywhere and she flailed with the tactical shirt trying to keep them off of her exposed skin. Finally she stopped and pulled the long-sleeved garment over her head, keeping the collar just below her nose to avoid inhaling a mouthful of bugs with every breath. Occasionally there was the lower-pitched buzz of large, slow-moving greenhead flies which dive-bombed her eyes and bit at the backs of her legs before she cold dislodge or squash them. Tiny black spots appeared on her hands which she figured for ticks or chiggers. They seemed to appear faster than she could wipe them off. Only the sound of crickets told her she was not actually crawling through hell. She wondered what Ronnie was doing and where he was, which was definitely not right behind her. She thought of what he'd said about it not being her jungle yet and decided that if it wasn't before, it was definitely her jungle now.

Mickey couldn't process exactly how much time was passing, how long she'd been crawling – two minutes or twenty? When a cloud of gnats enveloped her face she decided she'd had enough. She stood up and let out a scream. Her ankles were twin bracelets of red welts and she dropped the knife and slapped at them and her bare legs in a frenzy. She took another stumbling step and saw a fence post with a few strands of broken and rusted barbed wire still clinging to its rotted, nail-spiked length. Leaning incongruously against it was a large silver hubcap. It had a complicated bicycle spoke design and what looked like a wingnut or a tiny two bladed fan in the center. Mickey squatted next to it, pulling the tactical shirt over her knees and as far down as it would stretch. She picked up the bayonet and peered into the darkness looking for Ronnie.

She saw the lightning before she heard the thunder.

* * *

Ronnie stretched his long, sprinter's stride and, after he counted his steps, surf-slid on his belly into a patch of prickly foliage. He covered the back of his head with both hands, his elbows triangulated like someone surrendering. He felt the heat first and then watched the ground around him glow in a shimmering second of white light. He heard the explosion and then a concussive wave of heated air rolled over him. There was the sound of crackling, like a beach fire and then a piteous high-pitched scream which seemed to go on for seconds, wavering like an air raid siren. "Willie Pete" was grunt slang for White Phosphorous, a substance which burned whatever it stuck to intensely and incessantly for as long as it remained exposed to air. The burns it inflicted on human skin he'd seen first-hand and they were horrific. The *m34* he'd tossed at Billy Bowker contained fifteen liquid ounces of Willie Pete that ignited the instant the case split open. A thick cloud of smoke rumbled toward him like an approaching train and his back and legs felt suddenly sunburned.

There were pings and pops and then a low hissing sound. Ronnie thought of the rusting propane tank he'd marked when he first circled the shack in recon. He jumped to his feet and took off running.

* * *

The second explosion shook the ground and knocked the hubcap from the post. Acrid black smoke obscured her vision and made her eyes water. The whining and the biting instantly ceased. Mickey tucked her head to her knees and waited. If Ronnie were hurt or dead, she realized, she had no idea where she was or how she would get out. Ronnie had told her himself how vast and how trackless the Pine Barrens were. She thought of the scene at the station. Her father down, bleeding; probably dead by now. Speziale dead, shot, she remembered, with her gun covered in her prints. Shots Caputo lying dead at the lighthouse. How could she possibly explain all this, she wondered? *Who* could possibly explain all this? And who would ever believe it? Part of her desperately wanted to cry but she decided she was done with all that now. She wouldn't cry and she wouldn't quit. If Ronnie didn't appear soon she'd head back through the smoke and the bugs and the grass – she'd walk through the *fucking jungle* to find him. Mickey palmed the bayonet grip and stood up. The wave of smoke had cleared enough for her to make out the path and she began to walk. After a few steps she heard the rustle of wildlife moving on either side of her. Moving fast, she thought – running. Then a white-tailed deer flashed by so close she could have touched it. It took just her another moment to realize that the animals were all running in the opposite direction.

Surf City

The pulsing roof lights, flashlights and strobes gave a carnival appearance to the surrounding buildings and pavement. Red, blue, amber and white flashes and beams blended asynchronously in an arcing, kaleidoscopic display that bounced crazily off windows and bricks and the faces and eyeglasses of bystanders. A pale yellow Cadillac ambulance whooped its siren, pulled out and accelerated immediately, headed, for the big hospital in Atlantic City. Cruisers from every Long Beach Island municipality crowded at uncertain angles against a half-dozen State Police vehicles. Orange cones and cordon ropes appeared, sequestering a block square around the station house. All four doors and the trunk were flung open on the Galaxie. The Danube Blue Chevelle was lit by two sets of squad car headlights and an old Chevy Bel-Air stood silent guard on the side of the building, its engine still idling. Troopers with high-powered, long-barreled silver flashlights combed the parking lot for shell casings and tire marks. Intermittently the interior of the station was lit by the incandescent explosion of a giant flash bulb as the crime-scene photographer chronicled the grisly panorama.

A New Jersey State Police captain stood outside the station door talking to Billy Tunell.

"Where is Chief Cleary?" Tunell asked. "I'm the mayor of this town and I demand to know the whereabouts of my Police Chief."

"I understand," said the captain, a tall man with military bearing, peering down at the six-inch-shorter Tunell. "But I am under strict orders not to share information or to disturb the scene further until the agents from the Federal Bureau of Investigation arrive here from Philadelphia along with their Forensics team."

"Who was taken away in that ambulance, then? Was it Mickey – I mean Chief Cleary?" Tunell asked.

The captain looked around. His brass name tag identified him as one M.J. Hernandez. His coffee-with-cream brown skin was beaded with perspiration. "We believe that the wounded gentleman was actually Chief Cleary's father. The car around the corner is registered to him. We assume he drove here from Philadelphia for reasons unknown."

"Where is Chief Cleary?"

"OK, all I can tell you is that Chief Cleary's whereabouts are unknown at present," Hernandez replied. "The troopers who arrived on scene first believe she may have been taken against her will or may have fled into the Pine Barrens. Who did you said say you were again?"

Tunell's face reddened. "I'm the mayor of the damn town," he said. "And I can guarantee you, sir, that she most assuredly did not flee."

Hernandez's shoulders stiffened. "There are two dead Federal agents inside the station. Both appear to have been shot with Chief

Cleary's service weapon. For her sake, Mister Mayor, I sincerely hope you're right."

The Pine Barrens

For a long second the figure in the doorway of the shack stood screaming, its arms flailing at the incendiary substance burning away skin and muscle at five-thousand degrees, hotter than the flame of an acetylene torch. Then it slumped and went silent as molten once-living tissue fused with the wooden floor. Within seconds the black smoke began to rise. The tarry pitch between the unfinished boards ignited and flames fanned out anew, consuming or melting anything in their path. They burst through the roof and licked out from underneath the shack. The dry brush and deadfall caught immediately along with the overhanging branches. A fire-whorl started to form, a brilliantly lit dust-devil of destruction. The blaze briefly created its own wind, pushing it further from its point of origin. The dry winter and spring had turned the carpet of pine needles into tinder and it came alive with a terrifying symphony snaps and snarls.

Twenty-one miles away in the not particularly sacramental town of Tabernacle, New Jersey, the metal steps of the fire tower at Apple Pie Hill moaned under the weight of Forest Fire Lookout Carl Czarnecki who had descended twenty minutes earlier to evacuate the remains of an ill-advised Sombrero Special he'd purchased at the 7-Eleven store. When he eventually conquered the nine flights of steps and the sixty vertical feet he would climb through the hatch that opened into the seven-by-seven foot observation post. From there he would be able to see the twinkling lights of the Philadelphia to the west and the moonlit blackness of the Atlantic Ocean to the east. Spread out in every direction below the tower and the two-hundred foot hill it sat on would be one-point-one million acres of desolate pine forest simmering in drought and murmuring with possibilities. The gray smudge he would see in the distance would probably escape the eyes of a newbie but this was his seventh season in the tower. He would spot it with the circular plane-table Alidade and then mark it on the large map tacked to the wall. The United States Geologic Survey map had been annotated extensively over the years with hand-drawn squiggles and X's or circles, most drawn by locals in exchange for a look at the view. They showed a maze of unmarked roads, trails and shacks. He would reach for the bulky black walkie-talkie but would not use it because the Sombrero Special was not finished with him yet.

♦ ♦ ♦

The smoke was getting thicker and her eyes were watering when she heard his voice. "Cleary," he shouted out of the billowing blackness. "Cleary."

"Right here. Right here," she shouted back. Mickey walked back to the post, grabbed the fancy hubcap and banged it.

Ronnie appeared as if out of thin air, a foot away. His face was smudged with dirt and soot; his bare torso and pants were caked with blood. He had, she noticed, taped the dog tags to his chest and the white adhesive strip was stained and beginning to peel away.

"We have to go," he panted. "This whole place is going to burn faster than we can run. The bike's over there." He pointed into the smoke that was now rolling past them. "Are you OK? Because we have to run."

"I'm OK," she said. "Where's Bowker?"

"He's a crispy critter by now," Ronnie answered and grasped her arm. "Stay with me."

He pushed ahead of her and began moving. Mickey had lost all sense of direction but Ronnie moved, she thought, like he had night vision. How far they walked she couldn't tell but suddenly they were at the base of a large pine tree and she could see the Enfield leaning up against it. There was a sense of increasing heat on her back and she fluttered the tactical shirt to cool herself. Ronnie pulled the bike onto the soft, sandy soil and hopped on. He kicked the engine into life and helped Mickey squeeze into the small space behind him.

"It won't be a fun ride," he said. "Tuck your head against my back and keep your legs away from the exhaust pipes." Mickey looked down trying to figure out how she was going to accomplish that particular feat.

"Where are we going?" she shouted as a low rumble built in the distance.

"We're going back," he said. "Time to end all of this crazy shit. They might still be there telling the troopers who knows what so be prepared. It could get ugly."

"That dirtbag Sesso shot my dad," she said. "One way or another he's a dead man."

Surf City

"We're getting choppers from Maguire AFB and Fort Dix," Hernandez said. "She didn't just walk into the Pine Barrens. If she's out there we'll find her."

Tunell walked over and sat down on one of the public benches. A dark Econoline van pulled up and individuals in blue coveralls emptied from its rear doors, "FBI" stitched in tall gold letters on their backs. The carried plastic cases that looked like oversized tackle boxes and hustled into the police station.

Hernandez walked over to him. "Would you mind sticking close by?" he asked. "Just in case Chief Cleary is hesitant to cooperate? Assuming, of course, she's still in a position to cooperate."

Tunell nodded and stared down at his shoes. Tucked just behind them and wedged against the stone foot of the bench was a creased and dusty postcard. He reached down and picked it up.

"*Greetings from Surf City, N.J.!*" was printed in happy red cursive over a photograph of pristine white sand dotted with striped umbrellas, beach chairs, blankets and chaise lounges and the crowd of people who sat on them and under them. The Atlantic was a color-adjusted indigo blue with bathers splashing in the surf line. With his thumb he pushed off some of the dirt and sand and smoothed out the creases. In the soft, circular glow of a streetlight he stared at the picture and then up at the station which had become a hive of activity. A much larger but equally dark van arrived on the scene. For the bodies, he assumed. Tunell thought of the St. Christopher medal and said a silent prayer that his traveler would return safe. He put the postcard in his pocket.

TWENTY SEVEN
The Pine Barrens

RONNIE WAS FLYING BLIND.

Overhead the familiar *whump-whump* of helicopter rotors filled the air. He'd heard them in the distance and immediately turned off the motorcycle's headlight. He wasn't certain they were looking for Mickey. He thought they could just as easily have been dispatched to check out the smoke plume that was now surely visible from afar. The moonlight gave him just enough visibility to see the peeling remnants of the center line paint. As they passed the occasional streetlamp mounted high on a telephone pole he slowed down and veered outside of its arc of yellow light. It would only be a matter of time, he figured, until they met a State Trooper driving the opposite way. He knew he couldn't outrun a big V8 but the bike could go places a car couldn't if it came to that. Mickey was wedged behind him. He felt her weight every time he leaned into a curve and she didn't. The Enfield wasn't designed for two riders but they were managing. The helicopters crisscrossed over them several times and seemed to be heading west now. The blaze had probably gotten their full attention and Ronnie was thankful for the unplanned diversionary tactic. He didn't think they would be looking for a motorcycle either, but with all that had occurred he didn't want to take the chance. Finally, he recognized the fishy odor of Manahawkin Bay and knew they were close. He heard tires and engines in the distance and pulled off into a grove of pygmy pines until the two State Police cruisers whizzed by them, roof lights crazily coloring the branches overhead.

"Where do you want to go first?" Ronnie asked when the sound of their whining motors had faded.

"Back to the station," Mickey said. "My station."

"We'll be walking right into a cluster-fuck," he replied. 'They don't even know about Billy the Piney yet and I bet nobody's found the guy at the lighthouse either." He rubbed flakes of dried blood off his chest and neck. "Quite the body count for one patrol."

"I want to go in alone," Mickey said. "This is my mess, not yours."

Ronnie laughed. "I think it's a little late for the whole *High Noon* thing there, sheriff. Besides, I talked to one of the troopers so they can ID me now. But that was how I knew where to look for you."

Mickey appeared confused.

"Your dad; he got a few words out. Just enough for me to hear."

"But how-"

Ronnie patted the motorcycle handlebars. "Your Piney friend was the guy I bought the bike from," he said. "I was feeling the vibe when I met him. Kind of a miracle I was able to remember where he was. Can't really explain it."

Mickey put her hand to her chest and felt the bump of the medal under the shirt.

"What did you-"

"Phosphorous grenade," he said. "There won't be anything to find."

"You just happened to have one lying around?" she asked.

"Among other souvenirs," he said. Then he searched the sky. The helicopters sounded far away now. "You ready?"

"My dad came here to protect me," she said. Her chin quivered slightly and she clenched her jaw until it stopped. "Now I've lost him, too."

"Maybe not," Ronnie replied. He flicked the headlight switch and the ground lit up in front of them. "It was a high shot, right side not left. Saw guys make it who took a lot worse." He started the engine. "Come on; let's go light these bastards up."

"You let me do it," Mickey said above the rumble. "Just get me there and then stay out of my way." As she said this a different sound filled the air. Ronnie killed the headlight and turned off the engine, duck walking the bike into the pine straw. "That's not fire trucks or cruisers," she said.

Ronnie did not reply. The sound grew louder until they both knew what it was. Engines, several of them if not more. Not big engines, but loud, unmuffled four-stroke ones. Motorcycle engines.

The first row of headlights approached and Ronnie turned the Enfield's lamp on and off several times. The engines slowed and a dozen bikes approached. One pulled off not far from where they sat. With the multiple beams on them Mickey could not make out the rider. She saw him make some kind of hand gesture and all the engines throttled down and quit.

"Dunn," a voice called out. "Is that you?"

"Fuckin A' it is," Ronnie answered. "That you, Lieutenant Stellwag?"

"You know it," the reply came. Mickey saw another hand signal and all the headlights went out. A figure she could barely make out dismounted the first bike and approached. "That the meter maid with you, soldier?"

"Fuckin' A it is," Mickey shouted before Ronnie could answer. "Didn't I tell you to call ahead?" The figure laughed and came closer until she could see him. No, she thought, not handsome but right now, not bad either. He saluted Ronnie who returned it sharply.

"Jesus," Stellwag said. "You look like you both went two rounds with an NVA platoon. And is that Willie Pete's sweet cologne I smell?"

"Willie was here but he's all done now. Just popping smoke wasn't going to cut it this time, LT."

"Roger that," Stellwag replied. "Well it's a certified shit-show in your little town, Chief," he continued. "Not sure it's the Welcome Wagon they've got ready for you, either."

"I don't care," Mickey said in a hoarse voice. "I'm going back."

"OK, but let us provide you with a fighter escort," Stellwag said in a matter-of-fact tone that told Mickey he was not a stranger to making decisions or giving orders. "Give us a minute to get turned around. Then fall in between the last two mounts." She watched him fade back into the darkness.

Shore Memorial Hospital
Atlantic City, NJ

Richie Liszewski looked at the large pale man on the stretcher. "Get some O Negative," he said. "Six bags. And three bottle of plasma. This guy's needle is bouncing on 'E' right now." Both his gloved hands were holding large sponges tightly against the man's shoulder. Blood stained his "Dr. Kildare" white tunic and pants.

"Chest X-Ray's up," an orderly said flicking the switch on a bright fluorescent screen. Liszewski looked at it.

"OK," he said. "Get me a chest tube tray and a drain bottle. The big two-liter one with sterile water in the bottom." With one hand he reached for more gauze sponges and tucked them underneath his other hand, raising it from the oozing bullet wound for only a second. "Call Maguire AFB or Fort Dix and see if they have a chopper we could commandeer. Then call Jefferson Hospital in Philly and ask for the chest cutter on-call. I want the doc, not the surgical resident. Ask them if Camishion is available." He rubbed his chin on his tunic and locked his elbows to place more downward pressure. "Jesus," he said. "I thought I was all done with this."

"You've seen something this bad before?" one of the nurses asked.

"Honey," he replied, "I used to see more than this before breakfast."

"In Philadelphia?"

"A little further west than that, babe" Liszewski replied. "Try Da Nang."

Surf City

A black, windowless van was pulling away from the station when they arrived. The incoming thunder of a herd of engines brought all activity around the station to a standstill .Gawkers stood at the perimeters of a rope cordon. Two by two, the Sons of Satan rode in and then parted ahead of the Enfield. But they remained closely spaced, forming a wall of hot, rumbling metal on each flank. When she and Ronnie reached the head of the formation Mickey saw Mayor Tunell alone on a bench, head down and hunched over.

She directed Ronnie toward him. Twenty yards short of the bench it was if a switch had been thrown. Movement started again as finally the Enfield rolled to a stop. The heads of onlookers and law enforcement officers turned. In the kaleidoscope of competing strobe lights the motorcycle's chrome constantly changed color like a frantic chameleon. Guns were drawn. Flashlights were pointed. All attention converged on the bike.

A rush of excited voices filled the otherwise quiet night, growing louder than the booming surf. Bystanders wore looks of surprise or shock. Fingers pointed. Hands went to open mouths.

Ronnie straddled the Enfield and raised his hands above his head, squinting as the lights converged on him. Mickey slid off the seat behind him and struck a defiant pose, hands on her hips, her gaze hard and straight ahead. Ronnie deployed the kickstand and swung his leg over. Seconds later he dropped to his knees, hands behind his head.

"Unarmed," he shouted. "We are unarmed."

Commands came fast and furious, all instructing the pair to get down. Ronnie lay on his stomach. Mickey took a step forward, ignoring the shouted orders to do otherwise. A young trooper assumed a shooter's stance and leveled his weapon. Mickey took another step. From behind her Billy Tunell came running. He called out to her. She took another step and extended her arms in front of her, palms facing forward. The young trooper was shouting now, his face a mix of fear and anger. Mickey slowed her steps but did not stop. The trooper's voice was hoarse, his hands shaking slightly now. Ronnie yelled something but she either did not hear it or ignored it. She angled toward the trooper and kept walking. The lights pulsed off the metal of other pointed weapons.

The shot rang out just as Tunell reached her.

* * *

In Mickey's head it was completely silent. It was if a small tunnel had appeared in front of her and she was following it. Mouths were moving. Lights were flashing. But her vision was coned down to a rectangle of light – the open door of the station. She held her hands out, fingers spread to deflect the bright lights directed at her. They were all watching her. She could feel it. She wanted to own this moment and she wanted them all to know it. What more could happen than already had? She would walk into her office and she would sit at her desk. They could do what they wanted after that. She reached into the neck of the tactical shirt and pulled out St. Christopher, palming him in her right hand. The action made her slow just a little and allowed Tunell to reach her. She watched the older man stumble as he came astride of her, his glasses falling off. Reflexively she let go of the medal and twisted to help him. His weight shifted to her and in the next instant she felt them both falling. Something buzzing passed by her ear and then she was on the ground. The weight that was suddenly on top of her was crushing.

TWENTY EIGHT
Surf City

THEY HAD TAKEN HER shoes off when they tied her up. Now, looking at them on the floor of the cell, she remembered.

"You understand your rights as I have explained them," Major Hernandez asked her.

"I don't need my rights, Major," Mickey said. "I've been shot at, kidnapped, threatened with rape, torture and murder, all in the last six hours. I came back here willingly and peacefully. Why would I do that if I needed my rights protected?"

"A federal agent is dead, Chief Cleary," Hernandez replied in a measured tone. "Shot with your service pistol. Maybe you should reconsider my offer."

Mickey's wrists were cuffed and she brought her hands to her face together to wipe away the dirt. "Agent Sesso, the fat one, he's dirty as sin. He shot Agent Speziale with my gun. Held it with a handkerchief so his prints wouldn't be on it. I was handcuffed and locked in this cell. I watched him do it. He's the one who should be worried about his rights."

Hernandez glanced at the trooper by Mickey's side. "Agent Sesso is also dead. And Agent Sesso was also shot with your service weapon. Again, perhaps you should consider carefully any further statements you wish to make at this time."

Mickey knew they saw the look of shock on her face. She just didn't know how they were interpreting it.

"Look, Sesso was alive the last time I saw him. He stuffed a rag in my mouth and they tied my feet with an electrical cord. Then

Sesso choked me out. Next thing I knew I was in the backseat of a car headed into the Pine Barrens."

Hernandez and the trooper exchanged glances again. He motioned for a youngish man in a khaki suit to come over. "When you say they tied you up, you mean agents Sesso and Speziale."

"No," Mickey protested. "You're not listening. There were three of them in here. Sesso, Speziale and Petroni. But Petroni was the only one in the car. I never saw Sesso again after he choked me." She pointed to the bruises on her neck. "If Sesso's dead then Petroni must have shot him. And Sesso's the one who shot my dad. He used Speziale's gun – kept it in his dead hand to do it. Check the slug they pull out of Patsy Cleary. It'll be from Spezialie's piece."

The man in the khaki suit moved closer. "Arthur Petroni, the attorney? Is that who you're referring to?"

"Who the hell are you?" Mickey shot back.

"I'm Agent Driscoll, special assistant to the Deputy Director. You do mean A. Louis Petroni from Philadelphia, correct?"

"Isn't that what I said?" she replied. "I woke up in the back seat of some fancy car trying not to choke to death on the rag. Petroni's driving and he's yelling at me while he's driving."

"What was he saying?" Driscoll asked.

"You know, I was trying real hard not to asphyxiate at the time. I don't really know. Crazy shit. Didn't make any sense to me but then I was still pretty groggy. Where's Petroni? He's the one who dropped me off out in the Pines to get capped by some seriously screwed-up hillbilly. You guys need to find Petroni."

Driscoll touched his index finger to his chin. "Mr. Petroni's whereabouts are currently unknown," he said. "His employer says he returned to Philadelphia earlier this evening and left immediately for a long-planned vacation overseas."

"So they killed him, too?"

"We don't know that."

"Yes you do," Mickey said. "Because he's the one who could tie them all together. Whatever this was supposed to be in the beginning, it got way out of hand and the only way to put a lid on it was to kill everyone involved. Including me. Sesso was obviously working for somebody other than the FBI, Driscoll. That's going to be a problem for you, I think."

Driscoll left his finger on his chin. "But what about the death of young Mr. Ragone? There is a school of thought that believes you might have had a hand in that. Payback of sorts to the Ragone family for your father's injury."

"You have to be kidding me. Did you really just say 'a school of thought'?" Mickey spit out dirt and some tiny remnants of dead bugs onto the floor. "I don't know what happened to the kid. All I wanted was to get him to the State M.E. for a proper autopsy."

"We understand the decedent's remains are no longer in your jurisdiction. Do you have any id-"

"Somewhere in Phiily by now. Try tracking down our local coroner if they haven't wasted him yet, too."

"Chief Cleary," Driscoll said, "There are at least three people dead-"

"Four, including Caputo," Mickey interrupted. "Five if you count the guy in the Pines. Six if they got Petroni already. Body counts are a big deal with you guys, right?"

"Make it seven," Hernandez said. "Including the retaliation killing in North Philly yesterday we believe was related to the death of young Mr. Ragone. Did I hear you say Caputo?"

"Yeah. They sent Shots Caputo to kill me out at the lighthouse but that didn't work out so well for him."

There were puzzled glances all around.

"Tomasino Caputo?" Driscoll asked."Tommy Shots?"

"Yeah, Shots Caputo, Ragone's button man. He's behind a sand dune in the Barnegat Light parking lot in case you're looking for him."

"How did Mr. Caputo-"

"Natural causes," Mickey replied. "Considering his line of work."

Hernandez motioned to the young trooper who left hurriedly.

"Major Hernandez and I need to confer briefly," Driscoll said. "And I'm confused about this person you mentioned in the Pines. I'll want you to tell me more about that shortly. Can I offer you a drink of water, Chief?"

"You can offer to take these friggin' cuffs off me," Mickey snapped. "I'm pretty sure you got me surrounded here, Tex."

Driscoll motioned to the trooper who stood at Mickey's shoulder. "OK, uncuff her," he said. "And get her some water."

Driscoll and Hernandez moved out of earshot while the cuffs

came off. Mickey rubbed at her scraped and bug-bitten wrists. "Thank you," she said. "What's your name trooper?"

"George, ma'am. George Joo." He pronounced his last name like "Joe."

"Well, Georgie Joo," Mickey said, "You're going to have yourself one hell of a story to tell the boys back at the barracks."

Driscoll and Hernandez returned.

"And where's my dad?" Mickey asked before they could speak. "I want you to find out right now. And you make sure they save the slug."

"He's on his way by helicopter to Jefferson. They have a surgeon and an operating room waiting for him when he gets there. I'll keep you apprised of his status."

"How was he when he left?"

"He was unconscious but he was alive," Hernandez said.

"I'm afraid we're still going to have to detain you, Chief Cleary," Driscoll said. "Again, it *was* your weapon that killed Agents Sesso and Speziale. The killing of a federal agent is a capital crime. And then there's the matter of the note. Deputy Director Durkin believes there may be extenuating circumstances but until we can establish some sort of timeline, he feels we have to-"

"The note is bullshit," Mickey replied. "Sesso wrote it and planted it."

Driscoll's brow furrowed. "We sent a Photostat of the note and a handwriting sample from your logbook to our analyst in D.C. I'm afraid, Chief, they're a match for your deputy."

Before Mickey could answer there was a commotion at the station door.

"I'm sorry sir, I don't care who you are, you cannot enter a secured scene."

"Don't tell me what I can and can't do in my town." Mickey recognized the familiar voice of Billy Tunell. "I have important information which I believe will fully exculpate Chief Cleary and you are going to listen to it, goddammitt." Mickey had never heard him swear.

"Are you an attorney?" someone asked.

"No I am not an attorney. Why on earth would anyone want to be an attorney? I am an elected official and a public servant and I will not be silenced."

Mickey watched as all the heads in the room turned and

uniformed bodies parted. Billy Tunell walked in accompanied by a statuesque redhead. She was easily six feet tall and even with a modest sweater on it was obvious her attributes were not limited to her vertical dimensions.

"Who is officially in charge of this fiasco?" Tunell demanded.

"I am." Hernandez and Driscoll responded together.

"Very well," Tunell said, "Then please accompany me and my guest to a place where we can talk privately. It's a matter of some urgency for everyone involved." He nodded to Mickey.

"There's a fire in the Pines," someone yelled into the station. "Jesus, you can see the smoke from here." Most of the troopers exited and soon there was the sound of gunning motors and wailing sirens. Soon the only people who remained were Mickey, the mayor and his guest, Driscoll, Hernandez and the young trooper.

Driscoll spoke first. "Please explain the meaning of-"

"Allow me to introduce Miss Irma La Deuce. Irma, which is the name under which she appears theatrically, is an *artiste*; a *danseur*, if you will."

"I'm a stripper," Irma said without apparent embarrassment. "It's OK, Billy, you can say it."

Tunell flushed pink. "Be that as it may, I made Miss La Deuce's acquaintance when one of the Laundromats I own tangled with some of her more delicate wardrobe articles."

"It chewed up my G-strings and pasties," Irma said. "They all have the Two of Hearts on them. You know, the deuce?"

"Miss La Deuce has come forward of her own volition to shed considerable light on an event which appears to have set this entire debacle into motion."

Mickey stood up and brushed more dirt and plant fibers off the tactical shirt. She wondered where Ronnie was. She hadn't seen him since he got off the bike.

"I wanted to do the right thing as soon as it happened," Irma said quietly. "That's what I told him. I mean it was an accident, that's all. But then he said we should just keep going and not say anything about it. He'd make sure it was all taken care of. Said he didn't want any trouble for Mickey."

Mickey spied the *Inquirer* Sports section still lying on her desk. She thought of the article tucked below the fold. The one she wanted to tell Kaylen about. Except, she now realized, he had already known. A story unfolded in her head that she thought even another Mickey – Spillane - might find implausible.

Two of the Ship Bottom officers were seated on either side of Ronnie in the back seat of one of their patrol cars. All four of its doors were open to the night air.

"I'd like to go inside and see what's going on," Ronnie said. "I might have some information that could help straighten things out."

"That State Police major said you stay right here with us until he comes and gets you," one of them replied. "You do *not* screw around with Staties."

There was the smell of wood smoke on the breeze. Ronnie had watched the cars peel out and he could hear the air-raid siren sound of fire trucks on the move. It occurred to him that in the space of less than three hours he had killed two people. In uniform, he would have been given credit for termination with extreme prejudice of two enemy combatants and would have received a commendation, maybe even a medal. Now he wondered if they would try him in state or federal court and whether his parents would help him pay for the legal help he was surely going to require. He thought they might even throw in an arson charge if the forest fire he started did any serious damage. Four days ago he barely knew who Mickey Cleary was; now he might have to spend the rest of his life in prison for trying to rescue her. Doing the honorable thing, he decided, was going to cost him dearly again.

Driscoll wiped his forehead with a red-monogrammed handkerchief.

Hernandez twice started to say something and then apparently thought better of it.

After several minutes of silence Driscoll spoke. "Thank you, Miss La Deuce. We'll need to discuss what happens next. Perhaps you could spend the night in one of Surf City's fine hotels in case we need to talk to you again."

"I didn't bring any money with me," Irma said. "I didn't think-"

"You will be a guest of the Borough," Tunell said. "You've done a brave and difficult thing in coming here. It's the least we can do. I'll see to it with the innkeeper myself."

"Am I in, like, really big trouble now?" Irma asked. "Am I going to jail?" She appeared on the verge of tears.

"I believe that there exist here some extreme mitigating circumstances," Driscoll replied. "I don't believe that any of this was your fault. We just have to decide how best to handle the situation. We would appreciate it if you didn't call anyone or speak to anyone about this matter. Have you discussed it with anyone since it happened?"

She shook her head.

"Does your, uh, passenger know anything about what happened?"

Irma dropped her chin. "He was asleep. Dead to the world, if you get my meaning."

Driscoll rubbed at his temples. "Alright. I think we can leave him out of it for the moment. They mayor will see you to your accommodations."

"I just did what the policeman told me to. I didn't try to-"

"We understand," Hernandez said. "And we truly appreciate your cooperation."

"He was very nice," Irma chirped. "A real gentleman. I didn't even realize who I was driving around with until the policemen told me. I don't watch sports very much."

Tunell took her arm and led her from the station.

"Well this is going to be a major problem," Driscoll said. "A *major* fucking problem." He looked at Hernandez. "Have someone take the Chief home and let her get cleaned up. I'll make a few calls but something tells me we're all heading for a pow-wow over the bridge tonight. I'm not making any decisions without clearance all the way from the top on this one. This is one live fucking grenade, boys. Major Hernandez, I think you need to inform the Superintendent immediately."

"Where's Ronnie?" Mickey asked.

Driscoll looked surprised, as if he'd forgotten about him.

"I'll bring him in," Hernandez said. "Two of the local officers are keeping him company."

"He saved my life," Mickey said. "But I saved his too, just in case we're counting. So I want a guarantee that nothing bad goes down for him."

"You of all people should know I can't make any guarantees at this point, Chief," Driscoll replied. "For anyone - and that includes you. We need to hear what Mister..."

"Dunn," Mickey said. "His name is Ronnie Dunn. And he already put his life on the line for you and this country in Viet Nam. He did it again for me tonight. You have, or had anyway, at least one dirty agent, Mr. Driscoll. That won't reflect well on you or your office. If the shit hits the fan here, everyone is going to get covered with it, including you and your Director. I'd be sure to keep that in mind when you start deciding who, if anyone, takes a fall."

Driscoll's jaw clenched.

Ronnie entered, trailed by Hernandez. "You OK?" Mickey asked.

"Yeah," he said, "Five by five. Never better." He was wearing a baggy Ship Bottom PD sweatshirt one of the police officers had given him. Hernandez escorted him to a chair.

"Who was the redhead?" Ronnie asked.

For a moment no one spoke.

Then Mickey laughed out loud, breaking the silence. "Soldier boy," she said, "You aren't going to believe it even when they tell you."

TWENTY NINE

The Roundhouse, Police Headquarters
Center City, Philadelphia

THE CONFERENCE TABLE WAS a new addition, dark maple with a high-gloss, lacquered finish. All but two of the chairs around it were occupied.

"I really think you should have included Ronnie," Mickey said. She was wearing her spare uniform without badge or gun belt, both having vanished during her abduction

"This is complicated enough," Driscoll said. "Major Hernandez is debriefing him."

"You mean he's guarding him."

Driscoll exhaled sharply. "Fine. He's guarding him. While he's debriefing him. He seems to be a most resourceful individual."

Rays of early morning sun gave the room a pale peach glow. Everyone at the table looked drawn and tired. A third pot of Mr. Coffee was hissing in the corner. A side door opened and J.J. Durkin entered followed immediately by Basil Jablonski. Durkin took a seat but Jablonski went straight to Mickey and folded his arms around her.

"I have two uniforms posted in the Waiting Room over at Jefferson," Jablonski said. "He's still in surgery. The officers have orders to call me every half hour with updates. Rudy Camishion is the best in the city – that's why he's the Chief. If anyone can pull Patsy through it's him." Mickey saw he was holding something in his hand. It was a picture frame. He held it in front of her.

"That's me and Patsy the day you got baptized. You hold onto it. You take it with you when you go to the hospital." He placed it in her hand and went to his chair.

J.J. Durkin spoke first. "We'll dispense with the introductions other than to welcome Surf City Chief of Police Michaela Cleary who, by all accounts, has had a most interesting twenty-four hours." There was an attempt at polite laughter which dissipated rapidly. Despite the early hour, Durkin was clean shaven and smartly dressed, with a perfect Windsor knot in his navy blue tie. Jablonski, Mickey thought, appeared to have just rolled out of bed. He wore a wrinkled short-sleeve dress shirt open at the collar with what her father always called a U-shirt peeking through. His hair was marginally combed and his eyes looked puffy. Mickey peeked over at Driscoll who was drumming his fingers nervously on the table. There were three other men at the table. Two she pegged immediately as FBI agents and the third was the Superintendent of the New Jersey State Police. He was an imposing man with gray, close-cropped hair and a linebacker's build. He sat straight up in his chair, almost at attention, his military style coat impeccably pressed, his leather Sam Browne belt traversing his chest diagonally from left to right. Mickey noticed that he kept his eyes on Durkin only.

"Basil," Durkin said, "Why don't you catch us up on the Philadelphia end of things."

Jablonski took a slug of coffee. "Both Dante Ragone and Carmine Rocca are currently being detained downstairs for questioning on minor, unrelated matters. We believe, based on what we know now, that the death of Dante Ragone, Jr. was not a premeditated action by the Rocca family, although it initially was interpreted as such resulting in the retaliatory murder of 'Frankie Numbers' Cherubini. The good news, if there is any, is that these two deaths appear to be the extent of any direct conflict between the two families. The bad news is that it appears Carmine Rocca sought to exploit the death of young Dante to lure Dante, Sr. into taking actions that would lead to his imprisonment, his displacement or even his death, allowing Mr. Rocca to consolidate power in our fair city. This involved the abduction and murder of Chief Cleary which, we believe the plan called for, would be blamed on the Ragone family. I don't have to tell any of you what kind of heat the murder of one of our own would bring down on the assumed perpetrators. This relatively ingenious plot was complicated by yet another erroneous assumption. Namely, that Chief Cleary was somehow collusive in the death of Dante Ragone, Jr." He nodded to Mickey. "Which, quite obviously," he paused a beat, "she was not. Chief Cleary was thus unknowingly placed in what amounts to mortal double-jeopardy. Her actions have been nothing short of heroic."

Durkin took over. "Before continuing, I'll remind everyone here that what is said in this room never leaves this room. This is in the interests of, if not national security, at least national well-being." He pulled on his tie as if steeling himself for what came next. "It appears that one of the Bureau's agents, Charles Sesso, had ties to both the Rocca and Ragone families that escaped even our intense internal scrutiny. He was acting, in effect, as what our Intelligence colleagues would call a double, or perhaps even triple-agent. We believe he duped the Ragone's into thinking he was their man on the inside carrying out their plan. We think Agent Sesso's choice of scenario was based solely on personal financial reward and not indicative of a larger compromise of Bureau personnel or information. A search of his home has turned up a one-way ticket to Honduras, a nation with which we do not currently have an extradition agreement. "

Mickey was impressed at how smooth Durkin was at delivering what had to be a devastating admission of ignorance. He took a drink of water and continued.

"After debriefing Chief Cleary and her companion Mr. Dunn about the events of May twenty-four, we surmise that these competing Machiavellian schemes broke down completely." Durkin's cheek twitched. "I believe that Agent Steven Speziale began to suspect Agent Sesso's true motives and in doing so, lost his life in the line of duty." Durkin paused, collecting himself. "In all my years I have never, ever encountered a more despicable act than Agent Sesso shooting his partner in cold blood. We assume that Agent Sesso planned to kill Mr. Petroni as well before taking Chief Cleary to her planned demise."

Her planned demise. Mickey considered the sterility of the last two words. Perhaps, she thought, the terms torture, rape and murder were not part of Bureau jargon.

"So who killed Agent Sesso?" the Superintendent asked.

"We assume that Mr. Petroni did," Jablonski said. "Using Chief

Cleary's nine millimeter. We believe, from information provided by Mr. Dunn, that Chief Cleary's father, who at this moment is fighting for his life downtown, burst in on the scene at the police station in Surf City. "If," he stopped himself, "*When* he recovers sufficiently I believe he will be able to tell us exactly what happened inside the station at that point."

The Superintendent leaned in. "All but one of the fatalities occurred on New Jersey soil and thus in my jurisdiction. It's a lot of bodies for one night at the shore. And don't forget the lamentable loss of Deputy Fairbrother. If I may pay all of you the compliment of being blunt, I don't really give a shit about career criminals biting the dust, even if one happens to be," he arched an eyebrow at Durkin, "a federal agent. I may be just a simple public servant, but it seems to me that we've waded into a bloody quagmire here over what is, to my mind, a vehicle-pedestrian accident complicated by an amateurish attempt at a cover-up by a local law-enforcement officer. Somebody please tell me that I'm wrong."

Durkin cleared his throat. "Sadly, Superintendent, you are not."

The Superintendent placed his hands on the table. "And the motivation for this botched cover-up and its aftermath?"

"Driscoll?" Durkin said.

Evan Driscoll stood up. "Gentlemen, Chief Cleary, we are, whether we want to believe it or not, in a time of national crisis. American values, *core* American values, are under constant attack. Protestors riot in the streets and on college campuses. Brave soldiers returning from war are spit upon and vilified. Splinter groups of our own citizens seek to sow terror with bombings and undermine not only the government but the very rule of law. I am about to share with you sensitive information about the accident the Superintendent referenced." Driscoll reached a hand into his pocket. "There are only a few precious things that still bring us together as a country. Only a few heroes who still inspire young and old; who remind us of the ideals we strive for and the things we in this room stand for and devote our lives to protecting. What we will decide in the next few minutes will be whether to deal yet another blow to our sense of ourselves as Americans. Whether we admit defeat and withdraw or whether we keep fighting."

Driscoll paused, wiped beads of sweat from his forehead with an index finger, and continued. "There was a tragic accident. But it was just that - an accident. The complicating factor in this situation is the identity of the unconscious backseat passenger in Miss La Deuce's vehicle. That individual was one Mr. Mickey Charles Mantle, an employee of the New York Yankees Baseball Club."

The air seemed rush out of the room. Driscoll fidgeted in the stunned silence.

"Mickey Mantle," the Superintendent finally said. "You're telling me that Mickey fucking Mantle is mixed up in a hit and run fatality in my state?"

Driscoll glanced nervously at Durkin who merely nodded for him to go on. "As I said, Mr. Mantle was unconscious in the vehicle's back seat and completely unaware of any of these events. Miss La Deuce was driving him back to New York City. Apparently his teammates had more or less abandoned him in the Atlantic City establishment when he went to the bathroom to relieve himself. She was unaware of his celebrity and his stature and was simply acting as a Good Samaritan. Deputy Fairbrother came upon the scene and realized the, uh, sensitivity of the situation. At this point he apparently exercised his own discretion and embarked on an unfortunate course of action, sending Miss La Deuce and her sleeping passenger on their way. I don't think there's any way to hold Mr. Mantle culpable and Miss La Deuce was following instructions given to her by a uniformed officer of the law. Furthermore, Miss La Deuce was under the impression that the boy was merely knocked out and that Deputy Fairbrother would see to his welfare."

The silence was broken only by coughs and throat clearings. Mickey thought of Kaylen and pictured his desk and all the things that had been staring at her the whole time. She thought about the note Sesso had made her read and felt the blood drain from her face. A cold sweat appeared on her brow and she dabbed at it with her uniform sleeve. This was the second time she'd heard the story and it still broke her heart. Mickey set the picture frame in her lap, covered her eyes with both hands and looked up only when she heard the squeaking of a chair. The Deputy Director of the FBI slowly stood up and adjusted his necktie. Evan Driscoll took a seat, a look of relief on his face.

"Thank you, Evan," Durkin said. Then he addressed the group.

"Some actions are undertaken with the specific intent of doing harm or promoting evil. I don't believe that is the case at all here. I believe this represents a moment of misguided loyalty, not just to a person but to an ideal. An ideal, as Evan said, that we strive to protect every day. Our decision will not be an easy one but it will have repercussions far beyond this room and this moment. I have spoken with the Director in Washington and he with the Attorney General. The United States Government's position at this time is to take no further action for the good of the country. If you agree with this course of action your cooperation and your discretion will be recognized and appreciated."

Mickey thought of the autographed picture hanging on the station wall. The answer had been right in front of her. Jablonski rose and thanked everyone for their efforts. He nodded to Mickey. "And if you gentlemen will excuse me, Chief Cleary and I have some catching up to do."

* * *

In the gauzy sunlight streaming into Jablonski's private office Mickey thought he looked old and worn-down.

"I failed you, Michaela. Failed you miserably. And for that I am truly and heartily sorry."

Mickey looked perplexed.

"Speziale called me. He said they thought you might have been involved in the death of the boy. He told me about the note. Now I love your father as if he were my own brother so I let myself imagine how his only child would feel if she knew someone hurt him. I could have ordered them back here immediately but I, and I am ashamed to admit it, worried about what would happen if it came to light that you were my godchild. That it might look like I was protecting you, covering up for you. I worried more about myself and my political future, which is tenuous on a good day. I put my own interests before your safety – which is not what I promised Patsy and your sainted mother Eileen at the font in St. Peter's Church that day." He pointed to the picture she held.

"But you couldn't have known that Sesso was-"

"I warned Speziale to keep an eye on him. I had suspicions but nothing more that I could act on. I thank Almighty God that Sesso was a Fed and not one of us."

"It all went to hell in a hand basket," Mickey replied. "You couldn't have predicted what was going to happen. Dad used to call it the Law of Unintended Consequences."

Jablosnki rubbed the gray stubble on his chin. "In hindsight, I can almost understand what your late deputy thought he was accomplishing."

Mickey exhaled slowly. "Kaylen thought he was protecting something more important than himself; more important than the town. I have to believe he thought he was protecting the whole country in some way. But I should have put it together a lot sooner. He didn't have to blow his brains out in a motel room. I could have helped him."

"No, you couldn't," Jablonski replied.

"Yes, I could," Mickey said. "I knew the neck wound didn't fit the picture. It just looked wrong from the get-go. The M.E. would have confirmed it."

"And then what, Michaela? You either hide what he did or you send your young deputy to prison for obstruction of justice, tampering with evidence and probably abuse of a corpse. Once he made the decision to let that car leave the scene, the die was cast. But why do you think he bothered to make the neck wound?"

"He was smart enough to know if it was a hit and run they'd eventually find the car. I think he believed-"

"Believed it would be better if it looked like a murder?"

Mickey shook her head. "No, not a murder; he thought the neck wound would make it look like an accident with a boat. That's why he dragged it to the water. So it would appear that it washed up."

Jablonski turned off a pull-chain desk lamp as the morning sun brightened the room even further. "Durkin shared with me right before we came in that their lab people recovered hair and skin from the back seat of the deputy's cruiser. It's pretty basic analysis but they are apparently consistent with the victim's age and sex."

Mickey rubbed her eyes. She was about to ask a question when Jablonski's phone rang.

"Yes. Yes. I got it. She's actually right here. I'll pass it along."

Mickey leaned forward in her chair.

"That was Camishion. Patsy's out of surgery," Jablonski said. "He's lost part of a lung and lot of blood but he's holding his own right now. Says they almost lost him on the table a couple times but he didn't quit on them."

"Tell him Cleary's never quit," Mickey replied. She grabbed a Kleenex and wiped her eyes. "And tell him they never cry either, in case anyone asks."

Jablonski held up one finger and listened. "Yeah. OK, Rudy. Thanks. I'll bring her over myself." Then he hung up. "Your old man, he's like a Timex. And after all this I'd have to say that you're the same way. You both take a licking-"

"But we keep on ticking," Mickey finished.

"Listen, Michaela, it won't be public for a while but I plan to tell the mayor tomorrow that I'll be stepping down," Jablonski said. "This job is mostly about making judgments and I-"

"I think that's a bad idea, Commissioner" Mickey replied. "My dad could use some friends in high places for a while, don't you think?"

"So what do I do, then? Just say 'mistakes were made' and pretend like nothing happened?" Jablonski asked.

"I think that strategy will work for now. Besides, I'*m* asking you not to quit. Isn't there some weird Dago thing about a godfather not being allowed to refuse a request for favor?"

"Never heard of that," Jablonski replied. "It's a good story, though. Now let's go see my old partner. The Vine Street Expressway will be packed but we'll go lights and siren all the way. I'll even drive us if they'll let me."

"I thought you said you had Carmine Rocca and Danny Rags cooling their heels downstairs?"

"I do. But they can wait. I had them cuffed to the desk in the same interrogation room. Just to make it more interesting."

"Make sure Ragone knows I am sorry about his son," Mickey said. "But that I'm not sorry about anything else, especially Shots Caputo."

Jablonski leaned back in his chair. "That's still a missing link for me. Who took Caputo out? It wasn't you."

"He was a casualty of war," Mickey said. "Let's leave it at that. And tell Danny Rags that he's not welcome at the shore, not in my town or any other."

Jablonski rose from his chair with an audible grunt. "That's right, kid," he said. "You tell 'em. It's your town now." Mickey picked up her hat. She took the picture frame and looked at it.

"You were both very handsome, you know," she said.

"*Are* very handsome," Jablonski corrected. "And your mother was an excellent photographer. She would be very proud of you." He took a step back and saluted her. "Let's go, Chief Cleary," he said.

Mickey tucked the picture under her arm and led the way out.

June, 1967

THIRTY

U.S. ROUTE 1
City Line Avenue, Philadelphia

"MICKEY? MICKEY ARE YOU awake?" the driver asked.

John Michael Murphy had started his career as a dormitory security guard at St. Joseph's College, whose stone-walled campus they were now passing. The traffic light for Cardinal Avenue was less than a mile ahead but traffic was heavy and the car had no lights or siren. As the City of Philadelphia's current Chief of Police, Murphy had undertaken many unusual diplomatic assignments but none, he thought, stranger than this one. Jablonski had shared some but certainly not all of the details with him. What he wasn't told outright, he pieced together as best he could. He would not have an active role in the upcoming meeting and this was of some relief to him. He was to let His Eminence set the tone of reconciliation, forgiveness and acquiescence to the greater good. His job was to act as witness to the accords and the pledge of silence by all parties. In preparation, Murphy had gone to confession and attended morning Mass at St. Rose of Lima, his home parish. It was murky moral territory for someone raised on the Baltimore Catechism. The idea that he would carry a secret to his grave weighed heavily on him as the car crawled up the hill.

"Mickey," he said again. "Time to rise and shine. We're almost there."

The big man slumped against the passenger window stirred and blinked his eyes. "Sorry," he said with a slow drawl, "Dozed off I guess."

His seatmate filled more than his half of the Lincoln Continental's front bench. He looked more than uncomfortable in the suit and tie Murphy had helped him pick out for this visit. His shoulders were massive and even with the electric seat pushed all the way back he seemed folded into the confined space.

"What do I call him?" he asked. "Sir Cardinal or Father Cardinal?"

"You're not a Catholic, I take it, are you?" Murphy said.

"No sir," the man replied. "Methodist by birth but not much of anything anymore. Sunday mornings are for hangovers, like Billy Martin says."

"You address the Cardinal as Your Eminence."

The big man laughed. "Did you say your M and M's, Chief?"

"Your em – in – *ence*," Murphy replied, sounding out the syllables.

"I hope I don't have to do much talking," the man replied. "Unless they want to hear some stories. But I might need a few belts before I can tell the good ones."

Murphy smiled. "You just smile and say as little as possible. We'll make our visit short and then we'll get you right back up to New York in time for BP. They'll all be honored to meet you and that will be enough. This little conclave is really about their business, not yours. Washington Senators tonight, right?"

"Yeah," the man said and looked out the window. "I feel really bad about that kid."

"You were asleep in the back seat. It wasn't your fault. And it was a very honorable thing that that your lady friend did – what was her name?"

"Irma, Irma La Deuce is what she said, but that was her dancer's name. Prob'ly not her real one though, huh?"

"Probably not, but it's good enough for our purposes. If any of the people at this meeting ask you about her just tell them she's a professional dancer who was giving you a ride back to your hotel."

"I don't even remember leavin' the titty bar, so, just for the record, there wasn't any funny business between Irma and me. Martin and Ford were supposed to get me home. When they left, she was gonna drive me all the way back to New York, bless her heart. She took a wrong turn tryin' to find the Expressway, I guess."

"Funny business never crossed my mind," Murphy replied. "Just for the record."

"She said she never saw him, Mr. Murphy. Said he just walked right out of the dark and into the road in front of her. She wanted to report it but then the cop – the Deputy, I guess – he asks her who's in the back seat and then says he'll take care of it and she should just take me back to Atlantic City and not say anything about it."

"And you were asleep."

"I wasn't asleep, Chief Murphy. I was passed out."

"Well, passed out is just very deeply asleep. We won't split hairs here, but I don't think any of that is going to come up. An agreement has already been made amongst the interested parties."

"This a party?"

"No, think of it more like a ceremony and you're the guest of honor."

"Irma, she won't get in any trouble now, huh? I mean, she tried to do the right thing. She tried twice but only the second time took."

"Irma has been vindicated and can go on with her life and her chosen career. Just don't mention to His Eminence that she was a-"

"A stripper?"

"A professional dancer. It's not germane to the current discussion."

"Is that her real name – Germaine?"

Murphy hit the left turn blinker which clicked loudly in the quiet car.

"Just shake hands, smile a lot and tell them you'll hit the next one out for them."

The big man looked wistful. "Might be a while on that one. My best years are likely behind me now. It just how it is in this game. Sometimes it seems like yesterday I was still young. Other days it seems like forever ago." He rubbed at his knee. 'Who's all gonna be at this thing again?"

"His Eminence of course, his aide Father Lannon, and two prominent Philadelphia businessmen, Dante Ragone and Carmine

Rocca. It was Ragone's son who was killed in the tragic accident so be sure to offer your condolences."

"My-"

"Tell him you're very sorry for his loss. Did you bring enough baseballs?"

The big man kicked at the dusty canvas bag by his feet. "And a brand new Magic Marker," he said. "But I don't know what they're gonna do with a bunch of scrawled on batting practice balls. Probably worth more the way they are right now."

Murphy made the left turn at the light and pulled up to the massive iron gate which guarded a circular driveway leading to the Cardinal's mansion. It slowly separated in the middle. When it had parted sufficiently Murphy tapped the gas pedal and climbed the inclined drive. He pulled to a stop beneath the marbled portico.

"Everything's already taken care of," Murphy said. "So just be yourself, shake all their hands and flash that big grin. They'll be telling people about the day they met you for the rest of their lives. You're a hero to them. Don't forget that. " He patted the big man on the knee and turned off the engine.

Surf City

The mayor had been wrong, Mickey thought, as the sound of another light plane engine made its presence known. They were buzzing the island at least every ten minutes now. She enjoyed seeing the old biplane the most, but this one looked like a Cessna or maybe a Piper Cub with the strutted wings on the top. It took another full minute until she could read the banner.

"LEVON & THE HAWKS ALL SUMMER LONG!"

It fluttered and swayed as the little plane bucked unseen waves of turbulence in the stiff offshore breeze. Soon Mickey heard the buzzing of second motor, a little lower pitched. The biplane appeared, trailing the Cessna by what appeared to be an unsafe distance.

"AT TONY MART'S FOLL W THE ARROW"

Mickey pictured a large cloth "O" floating somewhere out on the green Atlantic. The Showplace of The World must be doing alright, she figured, if Tony could afford to run aerial advertisements two at a time.

The visit with Kaylen's family had been difficult for her. They didn't know her at all and, when all was said and done, she had barely known him. His sister JoLynne had been gracious to a fault, saying several times how "cool" her brother thought having a real city cop as a Chief was and that he seemed to really like and respect her. His parents, Mickey thought, were still deeply in shock and avoided direct eye contact whenever they could. She had been afraid they would ask her questions she was not at liberty to answer but they hadn't. Maybe it was best, she thought, that suicide was such a taboo subject. The fewer questions asked in this case, the better for everyone involved.

Mickey thought of the mayor's offhand account of the shore's only previous homicide. "Like it never happened," was the phrase he had used. Over the past two weeks, Mickey mused, it could have been the town's tourist motto. She had relocated briefly to the City Clerk's office while a small band of workmen "remodeled" the police station. The updating had given the place an efficient, modern appearance but she sensed that something tangible had been lost forever. The push-button phones and the updated police-band radio that monitored all the municipalities were nice but now there was no room and no reason for a record player and a stack of 45's. "Spiffy," the mayor had proclaimed, bestowing his highest accolade upon seeing the result. There was even a new "hotline" to the State Police barracks in Hammonton. Someone, she realized, was taking no chances.

The wind was whipping whitecaps far out past the breakers. The beach would be blanket-to-blanket in an hour. Mickey grabbed the wooden railing with both hands and leaned out, breathing deeply the salt air. A door creaked open below her and she saw Loretta, who looked up at her with one hand shielding her eyes.

"How did it go?" she asked.

"Better than I expected," Mickey replied.

Loretta cupped a hand to her ear then gave a dismissive wave. "Stay there," she said, "I'll come up."

The narrow deck quivered with each of Loretta's steps on the risers. When she reached Mickey she put out her hand. "Doing OK?" she asked.

Mickey took her arm and squeezed it. "Doing OK," she said.

"I didn't know your deputy but I can scarcely imagine what

the poor parents are going through. Did they ask you-"

"No. And I didn't volunteer anything other than we were all shocked and saddened. Thank God they're not Catholic. He's buried in a church cemetery and nobody's telling them he's suffering the eternal torments of Hell for his actions."

"Amen to that," Loretta replied. "You know, for as tight-lipped as everyone has been about this you're becoming something of a local legend."

"I hardly think-"

"I'm serious," Loretta said, brushing sand off the railing. "About the only thing I haven't heard is that you can leap tall buildings with a single bound."

Mickey smiled. "I had a lot of help when it counted. Plus I was lucky."

"We make our own luck, honey," Loretta replied. "And don't sell yourself short. Don't belittle your courage. Little girls and young women don't get many heroes that look like them. Mayor Billy says the hot item in the toy aisles is plastic police badges and snub-nosed water pistols. And it's not the little boys asking for them."

"I'm not sure that's a good thing," Mickey said.

"Are you kidding? It's a great thing," Loretta answered. "If the people at Mattel had any brains they'd be cranking out Police Chief Barbie right now."

Mickey's back stiffened.

"I'm sorry, honey. Did I say something wrong?"

Mickey swallowed hard and shook her head. "No. No, you didn't. You just reminded me of something and gave me an idea."

"Working tonight?" Loretta asked, pinching the short-sleeve of Mickey's uniform blouse.

"Yeah. I have to go in a few minutes. It's sure been nice having extra help."

"Billy says those three handsome probational officers are from the State Police Academy over in Sea Girt. How'd you finagle that one?"

"Let me tell you something. Those boys are basically Green Berets with badges. And I had nothing to do with the change in assignments."

Loretta craned her neck to look at the ocean. "You know, we can all pretend that what happened didn't happen. As long as we all agree to pretend together. People don't come to Long Beach Island to be reminded that there are bad things and bad people in the world, sweetie. They come here to escape them for a day, or a week, or a month, or a summer. They come here to jump in the ocean and sizzle on the sand. Then they go home with-"

"Sand in their shoes," Mickey finished.

Loretta leaned over and pecked her on the cheek. "That's right, Chief. Now you're starting to sound like a local."

Mickey reached for her Ray-Bans. Loretta pointed to the two freshly waxed cars parked side-by-side in the lot.

"You do realize, I hope, that you now have the *two* coolest automobiles on Long Beach Island," she said. "That '57 Chevy of your dad's brings back some memories for me. Don't be at all surprised if His Honor makes you a generous offer on it."

"I think I'd like to see my father behind the wheel again," Mickey answered.

"Billy says he's making progress. And that you've been able to visit him."

"Jablonski, the P.C., he sends a squad car with two uniforms to take me over anytime I want. And the PBA has someone sit with Dad to keep him company during the day, now that he's out of Intensive Care."

"The bills must be-"

"Mysteriously non-existent," Mickey said.

"You didn't hear this from me of course, but Billy's afraid you'll go back to Philadelphia's police force to be, you know, closer. He says they've approached you about being a detective."

"I've had several interesting offers recently." She thought of Evan Driscoll's business card tucked in her pocket. "But he shouldn't worry. I can picture my dad in a beach chair down here a lot easier than I can picture myself in a squad car back there. He'll definitely wear long black socks with his sandals, though."

Loretta laughed out loud.

"So, how's your soldier friend holding up?"

"You could say that the military had a lot more questions they wanted answered. It appears he must have answered them all correctly. And I guess they're reviewing his discharge status."

"Have you seen him lately?" Loretta asked. "Not that it's any of my business, you understand."

"At the moment I believe he's engaged in peace talks with

his father at a bar in Stone Harbor. Apparently beer and steamed oysters are involved. But I'm looking forward to a full debriefing on my next night off."

"Yes, I imagine you are," Loretta said with a sly smile. She patted her hands together and then looked at her watch. "I'll make you late if I keep asking silly questions. Don't want you to set a bad example for the new troops. But remember, I have Tab and Fresca if you get thirsty. And Ballantine if you need to talk."

"Wait," Mickey said. "I have something to show you. Stay right here." She went into her apartment and returned holding a shopping bag with Strawbridge & Clothier department store markings on it.

"You didn't," Loretta said putting a hand to her mouth.

"I did," Mickey replied. She reached in and pulled out a summer dress the color of the setting sun. "I go do a little shopping in Center City whenever Dad takes a nap. Beats the heck out of the Clearance table at Woolworths. Oh, and I got this, too."

She lifted out a plastic hanger with a two-piece swimsuit in vivid blue.

"Well it's the right shade but there's no place for your badge, dear," Loretta said.

"Exactly," Mickey replied. She dropped both back in the bag and reached out her hand. "Thank you for being here for me."

Loretta squeezed it and headed down the stairs. Mickey pulled the door to her apartment shut and watched the light glint off the newly installed Yale double lock system. She descended the steps and walked to the Chevelle. Another plane towing another banner whined overhead.

"RAY CHARLES   STEEL PIER AC   JULY 4TH   TIX ON SALE!"

Again, a second plane was close on its tail.

"THIS IS... THE SUMMER OF LOVE ON WFIL"

Mickey started the engine and flipped on the Delco. She punched the tuning buttons and when a bouncing riff hit her ear, she cranked the volume knob. Eric Burdon and the Animals were pleading not to be misunderstood. She thought of Kaylen and the dangers of good intentions, then shifted the cruiser into gear and pulled out onto the newly paved road.

July, 1967

THIRTY ONE

Catholic Home for Destitute Girls
West Alleghany Avenue, North Philadelphia

THE DAY WAS HOT despite the early hour and the fans still weren't working. Six Sisters of Saint Joseph gathered around a bare table where a large cardboard box had just been set down. Sister James Michael, who had carried the heavy item up the fifteen stone steps by herself, pulled a white handkerchief from her sleeve and dabbed beads of perspiration from her face.

"Who brought it?" asked Sister Mary Lambert. The dark blue tunics swished with movement. The veils were as square as tabletops and gave each white bandeau a peaked, triangular appearance. The coifs all had small sweat-stains but the starched half-moon wimples were spotless and stiff as mortar boards.

"A young woman," Sister James Michael answered. "She said it was something for the girls."

"Ooh, it's from Gimbel's," exclaimed Sister Sylvia, a novitiate and so, by more than a few years, the youngest member of the group.

"We should wait for Sister Constance," Mary Lambert said. "You know how she is about these things."

"Oh, for God's sakes, just open it." The gravel-voiced

command came from Sister Innocentia, the House Mother. She stubbed out her cigarette in a battered ashtray. "I really doubt it's a bomb. And if it's for the girls then it's probably not booze, unfortunately." She sauntered to the table. "Sylvia," she said. "Go grab the big scissors from the kitchen."

The young nun disappeared. Innocentia picked up the box and shook it. "I just hope to God it's not more crocheted doilies," she said. "If I have to put one more friggin' doily around here I swear to Christ I'll have a stroke."

"What did she look like?" Mary Lambert asked. "The woman who brought it?"

"Young. Pretty." James Michael answered. "Oh, just the prettiest thing. Dark hair, but it was kind of red in the sun. And wearing just the loveliest yellow dress."

"You sure it wasn't a hooker trying to make up for her life of sin and mendacity?" Innocentia asked. There was silence. "I mean, it wouldn't be the first time, right?" She produced a pack a Lucky Strikes from under her tunic and drew one out.

"I don' think she looked like a wayward girl," James Michael said in a meek voice.

"Just checking," Innocentia said, a silver Zippo appearing magically from the pleats of her habit.

Sylvia returned with a large pair of gardening shears. "This was all I could find," she said.

"Those'll do," Innocentia said. "Give'm here."

They all crowded around. Innocentia grabbed the shears in one leathery hand and ran the blades along the tape strip at the top of the box. Then she handed the shears back to Sylvia and pulled the leaves open. Brown paper obscured the contents. The Sisters waited.

"Grab it and dump it out," Innocentia said. James Michael and Mary Lambert picked up opposite corners and inverted the box. Shiny, new, unwrapped packages tumbled out and covered the table.

"What in the world?" Mary Lambert said.

"Oh my Lord, they're Barbie Dolls," Sylvia squealed. "They're all brand new Barbies. And look… " She rummaged through the pile, picking out smaller packages and holding them up. "These are more clothes. And little pairs of shoes and purses and hats."

"I think they call those accessories," Innocentia said. The other nuns looked at her. "What? I got little nieces, you know."

For the next twenty minutes they sifted through the treasure trove.

"How many girls do we have in-house right now?" James Michael asked.

"Nineteen inmates," Innocentia replied, the Lucky Strike dangling between her lips. She brushed ashes from her habit.

"And how many dolls are there?"

Sylvia began to count, mouthing the numbers. "....twenty four, twenty five. There are twenty five. That means every girl can have one of her own. Every single one. Won't they be happy? It's just so wonderful."

"Yeah, it's a friggin' miracle," Innocentia said. "A regular Joyous Mystery"

"It is a miracle," James Michael echoed.

Innocentia took a drag. "I meant it's a miracle it's not more doilies." She blew out a stream a blue smoke. "OK, ladies, box it back up. Don't say anything to the girls and we'll give them out after the evening rosary. Although now none of us will get any sleep tonight, you all realize that, right?"

The nuns busied themselves with the task, chattering happily.

Sister Innocentia walked to the barred window and looked out. On the curb stood a woman in a yellow dress. She looked almost like an apparition, her bright aura out of place against the bleak and crumbling landscape of the surrounding neighborhood. She waved up at the window. Innocentia's eyes were not the best anymore and her pince-nez glasses needed a stronger prescription that she could not afford. But there was something about her, Innocentia thought. Something she couldn't quite put her finger on. Something vaguely familiar. She waved back and bent to clean her glasses.

When Innocentia looked again, the woman was gone.

♦ ♦ ♦

The drive back from Philadelphia had been fun. The old Bel-Air didn't have the power of the Chevelle but her tinkering had at least given it a little more pick up. She'd even gotten the old Wonder Bar radio to work again. Jackie Wilson's "Higher and Higher" was bouncing through its little speaker. It made her think about Ronnie. Mickey wondered what would happen between them. Their courtship, such as it was, had been a literal trial by fire. Where, she asked herself, does anyone go from there? Ronnie had taken her on a few real dates and she had even met his parents. She'd talked with his father about sidearms and muzzle velocities for almost an hour. They'd snuck off and spent a day on the sand in Ocean City, Ronnie teaching her how to body surf the breakers. They strolled the boardwalk and gorged on freshly made Shriver's taffy and fudge, then had dinner at the Tuckahoe Inn. She liked the feeling of being just a face in the crowd for a while. On the way home they'd stopped at the Showplace of the World where she was treated like a celebrity by Tony Mart himself . But there was something between her and Ronnie that she couldn't quite name. Something that kept poking at the edges of their fairy tale.

As she wound through the Pine Barrens she no longer felt the weight of dread that it carried before and she was starting to appreciate the stark beauty that lived in the majestic solitude. When she crossed the bay she slowed, climbing the first bridge like a roller coaster car and waiting for the "damned Atlantic Ocean" to appear before her. Moving further along the causeway she tried to take it all in. She had sand in her shoes now and it felt really good.

Back in Surf City, Mickey drove Long Beach Avenue through town, honking at Mayor Billy as he politicked on the hot sidewalk outside City Hall. The Ebb Tide's parking lot was full and the beach was jammed. Lifeguards' whistles wafted on the breeze like screeching birds. It felt like home, Mickey thought. At least for now. And maybe now was all that mattered.

Evan Driscoll had wanted to meet her for lunch in Center City to, as he put it, "discuss her future possibilities." They were never made public, but he apparently knew all about the commendations she'd received from the Bureau and the New Jersey State Police. The idea that she could be one of the FBI's first female field agents secretly thrilled her but she had begged off the meeting, unable to even think about leaving either the job or Ronnie. She also wasn't sure that Driscoll's interest was purely professional and wondered if maybe Ronnie was feeling the same vibe. She'd run away from something once, Mickey thought. She didn't want to run again.

Mickey was about to pull into her apartment's parking lot when out on the bay road a candy apple red Mustang convertible with Jersey plates whizzed by, a middle-aged couple in the front buckets. The woman was in the driver's seat and her black hair twisted and bounced in the slipstream. Mickey reached to switch on the cherry toppers then remembered, with some measure of embarrassment, that she was driving a ten year-old Bel-Air sedan and not her Chevelle cruiser. For a moment she hesitated. She wasn't on-duty and she wasn't in uniform, although her badge and her creds were on the front seat next to her. She should just go home, she told herself. Maybe have a beer with Loretta. On the other hand, she considered, she was the Chief of Police in the very popular resort town of Surf City, New Jersey and some of her questions were still unanswered.

Mickey punched the gas pedal and headed off in the direction of the Mustang.

BoDean Bowker sifted the remnants of the shack. A mange-ridden coon hound nosed nearby. The ground was almost bare except for the soot. The burnt pines looked like spindly black skeletons in a woodland nightmare. The fire had not leapt the road for reasons unknown, limiting the burn to less than five square miles. BoDean had waited until he was sure the cops and the troopers weren't coming back.

No one was asking about Billy. BoDean wasn't asking either although he knew. He was afraid of the guys Billy dealt with in Philadelphia. Afraid with Billy gone that he was now a liability.

And he knew first-hand how they dealt with liabilities. The old dog was nosing in the charred remnants of the floorboards. There was little identifiable remaining after the State of New Jersey vans had pulled away with their yellow plastic trash bags full to the brim. BoDean walked over and poked with the barrel of his rifle, cuffing the dog in the process who then yelped and skittered to a blackened bush to pee. BoDean knelt down and brushed away detritus like a backwoods archaeologist on a dig. He picked up the small objects, slightly larger than gambling dice and rolled them in his hands. A couple of them were fused together.

Bone fragments, he knew from years of tracking. Wrist, probably.

Something sharp-edged brushed his fingers and he dug deeper. It was char encrusted and held tightly by the thermally-compacted soil but after a few tugs he had it liberated. BoDean held it in the palm of his hand. The heat had warped it a little but he knew what it was. With a thumb he scraped some of the carbon-black from the surface. Any paint on it had been vaporized but the detailed embossing was still intact. He bet it would clean up OK with a little work. BoDean tucked the badge in his shirt pocket and walked to the narrow stream of blood-red water.

Billy, he thought, Billy would do something to make it right if it had been him.

They were twins, after all.

ACKNOWLEDGEMENTS

As with any story, translating an idea in the author's head into something the reader can personally experience requires the help of numerous people with numerous talents the author does not possess. A special thanks to Sheldon Siegel for his advice and guidance on the ins and outs of publishing; Terry Persun for his expert help in formatting the manuscript; April Eberhardt, Jersey girl and literary agent for her encouragement and introductions; my gifted teachers and classmates at Lenoir-Rhyne University, especially Maddy Edwards for her good-cop critique and moral support and Dale Neal for his bad-cop challenges to constantly improve the story during the Workshop phase; Kelly Jo Heimer and Les Seltun at Control-Print Creative; Kate Galluzzi for her critical reading, proofreading and manuscript suggestions; Kristin Ollenburg, Esq. for her sage legal advice; Tony Brown of *AnInspiredImage* for his brilliant cover concept and layout; a special and heartfelt thanks to Bob Dugoni, author, master teacher, mentor and friend for his help and encouragement at every step.

I also want to thank those individuals who graciously agreed to lend their names to the fictional and sometimes nefarious characters portrayed in the story: William P. Tunell, MD, illustrious and now retired pediatric surgeon *par excellence*; high school friends and classmates Louis A. Petroni, *Esq.* and Daniel J. Ragone, MD; HS writing mentors Joe Marquart, Ann Donahue Croce and Bob Rocca; James C. Guidice, DO, master physician and clinical teacher; Rudolph C. Camishion, MD, legendary Philadelphia and South Jersey heart surgeon; Richard Liszewski, DO, retired general surgeon and early mentor and Karen Durkin, Esq. on behalf of the families of John Durkin and David Kelly; plus an affectionate nod to the late Mrs. Loretta La Marro, my real third grade teacher, who introduced me to the world of stories.

Surf City, NJ is a real town and Long Beach Island is a real island (God willing and the Sea don't rise) where, fortunately, absolutely none of the events described in this book occurred. For the sake of the story, liberties have been taken with the historical timeline, specifically the appearance of female patrol officers in metropolitan police departments. I hope the reader will find this a forgivable use of literary license.

I spent and later misspent many happy days, nights, and weeks of my life "down the shore". This story is for all of us who still have sand in our shoes.

ABOUT THE AUTHOR

DANIEL J. WATERS is a native of Southern New Jersey. He graduated from St. Joseph's College in Philadelphia and the University of Medicine and Dentistry of New Jersey and has been publishing stories and essays since 1981; his work has appeared in the Journal of The American Medical Association, The New Physician, The Examined Life (University of Iowa) and Intima: A Journal of Narrative Medicine (Columbia University). He has practiced open-heart surgery for thirty years and is the author of A Heart Surgeon's Little Instruction Book and A Surgeon's Little Instruction Book, pocket collections of surgical advice and aphorisms. He holds a Graduate Certificate in Narrative Healthcare and a Master of Arts in Writing from The Center for Graduate Studies/The Thomas Wolfe Center for Narrative at Lenoir-Rhyne University in Asheville, NC. He and his wife Pamela have three grown children and live in Clear Lake, Iowa.

Visit our website at www.BandagemanPress.com

Made in the USA
Middletown, DE
28 July 2018